Jake & Emma
# The Carrero Effect
## The Promotion

### L.T. Marshall

Copyright © 2017 L.T. Marshall
New edition copyright © 2018 L.T. Marshall
Published by Pict Publishing

ISBN: 978 1 9803131 5 1

This book is a work of fiction. Names, characters, places, and incidents are the product of the author's imagination or are used fictitiously. Any resemblance to actual events, locales, or persons, living or dead, is purely coincidental.

All rights reserved. No part of this book may be reproduced or transmitted in any form or by any means, electronic or mechanical, including photocopying, recording, or by any information storage and retrieval system, without the author's permission.

Cover copyright © Pict Publishing/L.T. Marshall
Front cover image copyright © Adobe/Natalia Klenova
Back cover image copyright © Adobe/Korionov

# The Carrero Series

### Jake & Emma
The Carrero Effect ~ The Promotion
The Carrero Influence ~ Redefining Rules
The Carrero Solution ~ Starting Over

### Arrick & Sophie
The Carrero Heart ~ Beginning
The Carrero Heart ~ The Journey
The Carrero Heart ~ Happy Ever Afters

### Bonus Books
Jake's View
Arrick's View

# Other books by L.T. Marshall

Just Rose

# Acknowledgements

I am surprisingly bad at writing acknowledgements (go figure). So bear with me while I bumble through my bad attempts at thanks. You all really mean a lot to me and I appreciate the help that I got in getting this out there.

I have a list of like a million people, so I am going to be diplomatic and try to cover all of you without actually turning this into a tick list. So if you recognize your group title then you know I mean you!

To all my little Weirdoes and Warriors—you keep this fun and rewarding and boost me when I want to give up.

Grace, Jackie, Heather and Wendy, for every single moment you spent keeping me sane and fuelling me to get to this point. You are my friends and my sounding boards. My girls!

Emma—editor extraordinaire with the patience of a saint and a compassion and understanding that means so very much to me. You rock!

Sarah Marie—sidekick, book wizard and more, there are not enough titles to encompass all you do so I am sticking with your pet name—wing commander!

Suzie—PA who needs a medal. For the laughs, the pep talks and the fangirling. I know I am your favorite (wink wink).

Victoria—you deserve a mention too, you helped me when I had no clue what I was doing and you contributed to the Carrero brand. I appreciate it with big hugs.

My fans—you have no idea how many of you give me the strength and determination to keep writing. Much love xx

Team Carrero—you know who you are and how much I love what you do for me. Keep up the good work!

My family—the list is getting long and you know I have the feels, be happy I actually mentioned you. LOL x

*For the one I call my "other".*
*You fuelled many a dude line in this book.* xx

# Chapter 1

I smooth my hands down my pencil skirt and tailored, gray jacket before touching up my dark lipstick in the hall mirror with a look of resignation. My eyes scan and check my tawny hair is neat and sleek in its high bun and I scrutinize my reflection again, to make sure it's precise. Sighing once more I take a steadying breath trying to ready myself, pushing down the gnawing ache of anxiety and nerves deep inside my gut.
*I'll do.*

I look as good as I know I'm capable of, and I'm mildly satisfied with what I see before me; a cool, efficient image of cold poise and gray tailoring that exudes authority, with no hint of the turmoil of emotion inside me. I narrow my eyes to look for any flaws to my immaculate armor, any stray hairs, specks of dust, or creased fabric, and find none.

I've never been a lover of my own reflection, with my young appearance, cool blue eyes, and pouting lips, but nothing is out of place and I look right for my new role as personal assistant to my very high-profile boss. Professional and capable on the outside which I guess is what matters; calm and uncompromising with every detail in place and clothes flawlessly neat. I have always been good at shielding the truth about how I feel inside.

I slide on my stilettos with a slow careful motion, keeping my balance with one hand on the wall and hearing the movement in the room behind me, I check the mirror in response.

"Morning, Ems ... God, you look professional as always." Sarah stifles a yawn as she wanders from her room and rubs her eyes with the back of her fist childishly as I watch her in the reflection behind me. It's unusual for her to be up this early on her day off; Sarah's never been a lover of mornings for as long as I've known her.

She's wearing her baggy pink housecoat, and her messy, short, bleached blonde hair is sticking up at all angles from her head; casually loveable as always, and I feel a warm affection for that bundle of happy energy. Her bright blue eyes are heavy with early morning fatigue and she's watching me closely with a silly smile on her face. A little too closely for my liking.

"Good morning, Sarah." I smile lightly, I try to ignore the way she's looking at me and straighten up to stand tall. I turn, lifting my briefcase from the floor in front of me and head forward into our open plan apartment, ever conscious of my grace and mannerisms under scrutiny, even in front of her, and push out the sense of tightness in my nerves today; swallow down the listlessness and try so very hard to curb the swirling of my stomach.

"Remember you need to be here for ten o'clock ... the boiler repair." I remind her as she shuffles along behind me to the lounge area, trying to distract her from the open gawking she seems to be doing. Running through my schedule in my head like a mental checklist to give me something else to think about, besides my nerves today.

"I know. I know! You left me a memo on the fridge remember?" she giggles childishly and throws me a patient look, raising a brow with an almost indulgent expression. She looks much younger than her age and sometimes I forget we went to school together. I feel more like her guardian than her flatmate nowadays, but maybe I always did, if I am being honest. I sigh again, pushing down the tight knot of apprehension I feel inside and give her a small smile of bravado.

"Don't forget." I sound stern, but she doesn't react, she's used to my serious tone and my endless organization of our lives. She knows this the way I do things; my need to be in control and have everything just so makes me feel more capable.

"I won't. I swear ... I'm not working until tonight, so I'm going to stick around and chillax ... Watch some back-to-back Netflix." She moves lazily to the bright white and gray open plan kitchen to the side of me and begins making herself a coffee, lifting the mug I washed earlier this morning from the rack for herself, with another sleepy bright smile. I watch her casual, confident movements around the kitchen, her domain when she's at home, and it gives me a sense of calm.

Sarah was always good at making me feel a little saner when I needed it, never aware of how I drew from that uncomplicated relaxed manner of hers when I needed to ground myself.

"I'm going to work." I walk steadily into the small open plan kitchen by the side of the bar which juts out into the lounge and lift the few open letters from the counter I've yet to deal with today. I know that I'm lingering and acting indecisively, compared to my usual efficient routine every day, and normally I'd already be walking to the subway station, despite being early.

"Oh, here." She slides a white envelope out from behind the toaster and holds it out expectantly for me to take it with a blank look on her face.

"Before I forget ... I know you've probably already taken care of them, as usual." Her sparkling eyes flash at me with affectionate amusement.

"What is it?" I look at the long envelope, taking it from her slowly with careful fingers, eyeing it up with a frown and seeing no writing on the front.

"My half of the utilities and the rent ... I got paid early." She smiles brightly and sets about going back to making herself coffee, pulling a loaf of bread open to slide slices into the toaster.

"Right, and yes. I've taken care of it already ... Thank you." I take it and slide it into my bag to bank at lunch and mentally note down a memo to do so. I ritually pay our bills at the start of every month when I'm paid, having a very good wage in a great company with many perks makes it effortless to make sure we are always up to date.

"No surprise there then," she mumbles and throws me another affectionate look, all cute eyes and gentle sighs as she regards me from a sideways look that I clearly catch. I just shake my head at her, fully aware that she prefers that I take control of our living expenses and always have. She's never been good with money and I doubt she would remember to pay the rent on time without my ever-efficient presence to do so. Taking care of things is how I like it to be; it gives me purpose, control, and a focus in my life that I so desperately need to thrive.

"I won't be home until six o'clock, Sarah, I presume you'll be at work by then, so have a wonderful day." I turn from the breakfast bar and head for the main door of our apartment, lifting my warm jacket as I pass the dining table and turn with a smile when I reach the dark gray door.

"Oh, wait ... Good luck on meeting your super-hot boss for the first time, Miss. Anderson!" She beams at me excitedly, raising her eyebrows; leaning out across the worktop so all I can see is her head popping out from the kitchen at a funny angle. She looks messy but cute and far too awake for her today. I smile back emptily, not wanting to give my feelings away or show any weakness.

"Thanks." I feel my face heat slightly with the rise of nerves hitting my stomach hard again but ignore the sensation, swallowing it all down with the expertise of a seasoned actress.

"Are you nervous?" she probes with a little furrow of her brow, still leaning out a little too far to watch me adjust my briefcase handle and pull my outside jacket on over my suit. I frown back at her question, the tightening knot in my stomach intensifying somewhat but I shake my head with a "No" in reply. If I admit it to her then I admit it to myself, then I'll let my nerves get the better of me and lose my edge.

*That just wouldn't do at all.*

"Of course, you're not ... You never are!" she adds quickly with a grin and slides back into her little culinary world, oblivious to anything amiss in my behavior today. I smile again as I watch her recede and turn with a wave of my fingertips before heading out the door on my mission to get to work.

*Sweet Sarah.*

So sure of my capabilities and cool, outward confidence.

*I sometimes wonder if she even remembers the old me at all? If she even associates me with the girl I was when we met, so many years before?*

I close the door behind me quietly, holding onto the handle for a second as I take a deep steadying breath and take a moment to be still. Refusing to let emotion get the better of me and crack my armor. Looking down at the cool silver knob as a way of grounding myself once more, steadying that creep of inner nerves and pushing down all my anxiety and fears.

*I can do this.*

It's what I've been working so hard for; finally, my abilities recognized after years of hard work and climbing the internal ladder and I need to push down the inner doubts and the final traces of my adolescent Emma, to focus on the tasks ahead of me. The responsibilities I'll be taking on after today. It's heady and overwhelming, but I steel my nerves inwardly, calm my hands against me as I've practiced a million times in the last ten years. Everyday working toward this person I've become, this cool and confident persona known as Emma Anderson.

It takes a moment to be able to walk from the door, but as I do I feel the armor sliding up and the mask fully connecting with my face. Each step strengthening my resolve, back to my normal practiced demeanor and that inner me finding the will power and steady strength to pull this off, day after day, as I head to the subway station.

\* \* \*

*Floor sixty-five of the Carrero corporation—Executive house. Lexington Avenue, Mid-town Manhattan.*

My hands are clammy and hot and my heart's pounding so hard I may throw up. Its grating on me that I'm unable to reel it all back in so easily now I'm here. I've been watching the hands on the clock move very slowly for the last few minutes and all I can hear is the sound of my own blood rushing to my ears. I'm sensitive to every noise and movement around me in the stark modern office, and the fact the shiny new keyboard in front of me is gazing back expectantly. I've not even begun to start working.

*This is so unlike me.*

I've taken twelve deep breaths in a row, yet my hands are still shaking, and I feel like at any moment I may pass out. I'm disappointed at myself for letting my nerves get the better of me and I'm trying to pull back every single emotion one at a time, to stow into that neat box in my head.

*Don't fall apart, Emma.*

I chide myself and check my reflection again in the glass opposite me that serves as a wall to the office, to make sure I'm not betraying anything. I look self-sufficient, calm, and in control, despite my inner turmoil; As I always do. No hint of the conflict going on behind the cool blue eyes or sleek, smooth tawny hair. Years of practice giving me this uncanny ability to act my way through life, making sure no one ever got to see the turbulence below the surface of my calm waters. I will never let them again.

"Emma?" Margaret Drake's voice echoes toward me as the clip clop of her stilettos comes at me across the white marble floor from her internal office. She looks unflustered and ever graceful in a tailored, black pant suit and high shiny heels.

"Yes, Mrs. Drake?" I stand, unsure if I'm meant to. Suddenly nervous and shy of this woman who has been letting me shadow her for over a week, she seems very professional today. An air of purpose, and I steady my hands on the hem at my waist and fix the obligatory smile on my face with grace.

"Mr. Carrero will be arriving shortly, make sure there's fresh water with ice on his desk and clean glasses." She smiles encouragingly, possibly sensing my unease.

"Have the espresso machine on and ready in case he asks for one, and all his mail and messages laid out on his desk before he arrives. When he does, please keep out of his way until I call you for introductions." She pats my shoulder gently, a mannerism I've grown accustomed to, and with a bright wide smile.

"Yes, Mrs. Drake." I nod, trying not to still feel in awe at the swirl of platinum blonde hair effortlessly held on top of her head, or the severe tailored jacket revealing a perfect curvaceous physique. When I met her a few days ago I had been floored by her physical appearance. My previous mentor had informed me she was in her fifties and Mr. Carrero's personal assistant and I guess I expected someone colder and dragon-like, considering her key role in the business. Not this designer-clad cool temple before me, with breathtaking beauty and natural friendliness, who is now my mentor. Margo Drake is a very beautiful and intelligent creature that I can only look up to.

"Oh, and, Emma?" she pauses, turning slightly.

"Yes, Mrs. Drake?"

"This week you'll meet with Donna Moore, she's Mr. Carrero's personal shopper and she'll fit you out with appropriate work attire. Anything you'll need when representing him when you go on trips and such; events and all that red carpet crap he's so fond of." She smiles warmly with a little sigh and a raised brow, suggesting she doesn't approve of his public affairs.

I swallow, deliberately quelling the nerves once again. I am aware that my role requires me to be available on short notice for trips and functions, but I was never informed it would include the public side of him at all.

*Damn!*

"Yes, Mrs. Drake," I say, trying to work out how much I'll have to spend to be red carpet ready, worried it may eat into my savings a tad more than I expected. A lot more than expected.

"It goes on company expenses, Emma. Mr. Carrero expects his personal staff to look a certain way." She winks at me, "He considers it a necessary expense for all employees on the sixty-fifth floor." Mrs. Drake has this uncanny ability to read everyone's mind. I like her ability, it removes awkward misunderstandings and nervous hesitations, no second guessing, and I find I work well with her because of it. I inwardly sigh with relief at the thought that this won't affect my savings or my future hopes of one day buying myself an apartment in New York to cut my travel time.

"Thank you, Mrs. Drake." I nod her way as she moves to walk off.

"Emma?" she turns her head back to me with a half-smile.

"Yes, Mrs.—"

"Please," she interrupts.

"It's Margaret ... Margo ... From now on! Only my children's friends call me Mrs. Drake. You've been here over a week and I'm more than happy with your progress, we're going to be working closely—so please." She gives me a full warm smile before turning on her expensive high heel, back toward the huge door of her own office.

I feel warmer, calmer. I'm getting the strong impression Margo has taken a liking to me in my time here. I'm not sure I like the casual first name suggestion though, I like to keep things as professional and impersonal as possible. I'm good at keeping people at a distance and I happen to prefer it. Letting people cross the line from business to pleasure is a messy mistake that I never, ever let happen.

I absent-mindedly glance back at the monitor of my computer, the company logo swirling in front of me as a screen saver. "Carrero Corporation". As if I would ever forget where I worked. Surrounded by opulent settings and posters and prints of the Carrero products and ads on every possible surface. That familiar gold hexagon logo with a black C, shining back on everything.

Mr. Carrero comes to mind. Mr. Jacob Carrero.

Yet, I have only seen pictures of him and he's the main reason I feel sick with nerves. Men with wealth, power, and good looks make me uneasy; they're a different breed and harder to predict. They see women as a commodity and are far more dangerous than average men.

If I'm being truthful, then men in general make me uneasy, but my experiences with average men have taught me how to handle myself. Jacob Carrero is by no means average.

He's been away taking personal time since before I was sent up here to replace my predecessor, she's on maternity leave with a view to not returning and I'm who they recommended as a replacement.

Carrero is everything you want in a playboy billionaire, he's handsome in an ungodly, devastating way, confident, and publicly popular among the female population. He has an Italian meets American look about him, inherited from his parents. His mother has the same mixed look, and he's one of New York's richest heirs. The Carrero family are almost like royalty and he is the eldest of their two princes, who have grown up very publicly. He's been gracing the social news pages for years, always charming the cameras that seek him out, and always smiling in just about every picture they have caught him in.

I've done extensive research to prepare myself for working alongside him, but it makes me uneasy, despite not meeting him yet. I'm aware that he's incredibly attractive, even to someone like me who finds most men intolerable. He has a reputation for being a bad boy, thanks to a large chunk of his early adult years being steeped in scandal at his wild behavior.

He seems to revel in partying and playing in the public eye, bringing no end of shame to the Carrero name, until recent years. Since then he seems to have grown up a little, focusing on the family business, yet still finding time to string along endless women in his wake and make appearances at glitzy events. He is a completely stereotypical, playboy billionaire, and boringly predictable.

I know from pictures that he has the darkest brown almost black hair and green eyes although I'm sure Photoshop has something on the sheer brightness of the color. No eye color could be that breathtaking in real life, and I know how magazines like to air brush good looks into every image. He sports a rough, stubbly beard, with a cropped, messy haircut that suits his age. Usually styled fashionably, most likely with one of the expensive Carrero grooming products his face has graced in the most recent years. It is obvious he loves himself enough to put his face on their million-dollar ad campaigns every year.

He's twenty-eight and despite having worldly maturity about him, he looks younger than his age when you see pictures straight on and caught off guard. I can't deny that I see the appeal. He seems to have the body of someone who is graced with a good strong, tall physique, and he takes care of it. There are enough topless shots of him in the media to confirm that, and he's not shy about showing it off. He also seems to have a weakness for tribal and Aztec tattoos, which litter his body in a rather appealing way. He looks like a typical brainless model, too good-looking to be a nice guy and far too muscular to have a decent IQ.

There's no doubt he's been blessed with more sex appeal than necessary for one man, and this is the root of my nausea. He's someone who charms and strings along women effortlessly. Unlike all the men I've ever known, and that makes me distrust him.

I can handle men who leech and grope, whose intent is written on their faces and have cowardly natures. I've never been faced with someone with the capabilities Jacob Carrero seems famed for, the effortless ability to make women swoon at his feet, and follow him around doe-eyed and lust sick. The man seems to just click his fingers to find dates and they all scramble to get a go at him; its pathetic really.

I know it's a huge honor to get this position. I know that I'm good at my job, and I've pleased the right people downstairs to even get here at such an early age, but I feel sick and scared for the hundredth time. I'm doubting myself, despite my achievements; the curse of my self-doubts.

The old Emma still hidden in the shadows, shaking her head at me and trying to convince me that I am a fraud. I don't know if I've overstepped my worth. I don't know if I'm capable of the task ahead of me. Capable of working with someone so young and as all-encompassing as Jacob Carrero, the celebrity hotel tycoon and New York's most eligible bachelor.

I pull my focus back to task, putting my mind onto doing something manual always helps me get myself together. I do as Margo asked and ready the large expensive espresso machine in the white kitchen. It's small, modern, and sleek, if a little clinical, and seems to only be used to supply tea and coffee despite the huge refrigerators. I wipe down the surfaces of the machine and surrounding worktops, removing the dust from the coffee grounds and ready his tray with iced water. Taking some comfort in this calming task, my nerves still rattled, and this irritates me. I thought I had gained more control than this.

I arrange everything she has requested neatly on his desk, straightening things as I go and checking the room to make

# The Carrero Effect ~ The Promotion

sure everything is in its place. I like neatness, it makes me calm and feel more in control, as though somehow by everything being orderly, my life is more so.

I smooth down my blouse, now that I've removed my jacket, savoring the silky feel of the expensive pale gray fabric and return with the pile of mail and messages I took for him yesterday; they're only the ones that require his attention and place them on his desk in line with the leather seat sitting neatly behind it.

The office is spacious and airy. One wall of glass and through it, the view of New York at its finest, hindered only by vertical blinds that sit open. Large abstract prints fill the sea of gray expanse to the left. I can't help but let my eyes skim over the silver framed pictures to the left corner of the wooden desk, with various people in black and white stills. Beautiful women, celebrities, and one of his father, Mr. Carrero Sr. Someone I've seen from a distance before, during a huge function last year that required extra staff. They look only vaguely alike in that Italian way, although I guess Jacob must look more like his mother, as the resemblance ends there.

In pride of place is a large framed picture of, who I assume, is his mother. She's very beautiful, and the resemblance is striking. Same dark hair, gorgeous face, cool tan, same bright green eyes, and yet a gentle warmth in that face.

In comparison, Carrero senior is fairer haired with deep brown eyes and a tight, harsh face, etched with lines as though his skin is weather beaten. In the picture of father and son, there's a coldness between them, despite the fact they're standing close, holding a champagne bottle in front of a ships stern. It sends a shiver down my spine. I know cold looks on men and the memories are completely unwelcome.

I look around quickly making sure there's nothing else

that requires my obsessive attention to detail and slide back out gracefully, assured everything is ready.

It's almost 9.00 a.m.; he will be arriving shortly, and my nerves are so taut I may actually snap with the tension if it isn't over soon.

# Chapter 2

I'm absent-mindedly twisting my pen in my fingers back at my desk, and it gives me a huge surge of anger—at myself. Stilling the pen sharply and laying it down with a smack and scowling at it as though it's the cause. Another habit from childhood that I'm permanently trying to overcome, and just one of the subtle tells that I'm not who I perceive to be. The only flaw in my perfect demeanor that I grasp so tightly onto.

*I fidget.*

And it's so at odds with the persona I've managed to create for myself since my teen years, getting away from the life I once knew. A stark reminder of how far I've come from my childhood in Chicago, and a habit that annoys me on a serious level. Not only because it betrays the confidence I seem to emit, but also because it's juvenile. My fidgeting occurs on many levels. For the most part, I've mastered it, but with my raw nerves this morning; I'm betraying myself.

I still my hands and focus on typing the documents Margo has given me to adjust, reminding myself to take steadying breaths as I do so. To stay calm while waiting for my new boss to appear.

Margo sweeps out into the foyer in a graceful cloud of Chanel No. 9, passes me at my glass desk near the entrance to our offices, indicating his arrival. She smiles my way fondly and quickly as she passes and gives me an encouraging wink as though I am about to meet royalty.

*Maybe I am.*

*Oh hell! Swallow. Deep breath. Relax.*

I can hear her running through his itinerary out in the hall as they approach. I know she's been emailing him back and forth, but this verbal being brought up to speed is something she told me he prefers, to recap. Something I need to remember as it will be my role soon enough.

I stay seated and keep my eyes on my keyboard, willing my nerves to stay under wraps.

I hear him speak to her and despite seeing interviews online, I'm taken by surprise by the natural sound of his voice. It's deep and sexy and has a boyishness to it that I never noticed in his interviews. The kind of voice you would recognize anywhere, even across a crowded room, and it draws you in. So crazily familiar and comforting. He sounds at ease with her and there's something alluring in it. Like a warmth sliding over you, completely throwing me.

I pause my typing as he laughs at something she says. Its unexpected and I flinch, shocked that it causes butterflies in my stomach.

*I don't react like this to men!*

Fumbling fingers on keys betray me, and I'm glad no one is paying me any attention.

*I need to get hold of myself. Get a grip, Emma!*

I feel my cheeks beginning to warm and I take my practiced steadying breath to curb my blush. There's gibberish on my screen and I quickly hit the back button to remove it, hiding the evidence of my stumble. Cursing the inability of my fumbling fingers, cursing that childish part of me that I'm forever pushing down and trying to gag into silence.

*Stop it, Emma ... Just stop. You are more capable than this.*

There's a group of them walking through the main area of our airy office toward Margo's desk, behind me in a separate room. Margo is nearest, concealing him fully from view, but I catch a glimpse.

He's still standing taller than her, despite her four-inch heels. There's two men with him; one in all black, suited and looking serious—he has some sort of wire in his ear, indicating he's most likely security. The other is dressed more casually, in a tan jacket and chinos and strolling along behind leisurely.

I realize this is Arrick Carrero, his younger brother. He's never in the papers much, but I recognize him. He hasn't really inherited the same masculine beauty or presence as his brother, and he seems rather publicity-shy, although he is only late teens. I notice that he's also only about five-foot nine, yet still muscular and has tawny hair much like his father's. That same weird nose profile too that Jacob Carrero does not have. Jacob seems to have a perfect nose, to match his perfect—well, everything. I wonder how Arrick feels, being the less attractive Carrero son, living in his brother's shadow.

Within a moment all of them are in his office, past Margo's inner door, and it's closed. I take a deep breath and try again to type this document out, meeting with my usual success, quick and swift skill with a keyboard now that I have no visual distractions.

It seems like an eternity has passed when my switchboard lights up, and the distant voice of Margot interrupts my concentration. I was unaware I'd been holding my breath until that moment and give myself another stern inner shake.

"Emma, please come into Mr. Carrero's office. Thank

you." The voice sounds distant and tinny on the remarkably high-tech machine.

"Yes, Mrs. Drake." I flinch at my use of her full name, knowing she asked me to call her Margo. I mentally scold myself to not repeat the mistake.

*I don't make mistakes. Ever.*

I slide up, smoothing down my clothes and putting my jacket back on quickly. Buttoning it up as I walk the small distance to her door which blocks entrance to his.

It takes all my willpower to walk into the office, and all of my acting ability, dredged up from somewhere deep, to pull off the undaunted calm demeanor that I try to present at all times. My stomach doing somersaults, and my throat drying up. I don't know why I'm having so much trouble with it today.

"Ah, Emma, here you are." Margo meets me as I pull open the heavy wooden door and slide in. Suddenly conscious of how short I am, even in my spike heels, next to her swan like body. She stands tall for a woman and I stand at around five-feet four.

"Jake, this is Emma Anderson. She's your new assistant in training. Your new number two." She smiles fondly at me and gestures me to come to her. I move beside her and feel the gentle familiar pat on my shoulder as she tries to put me at ease.

I blink a few times, at the use of the name Jake.

*Am I missing something here?*

It dawns on me he prefers the name Jake. Brain clicking with memories from my research. He corrected many interviewers and I remember he likes the informality and encourages using his first name; shortened first name.

All my thoughts slip away to nothing and I'm held grounded to the floor, unable to speak as the object of my nerves gets out of his seat. This is what I've been afraid of! My reaction when faced with someone I find attractive, and it's completely new to me.

I don't even notice the others in the room as he effortlessly glides toward me, he has the walk of someone who's never doubted his own confidence or abilities. Someone who knew from early in life that he was devastatingly hot and has the best kind of reaction on all women. It's mesmerizing in a way, but also disconcerting.

He towers above me as he approaches, putting him over the six-foot mark easily. Wearing all black; shirt and suit, minus a tie and top buttons open. The overall effect makes me breathless. He's beyond underwear model hot, he's like some female fantasy come to life.

*Jeeze.*

"Miss. Anderson." He extends an arm, and all I can do is reach out and shake the perfectly manicured, yet oddly masculine, hand. I'm aware of the way my heart quickens, and my breath is slightly labored at the tingling sensation of his skin on mine. I immediately feel betrayed by my own body.

I push it down, abhorred that I should react this way, it's alien to me and has me shifting on my own axis. I don't like being forced out of my comfort zone and into new experiences this way.

"Mr Car—" my voice sounds feeble. I'm so pathetic and obvious.

"Jake! Please," he cuts in, those green eyes taking me in with no clue to anything going on behind them.

"Margo informs me she's happy with you so far and will be training you a little more extensively in time, to step in fully when she retires. I guess that means we should get better acquainted on a first name basis." He throws me a charming, handsome smile, and I'm not immune to the effect. It's a smile that hints that he knows exactly what he's doing with it, though.

*So, this is how you win over women is it, Carrero? Melting them with seductive smiles. Ughhh.*

My insides lurch unexpectedly. His hand is smooth and burningly hot in mine, and I'm starting to feel clammy. Anxious Emma peeking her head out, only to be pushed back down with a firm shove.

*Be still, Emma ... Stay cool. Stop drooling.*

"I'm really grateful for the opportunity." I sound normal enough, only a slight waver in my voice this time and I feel relieved. If anything, my years of poise are saving me from myself right now.

He subtly looks me over. There's nothing in it, which surprises me. Just an interested appraisal as he tries to measure me up. I guess he's used to women going all weak-kneed and pie-eyed at his presence and it interests him that I don't appear to be. I'm glad he can't see my internal reactions, as they are behaving disgustingly right about now.

I'm unnerved that this close he's just as handsome, if not more than his Internet pictures, and his ruggedness is intimidating. The sheer power of his shoulders and toned body, straining behind the expensive clothing. I know from photographs he prefers more casual attire than suits and ties most of the time. He's sexually intimidating and so far out of my league in every way and now, in the flesh, it's so much more obvious.

"Can I get you a drink, Emma? You look flushed." His voice smooths over me like honey, and my mouth dries up. I'm blushing, and scowl at my inner-adolescent self. He removes his hand and walks away from me to his desk with a confident swagger.

I'm uneasy and try to regain my equilibrium, swallowing

several times to get the moisture back into my mouth and keep my eyes off his ass. A drink would be good right now, if only to release my throat.

"Thank you." I catch Margot watching me with a strange look in her eye, and I realize it's a touch of uncertainty. Mr. Carrero moves off to a bar at the rear of the room, to the side of his desk, with his back to us to fix me a drink.

*Shit!*

*She's thinking I'm just another receptionist with the hots for Mr. Carrero. Another woman to fall at the hurdle of meeting him.*

I try to pull myself together and smooth invisible wrinkles in my clothes and straighten my body up, trying to get back my professional air and grace. I hate that I've shown signs of being rattled. I don't normally break under so little pressure, and I'm not impressed with myself.

I see her expression warm, and I relax.

*Perhaps I'm overthinking this.*

I'm mindful that Mr. Black Suit is standing in a corner by the window, glaring at us; it's a little intimidating, but also reassuring. Just out of sight to my far left on the long cream Italian leather couch, the younger man is sitting below some huge prints of modern artistry depicting what might be naked women.

*Ughhh. Really? Could you be anymore playboy, Carrero?*

Arrick is disinterested in what's going on. He's playing with his cell, and I think I can hear the Angry Birds music that Sarah loves to irritate me with. An irritating, immature game, although Arrick looks late teens to early twenties so he can be forgiven for a juvenile game, I suppose.

"Here you go," Jake's voice cuts into my thoughts, bringing my attention back to him as he hands me a tall glass of something bubbly. I take a sip and give him a grateful smile;

it's a cold, clear liquid that tastes sweetly tropical with a hint of unexpected alcohol.

*I guess it's not iced water.*

It's a cocktail and I try not to show my surprise, but a tiny frown hits my brow before I can correct it.

*Surprising. He did this himself. Booze at work though?*

"Thank you, Mr. ... Jake." I correct, and he gives me a soft smile. I ignore the butterflies in my stomach rising again, with a minor annoyance.

*Stop behaving like a fourteen-year-old!*

"So, Emma, Margo tells me you've worked here for just over five years?" he sits back to perch on his desk, body casual and eyes fixed on me. Margo standing close by, listening. He is distractingly good-looking, more so when he relaxes all casual and charming, and very un-boss like.

"Yes. I've worked on various floors, but mainly tenth." I move place my glass on the table so my hands don't toy with the rim. I'm disappointed to be putting it down, it tasted amazing, but I'm not a fan of alcohol at work, or anytime for that matter. He has skills with making drinks though.

"You were Jack Dawson's assistant for a while?" his eyebrows dip as he questions, unusually cute and studying me non-intrusively.

*Get a grip, Emma!*

"Yes, Mr. Dawson." I smile, although I know it must look as forced as it is. Dawson is an unbearable letch who grabbed my ass at every opportunity and pressed himself against me whenever I tried to pass him. In his late sixties, small, and portly, I was surprised he still had those kinds of urges at his age. He's the type of man I'm used to dealing with, with his wandering hands and sleazy smiles. The kind of man I can handle.

"It was Miss. Keith who recommended you for this

position, I believe?"

I notice his beautiful teeth, white and perfectly lined up, just as a billionaire's mouth should be. I wonder how much he spends in dental work every year, to be Carrero model material.

"Yes. I loved working for her while her own assistant was on leave, she was easy to attend to, and I learned a lot." A surge of satisfaction at how cool and calm I sound once again rushes through my body. My nerves are settling and his effects on me winding down. I guess the shock of meeting him is abating.

I was wrong about his eyes, in person they're the most gorgeous, pure green I've seen, in fact, the photographs don't do them justice.

"She spoke highly of your efficiency and professionalism. It's rare for Kay to make an internal recommendation for a position like this." He smiles again, and the butterflies swoop back in. I blush, the heat rising up my face, and it annoys me as I try to maintain my professional maturity, but I'd loved Kay Keith as a boss. I was desolate when her assistant came back to work and I was demoted back to Dawson's office. The return to the letch and his slimy hands.

"Thank you." I'm smiling genuinely. It's not an easy thing to move from a lowly admin assistant through a company like this in just five years, especially with my meager qualifications. I have sacrificed so much in my life to get here.

"Well, so far, I've found her to be a joy. Efficient and capable, with a good understanding of the business. Don't think it will take long to get her up to speed with her requirements." Margo's smiling at me with an odd twinkle in her eye. I like her. She's still standing close, observing us and is oblivious to the other two men behind her. I know she's watching to see if we're a fit and is standing back to let us get to know each other. Her presence calming me.

"Glad to hear it—so, Emma, how has it been so far? Learning the ropes of life on the sixty-fifth floor?" There's a slight humor in his expression, a hint of that Carrero charm he's famed for. It's hard not to fall for it if I'm being honest, but I know it stems from years of schmoozing with the rich and famous, and probably fake.

"A breeze," I say coolly, avoiding that penetrative gaze he has going on now. "Nothing I can't handle so far." I allow a half-smile of confidence.

"Has Margo warned you about the frequent traveling you will have to undertake, or the unsociable hours we sometimes keep? This job can be full on, Miss. Anderson. It's not for the faint hearted." He's frowning now, still watching me closely, and it's a little unnerving.

"Yes, I'm aware that this is not a nine-to-five job, Mr. Carrero. I'm 100% committed to my career, so it will not be an issue." I reply without emotion, lifting my chin a little.

"You're young ... What about a social life?" Still frowning at me. Still trying to scrape away at my surface and figure me out. I would never give a man like him that chance.

"I haven't much interest in many social activities ... I left my home town to come to New York, and I don't know many people outside of work." My voice sounds unsteady, but I doubt he has noticed. He looks at me contemplatively.

"Career oriented? Can be lonely." He tilts his head to the side and lightly hunches his shoulders in a move that's devastating to my hormones and makes my body tingle and my temperature soar. I gaze down to the floor for a second and take a breath to combat these alien feelings.

*Stop eye raping him, Emma. Have a little more professionalism.*

"I'm never lonely, Mr. Carrero ... I'm an independent

person who doesn't need assurances, or company, from other people to be happy." I realize I've let my mouth shift into gear ahead of my brain and revealed more than I intended to. Another "old Emma" habit that grinds on me, despite years of trying to overcome it.

It's true though, I've been self-reliant from an early age. I keep people at arm's length, even Sarah, because it suits me to do so. Relationships bring complications, disappointment, and pain.

He narrows his eyes and studies me again, more probing as this excruciating "chat" continues.

"Oh, Emma, that's not the way a young girl like you should live her life." Margo cuts in.

"You're so pretty ... You should have young men romancing you around New York." She reaches out, touching my shoulder with a motherly squeeze, before returning to her previous position. I smile and ignore the urge to grimace at her words. If only she knew how that thought repulsed me. One thing I learned from my life was that romance does not exist in the minds of most men. Only sexual gratification whether or not you consent to it.

"Sounds like you're trying to talk her out of stealing your job, Margo." Jake laughs, lifting his boyish expression to the older woman, a complete change to his first smile; this one seems more natural and even more devastating. I see the affection flicker between them and it surprises me. She shakes her head at him.

"No. Emma knows I value her here. I think she's a perfect fit ..." She turns her gray eyes to me with a genuine warmth that thaws me a little.

"Not too sure how much you'll like it once Jake starts running you ragged, mind you." She winks at me and places a hand on his arm, showing the special bond they seem to share, and I wonder at it. They have a casual and comfortable ambience between them, almost like a mother and son.

"I'm sure I can handle the demands," I cut in confidently.

"Despite Jake's public playboy reputation, Emma, I'm afraid he's a workaholic ... Surprising, I know, but you'll get used to it; you'll rake up plenty of air miles in the next few months." Margo smiles again, this time patting Jake on the shoulder. There's a silent communication between them; secret smiles and glances, and I wonder how I will ever take her place.

"You'll soon get fed up with seeing the world." He gives me a comical frown, those alluring eyes back on my face and I hate the way it makes me feel naked.

"And the inside of hotel rooms." He adds with a cheeky smirk that heats my stomach with a flash.

I try to ignore the remark. Hoping to take him at face value and hope this internal wave fizzles away as quickly as it appeared. I'm sure I'll never see the inside of *his* hotel room. In fact, I can promise I won't; despite his reputation.

"I've seen enough of those to last a lifetime." Margo waves her hand, throwing him a glance I cannot translate.

"Right, we have work to be getting on with ... Emma, you're with me for now." She gestures to the door behind me, and I nod. Mr. Carrero stands from the perched position of his desk edge and smiles, lifting his hand out again while never breaking eye contact.

"To our working relationship, Emma." I accept it, ignoring the same tingling sensation his touch creates and smile tightly to disguise all the sensations. Sighing with relief that this meeting is over, I nod before I turn and follow Margo out of his office.

*Well, I survived meeting Jacob Carrero for the first time. My underwear didn't self-combust, and I remained intact.*

# The Carrero Effect ~ The Promotion

*Strike one to me.*

# Chapter 3

It's after twelve. My head feels a little woozy and stuffy, it's ridiculously hot in the office now, stiflingly so, it's making me feel nauseous. I've called maintenance twice to find out why they still haven't fixed the AC yet, it's blowing out tropical heat, rather than cold air. My face is flaming, and my pulse is beating so fast and hard, I feel like I've been running. My clothes are almost clinging to me, and I feel irritated because of the inability to breathe or find relief.

Margo has left the floor for lunch and I'm to follow on her return. She was wavering in the heat as much as me, but I told her I was okay to stay.

*Ever the hero, Emma! Good move.*

This is a huge sign of trust, and I think she's testing my capabilities, leaving me to man the fort and cope alone during a very busy schedule. It's been three days since Jake returned and I feel like Margo is relying on me a little more. Living up to her expectations and taking it in my stride.

I can feel the heat on my cheeks and my blouse is clinging in places it never has before. I'm obsessively clock watching for her to return, to relieve me for an hour, from this damned infernal heat before I pass out. My switchboard lights up, my insides tightening as his voice comes across the buzzer, "Emma, can you come in here please?" deep and sexy, the now familiar tingle in my stomach at the sound of his voice which I still have no control over.

I falter but reply with a, "Yes, Mr. Carrero." This is not what I need when I'm melting into a puddle on my seat and already out of sorts.

*Crap. Crap. Crap.*

I'm on my feet trying to pull my blouse from between my shoulder blades and smoothing it down without success. I pick up my notebook and pen, and glide past Margo's open office door and into his, pushing the heavy dark wood open and sliding in, I want this over quickly.

"Yes, Mr. Carrero?"

He looks casually seductive, sitting behind his desk amid an open laptop and piles of folders. His pale blue shirt has its top two buttons undone at the neck, his dark hair ruffled out of its normally perfectly spiked style, as though he's been running his hands through it, and his sleeves rolled up, revealing one of the tattoos on his inner left arm. A reminder of his rebel teen years. I know from images I've seen online that he has a few across his body. All tribal black tattoos and symbols; the effect is devastating even on me and I try not to react, annoyed that he still affects me.

"Are maintenance any further forward with fixing the AC? ... It's way too hot up here!" He leans back, putting his hands behind his head in a very "guy" manner. Stretching out and showcasing that perfect physique, making his biceps increase in size, straining at the fabric of his shirt. It's hard not to get a little heightening of the pulse rate.

*Eyes down!*

"I've called down twice, sir ... they're apparently on it." I keep my eyes averted, my tone level and sound as normal as possible.

"Emma, you look like you're about to pass out, I think you need to head to another floor and cool down." His eyes run over me over, I'm already conscious that I must look disheveled; I feel disheveled. But the passing out has more to do with the way he's sitting now, and my body becomes aware of how much sexier he is in just a shirt.

*Really, Emma? He's your boss!*

"I can't leave until Margo ... Mrs. Drake, returns, sir." I blink at him and resist the urge to let my eyes wander.

"When is she due back?" he frowns at me, oblivious to the riot of hormones raging through my body.

"Soon, maybe fifteen minutes or so. She's on her lunch early, I've to go on her return." I sound polite and factual. Trying not to squirm in my damp shoes and hoping I do not look as awful as I feel.

"Soon as she's back, I want you to go cool down, it feels like it's melting up here ... In the meantime, I need to dictate a letter. Maybe you'll feel cooler in here, I have the air vents open." He gestures at the wall of windows and I note the blinds moving a little as the small amount of air gets in. He's right, it is cooler in here—marginally. Well, it would if he wasn't sitting looking like that.

*Emma, again? Really?*

"Ready when you are." I hold up my notebook to move things forward and kill my train of thought. He turns his chair so he's facing the couch to the left of me and gazes at it, deep in thought.

"It's for the CEO of Bridge-stone ... A man called Eric Compton. You'll find his details on the system." He is in business mode, tone serious and face focused.

"Yes, sir." I scribble down.

"Emma?" his voice snaps my attention back to him.

"Yes?" I look up, at the tone of his voice, sure I've done something he doesn't like. Momentarily phased.

"You can sit down you know?" he's smiling at me and nods at a chair at the side of his desk, pretty much in his line of vision. It's why he turned his chair. I blush and come around to sit in front of him, I hate that since coming to work for him my inability to control my blushing has returned, he has a knack for making me feel childish.

"I don't bite ... much!" He smiles with his "I know I'm hot" look. My eyes flash up at him alarmed and see the humor. I give a short, embarrassed smile, to cover my reaction, my heart upping a gear and inwardly chastising my stupidity.

*Don't take things so literally!*

"I know you don't. " I smile coolly. Outwardly un-phased, despite irregular heart pounding and crazy goosebumps hitting my skin.

"You don't need to be so ... stiff, around me, Emma." He relaxes back in his chair, dropping his hands on the arms, casually so.

"Stiff?" I stare at him. A mild irritation fluttering within that successfully dampens anything else; I'm not good with male criticism.

*Especially about my demeanor.*

"You can thaw a little. I know you're efficient. You won't get sacked for relaxing." He looks amused, but I feel annoyance churn low inside of me. I came to do a job and I have pride in my professionalism, it's the one area I know I excel at.

*We can't all be laid back, Mr. Born Into Money. We don't all have the ability to sway people with a smile, have charmed lives with perfect childhoods, and irresistible faces.*

"This is me relaxed," I say tightly, training my expression to not betray my annoyance.

*As relaxed as you'll ever see me, Mr. Carrero, seeing as I'm paid to do a job, not pander to your ego.*

I pout inwardly, avoiding a direct look. He raises an eyebrow at me and breaks into an unguarded smile, confidently sexy and yet this time it irks me more.

"If you say so." That irritating smug look he has, that's the other side to Carrero. It's that face that makes women drop their panties in a blink, he also has this annoying male "know it all" cheekiness. Like he's always on the verge of a good joke, and it has to be one of his most infuriating qualities.

"So, to the CEO of Bridge-stone ....?" I raise my eyebrows, tapping my pen on my notebook, indicating we should move on, with a tight tone. I disapprove of his overfamiliarity. As much as I've seen him this way with Margo, I'm adamant that this working relationship will stay on a professional level. I have too much to lose. I've worked too hard to get here.

He frowns at me, holding my gaze for a moment, but I ignore him, looking down at my paper expectantly; relieved when he sits back and dictates what he wants me to note down.

* * *

"Is that all Mr. Carrero?" I finish my notes and push the pen in the top of the notebook with a sigh.

"I'd like a copy of the letter sent to my father's email and I would like it if you would call me Jake! ... Like I asked!" He lifts his feet to his desk, swiveling his chair back to face it and regards me with a relaxed, smug look, on his face.

"If that's what you prefer?" I'm not used to employers showing so little concern for titles, or who behave so casually.

I'm more than a little disappointed in the laxness I've seen from both Margo and Jake so far, in the way they behave with each other and it has me a little at unease. Here he is, sitting with his feet on his thousand-dollar desk, like a lounging teenager and it kills the image I once had of him.

"I'm not Mr. Carrero ... That's my father." His eye flicker to the photo on his desk and in a I see a dark shadow in them. He slides his feet back down, as though not so relaxed with that one tiny flicker. It's gone before I can decide if I saw it or not and I shiver inwardly. Men and their dark looks don't bode well with me, it's one of the few things which unnerve me deeply enough to bring me out in a cold sweat.

"Okay, Jake!" It's almost painful to use his name, even if he insists. He smiles again, looking more pleased as I stand, indicating my departure.

"Do you like working here, Emma?" he leans forward onto his desk, resting his arms in front of him and halting my escape for a moment. I pause, stunned by his question.

"So far," I answer, wondering why he even cares.

"Five years is a long time to work for this company," his voice is soothing to listen to, despite my reservations about him and I note how his tone changes when he's not talking business. He has this way of capturing you with just a subtle tone change, drawing you in. His relaxed natural voice is almost sensual, but overall comforting, genuine, he seems to have the art of relaxing people down to a finely-honed skill, the art of making women want to chat to him effortlessly.

*Very good, very clever. Win over women with conversation. Smooth player.*

"I guess I'm someone who likes to stick to something and work at it. See where it takes me." I tap my notebook against my hip in distraction, trying not to react to the way he sounds.

"You don't care that you're spending your twenties missing

out on life?" He's appraising me again, something he does a lot whenever I'm faced with him and I still never get used to it. Eyes eating me up as though I'm a puzzle to be worked out. I guess I interest him on some level.

"Perspective, Mr. Carrero ... This job offers me opportunities most twenty-six-year-old women never get the chance to experience." I shrug. Trying to will those sharp eyes to look elsewhere and stop tearing into me.

"You never aspired to be anything different?" he watches me thoughtfully, if not a little intensely.

"Such as?" I shift on my shoes, that internal rising awkwardness at his attention, getting a little extreme.

"Managerial role?" he grins. He's amused with his remark but I fail to see the joke so I smile emptily.

"I don't have the qualifications to be in a managerial position, Mr. Carrero ... I worked hard to climb from admin assistant to here ... This is where I want to be." I say, easily irked by him again.

"I guess that's lucky for me then." He throws me his "I can charm anyone with this" smile and I feel myself bristle. I want to get out of here. He obviously knows he's hot and he uses it to his advantage a little too well. I've seen how he turns it up on women, seems to like the reaction and turns more "Dude" with men.

"Perhaps."

"Time will tell, Miss. Anderson ... You can go now, see if Margo is back to relieve you. That letter is not urgent so take lunch first." He smiles me away, obviously bored with my lack of female swooning, with what I assume is his "charming" look and I turn to leave.

"Very good, Mr ... Jake." I throw him a tight smile and catch the flicker of amusement in his eye; aware now that he knows how much I dislike the informality.

*Very good, Carrero ... Here for your fucking amusement.*
I walk toward the heavy door, mood ruined by his smug face.

"Wait. Can you book a table for two tonight, at Manhattan Penthouse at nine, in my name?" he adds quickly, and I turn back to nod that I have heard him.

*Wonder which playmate is being wined and dined tonight?*

I've got used to the special date entries on his schedule and the list of current playmates gracing his bed. I'm sure he, long ago, ran out of headboard space to keep a tally of notches for his conquests and it's just another reason I will never warm to him.

"Yes, sir." I pull the door closed behind me and scowl through the closed dense wood. The urge to stick my fingers up surprises me. I guess I'll have to get used to the reactions he pulls out of me. Work harder to remain impassive. Seems he has an ability to piss me off without effort or without real reason and I don't even want to analyze it.

Twenty minutes later, Margo returns and I am free, just as I feel the AC finally breathe a fresh coolness over me from the ceiling, like a wave of relief. I'm sticky, hot, and flushed, and I need a change of clothes.

I head to the bathroom for a quick freshen up and gaze at the badly lit mirror on the wall, to see I'm glowing red. My cheeks are flushed, there's high color across the nape of my neck, and I have a dewy complexion where my make-up has melted. My hair is no longer slick and smooth in its bun but is weaving its way loose, despite the products I use to keep it sleek. I have natural waves which I straighten to get my hair this smooth and manicured.

*Dammit. I can't continue with my day looking like this.*

I look like I've done a workout in my work clothes, and

I'm melting away. Looking like a panda with the way my eyeliner has collected under my lower lashes and my normally perfect lipstick is looking smudged and damp. I wash my face and release my hair in an effort to minimize the damage. The humidity and heat have caused it to pull back into waves and it's covered in bumps and creases made by the hair ties. Without my straighteners it will never look right, unless I wash it. The company has showers on the fourth floor within the company gym, maybe I should sacrifice lunch and get a quick shower to cool off. I feel like I've been in a sauna.

I check my watch and work out how much time I have and decide to go for it. I have a forty-five-minute lunch break and I can shower in less than half that time. Luckily, I keep a change of clothes in the office, a suggestion from Margo, in case I'm ever asked on an overnight trip at short notice. I know I have toiletries in the bag too.

I go back and retrieve the bag, with my hair held in a loose ponytail, glad that Margo is focused on her laptop while taking a call and doesn't see me. Mona, the outer receptionist, throws me a funny look but says nothing.

I head down in the elevator with my bag and enter the floor that has the employee fitness facilities and shower block. I work for a company that's invested in hotel, fitness, and spas, and these facilities are standard in Carrero buildings, free for all employees. Another perk of this job, among the many.

When I emerge I look brighter and cooler, make-up residue gone, fresh clothes, and hair falling into long, natural waves in its blow-dried state. Unfortunately, there was nothing to straighten my hair within the women's locker room, but I feel cooler. Make-up back in perfect place, clothes a little less stifling, and a little fresher from being steamed and deodorized. Having my hair down bothers me, it's part of my uniform, part of my defense; being up and neat helps me feel more in control. Part of the image I present.

Having it down like this makes me nervous. I know how often I tug at my hair and twist it when I'm home on weekends; another nervous, old Emma, habit that I've found no control over. Anxiety related and childish. There's nothing for it; tying it up without my products and straighteners will look messy. I've got to cope with it for half a day. Even I can get through that, I assure myself as I head to the cafeteria for lunch. People looking at me as if they don't recognize me and it makes me more uneasy.

* * *

Back at my desk after lunch, the switchboard is flashing like mad and I Margo and Jake's lines are busy. Nina has a few calls on hold, so I buzz her to tell her to put one through to me too. I sit down to deal with the first call and catch sight of Margo waving through to me, smiling widely. She points at her head, then mine, indicating my hair and gives me a thumbs up, which makes me grimace. I don't think I've worn it any other way than up, during my five years working here. I feel like I'm not dressed properly and it bothers me far more than it should. I focus on the call.

Half an hour later, I'm lost in thought, absorbed in a financial spreadsheet Jake needs by this evening. I've already plowed through a mountain of work today, making light work of it and not conscious of eyes on me until I hear the movement of feet. Looking up absent-mindedly, more from reaction than any actual realization, I see Jake Carrero is standing staring at me. Six feet from my desk; I jump with fright and feel my face flush with heat.

*Crap.*

"Sorry Mr. Ca ... Jake ... I didn't see you there ... Is there something I can do for you?" my voice is all over the place in my floundering panic. Heart thundering through my chest at a rate of knots.

*How did I not realize that my boss is hovering by my desk?*

I'm supposed to be constantly aware and attentive to his every demand, this is such a faux pas on my part. I'm on my feet trying to plaster on my most friendly and efficient smile. I'm breathless. It's the fright he gave me, I'm flustered and trying to recover quickly. Body trembling with the shock I gave myself noticing his presence.

"Emma ..." He too seems at a loss for words, looking at me peculiarly.

"I was coming to give you these ... You look different!" His expression is unreadable. I can't even say what it is ... I remember my hair's down and flush, because I'm not prepared, I feel vulnerable and falter.

"It won't happen again. I took a shower at lunch, because of the heat from earlier." I need to reel myself in and claw back cool and controlled Emma. I try a steadying breath to stop myself looking like a complete idiot.

"You look ..." his green eyes are piercing through me and its sheer agony, all my little insecurities peeking up in one fell swoop.

"Untidy? It's not how I would normally come to work." I'm rambling, and I'm fidgeting like crazy, unable to just regain control.

*Fuck, fuck, fuck.*
*This is not me!*
*Don't fall to pieces, Emma, not now ... Please. Get a grip and pull yourself together.*

I know it's because he startled me, because I feel

undressed, and I'm at a loss because I feel out of my comfort zone, and he's acting ... odd. My breathing is labored and I'm trying to steady it without making it too obvious and doing a terrible job.

"I was going to say ..." he clears his throat and looks down at the papers, changing his direction of conversation probably because I'm making him uneasy.

*Great job!*

"So, here, I need these copied, emailed, filed ... I'm sure you know the drill." He glances up and away again, as though he isn't comfortable making eye contact right now.

*I do, yes. I do, of course I do. I don't need direction. I need a focus.*

I reach out taking them from him, stopping myself from grabbing.

"Yes, sir."

"Emma ... you look nice," he says softly, glancing at me only to make the remark and then back at his cell, which is now in his hand. I ignore the strange look of apprehension on his face and the tingle inside me ignites. Shifting nervously and try to steady my hands on the folder. This escalated quickly and I'm so angry with myself. I've literally just lost my cool and capable persona in milliseconds, all because of my stupid hair. I plaster on my cool expression and smile tightly.

"Thank you, Mr. Carrero." It's out of my mouth before I realize I didn't call him Jake and it's yet another reason to silently groan.

*Try and regain composure. Years of control, Emma, and you go to mush in seconds.*

I'm beyond livid with myself.

Margo appears a moment later, carrying a briefcase and a jacket. I'm grateful for her sudden appearance and instant calming abilities; I look at the wall clock and realize it's not even 2.00 p.m. I forgot they had a meeting across town at the second Carrero building and are leaving me to man the office. Carrero Tower HQ with Senior, something to do with quarterly finances.

*King Carrero in his ivory tower.*

He prefers to lord his empire in a separate building from Jake, several blocks away. I wonder if the coolness between them is why.

"Emma, divert any important calls and email me if you need anything. I've left you a pile of folders here." She taps a small pile she has placed on the desk, oblivious to my making a complete fool of myself.

"Work through and leave by four thirty." She smiles, her hand coming hooking a stray tendril of my hair and catching me by surprise.

"I like this, it's softer. You look so much prettier and more carefree and young." She smiles again, eyes alive with genuine affection.

I try to smile and force back the grimace I feel, uncomfortable with the attention this slight change is getting me and fully aware it will never happen again. Not entirely comfortable with the way Jake is still looking at me as she fiddles with my hair and I smooth it out of her grasp gently.

I sigh with relief when they utter goodbyes, turn and leave. Thank god, it's over.

*For god's sake.*

I haul over the folders to the front of my desk and throw my hair back over my shoulder angrily.

I'm angry at myself, I'm angry that Jake made me lose my cool without even meaning to. I'm angry that for a split second old Emma resurfaced; teenage Emma. Stupid, idiot, nervous, fidgeting Emma, raised her dumb head.

I've spent years pushing her into the background and

trying to replace her with the more capable and confident me. I don't need her presence or her anxiety and insecurities near me. She's a broken little girl who held me back, and the last thing I need is to see her again.

# Chapter 4

It's raining by the time I get home and I'm soaked walking from the station the few blocks to my apartment. Sarah's out when I get into our third-floor apartment; I take in the coziness of the small rental and feel more relaxed. I'm glad to be home, surrounded by our home comforts and bright rooms; our feminine haven. I'm tired, it's been a long day and I want to take a bath and go to bed.

I screw up Sarah's note, informing me she has made Mac "n" Cheese, from the counter. It's in the refrigerator for me and I throw the paper in the garbage.

The perks of living with a chef. She works late most nights and I can't remember the last time we spent more than five minutes in each other's company. Our lives comprise occasional brief conversations in passing, and notes on the refrigerator which suit me more than when I had to keep her company every evening.

Sarah has been my best friend since forever, we came to New York together five years ago and were lucky to get this place. She'd been accepted to an elite cooking school and I had a temporary admin role in the Carrero corporation, as a receptionist even though I had zero experience and hardly any qualifications. I had been nothing more than a tea and coffee maker back then, eager to do anything to keep me here in this crazy city. My fresh start. My escape from who I didn't want to be anymore and reminders of it. Sarah was thrilled that I wanted to come with her, un-phased at leaving Chicago to go into the world on our own, but our relationship has changed since then. We've drifted apart in so many ways; I guess we don't need each other like we used to; the apartment is the only thing holding us together.

I kick off my shoes and head to my bedroom to get changed, haul on workout leggings and a sports bralette and towel dry my hair back to dampness before my short after work exercise regime, I find it helps me unwind from the day's stress and gets me in the mode for sleep.

There's a flashing light on the answering machine and press it, a surge of anxiety in my stomach as I hazard a guess at who it will be.

It's Marcus.

Sarah's on-off boyfriend—it's who I expected it to be. They have been off again lately, much to my delight, but this call means he's back on the scrounge to hooking up again. I delete the message. She will never know he called. Marcus is as sleazy as they come, but Sarah can't see it; he's slimy, over-friendly, and makes lewd comments and sexual innuendos when he's around. I think she can do better, he makes my skin crawl, but she tries to tell me that my experiences with men are the reason I can't warm to them. I know deep down it's partly the reason I'm this way, but he's still a creep. I try not to linger on it and switch on my iPad for some workout music.

\* \* \*

I'm tired after my workout, meal, and hot bath, yet I know I won't be able to sleep, I've never been a good sleeper, not since childhood, as far as I can remember anyway. I have vivid dreams that make no sense, full of darkness and anxiety that leave me ravaged upon awakening. Working out before bed helps, but doesn't eradicate them and I've learned to live on the erratic, fretful sleep I do get. I still wish I could sleep like a normal person but I know that I may never lose the night terrors, my mind just can't let go of the past, no matter how hard I try to move on.

My cell vibrates, I realize with a small surprise it's a text from Margo. I've been waiting for my job to infringe on me outside regular working hours; I know they've been going easy on me so early into the promotion. I wonder if this is the start of full on PA mode.

*Emma. I need you in an hour early tomorrow, you'll be paid overtime. There will be a car for you, so you won't be late. You're meeting Donna Moore. x*

*That's fine, Margo. Thank you.* I reply uneasily.

This side of the job is new to me; Working early/late, specific outfits— the executives I handled on the lower floors weren't as important, I suppose.. I'm aware that working directly for a Carrero is a whole different ball game and in a way, I'm eager to start properly. I need a new challenge, things on the tenth floor had become stale and predictable.

\* \* \*

The car arrives bright and early next morning, a black four by four; a typical Carrero choice, and the driver is dressed in a black suit, similar to the security who had been in Jake's office. Their appearance makes me roll my eyes, the guy just loves all things black. I have since learned the guard that day was Arrick Carrero's personal bodyguard; Jake doesn't seem to require such things.

Dressed in cream slacks and a dusky pink, silk blouse, a present from my mother for my birthday, which isn't until next week, but she mailed them early to be sure I got them. I don't celebrate my birthday and Sarah knows not to even mention it when it comes around. I was surprised by my mother's gift as she doesn't normally bother, but for some reason, she did this time.

They're not as crisp and tailored as my usual attire but still passable and I feel obliged to wear them at least once as I know how expensive they must have been. I hate that she felt the need to buy me things like this, motherly guilt of some sort no doubt. It's her style, not mine, but she has tried.

My mother is an eternal hippy, romantic frivolity is more her forte and part of her appeal to men. Even in her forties, she's still attractive and men find her desirable; although the less I think about my mother's taste in men, the better. I shake away that memory, pushing down the revulsion in my stomach.

The car drops me at the familiar building; it's gray and wet this morning and there's a cold to the air, New York is coming up for a season change.

I run through the necessary security passes before I'm on the sixty-fifth floor, the building is eerily quiet, due to the early hour. Shivering, I pull my wool coat further around my shoulders to try to warm up, although the building has state-of-the-art temperature control.

Margo greets me at the office door with a blonde woman clad in expensive clothes and an air of seductiveness. Tall graceful and dressed all in red, Margo introduces her as Donna Moore, the personal shopper, and informs me I'm to be measured. Mr. Carrero insists that his closest staff receive this perk, as his public image often sees him on red carpets and at the center of media interest. He expects anyone who might accompany him to be appropriately dressed, always.

His father cashed in on his son's natural sex appeal from an early age, using him as the front man for their range of high-end grooming products and aftershaves, which means a never-ending media interest. The boy is basically a super model for his own company. Still New York's poster boy, even now, he can't seem to move without a camera flash or adoring fan appearing from nowhere.

I stand on a stool feeling hugely uncomfortable at her invasive measuring as she flits around me with a tape measure and questions me things I wear, colors I like, and such. She pulls out her cell and snaps a few pictures of me from all angles. Unhappy with the images, she fusses at me to untie my hair. I hold my patience and irritation in check, and follow her instructions, I'll never get it back in its sleek style without a lot of effort.

*There goes another day enduring it around my face and having everyone croon about it. Just great!*

"For my file, darling ... So I remember your beautiful coloring and bone structure, and how you look with your masses of soft hair." She smiles at me, eyes dazzling like a kid at Christmas. I've no idea why that's a necessity at all.

"I love your hair down." Margo smiles at me, eyeing me up.

"It makes a world of difference, Emma, really, it softens your whole face." She regards me with a warm expression and keen eye which adds another layer of uncomfortable to my mood.

"You don't think it's unprofessional?" I smart. I want them both to back off and stop scrutinizing me, making me nervy.

"Nowhere in the office uniform manual does it say—have your hair tied up like a school mistress." The two women giggle rather surprisingly, killing the whole aura of mature professionals.

"We work in a very high-profile business, that requires a certain attention to image." I can feel the heat in my cheeks rising with irritation, at the giggling, and the fuss over my hair.

"Emma, darling, do you realize how gorgeous those waves are? You've such a lovely color of hair, like pale autumn leaves." Donna chirps.

I look at her blankly, trying not to dredge up images of moldy sodden black and brown splodged leaves, on the New York paving stones last fall. Ignoring how uncomfortable I feel looking "softer".

"She's right, Emma. I think you look so much more natural and pretty like this. I think Jake agreed yesterday." Margo says, a twinkle in her eye.

"Did he now?" I scowl, meeting with amused looks. Ignoring the warm sensation deep in the pit of my stomach.

"Oh, I adore your pout ... You're adorable," Donna gushes and I sigh, realizing arguing is a lost cause. Donna is grinning at me in a mother hen kind of a way and it's the first time I notice the lines around her eyes, giving away a slight hint to her age.

"Emma, I merely meant that you do seem a little severe and uptight when your hair's back. I know that's ironic, considering how I look, but you're young and pretty. You've a natural beauty that you shouldn't hide, it doesn't make you look incapable." She's gushing all over me.

"I look like a child like this." I feel my temper fraying, only too aware how young, having my hair loose makes me look.

"Well, doing that, you do!" Margo tugs my hair from my

fingers and I flush, realizing I have been tugging at a strand under the scrutiny of two overbearing women, annoyed and slightly embarrassed at being caught unawares.

*Crap ... This is them ... Anxiety! Making me feel pressured, putting me on a stand and fluffing around me, knocking me off kilter.*

Taking my hair down is like undressing me.

"Yeah, just don't do the hair twirling and lip pouting." Donna nods in agreement, studying me with a finger on her chin.

"You're a woman child ... It's surprising." She laughs, but it only chafes my already frayed temper.

*I don't need the hair twirling pointed out, thanks very much. I know how bloody stupid it is!*

Teen Emma scurries to hide from my glaring wrath inside the depth of my head.

"Oh, to be that young and beautiful again!" Donna sighs, but Margo throws her a shocked look, exclaiming that she's gorgeous and they go off on a tangent of how fabulous each other look. I find it tiresome. I feel like I'm in the twilight zone.

"Okay, I'll start on your wardrobe darling. Margo has given me a list of the events you need to attend, and some work basics. I'll be back by the end of the day." She waves her hands in excitement.

"We shall trust your judgment, Donna," Margo gushes, we watch as she sweeps out in a flurry of red chiffon and a clip clop of heels. The cyclone that is Donna Moore. The energy in the room calms and I almost sigh with relief.

"Is this necessary?" I get off the stool, relieved at being released, feeling like a full-size Barbie doll.

"Yes, I'm afraid so ... Jake's image is important, the Carrero name envisions luxury and wealth. If you're to attend events with him you need to represent the same image, my dear." She smiles at me with a note of sympathy. "Jake knows asking his staff to spend thousands of their hard-earned pay on an image is ridiculous, so just enjoy the perk." She tries to appease my doubts as I try to calm my internal bristle, and urge to refuse.

"I don't like other people choosing what I wear." I like to be in control of every detail of my life. It's how I function. How I keep calm.

"Hush now. Donna is the one who helped me discover my inner goddess and made me look like this." She twirls like a teenage girl. She's wearing a fitted black suit today, molded, knee-length skirt and low buttoned jacket over a silky, silver camisole top, and perched on high black stilettos. Her blonde hair is a flawless French twist. She looks amazing.

"Really?" I feel slightly appeased. She's the picture of sophistication and control that I aspire to achieve, maybe Donna won't be so bad after all.

"Oh yes, I was hopeless with my style when I started here. Fifteen years on and here I am." She beams at me.

"Fifteen years?" the shock obvious in my tone; that would mean she worked here before Jake was even old enough to help run an empire. He would have been thirteen!

"Yes, I used to be Carrero senior's assistant." She's now clearing up the papers left askew, by Donna, on my desk.

"What's he like?" I've always been intrigued by the older man and meeting him last year quelled none of the interest. He seemed to be a force to be reckoned with.

"Like someone you never want to willingly meet." The deep smooth voice is so unexpected and close, I jump and spin around to see Jake striding in the door casually. The flutters in my stomach come back full force, reminding me I'm still standing in the middle of the room and I move to my desk.

He's wearing designer jeans in a soft, washed-out color, a white T-shirt with a graffiti print logo that is slightly too neat on that body, modern leather jacket, and his trademark shades. He doesn't look like a guy who's coming to the office for the day. I'm not sure I'm impressed, despite how much it suits him; bad boy biker style, it's not exactly professional.

"Mr. Carrero ... I mean—Jake ... Good morning." Controlled Emma is back in play, despite the hair tickling my face and the breathlessness at his appearance and attire.

"You look really nice today, Emma." He smiles, allowing his gaze to travel over me from head to foot, it makes me uncomfortable, yet still my face flushes with heat.

*Traitorous body!*

"And you, Margo." He turns his head toward her, it almost seems like an afterthought, but she smiles.

"Don't I always?" she smirks and throws him a wink.

"Of course." He grins at her and lifts his shades to the top of his head to nestle in his hair. I try to ignore the slight flip low in my stomach, hate that I react to him this way and quash it, looking anywhere but at him.

*He probably practices every sexy move and mannerism he has in the mirror a dozen times a night for ultimate appeal!*

"What's with the outfit?" she enquires, looking him up and down questioningly.

"Even for you that's rather casual for work."

"All work and no play, makes for a very sad boy." He grins back at her.

"Touch of espionage today, Margo, *Bambino*." His term makes me cringe.

*Baby? Really? Is this a hint of Casanova Carrero peeking out?*

I look down at my desk to hide the revulsion I know fleets across my face.

"Do you need me to come with you?" she looks him over intrigued and completely un-phased by his pet name.

"I actually need Emma, if she's up to it?" he turns, throwing me one of the heart aching "Yes, I know I'm hot" smiles, but I don't react. I've seen this smile in action when I researched him, and it does little for me.

*Liar.*

"I'm up to whatever task you ask of me," I respond.

*Within reason!*

The smile is making me uneasy.

"Intriguing." Margo frowns at him, still trying to work out what he is up to. "Is this the Daniel Hunter meeting? I thought we scheduled it for next week?" They're both standing at my desk, a little too closely for me to ignore, so I keep my eyes on the screen in front of me instead and try to appear busy.

"We decided to do it this morning ... He's free for a couple of days. Next week he's flying to Paris."

She nods, understanding what he's talking about; I'm not yet privy to the inner office secrets between them, which happen frequently.

"My office, Emma, please." He walks away, and I can only follow. I match his purposeful stride, even in heels, he waits until Margo and I've followed him in and closes the door behind us; she goes straight to his laptop, pulling it across the table to access, leans over the desk, pulling up files as he turns to me, "Do you have anything less ... *PA* ... to wear here?"

I falter and feel my face warm as he looks up at me with a smile.

*What now?*

"Emma, yes, dear. You'll be accompanying Jake today, but you need to look like a date rather than an assistant." Margo crosses to the printer to retrieve the files she's printed off.

I pause and muster all my willpower to keep my lungs moving in and out.

*Again ... What?*

I don't even know how to respond to that.

"You are going to be his number two today ... everyone knows I'm his PA, whereas, you my dear, are new blood." She smiles encouragingly, but it does nothing to my inner concerns.

"We're up to no good." He smiles at me in a very disarming way as I try to gauge his expression and hers, not convinced they're being serious.

"No, I don't have any other clothes here," I say quietly, the irritation rising within me.

"Maybe we can stop at your apartment and let you change?" Jake's looking at me now and I frown in confusion.

*Why would I?*

"Change?" I say icily. My stomach dropping at speed.

"Yeah." He stands and walks toward me, eyeing me up as though trying to picture me in less formal clothes. Pushes his hands into his jean's pockets, which only further emphasizes his muscular body and lack of formality. It's distracting.

"Something more casual." He chews his bottom lip while thinking and staring, a lot of staring. I glance down at my tailored cream trousers and spiked heels, I look exactly as I should.

"What? Like jeans?" I try to control the edgy tone in my voice this time.

"I was thinking more ... feminine ... a dress." The humor in his voice grates on me, I thought I was done being Barbie already.

*Why does my being in a dress amuse him? Am I that un-feminine?*

"If that's required, then yes. I have access to dresses." Sarah has a closet full of them, the kind of romantic clothes I avoid like the plague.

"We'll go there first then ... I need this meeting to look more of a breakfast date between friends." He straightens up, pulling his hands free and crosses them across his wide chest instead.

"Am I to be enlightened on my role in this?" I ask stiffly. I didn't think I would be subjected to dress up.

"I'm meeting with Daniel Hunter ... He's a player in his family business." He keeps his voice low, despite being closed in his own office. "I'll not say why until we work out a few particulars bu thanks to his very public break up, the media is all over his ass and he can't shake them to meet in private—"

"You're his fake date! Daniel will have a girl with him too, so it will appear as though four friends are having breakfast at the Waldorf." Margo cuts in. "You'll need to take notes and get acquainted with the particulars of the proposed merger, Emma, this is your first big responsibility. I'm taking a back seat on this."

*Crap.*

I'm to do this while being stripped of all that makes me comfortable and confident.

"I see."

"All you need to do is smile and look adoringly at me until we get into the suite where Daniel is staying." Jake shrugs with one shoulder.

*Yes, I'm sure that's going to be easy.*

"When are you leaving?" Margo presses, turning his hazy green eyes away from the scrutinizing he is doing over me.

"Now, if she needs to go home first ... Where do you stay, Emma?" his eyes are back on mine, once again making me uneasy as he scans my attire.

I tell him where in West Sunnyside and he nods before moving off to call his driver, I hear him telling him to meet us at the rear of the underground parking garage.

"Take a notepad and pen in a handbag, anything else will look odd ... It's a preliminary meeting to thrash out the proposal, so take notes." Margo soothes my nerves with a warm smile.

"Yes, Margo." I answer blankly, head reeling with all of this and feeling overwhelmed suddenly.

"Emma?" She halts me with a gentle hand on my arm.

"Yes?" I pause at her sudden intense look.

"Try to relax around Jake ... He's actually very easy to hang out with." She grins, but it does nothing to remove the tension building up inside of me.

*I don't want to hang out, I want to do my job.*

\* \* \*

Less than twenty minutes later, I'm in the back of a large SUV with tinted windows and I'm sitting mere inches away from him. My briefcase on my lap and a pen in one hand. I'm preoccupied, mulling over the weirdness of this request.

"That habit is at odds with how you present yourself, you know?"

I look up at his remark questioningly. The way he is regarding me, and half-smirking my way.

*What the hell is he talking about?*

I realize I have a strand of hair between my fingers, absent-mindedly twisting it. I drop it and still my hands on my lap, internally cursing him out.

*For god's sake ...*

It's the being unprepared, it has me on edge.

*Nice move, Emma.*

I scowl at teen Emma, always peeking at me from the recesses of my mind and smile tightly in response.

"Nervous habit?" he presses further, looking smugger.

"I don't get nervous, Mr. Carrero," I respond drily.

*Because I've spent many years perfecting the art hiding it, and for some reason, you bring it out in me when I'm not focusing.*

"Do I make you nervous?" he smiles, he's leaning back in his seat comfortably, an arm on the window ledge and looks effortlessly casual.

"I would not say that, Mr. Carrero."

*What would I say?*

Because he does make me nervous, if I'm being honest; I don't know how to act around him sometimes.

"Do I intimidate you?" his tone is steady and quizzical, a hint of playful and it's already tiring me.

*Are we really doing this?*

"I just don't know you well enough to feel at ease around you yet," I answer, impressed with my diplomatic response under the pressure of his gaze.

"I don't think any woman has ever told me I'm intimidating before." His eyes twinkle mischievously, his focus on me intense.

"I don't believe I actually said that," I say.

"You didn't say no."

"If that's how you perceived what I said." I smile tightly, but he laughs that only further grates on me.

"I've never met a woman who acts like you do around

me," he says, pushing a foot against the door so he can lounge some more. I throw him a wary yet questioning glance.

*What's that supposed to mean? Because I don't throw myself at you, begging to be mauled?*

"Women usually flirt ... Make their intentions clear, or just quiz the crap out of me." He shrugs, un-phased by the statement he made and oblivious to how much of an ass it makes him appear.

"Women openly tell you they want to bed you, Mr. Carrero?" I ask. I already assumed this was the case, the fact he expects it is a little repulsive. The fact he expected it of me, makes me irritated.

"Something like that." He grins at my honesty, watching me closely still, his body turned toward me slightly.

"That must be nice." I look out at the passing scenery, completely uncomfortable with the direction of this conversation, finding him highly inappropriate and praying to just get to Sunnyside quickly.

*Only one more block to my apartment and I can get a reprieve from this crap. Why did I have to live so far?*

"It gets old ... I like being intimidating ... That's one I haven't heard yet." He laughs at me again and I try to ignore it, hating that his laugh is nice to listen to.

I cast him a shady look.

*Must be so boring having women fall at your feet every day and tell you how sexy you are. Must be so hard to have been born with a silver spoon in your mouth, and no real problems in life, except how sexy your outfit is that day.*

"In what way?" he says in afterthought, turning his gaze back on me once more.

"What way what?" I feel tense. I hate feeling tense and watch my fingers carefully, making sure they stay steady on my lap.

"In what way do I intimidate you?" he's finding this highly amusing, judging by the expression plastered over his smug face, and the tone in his voice which screams tease.

"Is this necessary?" I bristle.

"What? Wanting to get to know my PA a little better? ... I think so."

*Sure, if that's what we call this ... Ego fluffing.*

"Probing." I say evenly.

"I don't think wanting to know why I make you so uncomfortable is probing ... We're going to spend the next few hours together, I think it's necessary. It's a novelty for me." He looks smug without smiling.

"I never said I was uncomfortable, you've summarized what I said and concluded what you're now pursuing. I merely said I don't know you well." He's exasperating me now and getting pissed at your boss is never a good career move. I try to keep my tone steady and unemotional, but I even hear the note of agitation in my own voice.

"My apologies." He laughs in that disarming way he has, and I sigh angrily. He knows how to get under my skin.

"Are you always this defensive?" he asks.

*For the love of god ...*

I need to muster all my strength to remain impassive.

"Are you always so informal with staff?" I retort defensively. Gripping my jacket hem to try and keep my temper low.

"Emma, my staff are people I respect ... People whose skills benefit me. I don't see a need to act like a stuffed shirt because I employ them. I'm not my father." I hate the way he's studying me, I can feel his eyes on the side of my face and I continue to ignore it.

"You're not like him ... I met him ... You're nothing like

him."

*In that he knows how to behave. He understands the boundaries between boss and employee.*

"Good. I don't aim to be." I feel him shift in his seat. "We don't exactly see eye to eye on most things."

I give him a cool look and notice he seems a little less relaxed. Maybe talking about his father makes him uptight. I can relate to that, not that I would call the sperm donor a father; the absent sperm donor of my childhood.

"You're not curious?" he looks at me quizzically, green eyes once again boring into the side of my face and making me uncomfortable.

"Curious about what?"

"Why I don't get along with him? ... Most women pry ... They want the juicy details." A hint of a smile in his voice, a gross generalization of my sex. I curb the urge to eye roll at him.

"No. It's not my business." I smile tightly; I'm not most women. It's a relief when we pull up in front of my building and I see my chance of escape for a few minutes.

"This is me." I point up at the block of attractive brown apartments rising above us, he regards me for a second then gestures I should go.

"I'll wait here, go get changed ... Something feminine and soft ... Something you wouldn't normally wear." He gives me an odd look, hiding his amusement and I have the sudden urge to throat punch him.

*Something feminine? Really? I'm pretty sure any clothes made predominantly for women are classed as feminine!*

Once in my apartment, I go straight to Sarah's room, she's still sound asleep in bed, so I quietly pull two dresses from the back of her closet with a grimace. This doesn't sit well with me, but I pick the floral floaty number my mother would approve of, it's not as short as the other one and I know she has shoes that match this. I go to my room so as not to disturb her and change quickly, despairing at my reflection with a curse and return to the SUV looking like some floaty hippy girl in love, in less than ten minutes.

"Better," he says, his eyes appraising me as I slide in. I ignore it. Dressed like this I feel exposed, I need my armor ... my tailoring and hair to keep my PA persona with me. Dressed like this I feel like teen Emma and it scares me, takes away my defenses. I don't like to be unprepared.

The car moves off again and I sit back, trying to relax. It's hard to do when every one of your nerve endings is on high alert. My legs are exposed a lot in this floaty dress and I pull them in tightly against the seat, pulling the hem toward my knees sharply.

"Why all the secrecy?" I ask in attempt to interrupt the way he's watching me, if I didn't know better, I would think he was checking my legs out. His gaze has certainly swept the length of me twice since I returned.

"His father, much like mine, owns a majority share of his business. Family money. If either gets wind of what we're meeting about then they would oppose this before I can get things in place. Once I maneuver this a certain way they will be unable to refuse." He sits back, turning to stare ahead, instead of at me, thankfully.

"So, you're going behind your father's back?" I say, blinking at him as though I have no real sense of this.

"For now. He would refuse to even consider it." He shrugs and starts pushing at something with the toe of his boot on the door.

"Why?"

"Hunter and my father have a history. They let their rift cloud what's good for business." He leans closer to me, abandoning whatever he was kicking at.

"And you think a merger, with someone your father hates, is a good business move?" I sit back in my seat trying to keep the distance, trying not to inhale that aftershave or unique Carrero scent. He smells too nice for my liking.

"If I do this right, then yes ... We stand to make a lot of money." He shrugs and goes back to looking out his window at passing scenery, moving back again.

"What exactly are you going to be merging with?" I relax, glad to have my breathing space back.

"They're primarily ship builders. I want to take our hotel experiences and build luxury, floating hotels and spas bearing the Carrero name. Modern conveniences with luxury fitness amenities onboard ... Super boats."

"Like cruise ships?"

"High-end cruise ships, only a lot bigger and more *pamper* based."

"What makes you think they will be a success?" I'm intrigued by his plan.

"The Carrero name ... It's what Hunter needs for this venture to be plausible. Their reputation of late has suffered. They had a few multibillion dollar disasters. They get our reputation and our name, and we get rights to the designs they have in progress."

"So, this meeting ...?" I'm impressed with his idea and know only too well the rich clients of Carrero would jump at a chance to stay on a floating spa.

"To outline my plan ... How I'm going to maneuver my father to agree to the terms. He could dissolve the whole thing." He looks serious, a return of boss mode.

"I see ... What's expected of me when we get there, Mr. Carrero?" Best to know my part and be prepared so I can act accordingly.

"I just need you to look adoring if we see any lingering photographers, there may be press hanging around. Daniel's going through a bit of a media scandal ... Caught screwing someone of importance and then she dumped him publicly."

"Then, when we're inside, I need you to keep detailed notes of what's discussed so I can backtrack later."

"Great." I grimace, wondering what looking adoring entails.

"You'll just have to follow my lead, Emma, and don't get too insulted if I need to touch you." He throws me a smile, watching for a reaction, a little too closely.

"Touch me?" I flinch at the tone of my own voice betraying me. My heart rate ups a few notches and my palms become clammy.

*I never signed up for touching.*

"You're my date remember ... I may need to hold your hand, or it might look weird ... When I take women out they're usually inclined to hang over me." He shrugs again, those piercing eyes back on the front of the car and giving me respite.

*Of course, they are.*

This makes me uptight.

*Great ... Now he wants to touch me and cuddle up for the cameras, nowhere did I sign up for that in my employment contract.*

"I have your permission?" He looks at me hesitantly, waiting for a response.

"Yes." It's my job. I feel anything but sure, but what harm could it do?

*Keep reminding yourself of that fact, Emma ... I'm sure I can tolerate hand holding for a few minutes, even with him.*

"Good."

As the car draws up to a grand hotel I'm not relishing what's coming, trying not to over-analyze any of this. Before I know it, his driver is opening my door. I step out as Jake follows behind me; we immediately see the hovering photographers with long-lensed cameras hung around their necks and they peak their interest as Jake slides smoothly up behind me, reaching his full height. Even without touching me, I feel him behind me. My body suddenly on high alert at his proximity.

"Ready?" he whispers and loops his fingers in mine as he comes around me to lead, pulling me toward the doormen. I can't concentrate on much else except the uncomfortable heat of his skin on mine and the way his hand practically dwarves my own. I've never let anyone hold my hand ... Well, my mother, maybe once or twice, but she doesn't count. It's not a welcome experience and I have to steel against the urge to recoil and snap my hand away.

Suddenly there's a small flash that startles me.

*Crap.*

I hear them call his name from the right side of us; he walks on, ignoring them, and pulling me toward our destination, pulling me against the side of his body, his grip tightening, keeping me close. I keep my chin down, watching my feet and for the first time glad my hair is down to shield my face. We walk on and I allow myself to be led, there's something disturbingly reassuring about it, despite my reservations. I feel safer than I had expected with him.

The photographers are denied entry beyond the huge glass doors by tall, uniformed doormen.

"Are you here to see Daniel Hunter, Mr. Carrero?" a faceless voice calls out.

"Are you consoling your friend over the break up with porn star, Candy Kane?" Another voice. I cringe ...

*What the hell? Someone of importance. A goddamn porn star!*

"Jake?" A male voice greets us from inside the lobby and I'm introduced to Daniel Hunter. Another billionaire playboy from a wealthy family. The two men fist bump in such a laddish way and do that whole guy arm embrace thing, where they bump shoulders in a macho manner. I watch in complete disbelief that this man is my actual boss, acting like a street thug while his buddy is tugging along a leggy supermodel looking creature.

*Got over his porn star pretty quick.*

Daniel takes in my appearance rather obviously.

"She's not your usual type?" he smirks as the two men greet warmly.

"She's definitely yours though." Jake smirks, nodding toward the disinterested bimbo, reminding him of their purpose here, and Daniel grins. I instantly dislike him.

He's tall and well built, like Jake, but he has sandy blonde hair and dark brown eyes. He's handsome in a classic American way, but something about his features make him seem shifty. Sleazy maybe.

The other girl looks bored, dark hair cascading over fake breasts, standing tall in stilettos and a short playsuit. She's picking at her red nails as we move on, following Daniel back into the hotel.

Jake keeps hold of my hand, throwing a glance back at the lenses pointed in through the glass entrance, he throws an arm around my shoulders, shielding my face from view and I inwardly freeze.

"Try to relax ... You're tense." He smiles down at me, close enough that most would assume he kissed me lightly and I know he's trying to give this impression. I hold my breath, suddenly assaulted with how good he smells and feels so close to me. It's unexpectedly sensual and the intimate closeness sends me into panic mode.

I react without thinking, to lift a defensive hand to his chest as my heart pounds crazily. I feel overwhelmed and scared. I don't like the proximity; instinct taking over. He grasps my fingers with his free hand and holds them gently, shielding my reaction and making it look like something else entirely.

I focus on my breathing trying to block out the creeping fear running over me.

*Don't fall apart,* I scold myself internally. *Hold your shit together, Emma. It's only pretend and he's barely touching you.*

"I have a room." Daniel winks at us as though implying something is going on.

"I figured I would have a use for it afterwards." He throws a glance toward the leggy, bored, supermodel, who looks like she's as excited for that as she is about being here. I grimace and flush at his insinuation.

Jake releases me when we're in the confines of the elevator and throws me a smile. I feel like it's meant as praise, but I don't respond, too busy trying to calm my pounding heart rate and get my breathing to normalize.

We get to the desired floor and follow Daniel, he already has his key card in his hand.

"I took the liberty of ordering a breakfast menu ... I know you like to eat, Jakey boy." He grins Jake's way and gets a smile in return.

"I'm starving, and I'm sure Emma needs to eat too."

I nod shyly. I hadn't had time to eat this morning, but I'm not sure how he could even know that.

Finally, in the hotel room, I feel stupidly disconcerted. It's knocked me for six. Jake's hands on me have left permanent heat where he laid them, a lasting sensation, as though they are still on me. I give myself an internal slap and pull myself together.

*I need to stop over thinking this.*

# Chapter 5

I sit and listen as we eat from the breakfast buffet, the business merger sounds promising and I take key point notes on things he will want to recap. I listen intently to them thrash through proposals and possibilities with enthusiasm and can see that these men are genuine friends. They have a rapport you can only find between men who know each other well, sarcasm and banter interlaced with business talk. Jake is one of the 'guys' when he's around Daniel.

I notice as I've been sitting cross legged that Daniel Hunter has not concealed his open appraisal of me, his eyes following my legs and arms intrusively, as Jake outlines some points of business. He makes my skin crawl and I'm doing my best to ignore him. I catch Jake glance my way a couple of times, with an unreadable expression before he looks back at his friend.

I look up occasionally from note taking and am intrigued with the differences between them. The friendship seems genuine, but I don't see the connection.

The way Jake just occupies a space, effortlessly cool and sprawled out; he always looks so laid back and comfortable in all surroundings, even at work. Right now, his feet, crossed at the ankles are on the low coffee table, he's sitting low down in the arm chair like an adolescent with his forearms resting on the arms of the chair, his head nuzzled in the cushioned back. Yet he still has an air of capability and command, he's just so at ease and still. I guess he's always been comfy in his own skin and probably had adoring girls throwing themselves at him from a very early age. A blessed life that instilled this self-assurance.

Daniel, on the other hand, is more hyperactive and fidgety. Sitting straight up on the couch and leaning forward away from the back. He moves a lot when he talks and behaves over energetically when his interest is peaked. I wonder if he's a firm member of the "Charlie" culture among the rich and famous. Cocaine use is common, I've seen a lot of it in the ladies' bathrooms at the Carrero glitzy parties, events, and promotions. I glance at Jake, wondering if he's someone who uses it too and feel a heavy ache in my chest. I hope he's not, I've always had zero tolerance to drug use.

When we're done, Jake stands and stretches out, revealing a tiny inch of the naked toned abdomen at his jeans waistband and it takes all my strength not to inhale sharply. I'm beyond mortified at my own reaction but hide it well. I've seen naked before. I'm no virgin and I'm pissed at myself for the stupid reactions I have to this man. He brings out such adolescent responses in me.

*Although ... that abdomen is worth an ogle!*

"I'll work out the finer points, Daniel and we'll meet again. Next time more formally, to discuss this further." He shakes Daniel's hand and they hug in a very "Bromance" way.

*Nice. Male bonding over stabbing your fathers in the back. How admirable.*

"Dude, we on for a drinking session when I get back?"

"You need to ask?" Jake jokes as they stand a foot apart.

"Yeah, guess you need your wing man to help you pick up on the pretties. You're pretty useless solo." Daniel laughs and pushes Jake in the arm playfully.

"We both know I'm the one with the moves, women just like your pretty boy smile and fat wallet, Princess." Jake pinches his cheek and is rewarded with Daniel's middle finger.

Daniel turns to me with a sideways crooked smile and a glint of sleaze in his eye. I steel against an eye roll and remain impassive under his scrutiny, standing up slowly and pulling my bag to my side.

"Emma, it was really nice to meet you, I'm sure Jake would let me take you out to dinner." He smiles my way.

*Does he realize his slinky, sexy, bored woman is ten feet away lounging on a couch and watching a movie on her iPad?*

My skin crawls.

"I wouldn't let you anywhere near her Hunter! I know your MO remember." Jake cuts in smoothly and easily between us, saving me from a refusal.

"Bro?" Daniel frowns with mock shock, holding a hand to his chest as though he's deeply wounded.

"Forget it ... I wouldn't let you near her with anyone else's, let alone yours." Jake's still joking, but there's a slight edge to his tone.

*He's serious.*

"I forgot you don't mess with the staff." Daniel laughs smugly. I miss whatever look passes between them as Jake stands in front of me.

"I don't mess with good girls—Period." Jake turns, throws me a cavalier wink and my heart stops mid-beat.

*He thinks I'm a good girl? What does that even mean?*

*Boring, uptight? What's wrong with good girls?*

"Amen to that!" Daniel cuts in and both men high five in a show of male camaraderie. This time I don't quell the urge to eye roll and catch Jake grinning back at me.

I feel a swell of relief as he turns, placing a hand on the small of my back to guide me out. It's the first time skin contact has been acceptable between us, he heads me out of the room, along the hall, and finally to the row of gold colored elevators leaving Daniel behind in the room, to do whatever with his date.

"I'm sorry I answered for you," Jake glances at me in the elevator.

"I just don't think any good would come from dating Daniel Hunter ... I know him too well." The look of conviction and honesty is endearing.

"I don't want to date Daniel Hunter." I smile tightly, suddenly warm and a little claustrophobic but also deadly serious.

Why does he have this knack of tilting me off keel? I don't like it."He's bad news with women." He frowns at me, watching me a little closely and I have to look away for a second to stop the creep of heat running up inside of me.

"Bit like you then?" I smirk and catch the full width of that jaw-dropping smile from the corner of my eye. It's unexpected and makes me smile too.

"I'm not bad news for women ... I know how to treat them, whereas Daniel does not. He's a typical playboy, he doesn't care whose feelings he hurts."

*Irony.*

He slips an arm around me, pulling me in against him, shielding me as we leave the elevator amid more flashes and clicks. This time I anticipate it and feel more relaxed about the contact. I keep my eyes on the floor and try not to react to him, which is hard, considering he has me pressed very securely to that muscular frame and it's not exactly unpleasant.

Outside I look up, blinking harshly as the sun glares, I lift my hand to shield my eyes. He slides his shades from his head onto my face in such a fluid movement that I'm taken by surprise. He registers nothing on his face, just guides me to our car as it pulls up and he deposits me in the back before following me in. I suddenly get a little inkling of how the women he dates must feel; he's attentive and in control, with great manners. He's a gentleman.

*Very smooth, Carrero, unexpectedly smooth.*

I hand them back in the dark confines of the car and he pushes them back on top of his head with a smile.

"Back to the office?" I enquire, clutching my briefcase to offload my notepad.

"Not yet. I've some things to do and I figure we could use the bonding time, Margo agreed we should get better acquainted." He looks out the window as we move off, watching the photographers fall back. Tinted windows concealing us fully.

"Why? I'm only your PA." I'm surprised and too quick verbally to curb my stupid question. I know I should never quiz the boss.

"And that job entails a lot more than typing, Emma. I know you're used to working for the execs on the lower floors, but I've certain tasks that my staff undertake. It's why I took you on a recommendation and didn't just dip into the temp pool." He studies my face seriously.

"Tasks? Beyond those of a PA?" I ask carefully.

"You'll accompany me on business trips, dinners and such. Sometimes I prefer my PA to an actual date. Less hassle. Your being unmarried and having no kids are part of the reason Margo singled you out from the list. She recognizes that you're career oriented and like to go above and beyond for your position."

*Above and beyond? What the hell does that mean?*

"List?" I query instead, trying to not mull over the fact he sometimes replaces dates with his PA. Trying not to read anything into what he just said.

"There were more than thirty employees recommended for your role."

"I'm not surprised, I guess this was a job worthy of fighting over."

Of course, there would have been a list; every woman this side of Manhattan would want to work for Jake Carrero. Work with him closely, very closely.

"You'll soon get sick of the flights and hotels, Emma. I practically live out of a suitcase." He sighs and once again finds that something with the toe of his boot at the door to start pushing. It's oddly juvenile.

"I will?" The thought is a little exciting, I long to travel, long to experience things beyond New York.

"Margo has a husband and family, she can't be my chaperone anytime I need her. She's missed out on so much of her kids' lives." He looks genuinely guilty about this.

"Now her husband is retiring, and I think she feels it's time to rekindle her marriage. So, she took the opportunity to find a more suitable assistant. Natalia has already decided that on her return, she won't return to my office, she wants to offload some of her responsibilities and concentrate on family." He throws me another disarming smile.

"Not everyone can handle the intensity of this job, Emma ... Or the hours, and once you're ready to move up to Margo's position, we'll find someone else to work under you." He stops with the fidgeting and rests his focus on me once more.

"I hope I don't disappoint. I aim to work my butt off," I say, honestly, starting to relax in his presence, somehow seeing a new side to him after this little encounter. Time alone has made me a little less intimidated by him.

"Over the last couple of days I've been observing you; trying to find out if we're compatible enough to have the same kind of working relationship that I have with Margo."

"And?" I'm surprised by this.

"You're still my PA, aren't you?" He smiles warmly, that devastating natural smile of his.

"Early days, Mr. Carrero." I smile back, feeling a little bit of my relaxed humor seeping into my tone, feeding from his casualness for once.

"Reading people is a gift of mine. I recognize ability. I think once you relax and thaw a little, we'll get on fine. Your skills are on point, you follow instruction and you take initiative."

I'm stunned. I don't know why his praise shocks me, I know how hard I work, I know how good I am. I guess I'm shocked that he even noticed. He seems too relaxed to sharply watch people. I guess it's another of his hidden skills, a silent observer who is very good at hiding it.

"Margo aims to hand over to you eventually ... I want to make the transition smooth, so she has no reason to backtrack. Margo deserves her retirement." I see the affection in his face, I don't think I've ever seen that kind of connection between co-workers that wasn't sex based.

"I'm sure I won't disappoint her," I say.

"You need to learn to relax around me."

"If you're implying I adopt your casual posture and manner, then I don't think the transition will go as smoothly as you want." with an edge of seriousness in my tone. I want him to understand that I'll never be as lax as Margo in our work relationship.

He just grins at me, all white straight teeth, and chiseled handsomeness.

*Annoyingly so.*

# Chapter 6

It's been twelve weeks since I met Jake Carrero and I'm no longer unsure around my over-familiar boss. In such a brief time, the forced proximity and grueling demands has carved out an amicable relationship that doesn't completely offend me. I find him tolerable, sometimes even amusing, I'd go as far as saying companionable. I maybe even like him a little more than I ever imagined I could.

The full force of my job requirements came upon me in a tidal wave after the Hunter breakfast. Margo decided to throw me in the deep end as it was the only way to test my resolve and she has slowly been receding from the picture, until now. Now she is completely absent.

I run after him to meetings, carrying files and folders, a wealth of information always at my fingertips. Awaiting his commands, always up to speed with every detail he's dealing with, always involved. He's an exhausting workaholic, with a very hands on approach, yet I've never been happier or more challenged.

Trips are frequent and tiring and I spend my days in an endless flurry of typing, answering phones, having orders tossed at me, and dealing with a hundred people via my iPad, iPhone, and laptop, all of which he thrust at me rather ceremoniously after the Hunter meeting.

I'm excelling at the control and efficiency and am starting to take it all in my stride. Despite acting like he's Mr. Cool and laid back, and takes nothing seriously, I was pleasantly surprised to find Jake is deeply embroiled in his father's business. Surprised to find Mr. Carrero does in fact possess a very shrewd business brain and high IQ that contradicts how he presents himself. I guess that's a part of his allure, he's smart, sharp, and attentive, but wrapped up in casual charm and sexiness normally associated with dumb underwear models.

I've been privy to so many contracts and papers in such a short time that my head reels every night when I go to bed. I've lost the ability to switch off and I now lie awake restless with things I need to get done the next day. Eager to go back to work; I've found so much more enjoyment in submerging myself in my new role than I ever found on the tenth floor.

Jake was right about identifying my skills, he pounced on them and uses them to full capacity every single day. He's never dull to be around, that's for sure.

My wardrobe has expanded hugely thanks to the skill of Donna Moore and I can't say it's unpleasant. Her taste is impeccable, and she has chosen things I would have bought for myself. Margo was right, it's a perk I am enjoying. I looked forward to her frequent visits, laden with bags of clothes Jake has assured her I need.

"Emma?" Jake's voice cuts through my thoughts as I run through my schedule on the iPad in my hand, engrossed on shifting appointments to fit in an impromptu trip and emailing the changes to Rosalie to organize. She's my new assistant, replacing me in my old position, now Margo has retired. He's just arrived back from an early lunch with one of his brainless bimbos.

"Jake?" I answer without looking up, aware of his body heat close behind me.

"I need the Hunter file." His voice runs over me smoothly.

"Already on your desk" I smile graciously, pulling down the back of my tailored jacket, a gray woolen Dior courtesy of Donna; standing in the middle of my office, which is right outside his. I walked out from placing those exact files on his desk when my email beeped.

"Thanks, did you call and arrange my dinner booking with Clare?" His girl of the moment, yet not the lunch date; some Hollywood actress turned country singer with endless legs and oversized boobs. I dislike all of his girls, and the frequency in which he replaces them.

"Yes. You're in at eight at the Plaza, where she's staying. I've arranged for the car to collect you." I respond drily, trying to keep the disdain from my voice.

"Good girl." He pats my back childishly and I give him an indulgent look ...

*"Good girl?" Like I'm some sort of puppy. Next, he'll be giving me a biscuit.*

"Emma?"

"Mmm-hmmm?" I look down distractedly as an email reply from Rosalie pings to the top right corner of my tablet. She's down at accounting and not at her desk, ten feet away.

"Fuck!" Jake breathes right behind my head, his breath on my hair and it sends tingles from the contact.

"What?" I look up in surprise at him, craning round to see his face behind me, he's glaring past me toward the wall of glass in the outer hallway as a group of suited men and women make their way toward us from the elevators. They

## The Carrero Effect ~ The Promotion

haven't seen us yet, as their view is impaired from the angle. Jake swipes me around the waist and halls me backward, making me almost drop my iPad. Pulled into his office, he shuts the door as I squeal in surprise at being man handled in such a Neanderthal way and make a protest.

"Jake!"

"Shhhh." He covers my mouth with his hand, still caught in his arm, he pulls me backward, lifting my feet from the floor. My arms flail with the sudden kidnapping, and I grip my iPad tighter, struggling weakly.

I hate when he does stuff like this, he has no concept of personal space or how inappropriate it is to manhandle your PA. He manhandles me way more than I ever thought possible. This is often a daily occurrence in some way or another.

"Just be quiet and do as you're told." He drops me from his embrace, grabs my free hand, hauling me toward the rarely used door of his office into his second room, with apology. It's a changing room come office that I've never actually understood. He stores clothes, art, and random crap in here, including the couches which used to grace the office floor.

He latches the door behind us and sits on one of the cream couches, leaving me heaving in the middle of the floor like a crazy person.

"Jake are you having some sort of mental breakdown?" I snap looking around the room he has us caught in, while I steady my breath. I run my hands down my skirt, trying to unwrinkle my clothes now I've been unceremoniously released, to regain my demeanor.

"It's my father ... I don't want to see him." He shrugs at me as though it's all the explanation I need.

I know that several heated calls have taken place in the last few days, when the Hunter merger become public. I learned quickly how strained the father-son relationship is and it's not the first time we have evaded Carrero senior. He either evades him or insists on antagonizing him in heated rows. Usually public rows. They have a deep rooted conflict I've never pressed him about.

"Why didn't you leave me out there to tell them you're not here then?" I snap and keep my voice low. I hate when he grabs me, it's something he does frequently, when he wants me to move in a hurry, or get out of his way.

*Wouldn't kill you to just ask me to move!*

"Because wherever you are, is where I usually am. He knows that!" I can't argue with that logic, Jake seems to require my presence a lot more than I ever saw him with Margo.

I hear his cell ring in his pocket and he slides it out, sighs and slides it back down onto the couch, silencing it. I feel my temper dissipate and push my cool facade back into place as I watch the hopeless look on his face.

*So boyish at times.*

He stretches his hands behind his head in that casual way he has, closes his eyes as I watch, bemused, but still irritated.

*My boss, the man-child.*

Sometimes endearing, but generally a huge irritation to my day.

"If we hide out here for ten minutes, he will fuck off." He says through closed eyes, hands tucked behind his head and mimicking sleep.

"Jake." I warn lightly, he rarely swears at work. He opens one eye and smiles at me, sliding to his left he turns, lifts his feet onto the couch and slides down to get comfy. A slide into a laid down position.

*Yes, this is the CEO of this empire!*

"Power nap until he leaves my floor." He smiles; even through tailored suits, I can still make out the perfect lines of his body and look away to steady my focus on the rail of clothes in here. Distraction always works.

*When was the last time he used any of the suits hung in here? Focus on the suits!*

I'm pretty sure the black Armani is the one he had sent in for the banquet we never attended. I should have it returned, I think to myself, and make a note on the iPad.

He pats the sofa next to him suggestively, a cheeky Carrero glint in his eye but I continue with my notes, refusing to make eye contact.

"I think not, Mr. Carrero." Sighing inwardly at the man I have to deal with every day, he's never dull anyway.

"Your loss." He closes his eyes again. We pause as we hear voices in the room next to us, faint and distant, that quickly evaporate as the intruders leave again.

"You've a meeting in about fifteen minutes, I'm sure half those suits are going to be in it." I point out, sounding unamused and bored.

"I'll just imply I was busy elsewhere." He shrugs, refusing to open those eyes and managing to look crazily hot.

"Busy doing what?"

"Busy in a cupboard with my PA, trying out the softness of the couch." He smirks, opening one eye and then the other slowly, to grin at me.

"I'm not having you imply we were up to no good somewhere in this building. Do you know how quickly that would get around the temp pool?" I say calmly, this is a repetitive conversation which only makes me sigh again. Only I would be lumbered with a boss as trying as this, who loves nothing more than to stress me out. The sexual innuendos never run out with him.

"We *are* up to no good, may as well get on the couch and make it worth your while. I'm sure I could help un-wrinkle that skirt." I roll my eyes, he's in his playful mood. I probably won't get much work done this afternoon, he's trying at the best of times, but worse in playful mode. I check my watch in irritation, we should get out of here.

"In your dreams," I respond drily, trying my hardest to ignore him.

"Always." He throws me a quick eyebrow lift; cheeky smile. I remain impassive. He's tiresome and we have a meeting we should already be arriving at. Needless to say, he no longer intimidates me, and his overly familiar behavior is a sign that we have grown somewhat closer in the past weeks. He stopped behaving quite so properly a while ago and I gave up objecting because he is simply too exhausting.

He's watching me as I smooth a stray hair back into my French knot, aware that his eyes are on me, I raise mine in question. Throwing him my haughty look. My silent, "What?"

"I miss it sometimes you know?" He's watching me now, a strange look on his face and a faraway glaze to his eyes.

"Miss what?" I mumble trying to sort my jacket out. He really did a number on making me look rumpled this time.

"Being able to intimidate you." He's grinning again and eerily reading my thoughts of a moment ago. Something he does a lot.

"Shame," I respond flatly. I add a note to my planner for a reservation next week and pull up a new email I received, it's finance asking for the spreadsheets we finished this morning. Rosalie is obviously having no fun with them today.

"I think it's safe to leave the closet with you now, Mr. Carrero." I close my iPad inside it's protective cover.

"We're back to Mr. Carrero are we? Have I made you pout, Miss. Anderson?" He throws me his most innocent look.

I'm fully aware of my using his title when he pisses me off, he thinks I'm mad at him.

*Maybe I am. He did haul me into a cupboard after all.*

"I think you need the boundaries redefined, seeing as you just manhandled me into a closet." I pout at him.

"Point taken. I'm so very sorry for my terrible behavior." He's still smiling at me and I can feel the urge to smile tugging at the corners of my mouth. This annoys me immensely. I hate that he always manages to make me smile, even when he's pissed me off. He's incorrigible and exhausting. I don't know why I endure this every day. I push it down; I would rather stay pissed or appear to be, as it usually gets him to behave a little more demurely.

"Anytime soon?" I gesture at the door impatiently, crossing my arms.

"You go, I may stay here for a bit and watch you walk out." He turns, getting comfy again to watch me walk out. A look of wickedness gracing his face and I sigh.

"Enjoy the view," I retort. "I'll leave my resignation on the desk as I pass." I smile sweetly, upper hand as always. He couldn't run things quite so well without me.

"Reason being sexual harassment ... ... Again!"

"You couldn't leave me, Emma ... You adore working for me too much. You would miss my sexual harassment." The laugh in his voice indicates he is still smiling my way.

*Ass.*

I raise an eyebrow back at him and turn away as though I'm serious, I fight the urge to smirk. He has a way of getting under my skin even when being juvenile.

I open the door and slide out, looking around cautiously. I notice that his office door is ajar, and I head out to peek around; everything is clear. A small walk to my old desk and I can see most of the floor is vacant, with only the regular secretaries milling around and paying no heed to me. I pull out my cell and text him that all is clear rather than venture back in.

I can't believe he made me hide in the closet from his father. Sometimes he acts like a two-year-old not New York's most eligible bachelor!

He appears a minute later, looking cool and collected and smiles as he tugs a strand of my hair back down from my French knot. I could slap him, he knows how much his fussing my hair annoys me, yet it's something he does several times a day. I smooth it back in place and curse under my breath at his back, resisting the urge to throw him a finger. I pick up the files for the meeting and check my watch again, we should make it if he moves his ass.

* * *

The meeting is eventful to say the least. His father makes a grand entrance halfway through and everyone clears the room quickly. The two Carrero men go at it like raging bulls as I stand outside, observing the many eyes watching them through the glass. I stand with my back to them, iPad in hand as I reply to emails and I can hear them arguing in Italian so that no one else can understand what they're saying.

His father is pissed, but Jake is antagonizing him, I can tell by his tone of voice and a quick glance confirms it with his aggressive posture. He never knows when to stop. The merger could still be called off, he should be smoothing things over, not letting his feelings get the better of him.

Finally, Senior storms out, yelling something in Italian and I hear Jake snort in answer. Senior glares back at him before stomping off with a flurry of nervous assistants running after him without a backward glance, the air crackling with tension.

"Emma!" Jake's voice makes me jump. He sounds pissed and I snap around as he wanders out, loosening his tie, his eyes normally so still are stormy and dark and despite his controlled, cool tone I can sense he's aggravated.

"The merger is going ahead." He almost growls it at me, looking a tad ferocious.

"He isn't stopping it?" I'm surprised by this.

"He can't." He frowns and takes my arm, pulling me back into the board room and sliding the door closed. Holding me close to his face. Another example of his hands-on approach.

"It's gone public, just like I planned. If Hunter or my father back out now, it will damage both of their reputations. They both stand to make a lot of money and a lot of jobs ride on this merger. Hunter can't refuse, his business will go under if he does."

I realize that the last few weeks maneuvering this deal in certain ways, and letting certain facts leak, has been deliberate. Brain behind the brawn, and one of the reasons his father always pushed him to get involved in the family business. Funny that it's backfired on him.

"If he stands to gain from this, then why is he so angry?" I query. I know Giovanni Carrero values money above all things.

"He despises Carl Hunter, you know this." He shrugs with one shoulder. Casting a look over my head and frowning at the meandering staff.

"Why did you choose to merger this deal if you knew it would be this way?" I've been dying to ask him that question for weeks but never felt it was my place to interrogate his decisions. Jake's expression closes, and he looks thoughtful.

"Let's go for food ... I don't want to talk here." He glances up and out one of the long windows again, as though insinuating he doesn't trust nearby ears.

"You just had lunch an hour ago, Jake," I point out, but he shrugs in response and I know it doesn't matter. He has the appetite of a horse.

The boy could eat all day and still find space for seconds.

# Chapter 7

I'm sitting across from Jake in Eleven Madison Park, a bustling popular restaurant, his current favorite place to eat and watching him mess with his cell while we wait on our food.

"Jake?" I interrupt gently.

"Emma?" He responds without looking up. He's deliberately being evasive.

"The Hunter merger?" My curiosity has been niggling all the way here and I have been extremely patient. He sighs and looks down at his cell, puts it inside his jacket, bringing his steady green gaze back to me. His face unreadable.

"My father and Hunter are not what you would call the best of friends anymore," he says quietly.

"Anymore?" I repeat flatly.

"Yes, Emma, anymore. They used to be as close as Daniel and I." He leans back, sliding down into his chair a little and I feel his feet come to cage mine under the table on either side. Our upper ankles touching slightly. Jake is a toucher, he always has to have some sort of contact it seems. It no longer bothers me.

"What happened?" I watch his face carefully, he's good at giving nothing away, amazing poker face.

"My father had an affair with Elsa Hunter." Daniel's mother, and Hunter's wife.

*Crap.*

I wasn't expecting that.

*Is that the basis of his bond with Daniel, shared anger at their parents?*

"It's not exactly common knowledge." He sighs and moves his water glass, he needs a point of focus. I can tell this is something he hates talking about. Jake only fidgets when he's very uncomfortable and it's his biggest tell, watching items he moves around, as though for distraction.

"When?" I know I shouldn't pry, but Jake rarely denies me knowledge, on any subject.

"When I was in my early twenties ... My mother forgave him, but I didn't, not for a long time ... I'm not sure I've forgiven him, even now. He broke her heart." Jake's relationship with his mother is unparalleled. I can see why he harbors so much anger toward his father and I also see why Jake's a little apprehensive when it comes to real relationships.

"Is that why you pushed for this? ... To get at him?" I nudge his ankle gently with mine, so he'll look at me.

"Yes ... No ... We stand to do well with this, but I guess it's always been a factor." He shrugs and avoids my gaze, signaling that the money hasn't been the main reason. Jake's also a "shrugger"; it has to be his most common mannerism, annoyingly so. It does, however, emphasize his shoulders and the sheer solid mass of them.

"How did you find out?" I try tearing my gaze from his upper body.

"Carl Hunter caught them in bed together, in his own house." He's still focusing on his glass and turning it absent-mindedly.

"So, that's why there's a weird atmosphere when he's around?" I watch his every movement, a little empathetic to how young he looks when he does this.

*Makes so much more sense now.*

"I don't think I can ever forgive him for hurting my mom like that. She deserves better than him." I know Jake's close to his mother, he visits her often and he has me send her flowers every month. A dozen colorful Gerberas ... her favorites.

*A thoughtful son.*

"She stayed with him though? She could have left him if she wanted too." I point out, feeling a little enamored with how deeply he feels for his mother's heart ache.

*Sensitive and loyal. Who would have guessed it?*

"You try leaving a publicly famous billionaire when he's been caught with his finger in someone else's pie, *Bambino* ... She knew he would have caused chaos for her if she tried. It's one of the reasons I feel like I do about him. He's a fucking control freak and all about his reputation." The flash of anger surprises me, Jake isn't one to lose his cool so easily. He shifts in his chair, taking a deep breath and quells his outburst a little, his eyes are still stormy, but his awareness of the surroundings causes it to burn out quickly.

"He forced her to stay?" I understand why he feels that way.

"In a way, I feel he did." He gazes across the restaurant as though trying to find his inner calm in the sea of strange faces around us.

"And now?" I urge.

"She's in her fifties, she's resigned herself to the fact she won't ever be able to find someone else and I guess she still has feelings for him. She's trapped in a loveless marriage." He looks back at me, a small sardonic smile. I see the hurt in his face and it makes me want to reach out and take his hand, but I hold back.

"A loveless marriage?" The thought is so sad, especially for someone as lovely as Sylvana Carrero.

"It's been loveless on his part for a long time, Emma. I think even before the affair there were cracks in the facade. My father married her after a one-month romance." He finally stops looking around, his eyes coming to rest on my face.

"Do you think Elsa was the only affair?" I ask, wondering why he's telling me this now.

"Probably not, but it's the only one I found out about."

"It explains why you're always so off with him. Your parents seem fine when I've met them at events." That is true, a beautiful woman and her adoring husband is what they excel at portraying in person. How odd that the truth is so very different. I know all about hiding true appearances. I am a master of deceit.

"A carefully played ruse, Emma. My father is all about appearances, my mother knows her place and how to play her part." Jake looks angry again, but his demeanor is still cool and controlled, he moves his glass for the tenth time in a show of discomfort.

"Your behavior in your younger years? ... Rebelling was payback?" This has interested me for a while, his rebellion and then reform always seems at odds with how he is now. He shrugs and drinks his wine thoughtfully.

"Some ... I had other reasons too." He looks anywhere but me, and I can tell he's hiding something.

"Such as?" I nudge again with a soft smile.

"Italian blood." He smiles, trying to pass off my question and I can see it doesn't reach his eyes. It's the first time I've ever seen him truly evasive when it comes to our personal chats, normally he's so open with me about everything. I push down the tremor of doubt, gut telling me that maybe I'm over thinking it.

Our steaks arrive, and we sit silently while the waitress lays them out on our table. He gives her one of his seductive smiles and I watch her literally slump with desire.

*Jesus, you're being so obvious, it's actually pathetic woman!*

I frown across at him, he likes to invoke the reaction for his own amusement, the eternal playboy with the childish temperament. He likes the effect he has on women of all ages.

"She may have trouble finishing her shift now," I scold after she wanders off.

"Jealous?" He winks at me, but I just glare at him coldly.

*No. Maybe?*

"Your un-flailing libido never fails to impress me," I say sarcastically.

"Least I have a sex life." He takes a mouthful of food, giving me that teasing eyebrow lift of his.

"Meaning?" I pick up my fork and clean it on my napkin before I start with the salad, still watching him with a very serious expression.

"Meaning, I've spent many intimate hours with you and am yet to see any form of date or fuck buddy keeping you cheerful." He raises his eyebrows then digs into his food again.

"I've more important things to do and no desire to date or find a "fuck buddy"." I grimace at his term, throwing him a furrowed brow.

"Might put a smile on your face." He's grinning. I look up at him and throw on a mock smile, as widely as I can muster.

"There. See. No man needed," I say as he laughs and

shakes his head at me in amusement.

"How come you never seem to date anyone? I mean you're not exactly unattractive, you could easily pull ... I've seen the way men check you out. Are you holding out for me to hang up my playboy hat and settle down?" The thought makes me feel odd inside, but I remain impassive.

"I've more than enough testosterone to deal with, having you glued to my hip on a daily basis, Carrero. And no. I don't ever see you taking that hat off and being happy with only one woman to keep your interest." I'm trying to keep my focus on my food as my cheeks warm up, I'm not comfortable with this ever-probing fascination with my lack of boyfriend. It makes me squirm in my seat.

"Emma?" he looks at me seriously, that hint of serious coming through the boyish charm.

"Even women have needs."

*Do they?*

I think sourly. I'm pretty sure I've never needed to go there. I tried it when I was young; non-serious boyfriends and the pressure of other kids doing it. I didn't like it much and it only left a sour taste in my mouth.

"You would know, of course, being one hundred percent hot-blooded male." I laugh at him, raising a brow at the man who is as far from feminine as any guy can get.

"I go to bed with enough women to know it's not only men who crave sex. There's no way you can tell me you don't get the raging horn, at all?" He's a little too focused on me now and looking serious.

"Jake, can we talk about something else? I don't think I want to talk about sex with my boss over lunch." An anxious knot has moved up into my stomach at the topic of conversation and I feel uncomfortable, like I always do when any conversation is turned on me and my life. Something he often does.

"Do you need me to set you up? Are you secretly man shy? Or maybe I should show you what a real man feels like." He winks at me and I just roll my eyes, suppressing a smile at his humor.

"Like I would ever trust your choice of men ... Or you! ... The Daniel Hunters of this world don't do a thing for me." I smile sweetly.

*That's an understatement.*

"So, what is your type of man?" he asks curiously, focusing on me instead of his food now. I throw him a dark look, indicating that I really mean we are done with this topic.

*My type? Far, far, away from me.*

"Okay, okay ... Are you going home to visit your mom anytime soon?" he pushes in a new direction instead, but I just drop my fork, mood dying, and temper punching me in the stomach.

*For god's sake.*

"This again?" I shake my head at him feeling irritated, being too sharp with him.

"Don't roll your eyes and wave your hands at me!" He shoves my foot with his under the table, and I kick him back, feeling a light satisfied smirk as he grimaces with a glare. Relieving me of my temper a little.

"Why do you always bring her up?" I ask.

"Because I find it weird that you never go home to see her, Emma ... She's your mother, and Chicago is two hours on a plane. It's hardly on the other side of the world. You know you can use the jet whenever you need it." He's frowning at me, all green eyes and stiff, squared jaw, looking wounded at my anger over this.

"I don't need to run home and see 'Mommy', Jake. I'm a big girl with my own life." I scold. I hate that he always presses me about this at every opportunity.

"I go see my 'Mommy' every couple of weeks ... She gave birth to me and raised me. I can't imagine going five years without one trip home ... it's odd." He narrows his brows at me and that green gaze just penetrates mine.

"It's not like she hasn't come here to New York. I don't need to go home." My food isn't satisfying me like it normally does, and I realize the conversation is souring the taste. I put down my cutlery now I've lost my appetite.

"You grew up there ... Don't you miss it?" he's still eating and trying to come across as non-intrusive, but I'm not fooled. Jake is one of the most intrusive people I've ever known, he has a severe craving to pry into my life every day and he is as subtle as a bull.

"No," I snap. Finally letting the irritation rule and losing my cool with him.

"Did you leave for a reason, and that's why you get so pissed about this?" My eyes flash up as though he's struck me, but I quickly look back down. I won't have this conversation, he needs to leave it alone and know when he's crossing the line—again.

"Drop it," I say quietly, feeling the rush of emotion run through me, dampening all of the happy I had on arriving here. It's not a good feeling.

"You never talk about you, Emma ... You know everything about me," he almost pleads.

"I never knew your father had an affair before now!" I snap a little more harshly this time, looking at him accusingly and hoping to push this back down.

"But you do know now." He sulks a little, his green eyes narrowing under furrowed brows. Little boy scolded comes to mind.

Sometimes we bicker, it usually goes a lot like this and

usually for similar topics. I sigh heavily, annoyed, at well, everything. Guilty at making him like this and regretting my harsh tone immensely.

"I'm sure there are things you haven't told me, Jake ... Everyone is entitled to privacy." I remember the fleeting look earlier in our conversation and see it reflected in his eyes once more. Something is there after all. It seems to cause him to back off, thankfully.

"Fine ... But it's just weird." He looks down at his plate, definite sulk face on. I cannot help the tug of affection that softens my whole attitude.

*Man-child returns.*

"You are the king of weird, you attract massive amounts of weird, so you have a cheek." I try a friendlier tone, efforts to bring humor back into the conversation. I hate when we bicker and argue over pointless things and I see his frown smoothing out to be replaced with humor, he knows what I'm hinting at.

"You're talking about that freaky Lisa?" he smiles slightly, mood dispersing too.

Yes, he got my hint.

"You didn't say no to her weird fetishes ... You asked your PA to research them." I narrow my eyes accusingly, but can't help the giggle that springs from my throat. Mood lifted, and irritation gone, just like that, as is our way. We always recover quickly, effortlessly. He laughs too.

"I didn't actually partake, Emma, I just didn't think she was being serious ... I thought I was missing some joke." He smiles, his natural sexy Jake smile, and it makes me smile too. Glad that he is once again his normal, infuriatingly smug, and cheeky self once more.

"You called me at four in the morning to ask me if diapers would turn me on." I reminisce while laughing, remembering the shock that had run over me when I had been rudely awakened with that drunken question.

"I needed another female perspective. A normal female perspective. She scared the shit out of me." He flinches at the memory which only makes me grin more.

"How do you think I felt ... I got a wakeup call from my drunk boss asking me about weird crap to do with adult babying fetishes, and diapers." I point out.

"You were very cool on the cell ... Efficient as ever ... Serious about the whole thing. I think it was the first time I figured you and I were going to be best friends." He's laughing at the memory, my heart ups it's beat on the best friend comment and warms slightly. He has said something similar several times before. I guess the feeling's mutual. I never really thought about Jake and I being real friends before that.

I remember that night well, I had tried to gauge his seriousness and even attempted a rational factual conversation while skimming Google for answers. I shake my head, grinning too.

"Only you could pull the freaky one in a nightclub full of normal women, Jake." I point out, relaxing once more.

"She ended up going home with Daniel and he still doesn't mention it."

I burst out laughing and that does make me feel better. Daniel still gives me the creeps and the thought of him tied up in a baby's crib with some weird diaper wearing crazy makes me laugh. Jake is chuckling too.

He leans over, topping up my now empty wine glass, we're only halfway through our food and I haven't noticed how much I've drunk already; his bad influence on me has turned me into a wine with food type of person. He always orders by the bottle wherever we go to eat. I never drunk much before

Jake.

I pick up my fork, starting to eat again, now that my temper has improved along with my appetite. Feeling light and merry now, and ravenous once more.

"I like you when you're like this." He looks over at me, a happy expression on his face, eyes almost twinkling.

"Like what?" I look up innocently, the steak is so tender that I'm now savoring every mouthful. Appetite fully restored.

"More relaxed. PA mode on hiatus. When you forget to play cool." It sobers me slightly, he has a way of making me forget myself when we are kicking back and much like now, it startles me. I didn't like letting that mask drop, I don't like people seeing too deeply. Especially not him.

"It's hard to focus when you ply me with alcohol," I say a little too quickly, trying to reel in my controlled facade once again, pushing the glass away from my plate.

*That's enough wine.*

"Maybe that's why I do it." He smiles softly, but it makes me suddenly uncomfortable. I ram food into my mouth and stare across the restaurant, looking for a diverting topic.

I gesture toward the far window with my fork, and he turns to look at what I'm pointing at, spotting the movie star too, he looks back at me shrugging.

"He's an asshole ... I've met him. He's a bit of a diva, and I mean look at him; he's wearing a god-damn flower brooch ... If that doesn't scream closet gay, then I don't know what does." He shrugs nonchalantly, but for some reason this makes me laugh unexpectedly and causes me to choke on my half-chewed steak. I erupt into a coughing fit which has me grabbing for my wine, in an effort to dislodge the lump in my throat before I die.

"Jesus, Emma, don't have a coronary over seeing some asshole Hollywood big shot." He's laughing at me now and I throw him a pained look. I gasp for air, thumping my chest to push my steak down and inhaling heavily.

"Fuck you." I manage weakly, with a smile.

"Swearing at your boss is good grounds for dismissal ... gross misconduct." He jokes and tops up my glass again with a wink, highlighting the fact I just drank it all without meaning to.

"So, fire me." I throw back, slugging down my red wine and finally clearing the food that is still caught in my throat and intent on half killing me.

"Can't fire my future wife!" he acts shocked, and grasps his chest in mock horror in response, before he chucks his fork down on his plate, also finished with his food. I ignore the wife comment, another frequent joke he makes.

"Dessert?" He looks at me with a questioning brow. I shake my head, I've drunk too much wine, feeling a little tipsy now I need to get out of here. I need coffee.

"Back to the grind, *Bella*." He offers me his hand as I get up, chucking my napkin on the empty plate; I take it without hesitation and let him pull me with him, then immediately wonder when this stopped being weird.

*How many times have I let Jake touch me without repulsion coursing through me?*

I walk behind him contemplating this fact, staring at our loosely held fingers. It's become something as familiar as being around him now. Maybe it is just the nature of our relationship ... Platonic and safe. We are real friends.

The jokes about sex, the best friend comments, and wife vibes are frequent, but I know it is all play. Jake is never anything but a complete gentleman, well, minus the man handling, but even that is not so bad. I've never had a platonic relationship with men of any age and it makes me feel slightly strange now that I'm examining it.

* * *

The afternoon is chaotic. For the first time, I'm glad of my assistant, Rosalie's, lingering presence, it feels like I don't get a second to think.

Jake's in his office with just as much going on as me; I've walked in there a dozen times with files and notes and each time he seems to be shedding clothes. He's now sitting with his shirt pulled out, unbuttoned at the collar and his sleeves rolled up. His normally styled hair is ruffled, messy, and his tie and jacket are strewn across his couch. His shoes are lying in the middle of the floor, a sure sign he's stressed.

I pick up his tie and jacket and hang them neatly on the hooks behind his door, shuffling his shoes to under the edge of his desk with the toes of my stilettos. I move all the papers from the left side he's been through and pile them neatly into an open box file, before laying out some stapled contracts he needs to sign, to send down to legal. He smiles up at me briefly, leaning back so I can move the papers in front of him, before setting to sign them while propping his cell to his ear.

I move around in companionable silence, straightening and removing things from his work space so he can take the new ones, noting he's done with the Hunter briefs, I scoop them up to take them. We have gelled this way for a while now, anticipating each other's movements silently, and wordlessly working around one another. It's something that just happened organically, over the weeks.

"Emma?" he pauses on the cell, throwing me a soft look.

"Yes?"

"Organize a flight to Seattle for tomorrow, early as you can. We'll need hotel rooms for the next five days and a car." He moves his cell into his neck some more and keeps signing papers.

"Yes, Mr. Carrero." I always use his title when we're in front of company, or he's on the cell.

*Another trip!*

I sigh. We haven't been back from London that long, and Jake was right; hotels no longer did it for me, even five-star suites. It's just another few days getting tired from jet-lag and a few days of grueling work with men in suits who look at me like I am worthless. We have taken so many trips already that it feels like second nature to me now. The novelty has well and truly worn off.

\* \* \*

It's been two hours watching him through the glass panels in the boardroom as I sit in a temporary office. So far, I've been in there several times with files, coffee, and whatever else he asks of me. I'm not needed right now, so I'm sitting in the next room.

I feel as fed up as he looks. My laptop is keeping my focus, if this meeting runs over any longer then it's going to be a late night and we have flights to catch in the morning. I have an hour on the subway to get home to Sunnyside as it is after this.

I see him lift his cell from the table in front of him and start touching the screen with a hint of amusement on his face, I wonder what he's up to. A second later my own cell buzzes and I pick it up seeing the email notification from Jake.

*Jake Carrero has sent you an iTunes gift.*

Frowning, I open the email and see he has gifted me a song.

*Jake Carrero has sent you an iTunes gift.*

*"Rescue Me" by The Raffetillies.*

I stifle a giggle and shake my head, looking up through the glass and catching his quick eyebrow raise before he turns his attention back to the meeting at hand. Biting my lip, I scroll iTunes for a suitable title and purchase a gift in return. I send it to him and wait to see if he will read it.

*"Cry Baby" by Melanie Martinez.*

I wait, watching for his reaction. I see him pull his cell over and slide the screen, a couple of presses, then he lets out a laugh and tries to cover with a cough. I see a couple of the stuffed shirts look up disapprovingly, but they say nothing, and the meeting continues. Jake throws me a wink with a small shake of his head.

*Back at you, Carrero. Not so funny now, are you?*

I smirk to myself, satisfied with our little joke.

* * *

Finally, the men all shuffle out of the boardroom, I stand dutifully by, politely saying farewells like a good little PA.

*Thank god.*

Jake emerges with a smile on his face and immediately pulls me to one side.

"Effective form of communication ... Music." He grins at me, looking as gorgeous as he always does, if not a little tired.

"I can see this being abused by you, now you've found something else that you think is clever and amusing." I smile with a slight groan at the twinkle in his eye and can already predict this will become frequent.

"Say it with song titles ... They do say music can speak volumes." He winks, resting his arm on the door jamb over my head, so he's leaning into me, extremely close and smelling a little too divine. I'm aware of the odd glances a couple of passing assistants throw our way and try to press myself back a little, to make it look less intimate.

"Hmmm." I look down at the time and point out that we should head home, uncomfortable with the attention he's drawing. After all we have a flight to Seattle to get on tomorrow.

# Chapter 8

Seattle is miserable.

It's rainy and cold and the meetings drag endlessly; another boring board of directors, and another boring meaningless round of chatter. Something I learned working in my new role, is how much business men like to set up meetings to discuss nothing much at all and will take several sessions to conclude on something minor.

The hotel is like every other we have stayed in, a penthouse suite. Grand, opulent, and modern. Jake insists that when we travel we have rooms in the same suite, so I can be at his beck and call, as we usually work late from them. I spent the best part of last night having him dictate memos and running through his schedules and itinerary before he made me get up at the crack of dawn to jog with him in the rain.

Jake likes conversation when he runs, so whenever we leave home and his trainer behind, he harasses me into it. I have never jogged so much in my life.

I'm tired by the time we get back to the hotel, it's been a long day and I'm none too pleased, when upon arrival, we're met in the foyer by a familiar looking red head. I inwardly groan.

*Felicity Crane!*

This is the one with a voice like razor blades and I have a headache coming on, she's also a screamer and the reason I carry headphones and an iPod when I have to live in the same suite as Casanova Carrero.

I give him a withering look and catch his smirk, he knows how much I love Felicity. She's been on his date list for a few weeks, sporadic hook ups, because she understands the meaning of casual sex! Seattle is her home base, although she travels a lot and meets us in random cities.

"Miss Crane." I smile tightly and try to look elsewhere as she embraces Jake eagerly, with loud wet kisses.

*Gross. Have some class for god's sake.*

"Oh, Jake, you look so hot in this suit, so very business man of the year." She whines in that painful voice. I try to numb out the clingy baby tones as we hit the elevator. Like nails down a blackboard.

"You look nice, Felicity ... New hair?" Jake, as observant as ever, although he only noticed because I pointed at her hair with scissor motions as soon as her back was turned.

"Oh, Jake, you noticed." I can hear her beam, I shake my head at him and turn away. Even though I'm standing with my back to them I know she's probably curled around him possessively, like an octopus.

I don't get what he sees in half the bimbos he dates, he's not a stupid guy, he can't get any enjoyment out of conversation with the brain dead. I guess it's not the conversation he's interested in, as I turn slightly and see the endless legs and tight ass of Miss. Crane. His woman all fit the same standard: gorgeous, tight bodied, and dumb.

My cell vibrates in my pocket and I look down to retrieve it.

"Emma Anderson," I answer, not recognizing the number and glad for the distraction from the smoochy woman molesting my boss behind me.

"Emma?" It's a male voice, one I vaguely recognize, something gnawing at me in the back of my mind.

"Yes, this is Emma." My curiosity evident, I feel Jake watching me with interest, I can feel his eyes on me, because normally all calls relate to him in some way, and the fact that he is also a nosy git.

*Being a nosy shit, he probably thinks I have finally found a date.*

Felicity is babbling on incoherently, right behind me and it's distracting as I'm trying to listen to the hoarse voice on the other end, who is mumbling annoyingly. I have to plug my other ear to hear what he is saying.

"Emma, I wasn't sure if you would talk to me ... It's been a long time ... Emma it's your father, Frank Roberts." The faceless voice slurs and my blood freezes in my veins, the warmth drains from my face, inhaling fast and I'm at a loss for words. The suffocating sensation in my lungs momentarily knocks me for six but I push it down harshly and find some resolve to answer.

"What do you want?" my voice sounds alien to me as I regain my composure, I sound as shocked as I feel and know that Jake will notice it too. A tremor of teen Emma slipping out.

"Emma, I just want to talk ... I want to meet up and maybe if you give me a chance ..." His voice is weak and gnarly, it causes a creeping bile in my stomach to rise and an anger to swirl viciously.

"We have nothing to talk about ... Leave me alone." I snap aggressively and disconnect the call, my hand trembling as I fumble with it, trying to switch it off. Jake's hand is on my arm, trying to turn me, but I stiffen to stop him. Not able to look at him while feeling this prickly.

"Emma, are you okay?" he sounds concerned as my cell vibrates again before I manage to turn it off; it's the same number; I blanch at the screen then reject it, this time managing to switch the cell to mute and shove it deep into my bag. I am overcome with emotion, and I don't want to be closed in this elevator with Jake and Felicity the "Crone" anymore. I can hear Jake asking me what's wrong again but I'm fighting to get my head calm and straight before I can answer.

"Emma?" his voice is intent. He pulls me back against him, his hard chest against my back, his face coming around the side of mine to see me. I block him out, trying to get a hold on self-composed Emma before I can say a word.

*Deep breath. Steady, calm, composed.*

The closing walls begin to move back out and I calm myself, pushing out of his embrace and against the elevator door with a palm to steady myself.

"I'm okay ... Really!" I give him a quick glance back and a tight smile, but his expression stays the same, he looks worried and only frowns at my reply. Felicity watching us silently. Suspiciously.

*Yes, Felicity. My boss often manhandles me, it doesn't scream affair!*

He knows nothing of my father, he's never broached the subject. Not that I would ever volunteer the information if he did.

"You want me to send Felicity home?" he says it right in front of her and I hear her small intake of breath, followed by the indignation in her voice.

"No," we say in unison. I don't want this kind of awkwardness, I feign a smile and give him a reassuring look as we stop at our floor.

"It's fine ... it's nothing." I warn, impressed with how quickly I've managed to sound bright and normal. All those years of hiding, finally paying off. I head to the door of our suite and let us in with my swipe card, his eyes are on me; I can feel it. Felicity is, for once, silent, and I think she senses the oddness of the atmosphere.

"I'm going to bed. I'm tired, I'll grab a shower and a light snack and hit the sheets." I need to get away from his probing eyes, I know he will start to question me and we'll only end up quarreling about this.

"You don't want to come for dinner?" he sounds odd, tense; watching me intensely.

"No, I want to just stay here." I sound normal despite the hammering inside my chest and the tremble in my fingers, ever grateful for years of perfecting this. My whole body just feels weak and surreal.

"You want me to order you some dinner to the room?" The look of concern is still crossing his face and it endears me to him for a moment. I feel guilty that I'm clamming up, but I can't help it, it's who I am.

"Why, Mr. Carrero!" I smile at him, hoping to look amused. "I didn't know you knew how to do such things." I purr demurely, and he smiles back, relaxing a little. Finally, that look in his eye dissipating, mission accomplished. I've always been good at quick recoveries, no matter how bad the shock; the mask is back on and he's none the wiser.

"You would be surprised at my capabilities, Emma. Maybe some time you'll let me show you the extent of them." He's still eyeing me, only this time with that cheeky glint and I try a more genuine smile and shake my head. It's always sex with him.

"Do you want me to order food?" he asks again insistently. Serious tone back on.

"No, Jake. I can order food, go have fun." I head to my room in the suite now and throw my coat and bag over the nearest chair. I just want him to leave so I can sit down and process what just happened, alone. I need to think about what I'm going to do if Frank Roberts continues to pursue me. He can go crawl back to his hole and die for all I care.

Felicity makes a beeline for his room with her overnight bag, eyeing us weirdly, but he makes no attempt to follow; as she disappears his expression changes back to full blown frown mode.

"Who was it?" serious, no-nonsense boss tone.

*Ughhhh!*

I should have known better ... He's hard to palm off even on a good day.

*God dammit, Jake.*

I turn away breezily, I know he won't let up ... he'll cancel dinner and stay here if I say nothing. There's no point being evasive when he has that look on his face, I resign myself to caving.

"My sperm donor." I wave an airy hand as though I'm saying something non-important, but I can already feel the tension in my face. I'm glad I'm looking toward the open door of my room, away from him, and pull out my cell to cradle in the charging dock on the table beside it.

"Your father?" he sounds surprised.

*You and me both.*

"Yep." I look around quickly for a distraction, so I don't need to turn and look at him. I see his personal tablet on the table nearby and lift it to scroll iTunes, to turn on music. It's the best I can muster when he's moved so close.

"You've never mentioned a father." His tone is serious and gentle, body a little too close for comfort.

"I don't have need to. There's nothing to mention ... I

don't know him."

"So, why is he calling? It didn't sound like nothing, Emma. You definitely didn't sound happy." He's moved closer to me and I can feel his body heat emanating against my spine. So close he is touching me.

"I got a shock okay ... I've met him once in my life and it was brief. I don't know why he's calling." I lie.

I have a good idea why he's calling now, it's no surprise. He did this once before, a brief meeting at fourteen, when he thought my mother had struck gold. A simple picture in the paper about the "feed the homeless" charity she runs, he'd been disappointed to find that she was as penniless as the charity she runs. Sure, that she would be swathed in dollars, and able to help him out with a few hundred to tide him by. Here he is now, after I have been photographed more than a dozen times in the presence of a rich Carrero ... New York's royalty.

*Figures. He thinks I'm loaded and dating Prince Carrero.*

"Talk to me, Emma." He's standing so close to me that I feel his breath against my hair, I move away quickly, tense and jumpy; I need head space and solitude. Not probing Jake.

"Go. I really am itching to get in that power shower and let my hair down," I say sweetly, moving further from him to give myself some much-needed distance, and finally managing to look at him. His look darkens, and he presses his lips together. I know he's contemplating pushing me further. I know that look.

He seems to think better of it and the frown on his brow lets up as though the thoughts have floated away on the breeze. He doesn't want to argue either.

"Want me to help take your hair down?" he winks and there it is, back in full swing, that cheeky Carrero grin and amusement in his eye. I feel myself inwardly relax.

"I'm pretty sure I could sue you for such suggestions, boss!" I throw with a half-smile.

"It's only harassment if you don't like it, *Bambino*." He grins as he moves close to me again, fingers twitching at me as though making threats. I swat him away, he's not against tickle torture in times of need.

I just need them to leave, I hate feeling vulnerable in front of anyone, especially him. I need to be alone.

"Your ego is never shy, is it?"

He doesn't answer, just steps forward quickly and shoves me into my room, so that I almost lose my balance and he laughs at my angry scowl. Turns on his heel and walks away.

"Asshole." I yell after him with a smirk. He turns and blows me a kiss and a wave before walking across the suite to his own room and I feel relieved. I fooled him well enough; they'll go to dinner now and he probably won't remember anything about it later.

*I hope he won't, I don't want to talk about this, not with him, not with anyone.*

I watch him walk into the room with Felicity and I shut the door quickly. Leaning back against it for a moment to steady my nerves and reel a little from shock, I exhale slowly.

*Who the hell did he think he was, calling me after all this time?*

I stifle the lump of emotion in my throat and shake it off, I won't succumb to tears over that scum bag, he deserves none of my tears, or my time.

\* \* \*

My shower is hot, steamy, and satisfying. I come out flushed and breathless and figure I maybe should have gone easy on the temperature gauge. My head's swimming a little, and I'm still feeling fragile.

I haul on my nightdress and robe to try and cool off, pad out into the empty room and instantly know that I'm alone. I had been in the shower an hour and they must have left for dinner. It feels good to be able to chill out and have some alone time though. I mulled over the call enough in the shower and I'm tired of thinking about it. I'll have to screen my calls from now on, maybe change my number. I'll need to call my mother, I have an inkling that she was behind him getting it and it pisses me off immensely.

*Always a sucker for a goddamn sob story. She needs to get a grip.*

I have been in the social pages a lot over the last few weeks, on Jake's arm, at various functions. I guess he figures I've hit a goldmine and wants to see what he can get out of me. I push the bile down in my throat bitterly as I think about the fact that all I am to him is a meal ticket.

*He's a prick. A money grabbing asshole.*

He's never wanted any part of my life, except when he thought my mother could throw some cash his way and now, here he is again. Sleazing his way out of his dark hole once more.

I'm not my mother, I'm not some sap who can be pulled around by a garbled confession, asking to get back in my life.

I pace to the bar in the corner and slam my hands on the counter, that old familiar rage in me creeping out; teen Emma's rage. I hate him for that, hate him for making that part of me resurface. A part of me I try so hard to quell.

I reach out to the crystal decanters and pour myself a brandy. I'm not one for hard liquor, but I need to quell all these emotions funneling up my throat. I need to get back in control. Relax a little.

\* \* \*

I don't know how many brandies I drink, but the hotel floor gets really comfy and plush. It feels a little warm and I'm enjoying the soothing music coming from the surround sound. Jake's playlist is on repeat, he has an eclectic taste in music, but I like it; every song makes me think of him and I wish he was here on the floor beside me, enjoying this feeling.

If I don't move, my head doesn't swim too much but it feels kind of nice, like lying on a lilo on the sea, and drifting away into oblivion. I like the way my hair fans out and I can stroke its silkiness, mingled with fluffy floor.

*I never realized how soft my hair was before now, I should leave it loose more often.*

*The ceiling looks amazing from down here too, smooth like whipped cream that's been spread out over an expensive cake.*

I hear the distant noise above my head and feet come into view as I tilt back to see, upside down. Tall black stilettos on gazelle like legs, followed by black tailored pants over expensive shoes. Even his shoes and legs are sexy!

*They have returned!*

I giggle naughtily at being caught in such a compromising way. I wonder what they will make of drunk Emma, laying sprawled on the floor. I find it highly amusing in my current state, and really have no cares about it.

It's semi-dark with only the lights on dim and I can see they're walking toward me, maybe they can't see me. I giggle again with mischief and pretend to be invisible.

*If I close my eyes I'm sure they will go right on by, maybe they might even walk over me.*

"Emma?" his deep tone catches my attention.

"Jake." I smile, opening my eyes again.

*Oops, busted. He found me.*

"Emma, are you drunk?" his voice sounds husky with amusement and I giggle in answer, he moves toward me, stands over me looking down.

*Oh boy, is it a sexy view!*

His tie is off and draped casually round his shoulders, his white shirt open at the collar, his jacket discarded somewhere.

*Why did I never notice just how sexy my boss is?*

I hiccup, and it feels funny in my throat, sounds so alien to me, that it makes me giggle again.

I like being drunk, I feel lighter and more fun; it makes me think Jake is sexy and that's pretty funny. I don't find men sexy at all, so that's even funnier ... Well, except Jake! He's the exception to the rule in that everything he does is sexy and alluring, even standing staring at me, as he is now.

I hear a strange sound. I'm laughing; I guess I find myself funny and I sound so detached.

*I must be really drunk.*

"Emma, I think you better get in bed. Come on." He leans down to catch my hand, from across my stomach, but I leave it floppy and weighted, so he gets nowhere pulling at it.

*I don't want to hold hands today, Carrero. You're looking a tad too Casanova tonight.*

When he picks it up again, he tugs, but I refuse to cooperate.

*Nope, I'm not going to hold hands with my hot boss while he's swooning around looking all sexy on me.*

I giggle again. I feel too heavy and too comfy to move. I want to sleep on my fluffy floor.

"Wan sssstay right here," I slur, I can hear it now and it amuses me. I've never heard myself slur before, never allowed myself to drink to the point of slurring.

I spot my hand held in front of me and prod dementedly at the air as if I'm trying to make a point, fascinated at the uncoordinated motion of my own limb as it waves above me. Everything feels dreamlike and warm.

He frowns at me and I have the urge to poke him between the eyebrows. They are too even and straight to be real.

"You prefer the hotel rug to a bed?" he can't speak without smiling, so I guess he is finding me amusing this way.

He has a beautiful smile.

No! A gorgeous smile!

"Hmmm mmm hmmmm." That was almost an answer, I think.

*God, why did I drink so much brandy?*

Everything is swaying and soft. If I close my eyes, maybe I'll hear something soothing like the ocean, I feel like I'm on the ocean.

*Oh, yeah, the sperm donor and all those tidal waves of emotions I was trying to drown.*

"Right, that's it." He scoops down and slips his hands under me, hoists me up effortlessly, as though I weigh nothing. I'm too drunk to fight, or squeal, and I'm being carried like a baby toward my room. Freaky Lisa comes to mind, and I wonder if this is part of her fetish fancies, it makes me giggle some more.

*God, I feel amazing; why can't I always feel like this?*

"No! Don't want to go to bed." I sound petulant, like a child, and start struggling. If I go to bed, I'll stop feeling this way. I may lose this warm feeling and blank mind euphoria, I may start fixating on shitty fathers who abandon their kids in infancy. Pricks who only see dollar signs, instead of the damage they have caused.

"Emma, hold still." He fusses, struggling to hold me.

"No. Nope, nope." I shake my head and he finally stops and puts my writhing body on my own bare feet, outside my door, but upright isn't good. It really disorientates me as everything sways.

I giggle then have the overwhelming urge to "Shhh" him. Which I do with a grand finger gesture on my lips.

*He talks too much.*

He stifles a laugh, and it sounds good; looks even better. I like Jake's laugh, it's so free and boyish, uncomplicated and deep. Like him. I could listen to his laugh for an eternity, it always makes me feel like smiling too.

He frowns at me, but I know it's not a real frown, it's an, "I think you're a funny drunk," frown and it makes him cuter.

*Is my boss cute? I guess he can be, when he looks like that. God, that makes me feel sad. Why does he have to be so cute?*

"Emma? What is it?" he frowns at me some more, moving close; I guess my sad face is on show. I poke his dimple gently with my finger tip as if to eradicate the object of my sadness and feel the frown on my face turn to gentle accusation.

"Why do you've to be soooo ...?" my fingers wave and I notice there's a shiny sparkly thing on the table behind him. I always liked sparkly things as a child; I want to play with it. It looks like my cell and it's all lit up and memorizing, I'm like a magpie to a pretty sparkle.

"So? ... What?" he tries to pull me back to him as I attempt a grab at the object of my interest on the unit. His arms loosely around me, his upper body tilted back so he can look down at me. It's hard to walk in a straight line and harder to control my limbs when a strong pair of arms are hauling you back.

"Sooo ... What are you talking about?" I look back at him

confused, my head slightly spinning and I've no idea what he said. I look back at sparkly and see it's just my cell that I'm trying to catch and lose interest immediately. It's no longer lit up.

"Emma, I've never seen you plastered. You just decided to have yourself a one women party on the floor, without me?" he's still smiling and regarding me affectionately.

*I love Jake's smile ... It makes me sigh.*

I "Shhh" him again, except this time it's his mouth I cover with splayed palms. His lips feel soft and tickly under my hands. If I cut off the sexy voice, and adorable smile that goes with the cute look, then I can forget how hot my boss is.

I look around, seeing the cell again and I remember who called.

"My father called me you know?" I point out childishly.

*Yes, he did, that sad excuse of a human being dialed my number and connected to my cell. Asshole, scumbag!*

"I'm aware of that, Emma ... Do you want to talk about it? Is that why you got drunk?" Jake holds me against him, leaning back to see my face again; I look up, liking what I see once more.

*You're my dreamy hot boss.*

"No ... Yes ... No ... Who?" I forget the question while trying to give an answer, and he shakes his head at me. I feel perplexed, but I don't know why, and I'm sure he's holding onto me a little too closely suddenly.

*I wonder where Felicity has gone. I hope she's not the jealous type, not that she should be ... I don't do sex ... Or feelings ... Jake sees me as he would a sister, or a platonic friend, I guess. That thought annoys me a little.*

"Emma, I really think you need some sleep, or coffee?" he loses the frown, and a little seriousness clouds his tone.

"I don't like coffee." The stuff stinks and tastes worse. I

don't know why Jake drinks so much of it; I prefer brandy. I giggle as he pulls me toward the couch and maneuvers me onto the cool soft seat, lifting my feet up to the next space, laying me flat on my back.

*Smooth move, Carrero.*

The motion makes me laugh again and I like how it sounds. I never giggle like this. It feels very unlike me in every way. I've turned into a giggler with zero control over it.

"You stay like that while I make you a drink ... Tea? Water?" he asks.

"Brandy!" I never liked the stuff at all, it burns going down, but it did start to taste good after the third one, and the side effects are positively awesome.

"No, Emma. No more alcohol." He sounds stern, bossy and paternal ... Like a father should. It brings sperm donor back to the forefront of my swirling thoughts.

"Why didn't he want me, Jake?" I query. I talk to the ceiling, it feels a bit like I'm lying on a shrink's couch, like in the movies when sad people talk to psychiatrists in stark offices on green couches, and stare at boring ceilings. I note the ceiling no longer looks smooth and creamy, it looks shitty.

*Maybe Jake could be my shrink.*

"Because he's an idiot. Not all men are cut out to be fathers."

I can hear the clink of mugs.

*That's true. See, he's a good shrink ... he seems to understand.*

"What's wrong with me?"

*That's a good question to ask a shrink, as I want to know.*

His face appears above me and I jump a little in fright; I wasn't expecting him so suddenly, maybe it wasn't sudden. I have been taking long pauses to daydream between replies.

This is a weird angle, but even down here he looks gorgeous.

*Why can't you look ugly from at least one angle, Carrero? Even the odds up a little. Maybe have a double chin or something.*

"Nothing ... You deserve so much more than someone like him." He looks serious, and just hot.

"I'm part of him ... I have his blood ... But he didn't want to know me." I sigh dejectedly as he moves from above me and on to the couch beside me; he has a glass which clinks with ice and slides it on the low table to my left. He sits near my head, so he can look down at my face and he's no longer smiling.

"Does he want to know you now? Is that why he called?" he frowns once more, watching me pensively.

"He wants money." I point out, matter of factly.

*Yes, as much as he can lay his grubby little hands on, filthy, scum bag, gold digger.*

"Money?" he pauses to watch me. His tone that of surprise.

"He thinks I'm loaded, because I'm always in the paper ... with you ... Probably thinks we're in love." I laugh at this little fact, but Jake doesn't laugh, he just goes on watching me and sips from his own mug before looking lost in thought. I can smell coffee and guess he's not drunk.

"Why are you chewing your lip like that?" I ask him, reaching up and prodding him gently in the dimple again. Jake has a touchable face. I've never noticed before how much his face cries out to be touched; there's a beauty about his features, even his designer stubble, that makes your fingers itch to trace the lines and curves.

"I'm thinking, Emma ... stop poking me in the face, woman," he chides with a frown and I push at his frown a little harder, feeling irritation at calling me "woman".

# The Carrero Effect ~ The Promotion

*Asshole!*

"You're very touchy-feely when you're drunk, aren't you?" he catches my finger and pushes it down. He has a cheek calling anyone touchy-feely.

*Mr. Hands-On, Carrero!*

"You've a touchy kind of face." I giggle again but spinning starts to take over and I decide to lay still to see if it will pass, lay watching his green eyes in the dim light and wonder what he's thinking about. Mesmerized by the way his eyes change with his moods. Sometimes they're dark and almost brown, other times pale and almost aqua. Normally, they're a very bright, almost emerald, green.

"Hmmmm." He looks at me in a really odd way, and I can still see the hint of a frown; I stifle the urge to poke it again.

"Hmmmm!" I mimic in a mock deep male tone.

"What's 'hmmmmm' all about?"

*Jake can be exasperating! I like Jake. I'm glad he's my boss, I think we get on better than most boss-employees do.*

"It's just hmmm ... You're drunk. You're making very little sense, and your grabby hands are a little distracting. I think I need to put you to bed."

*What does he mean, "grabby hands"?*

I hold my hands up in front of me to look, they don't look "grabby" at all. I was merely having a little feel of a beautiful face. I hear him sigh and he's closer, leaning down to peer at my face, as if he's trying to gauge just how drunk I still am. I have the urge to say "Hello" or "Peek-a-Boo".

"Where's your hot Crone?" I laugh at my own joke. It's rather funny.

*Miss Crane ... Crone ... Get it?*

He smiles, sighing deeply as though he has no idea what to do with me anymore. I notice that when he moves his jaw in any little way, his ear moves slightly. I wonder if all men have this special talent.

*Would you call it a talent? Ear wiggling ... Special skill of sexiness.*

I giggle again.

"Emma, you've seriously lost your filter." He laughs at me, looking at me in a "what am I going to do with my plastered PA" kind of way. I reach to poke his dimple again, but he catches my hand and pushes it down.

*Damn, he's quick.*

"Mr. Cartierro, leave my fingers alone," I sound out properly.

*Now that's funny, because Cartier is one of his favorite places to spend huge amounts of money on leggy dates like Crone.*

I'm making him laugh, when he smiles naturally like that it makes me want to smile too.

*God, I could lick that smile, it's so delicious.*

"As amusing as this is, Emma, you're going to have to go to bed. As much fun as you are drunk, I think I'll get more sense out of you over breakfast." He puts his mug down on the table.

"I don't want to sleep" I pout.

"Tough, you're going to bed. I have a duty of care." He scolds softly.

"I won't go, you can't make me." I'm sure my childhood sulky face still exists, I'm pretty sure it's making a comeback. I try and swat his face and hands as he reaches to help me up.

"Aargh. Emma!" He runs his fingers through his perfect hair, messing it up. I think he's frustrated with me, but I don't care as I don't want to go to bed, to be alone with my own mind.

I look at his messed-up hair, I like it better like that, less groomed and perfect and a little rugged. It really does make him look so much hotter. That "just fucked" look.

*I didn't think that was possible.*

I reach out and tousle it some more; I've never touched his hair, it feels nice, kind of thick and smooth, a little stiff with product, yet sensual.

He catches my fingers, pulling my hands in between us and keeps hold of them tightly. He's giving me a testy look and I wonder again where his date has gone. She's lucky, because she gets to run her fingers through his hair anytime she wants and that upsets me.

"If I have to drag you in there and put you to bed, I will. I'm not against hauling you to bed and holding you down." There's seriousness in his eye. He looks like boss Carrero and that means no messing about.

"Promises, promises." I tut, wriggling a hand free to poke him again in the dimple, he's not smiling but I remember where it is.

*Bullseye.*

"Fuck's sake, Emma. What you do to me woman!" He scoops me up and I squeal. He's so fast it makes the room tilt. I grab on for dear life and try not to choke him with my vice like grip, my face almost pressed into his. He can walk fast and in a few easy strides we're already in my room and he's pulling back my sheets with one hand.

"Are you mad?" I suddenly feel tearful. I don't want my gorgeous, hot boss, angry at me.

"No, Emma, I'm not mad." He lays me in the bed and pushes me onto my pillow softly. He pulls up my sheets and tucks me in like I'm a child.

I don't remember my mother ever doing this for me. No one has ever done this for me.

"You don't like drunk Emma?" I ask warily.

He smiles down at me and runs a gentle hand across my hair then down my cheek and it feels soothing. The back of his fingers feathering softly across my cheek and erupting tingles on my skin. I don't think he's mad, and it makes me feel better. His touch has the same effect as a calming wave; that gentle look on his face making me relax.

"I do like drunk Emma ... maybe a little too much." He looks odd when he says it and his eyes darken, he frowns, then quickly smooths it away.

"I don't like drunk, Emma." I sigh and close my eyes. I'm jealous that Jake likes drunk Emma.

*She's a cow.*

I close my eyes, when I do, I see the face of that weasel man at my mother's table when I was fourteen. I had just walked in from school and she had figured a cozy dinner to introduce my father was a good idea. How wrong she was.

My brain swivels forward, drunkenness opening doors and letting my mind lose control. I see my mother with her various men, see their faces swimming past me in a rush, like a subway train, until it stops on one looming grin that makes me shiver inside. That looming face which sometimes wakes me in the night with terrifying dreams. The ever-present face of my nightmares.

"Why?" he asks, and I focus back on his face, pulling myself out of my head. He's sitting on the edge of the bed, twirling a strand of my loose hair between his fingers. It makes my scalp tingle and draws my full focus to his strong form, so close to me, smelling so very good.

"She thinks about things I don't want to think about." I sigh quietly.

"Like fathers who weren't around?" he sounds softer, warmer. Jake always asks me things about my past, I wish he didn't, but tonight it doesn't feel so bad. I want him to stay and talk to me, not go to his room with that awful "Crone".

"And people called Ray." I let out a long heavy breath at the mention of his name, the looming face is still watching me inside my own head. Evading my closing doors, his lip curling back to reveal his snarl. I feel the bile rise in my throat as the fear travels up my legs.

"Ray?" The confused husky voice distracts me.

"Ray, who beats up girls and tries to molest them." I whisper, afraid of saying it out loud.

*Why did I start thinking of Ray? Stupid, Emma, very stupid!*

I don't like brandy any more, it breaks down the walls of my carefully made black box and lets things that I locked up tight loose.

I feel a warm touch on my arm, it's soft and delicate and sends a soothing sensation through the fear, bringing me back to focus. It helps Ray's face move back into the shadows, where he belongs.

"Emma, why did you never tell me any of this?" Jake's voice sounds odd. I don't recognize his tone; soft and breathy, but I'm feeling the tug of drunken sleep falling over me, despite everything running through my head. His touch too soothing, and it's making me fall into peaceful darkness. My eyes get heavier and the bed sways like a cradle, pulling me away from his voice.

"Don't tell Emma I told you ... She will be really mad." I whisper.

*Naughty teen, Emma? How did you get out?*

I try and haul her back down into the shadows with me as darkness overtakes us both.

# Chapter 9

The sun coming in tiny slices through the drapes, is worse than having salt poured in my eyes. I feel the nausea hit as I try to sit up. My cell is by the bed, and I realize it's been switched off; I never switch it off, I don't even know what time it is, and I could have missed a multitude of calls.

I swallow down the bile and reach for the glass beside my bed, lukewarm water will have to do. I know I should remember last night, but after my third drink on the couch I don't remember much else; I don't do hard liquor, so it's no surprise.

*I'm a total lightweight.*

I know at one point Jake came back, I think.

*Maybe.*

I have strange images of him leaning over me, with his tie hanging free; I'm not even sure if it was a dream, or a memory from another time.

I shower fast to combat the dizziness and ram toast and paracetamol down my throat in the sitting area, in a bid to recover quickly. The place is silent, and I guess Jake is still in bed. I remember Felicity is here, I forgot about her; I always try and ignore his female guests. At least I slept through her screaming for once, the only upside to my hangover.

My head winces every time I move and I'm having to sip water to keep the gag reflex at bay. I'm regretting drinking brandy immensely.

*What the hell was I thinking? Why did I let it get to me that much? Why did I let that idiot get under my skin?*

I have more resolve than that, I think it was the shock. It's been twelve years since his last contact, and although I knew he would resurface one day, I hadn't expected it yesterday.

I'm wearing workout clothes, I intend to hit the gym when the nausea subsides, to sweat this out of my system. I'm glad we don't have any meetings today, nothing planned until this evening, with a late client dinner. I might be able to get through it, if we're working from here.

I notice it's gone 9.00 a.m. and wonder why Jake's not up; even on weekends he never sleeps past six, even with a hangover, and this isn't like him.

I don't have to ponder it for long, as he appears, walking in the door, wearing sweats and a T-shirt soaked in sweat, he's already been down at the gym and has a towel draped around his neck. He looks bright and cheery, as usual; he's a morning person, something I'm not and never have been. I smile as he walks in.

"Morning, shorty," he smiles back.

"Morning," I mumble.

"How's the head?"

"Sore." I sigh and wince almost in reply.

"There's painkillers in the bathroom." He flashes me a smile as he walks past the couch.

"I got some already." I shake a packet in the air as proof.

"Have you eaten?" he walks across toward the kitchenette

intent on whatever he is doing.

"Yup ..."

"Good. Quickest way to recover from a hangover. Can you order me some breakfast, I'm going for a shower." He's at the fridge drinking a bottle of water, before throwing me a Jake special "I'll floor you with my hotness" smile and raised eyebrow in way of thanks and stalks off to his room.

I wonder where Miss. Crane is, as I watch his rather too pert ass sauntering away and guess she's still asleep. Jake must have exhausted her last night, and it instantly pisses me off.

*Ughhh!*

\* \* \*

He eats breakfast in the sitting area, while reading through papers, in his trademark jeans and T-shirt, he's barefoot and his hair is still ruffled and damp from his shower. He looks nothing like the CEO of the company I first met, and every bit a random guy on a weekend. It somehow feels a bit domestic.

Felicity is sound asleep in his room, giving us some much-needed peace, before her screeching voice grates on my nerves again. I am glad of her absence, for some reason her presence today is grating on me, more than normal.

He doesn't seem intent on any kind of work yet, and I'm glad. I'm trying to stay as still as possible, laying in my space on the couch, beside him, it's the only way the nausea and sore head are bearable and I'm trying to concentrate on the laptop on my thighs. The screen won't stay in focus and I'm finding it unbearable. I sigh, sliding it onto the table and lay down properly, resting my head on the cushioned arm. He gives me a knowing smirk and I glare at him. I'm so not in the mood for him to take the piss right now.

*Yes, I'm hungover, Jake. So what!*

I should maybe remind him of how many times I've seen him legless and stumbling into hotel rooms at stupid o'clock. I've seen sunglasses wearing, grouchy, next day Jake, many times over the past few months.

He finally puts down his mug of coffee, and financial times, and throws a look at me. I see his shift in position, it's his "I'm getting ready to chat" pose and groan inwardly. I'm suffering, and I would really like to stay silent.

*Cool composed Emma is on holiday right now.*

"You want to talk about last night?" he looks me straight in the eye, all Mr. Serious.

"Last night?" A memory of it, for a start, might be helpful.

He watches me carefully and I shift in my space, a little uncomfortably, unsure what's so engrossing.

*What did I do last night, besides getting smashed? What does he want to talk about?*

"Drunk Emma, as fun as she was, isn't someone I've ever met." He eyes me accusingly.

"Or will likely to again, seeing as I feel like hell." I grimace and haul my arm over my eyes so I don't need to look at him, he's studying me a little too intensely.

"You want to continue our conversation?" He pushes on, regardless of my "go away" posture. Lays his hand casually on my bent knee, propping it up at the wrist and resting quite happily there.

"What conversation?" I ask, genuinely confused but stay concealed under my arm.

"You don't remember?" The surprise in his voice makes me a little wary. I shake my head and feel the color rising in my cheeks; Jake never presses for no reason.

*What the hell did I say to him last night?*

"I put you to bed."

*Well, that explains why my cell is off.*

He turns his off every night, whereas I normally don't. Just in case I'm needed.

"Thanks." I mumble. I want to ask him what I said, but I don't, because I'm scared. I'm scared I might actually have told him something I didn't want him to know.

"You talked about your father." He says matter of factly.

*Crap. Like that.*

I feel the anger rise in me unexpectedly and it's too quick to grind back down.

"He's not my father! ... He's just a donor to my existence, and nothing more." I snap, jumping to my feet, his hand falling to the couch. I feel the heat rise in my face; teen Emma's anger, renewed with a fury and I'm pissed at myself for her appearance once again. I angrily storm to the kitchenette, I need water.

*And a boss who stops bloody well digging into stuff that has nothing to do with him.*

"And Ray?" The question is so calm and unimposing yet has a devastating effect on me. Stomach lurching to my throat, I falter and drop my water bottle hard on my foot, giving out a shocked yell and jump back.

"Are you okay?" He leans around, looking at me. His eyes steady on me as I scramble back, my head reels as I bend down to retrieve the Evian bottle and try to take a deep breath.

*Control Emma ... Control.*

I stand back up slowly, and more deliberately.

*How does he know about Ray?*

"Fine." I say stiffly.

"Come here, we need to talk about this." He watches me

intensely, a no-nonsense expression on his face.

"No." I close him down and take a gulp of my water, it almost chokes me going down. I want to know what I told him about Ray, about my father, but I also don't want to know, don't want to talk about this. I feel sick, maybe I should tell him I need to throw up and lock myself in my room for an hour, make him leave me alone.

"Don't you trust me, Emma?" he sounds so hurt, it hurts me too.

"Of course, I trust you." I turn to him, flashing anger again. Incensed at the question.

*How could he ask me that?*

We're together almost constantly, I have to trust him, I do trust him.

I realize it's the first time I've admitted to myself that I actually do, and it startles me a little.

*I trust Jake! I trust a man! When did that happen? How did that happen?*

What's more amazing is that I trust playboy Casanova Jake Carrero ... my heart-throb boss with his string of women and his hands-on personality.

"Then talk to me, Emma," he presses further, refusing to give up; his eyes still steady on me. I shake my head and turn away; I can't look at him.

*Why can't he understand that certain things don't need to be brought up ... Talked about?*

The past is done, and I'm done with the past, talking about it only makes it linger. Brings it to the forefront of my mind, where it has no place to be.

"I don't need to talk about this." I huff.

He's on his feet and walks toward me and I feel trapped, I know if I walk off he'll follow me. He has that determined expression on his face, the one usually reserved for stubborn clients. He grabs my upper arm gently and pulls me to face him, he looks angry, but his manner is calm. I try to twist free, but he holds me tighter; I think he knows I'll walk off if he lets me go.

"You said he beat you and tried to molest you."

I gasp and withdraw from him, shocked that I even let that much out in my drunken stupor.

*Crap. I don't want him to know about this. What the fuck, Emma?*

I don't want him looking at me like some sad little victim, incapable of taking care of herself.

*Why would I tell him that?*

He seems surprised by my reaction and lets me go instantly.

"Please, Jake." Trembling with the unexpected bite of tears in the back of my eyes, I stalk past him. I can't do this, he has no right. I can't get upset and let him see weak Emma, she doesn't exist anymore; I've no will to let her come back now.

"I want to know, Emma, you're my friend." He follows me, and I feel the anger writhe inside of me, teen Emma raising her ugly head and losing control like she always did, hot temper flaring.

"Why? It changes nothing!" I snap a little too aggressively.

*Shit ...*

I'm falling apart; I don't shout at Jake. I don't shout at anyone like this. I've more control than this now, I'm no longer teen Emma.

"It affects you." He looks angry, but I don't care.

*Be angry. You started this, Jake. Leave me alone.*

"This doesn't affect my ability to work for you, therefore

it's none of your business." I snarl through gritted teeth.

"You are my business, we work together almost every second of almost every day, our relationship goes a little deeper than boss and assistant. It depends on trust and honesty, to be able to work this way." His voice is heated, he reaches for me again and I move out of reach, tense and prickling. If he touches me, I may lash out, I need to go to my room.

"I trust you with every detail of my life, would be nice if you did the same." His voice matches mine, tense and angry, temper bubbling between us and it feels like static in the air.

"You don't pay me to burden you with my past." I snap at him.

"If you don't tell me, I'll find out for myself." He threatens, and I see the darkness move into his eyes.

"What do you mean?" I falter at his threat. There's an edgy tone I don't relish, it stops me in my tracks, causing me to glare at him with uncertainty.

"I'll have security do a deep background check on you, and pull up old dirt," he snarls.

"You wouldn't?" I scream at him, panic flaring at what he might find out.

*How dare he! That crosses the line in so many goddamn ways, and I'm not even sure it's legal. What the hell is he doing? What's he even thinking about? I'm supposed to trust him, after he's just said that to me?*

I feel rage shoot through me at a hundred miles an hour and can't contain it, I clench my fists and march away from him. I need space before I break something over his head. Before teen Emma and her erratic emotional self, bursts forth and ruins my life. I'm reeling but I'm terrified.

*What if he does? What will he find out?*

I pale and feel weak. I don't want Jake finding out about

my past, about how damaged I am. My time in a children's home, and why. He would never look at me the same again.

"No. I wouldn't ... I would rather you wanted to tell me." He's shouting too. I can't even begin to start to calm down, despite his admission; it makes me feel slightly reassured, hysteria holding its breath, but the rage is in full roar. I feel the hot tears on my cheek and wipe it away furiously. I don't cry. I never cry, I hate crying. It's so weak and vulnerable and makes me feel inadequate and worthless; I bristle inside and turn on him angrily.

"This conversation is fucking over!" The rage in my voice seems to startle him and instead of yelling more, he looks taken aback, remorseful.

*Too little, too late, Jake. Go away and leave me alone.*

I turn and stalk away, stomping hard and pushing things out of my way. Felicity appears from the bedroom and I cast him back a haughty glare with intent. I think he gets the message. The "go fuck off and play with your fuck buddy message" and slam my bedroom door, closing out his view of me.

*ASSHOLE!!!!*

I want to scream it at him through the closed door; I've never had this wave of reaction toward Jake before, and I can't control it. I'm beyond livid. I'm reeling, angry, and hysteria isn't far away. I hate losing control this way, every emotion bubbling to the surface like an angry volcano, threatening to explode.

*I mastered this once, I can do it again. I can push it all down and force it back into its black box. Put it all back neatly and close the lid. Bring calm back to the surface and put the mask back on.*

But I can't!

*Because he knows!*

Because he saw a sliver of my shameful wretched past and I'm devastated. He will see I'm a fraud, that PA Emma, his number two, is nothing more than a facade for a broken piece of worthlessness that men liked to knock around and touch.

It makes me feel sick inside, and I hurtle myself onto the bed amid a flurry of tears.

*I hate crying, I don't cry! I won't give them my tears, I won't let them have that from me. They took everything else.*

I roll on my back and take gasping gulps of air, swallowing them down painfully.

*That's right, Emma, breathe.*

I hear myself telling teen Emma, as she lays on the floor of her Chicago room.

*In ... Out ... In ... Out ... In ....Out. Slowly, and surely.*

I force myself to focus on the light fitting on the ceiling above me and keep going.

*In ... Out ... In ... Out ... In ... That's right, nice and steady.*

I'm not in Chicago anymore, it's okay now. I regulate my breathing to match my count, bringing myself down from near hysterics.

*In ... Out ... In ... Out ... Slower, bring it down a notch.*

I've overcome this a million times, and I can do it again. I can fix this.

*In ... Out ... In ... Out. Take deep breaths in ... It's getting easier.*

*In ... Out ... In ... Out. Calmer, smoother breathing.*

The tidal wave subsides slowly, and the blackness fades out. I feel my lungs move easier, the heaviness lifting.

*In ... Out ... In ... Out.*

Like a chant.

I'm in control ... I'm not a child anymore. Ray is not here

to hurt me.

*In ... Out ... In.*

The room around me is safe and still.

No one can hurt me anymore, I'm stronger now, I'm more capable.

*In ... Out ...*

The tears disperse.

*In.*

*Out.*

The anger subsides and I'm left feeling raw. I stop chanting as I breathe, I'm back in control and laying so very still. It's easier than it used to be. I'm better at it and it takes less time now than it used to; new Emma is laying on the bed, staring at the ceiling and she's remorseful. Logical, clear thinking, back in full swing.

*I can't leave it this way with Jake.*

I screamed at my boss ... my friend ... I don't know if I can face him again.

*But if I don't, it will only get more awkward, I may get fired. I don't think Jake would fire me, but still.*

He can't work the espresso machine, and coffee is his lifeline. A small smile tugs the corner of my mouth as I picture him trying and I feel the inner calm of my regained self and sit up. I'm ashamed and embarrassed.

My iPad lights up on my side table, indicating I have an email and I see Jake's name from my view point. I lean across, sliding it over and pull it onto my lap. Opening the screen with a tentative slide, I click on the email notification.

*Jake Carrero has sent you an iTunes gift.*

I open the email, thinking back to the last time he gifted me a song, and feel my heart tug a little. Remorse hitting me hard, nervous at what this may say.

*Jake Carrero has gifted you:*
*"Please Forgive Me" by Bryan Adams.*

I feel a lump rise in my throat, and the threat of new tears, only this time they're not in anger or sadness. Jake is trying to make things okay with me and I can't just ignore him. The swelling of my heart at his attempt and his sweetness has me on the verge of tears. I need to claw back some dignity and face him, let him see that I'm still the same Emma I was, and maybe ask him to forget this ever happened. That I'm not an insane psycho with a troubled past, who screams at him and runs away to hide.

*Well, maybe I am.*

I stand up and walk coyly to my door and open it quickly. Like ripping off a band-aid and steadily walk into the sitting room.

I see him sitting on the couch, leaning forward with his cell in his hands. His powerful body looks tense and stiff and he's looking at the floor, lost in thought, it's his thinking pose, when he's trying to choose a course of action and I feel remorseful.

*I made Jake stressed. I did that.*

Felicity is standing in the space by the door pulling on her shoes and glaring at him icily.

*Maybe it wasn't all me.*

I wait until she slams out dramatically, expecting him to react, but he stays focused on the floor, lost in his own thoughts. She hadn't even noticed me standing here.

*Here goes!*

I take a deep breath and walk toward him slowly and unsurely. I have no idea what I'm going to say, we have never fought this way before. We argue and bicker, and we have disagreements, but we have never walked out on one another in rage. I look at him shyly as I get to four feet away.

"Jake?" I breathe softly, apprehensively. My voice startles him, his head snaps up. He must have been lost deep in his thoughts and I catch the uncertainty in his eye.

"Hey," he says warily. He looks so lost, it hurts.

"I ... umm ..." This is harder than I thought it would be, I can't look at him, so I look to my right, away from him, across the room trying to find a focus while I find the words. There's a noise from the couch and then I'm hauled into his arms, pulling my head against his chest with a warm hand cupping my skull. He envelopes me in a bear hug and I'm too stunned to react. I stiffen at the alien-ness of it and then slump with relief. Jake's not mad at me anymore, we're done fighting.

"I'm sorry." He breathes into the top of my head, his face buried in my hair.

*My touchy-feely boss!*

I'll have to forgive him again, for manhandling me, only this time it's not that bad; it feels good and it takes away all the anger and doubts inside of me. It seems to be restoring me to my former self.

"I'm sorry too." The emotion catches in my throat, I revel in the feel of him.

*Jake, my boss. Jake, my first real male friend. I don't want to fight with him this way.*

I've never been hugged like this by anyone. Not even my mother, and it feels so safe, so unfamiliar, but yet so right. I close my eyes and allow myself to breathe him in; I wonder if that makes me weird. Freaky Lisa comes to mind.

"I won't push anymore." His voice is still soft and warm above my head my arms have slid around his waist and I'm holding him as tightly as he's holding me. The realization makes me feel awkward and embarrassed by the intimacy, and I let go. I'm overstepping the mark. He senses my reaction and releases me too, sheepishly we stand apart and

I'm overcome with shyness.

*Crap. This is new.*

He shoves my shoulder like an adolescent and I know it's to cover our awkwardness, so I shove him back.

*For a twenty-eight year old he sure knows how to revert to fifteen at times.*

That gains me a Carrero grin and I shake my head at him, rolling my eyes, amazed at how easily we can just get over it. It reminds me of how easily Sarah gets over things and I suddenly miss her.

He's back in playful mode and for once it doesn't irritate me, it relieves me.

"Knew you couldn't hate me for long, *Bambino*." He's still smiling and trying to look convincingly assured.

*Yeah, of course, you were so confident when I walked in.*

I remember his stressed posture and lost look, only moments before.

"Hmm, the jury is still out on that," I say impassively, I could never hate Jake. He throws me a mock injured look and I push him harder this time, he falls back onto the couch with flailing arms and a shocked expression.

*Easy there, teen Emma, he's still your boss.*

"Hey, woman! Any more of that and I'll have to retaliate. I can promise you, my kind of physical exertion will put some color in your cheeks." He gets up as though he's going to grab me, and I squeal, throwing out my arms toward him and shoving him straight back down with more force than necessary. He falls into the couch and just laughs at me.

"Hey! ... Gross misconduct, Miss. Anderson." He throws a scatter cushion up at me, but I dodge it easily.

"Sue me." I throw it back with a smile as I walk to lift my cell and groan at the numerous notifications. I'm a little breathless, and a hell of a lot happier.

I push down the thoughts about sperm donor, Ray, and Chicago. Jake says he won't press me on this issue and I know he means it, I can relax again. We can relax again.

I glance at my work out clothes and realize I need to get changed, we have actual work to do; I look at him lounging on the couch, still watching me and I feel better, lighter; he drives me crazy sometimes, but at least Jake isn't someone who harbors moods or anger for very long. Well, unless you're his father. Generally, he has a pretty sunny manner.

*The thought makes me smile ... Sunny ... Never thought I'd associate that word with Jake Carrero.*

"Are you going to get changed?" I ask as I skim through my cell, I need to get my laptop open and check the email from Rosalie. She's text me, informing me there are file attachments, revisions to the Hunter–Carrero contracts Jake has requested, that require his immediate attention. I push the last thoughts of sperm donor away and get back into PA mode.

"Nope." He's laid out on the couch tossing the cushion in the air casually and watching me from his vantage point, I frown at his casual attire.

"Well, I'm going to get changed, so at least I can feel like I'm ready for work." I take my cell with me and walk back to my room, engrossed in replying to Rosalie's email.

"Emma?"

I freeze, a tiny tremor of doubt crosses my mind and I hold my breath. Waiting.

"Uhuh?" I try to sound non-committal.

"I'm glad we're okay ... Let's not fight about that shit again okay?" his huskiness betrays a slight hint of emotion.

"Okay." I turn and give him a genuine smile, I feel a warm tide of affection fill my stomach as he throws me a genuine natural smile in reply. No showy playful or "I'm just so gorgeous", but relief we're friends again and I feel myself returning it even more so. No one makes me relax like Jake does, sometimes it's a curse but right now, I don't mind it. It feels okay to sometimes relinquish a little bit of the control, to stop holding everything in, especially when that smile is the reward.

* * *

Jake has watched the most godawful movie on the huge flat screen for the last half hour and I can tell he's bored, he's been channel hopping, messing with his cell and laptop and moved position on the couch about a hundred times. He's restless.

I'm reading one of the proposals for a small start-up Jake asked me to consider, and I'm fully aware he's been avoiding conversation. I know that look on his face, a little wary and a little unsettled. He's still unsure that we're okay but I'm letting him stew by carrying on with work and avoiding chatter.

"Let's go running?" his listless tone drags me from the papers in my hand and I sigh heavily.

"No."

"Why not?"

"Because you drag me out at six most mornings to jog with you, and I know you're going to do it again tomorrow, so I'm not doing it now." I throw him my best moody glare.

"You suck," he sighs childishly.

"Jake?" I laugh. "You do realize you're my boss?"

"And?" he actually pouts, looking very much like a child about now.

"You're behaving like a moody teen … Don't you have any

new bed buddies to pester?" I say, sighing loudly.

"Hmm." He sounds uninterested, he never seems to find women that hold his interest long. I feel my irritation rise, he has that air of frustration which I know too well. I can practically time how long it will be before his mood starts to really tumble and I get to be on the receiving end of grumpy ass Carrero.

"For god's sake! ... Okay!" I snap. This could go on all afternoon and I can't focus when he's being this way.

He grins and jumps up to go get changed into sweats. He's a smug winner. Likes to throw his success at me with huge champion grins. I swallow down the tension inside of me.

*Back to normal then.*

I go to my room and change into workout clothes and running shoes, I grab a hooded top and walk back into the main room as he walks from his door. He's in gray sweats and hooded top, he always looks so much younger and carefree dressed this way. Less playboy billionaire and more normal, good-looking guy, going to the gym. He leads the way to the elevator, whistling the whole time, in a far better mood and we head down to the main floor in companionable silence.

My cell vibrates, and I haul it out to check, it's a text from Sarah.

*"Hey, are you home this weekend?"*

We're due to fly back on Friday so I reply that I'll be around.

*"I may need your DIY skills. I want to redo my room."*

I sigh; decorating is not what I planned with my first whole weekend off in a while, but Sarah is useless with a paintbrush.

*"Okay. I'll text later, I'm going for a run."*

I reply, not wanting to talk about this right now.

She sends me back some kisses and a smiley face and I

slide my cell back into my pocket. I feel myself smiling despite my mild irritation at her request. I do miss Sarah, despite how distant we've grown, lately I have started to feel it more than before. I have no idea why the change in me, but I am more aware of it.

We exit the Four Seasons Hotel into the gloomy afternoon and I fall into an easy pace beside him when we hit the pavement, it's wet and muggy and gray. The air is cooler than it's been the previous couple of days and it forces me to jog a bit more energetically to get warm.

"Trying to race me?" he grins and pulls up his hood against the rain. The street is quiet and practically deserted, yet so picturesque, despite the overcast sky.

"You'd have no chance." I pull my hood up too, the drizzle isn't too bad, sort of refreshing.

"First one to the museum wins." He lurches into a run and takes off without waiting for my answer, and I follow in hot pursuit. My heart is pounding as I try my hardest to keep pace, but his stamina and long legs soon beat me into retreat and I have to stop to gasp air into my lungs. My throat and legs are burning from exertion and I have to bend my head down between my knees to stop the rise of nausea. He comes jogging back, noticing that I've given up.

"Lightweight." He bends over beside me and pulls me over to him with an arm casually around my shoulders, making me stand up; he pushes his water bottle in my hand and I accept it gratefully. Tugging me with him, we start walking slowly in the direction we had been heading as I catch my breath; already I'm sweating all over. I'm not as fit as I thought I was, we have barely run three hundred yards at full speed.

"Shut up." I breathe finally as my chest stops heaving and the nausea subsides.

"You need to get in the gym with my trainer ... he'll sort you out. Take care of that wheeze." Grinning as he winks at me, he's barely panting.

"Boxing is not my thing." I shake my head, he still has his arm casually around my shoulders as we walk, our bodies leaning into one another, side by side. To the average onlooker, we would probably look like a couple.

"Maybe it should be ... It's better than therapy. Why do you think I'm such a happy go lucky guy?" He winks.

I hand him back his water, throwing him a look of indulgence. A look that says, "all that casual sex?" and he lets me go to take a drink. He empties it and throws it in a nearby trash can, impressed he met his own bullseye. That juvenile boy inside, fist pumping at his ability to dunk a plastic bottle.

"Do you really want me to learn how to beat you up, Jake?" I smile cheekily, watching him.

"*Carino.* Even if you became a pro boxer, I would still put you on your ass. You're half my weight class." He smirks and squeezes my shoulder lightly.

"I don't even know what that means." I stop, leaning back to stretch out my limbs and start jogging on the spot to signal I'm recovered enough to continue jogging. He pulls my hood further forward over my face and shoves me in front of him playfully, so that I'll lead.

"It means that you'll never be able to beat my ass, girly." He laughs with a huskiness that sounds a little too sexy.

"Don't tempt me," I warn.

"I like a challenge."

"Well if beating is what you're into?" I catch the cheeky glint in his eye and sucker punch him in the ribs playfully, before he can finish his sentence. He pushes me away and tries to trip me deliberately, catching my wrists, so I don't fall, and he receives a pout and glare. He rights me on my feet with a laugh and we set off again.

*He's in a childish mood this afternoon ... Great! That's all I need.*

We jog on in silence for two blocks before we round a corner, and head in a new direction. I look around at the unfamiliar streets and surrounding scenery, Seattle seems lower paced and more relaxed than New York. It hasn't got the same buzzing energy and I kind of like it. It's a welcome break in our hectic schedule lately.

"What are you thinking about, *Miele*?" his voice cuts into my thoughts. Jake's looking at me as we run, and he has to keep pushing his hood back at the side to see my face, the gesture makes him look childish and I smile.

"Wondering where I would dump your body if I beat you to death."

"It's like that, is it?" he grins.

"Yep."

I'm not prepared for the sudden lurch at me as he grabs me by the waist and tips me upside down in mid-air. With his muscles, I'm no more than a gym bag in weight, I squeal in surprise and choke on the sharp intake of breath. He tips me completely over onto my feet so that I'm still bent double but in a head lock, my butt facing away from him, my head against his abdomen. I'm squealing and trying to wrench myself free as he keeps walking, but I'm stumbling backward.

"Jake ... Stop it." I'm laughing and unable to fight as he has my arms pinned to my sides.

"I can't. I'm looking for a shady corner, so I can administer some much-needed discipline." He threatens, but I can hear the playfulness in his voice. He finally releases me and hauls me back up, pulling me against him with an arm around my shoulders, he drags me onward. My hood falls free, letting the soft rain cool my hot face. Breathless from his antics and disheveled from his manhandling.

"You know how many sexual harassment laws you just broke? I could haul your ass through the courts." I point out. Laughing hard as I do so.

"With my reputation, my lawyers would probably just settle." He smirks and winks; I shake my head at him and try to pull my clothes back into their rightful place within the confines of his arm and fail miserably.

"Should stop manhandling the staff then!" I snort, unable to stop giggling, he's walking fast and making me stumble to keep up.

"Where are we going?"

"A walk ... I'm bored at the hotel," he says dejectedly.

"Are you ignoring my suggestion?" I ask innocently.

"About manhandling my staff?"

"Yes."

"Yes ... There's no fun otherwise. You were made for manhandling, Ems." He throws his playful "I'm hot and it means I get away with it" smile and I fight the urge to sucker punch him again. I pull myself free from his grip and shove his arm off, so I can finally adjust my clothes properly. He has them all twisted around me and my hair is falling in my face. He tugs the hair tie out of my ponytail so that it all comes tumbling down and I throw him an exasperated look.

"It was coming down anyway." He offers by way of an explanation and tosses the hair tie in a dumpster as we pass it.

"Hey," I sulk. "I don't have another one with me."

He shrugs, which only makes me narky with him.

"You'll just have to leave it loose then, won't you?" He ruffles my hair, trailing his fingers through the length and down my back softly.

"Stop acting like a child ... Sometimes I seriously can't

understand why I work for you, or that you even run an empire." Watching him now, he's far removed from Mr. Business, or even Mr. Public eye. He's adolescent Carrero.

He reaches out a hand, ignoring me and tugs me closer by the hood so I'm within reach of his arm and puts it back around my shoulders. Only this time it's loose and casual, and my clothes stay neat and in place. I don't bother fighting this time; I'm so used to touchy-feely Carrero by now that I've stopped caring any more. He has very few inhibitions, and he's been raised by a touchy-feely, Italian, family.

*Why doesn't it bother me? It would bother me if it was anyone else.*

I guess because Jake is the first man I've ever known who touches me without intent. There's no threat, or ulterior motive. In the way that a child touches automatically, because they want to, and they don't see the issue with doing it.

In the way he constantly flirts or makes suggestions of a sexual nature, yet never follows through. It's harmless, it's just how he is. Saying that, however, he's a constant annoyance at work, forever tugging my hair or prodding me in the side and manhandling me into cupboards. Maybe I *should* sue him for sexual harassment; I smile to myself.

*Teach him some boundaries, that would show him.*

"We need a break, Emma ... I'm listless and tense all the time lately ... distracted." His voice is subdued suddenly. I appraise his expression and he looks distracted, even with his hood still up, making him look more street thug on the prowl, and less Mr. Business, there's an empty, lost expression just under the surface.

*I couldn't sue that face.*

"You're the boss ... You don't need anyone's permission." We're walking along an alley with no real idea of where we're going, and it's stopped raining. The sun peeks out between the dull clouds, threatening a better afternoon.

"Maybe somewhere to relax for a week." He's looking around, seemingly lost in thought.

"Where do you want to go?" I ask curiously, there aren't many places he hasn't been.

"We could be spontaneous," he answers quickly, and I raise a brow.

"Could *we* now?" I emphasize the "we", making it clear that taking your PA on holiday with you defeats the purpose of a holiday. Not to mention it being odd.

"You don't want to come?" he looks at me in the way a child would on finding you're no longer taking them to buy candy.

"Ummm, why would I come on holiday with you?" I stifle a giggle at his expression.

"Because you work as hard as I do and could use the break too. Because I want you to."

"I don't think it's appropriate" I hesitate, somewhat amused that he would even suggest it.

*He's actually being serious?*

"Emma, we have literally lived in hotels together for the past few months, you've stayed the night in my apartment more than once ... Why is it any different?"

"Because a holiday isn't work ... it's different!" I'm starting to feel uncomfortable with this direction of conversation.

*Why is he pressing this?*

I think of what kind of gossip would fly around the offices if wind got out that we headed off in the sun for a week together. Not to mention how it would look if the media took pictures of us together, relaxing on a beach, or a boat, or whatever he chose to do to kick back. I wonder if he ever took Margo on a break.

*I should ask her next time she checks in to see how I'm doing. Ask her if she ever got whisked away for a romantic time out.*

"Don't overthink things, Emma." He lets go and pulls my arm, indicating we should jog again. I can feel my limbs getting heavy, so follow without hesitation; we should slow the pace to warm "down." I guess it also signals the end of conversation, I observe drily, as he jogs ahead making it impossible to talk. I follow him as we round the corner and start heading back in the direction of the hotel, trying to keep up. I get the vibe from him that he's sulking about this and I stifle the urge to laugh at him.

*What the hell? Jake sulks? Actually sulks. Since when? And why? Because I won't go on holiday with him? Surely, he can't be pissed at that?*

I watch the straight, muscular shape of his back as we jog and think rationally, he's been tenser lately, maybe he's just stressed. Jake doesn't sulk. He's probably just tired, and eager to get back. It's been non-stop lately, with so much in the pipeline and he's right, we could use a break.

He stays ahead of me at a good pace, so that all I can do is jog to keep up, we head back to the hotel via an unfamiliar route and I can't help but feel a little miffed at his sudden cool attitude.

# Chapter 10

It's late, and he's out with some blonde bimbo who posed in *Playboy*, all fake boobs and Botox with an irritating laugh and a weird pair of overly plump lips. We fly home tomorrow so he's letting off steam Carrero style. Loose women, booze, and a nightclub.

I glance at the clock in distraction, noticing how quiet it is when he's not around to frustrate me. I don't get his fascination with nightclubs, all that loud, thumping music grinding bodies, and stifling air. But then Jake's fascination with jumping out of planes and down buildings is beyond me too. He's the original adrenaline junkie, and never seems to sit still for long.

It's a hot muggy night and I feel sticky in my sweats and T-shirt, my hair has been up all day and it feels itchy, my scalp screaming for release. I had a good workout session in the gym after dinner, but I regret eating first. I'm starving now, due to the energy burn off, but don't want to eat more. I'm always conscious of my figure, being on show all the time. Especially when paired with the Adonis known as Jake. Besides, food after 8.00 p.m. makes me feel bloated and restless.

A shower cools me off, but I'm too hot to put on more clothes, I look through my array of nightwear and pull out a short satin number that Donna bought me in four colors. My saintly shopper! She now takes my personal requests and I had thrown this in my suitcase in case it had been hot and stuffy.

It's strappy and slight, and looks cooler than my normal nightdresses, although, there's a lot less fabric to it than my normal style. I leave my hair down, but I blow dry it, soft waves hang around my shoulders and I realize how long it's been getting. I rarely keep it down, so it's hard to judge how much it's grown over the last few months. I should really get it cut to tidy it up and make tying it up less of an ordeal.

I go to bed around ten, taking my laptop with me, so I can check my emails and reply to anything urgent.

\* \* \*

I wake with a start, hot and clammy and my throat's parched. I was dreaming again of the darkness of my room and the creeping sensation of someone in the shadows, coming toward me. I remember I hadn't been able to move, frozen with fear and I shake it off, pushing it down with the other five million of these vague night terrors I've had over the years. Memories mixed with fear and imagination don't make for very pleasant dreams, even after twenty-odd years.

I reach for my glass by the bed and notice I emptied it when working on my correspondence, I'll have to get up and get a drink now.

The clock tells me it's 4.00 a.m. and still incredibly dark outside, I'm aware that the room is still eerily quiet as I slide out of bed, meaning Jake is still not back. He usually falls through the door anywhere between four and five when he's gone out, unless he's with Daniel Hunter. Then you see him when you see him, sometimes not until the next day. Daniel is the bad influence that Jake doesn't need, and I worry when I know he's with him. I'm glad we're still in Seattle and he's not with him now, getting up to god knows what.

I pad into the suite and across to the kitchen/mini bar area, I don't bother with lights as the dim glow from the lamp in the sitting area is enough, and if I wake myself fully then I'll never get back to sleep. I'm glad of the coolness through here and it feels good on my exposed skin after my clammy awakening.

The water from the fridge has a slight lemon taste and it makes me think of Jake and the endless bottles of water, with lemon slices, he goes through a day; he drinks as much water as he does alcohol and it's him who started me on lemon water.

I hear the noise outside the suite door and know that he's just getting home.

*Great! Let the fun begin!*

Leggy blonde will no doubt be falling around giggling and noisily attempting quiet. That's not what I need. I freeze by the fridge in an attempt to go unnoticed. Hopefully he will head straight to his room, and I don't have to endure another of his low IQ bed mates. I lean on the counter and concentrate on sipping the water slowly, the coolness of the surface makes me look down and tense, realizing I'm not wearing my robe.

*Crap. I'm dressed like a hooker!*

I'm standing in a scrap of lace and satin that leaves very little to the imagination and is pretty see-through in places, I suddenly feel overly exposed. I also can't run now as he's opening the door. I push down my anxiety and stay still and composed, maybe he won't even notice me standing here.

"Emma?"

*Shit!*

My eyes jerk up from taking in the shortness of my nightdress and I straighten, suddenly awkward; he's looking at me oddly and even at this distance I can tell he's really drunk, I can smell the booze from here. I squirm slightly, noting that he's looked me up and down in a slow, very male way he never has before, and I don't like it.

*Fuck. This stupid nightdress.*

I notice there's no accompanying blonde either.

"Hey ... Did you have a good night?" I try to sound bright and bring his eyes back to my face, he's still watching me, and I feel self-conscious. I gauge that he's on the upper limits of drunkenness. A ten plus on the Carrero scale, he's really overdone it tonight.

"You should have come, tiny." He slurs badly, I don't know why he always asks, as I always refuse.

*It's not my thing.*

I just smile tightly, willing him to go to bed so I can make a break for it and cover up. I move to walk past him, but he steps in front of me clumsily, he tries to walk to the fridge at the same time. There's an awkward pause and we both laugh nervously.

*Okay, this is beyond weird.*

I think he feels just as uncomfortable about seeing me so underdressed, this doesn't feel like our normal atmosphere. I'm feeling overly sensitive to his body and movements, so close to me, in a way I've never experienced, and I don't like it at all. The amount of naked skin on show I have is tingling with the heat he's emanating. I can almost feel a sizzle of electricity in the air, it's so tense.

"I'll leave you to it." He smiles and sways slightly toward me, I put out my hand to steady him. I've probably never seen him reach swaying point before and this weird, whatever it is, has us both acting odd.

*Just how much has he had to drink tonight? Jeeze, he smells like a brewery and then some.*

He looks alien to me and not like Jake at all.

"You're really drunk, aren't you?" Normally drunk Carrero amuses me, but there's something off and I'm aware of every thump of my heartbeat and my own shallow breathing. The weird tension that's making me stiffen, my body can sense the difference between us.

"I am!" He breathes but makes no effort to move away. I take my hand from his arm and wrap my arms around myself protectively, in a bid to cover cleavage and exposed body, really unsure now. All I manage to do is create more cleavage so I loosen my arms again. I don't recognize him, the heaviness of his voice, the darkness of his normally clear green eyes that most definitely take in a long slow look at the aforementioned cleavage; the facial expression and body language. I feel a huge pang for sober, normal Jake right now. As though he's gone away.

"You cold?" his hand comes up to touch my shoulder and I jump.

*Crap.*

I'm nervous.

*Why? It's Jake! I'm being stupid. Is it because I'm dressed this way and he's looking at me like that? Jake would never hurt me in that way.*

I'm exposed and self-conscious and it feels like I'm naked. I feel vulnerable, and vulnerable is not something I can do, it's making me edgy.

"Sorry ... I didn't mean to ..." His voice is breathy, and he steps back, slightly swaying again.

"No, it's okay ... Sorry, I'm just ..."

*I'm just what? Jumpy as shit! Freaking out over nothing.*

"Just what?" The expression on his face changes, I see the concern and I realize he does look the same. He's still in there, my sweet, safe Jake and feel stupidly relieved. I can't control the nervous laughter that bubbles from my throat in a very non-Emma like way.

"Nothing, I'm half asleep ... I'm going to bed." I step back from him with a sudden need for personal space and move to walk around him.

"Emma?" he slurs.

"Yes?"

"I like this." His fingertips skirt down the side of my stomach gently, causing me to inhale sharply. I flinch and move back, reeling, unsure. His touch feels so different ... So not Jake! It makes my skin tingle and erupt, then crawl back in revulsion, fear. I don't even want to evaluate whether it is good or bad. It's wrong. It's too intimate. He lifts his hands defensively, he knows he's overstepped the mark.

"I'm sorry ... Emma. I'm going to bed ... I'm drunk as fuck." He looks pained and uneasy.

"It's okay. It's fine. Go to bed." I know I'm stiff and tense, I feel the coldness in my own voice, my heart pounding erratically, like a scared deer caught in headlights.

"Don't say it like that." He moves forward gently, and I feel his fingers trace my jaw, his eyes locking with mine.

"I would never do anything to you, Emma." He sways forward again, bumping noses with me because he's too close and incapable of steadiness. His hand comes to my shoulder to steady himself and moves back slightly.

I can't relax, this is not my Jake. This is a glimpse of Casanova Carrero, someone I've only seen at a distance, someone who has never turned his attention on me. I'm motionless, focused on every touch and movement, pinned by fear. Memories of a million dark nights and hot breath near my face flashing through my head at a million frames a second. I feel as though I'm suffocating.

He leans in quickly, so quickly that I can't counteract, and his lips meet mine, soft and hot and surrounded by the smell of alcohol. His hand comes to cup my face gently and pulls me in against his mouth. I freeze, every piece of my body caught in time and I feel suddenly detached, like it's happening to someone else and I've lost the ability to do anything. To stop it.

His fingers tug my chin down, opening my mouth slightly as he fully connects, his tongue sliding lightly over my bottom lip ... gently ... slowly ... And I recoil.

The panic searing through me is like an electric shock and I shove him away, hard, I'm breathless and panicking. Teen Emma is making herself known, I feel like the room is spinning around me and the blood rushing through my ears is louder than I can bear. My head feels like it might explode.

"Shit. Emma ... Shit." He seems flustered, he tries to grab for my arms and I start struggling away from him, trying to avoid the contact.

"I'm sorry ... Emma. I'm sorry ..." he tries to grab me to make it right, but I can't. I can't let him touch me. I feel like my skin is on fire and everything is spinning out of control. I need air, I need space, I need solitude. I need away from him. I'm so confused that I don't even know how I feel right now and he's stifling me with his sheer closeness.

"I ... Need ... To ... Go." I finally manage a few struggled words, my legs aching to run far, far away from him, the instilled fight or flight instinct kicking into action. He releases my wrist, having finally caught it and quickly moves out of my way. I can't look at him, I can't trust myself to slide past him, so I take a huge arc, keeping him at arm's length.

I move fast and run to my room, slamming the door behind me, latching it and sliding to the floor in a crumpled, un-composed heap. Everything reeling and dipping around me and I know I'm either going to pass out or throw up.

I lean forward, putting my face on the floor, trying to calm the chaos of my mind in the darkness of my room. I'm panting. I need to pull in these reeling thoughts, rationalize what just happened.

*Jake was drunk, really drunk. I've never seen him that bad. I'm amazed he's still upright. I must have given him signals, encouraged it? I must have looked wanton dressed this way ... I asked for this! Isn't that what I do? I give off signals that make men want to do things to me?*

*But Jake's not like that. Jake doesn't need to do that, he's never given me any inclination that he ever would. Isn't that why I relax around him? He has every woman he could ever want, falling at his feet; this has to be me. I had to have looked at him in some way or sent some unintentional signal to him to make him kiss me.*

I'm racked with guilt and shame, just like so many times before, when my mother's boyfriends tried to touch me, tried to kiss me, tried to take my night clothes off. I can't even think about his mouth on mine. I don't want to. I can't even begin to process it; it didn't feel like anything I could compare it to. I had no point of reference to what I was feeling at that moment.

I have been kissed before, it's why I don't like it. Forced harsh mouths against mine, trying to pry my mouth open cruelly. I resisted them all; bit, squirmed, and clawed. But Jake's kiss hadn't been forced, it was soft, and for a fleeting moment, my mouth responded, opened and stilled as his tongue slid over my lip.

I push the memory away harshly.

*Stop it! This is fucked-up ... This is wrong; he's my friend. He's my boss!*

I hadn't let my two boyfriends kiss me at all, I turned my head, even when I finally felt pushed to have sex with them. And hadn't I only even done that because I felt I was supposed to? I hadn't wanted them to kiss me. It reminded me too much of things I didn't need to remember anymore.

*So why the hell did I let Jake kiss me just then?*

# Chapter 11

I don't get much sleep. I stare at the ceiling, listening to the silence in the dark, before dawn finally tugs me out of bed; I jog alone at 6.00 a.m., the familiar route I normally take with Jake, but he's still in bed and avoiding him is my only plan of action this morning.

I pound the picturesque streets of Seattle with my soft-soled running shoes and try to bring back all the calm and control that rules my life. We need to forget last night ever happened if we're to move on. I need to stop over analyzing and obsessing over it and forget it ever happened.

He was drunk; Jake's impulsive and sometimes irrational when he's drunk, he can be unpredictable and foolish, and I shouldn't put any weight on last night at all. He's a born womanizer and last night, with beer goggles on, I was just another possible conquest who was obviously giving him some sort of come-on signs.

I shower and eat in my room and pack my suitcase, we're heading home today, the flights set for noon, so we have some time to kill. Jake's private jet, so it's not like we have a check in to deal with.

The sitting room looks normal and serene, but it just feels claustrophobic to me. I try and settle with my laptop on the couch, it's still early, my bottle of water between my feet perched on the low coffee table.

"Emma ... I'm sorry about last night." His voice startles me from behind, I've been so immersed in thought, unaware he had even appeared.

"It's forgotten," I respond a little too quickly, and inwardly tell myself to calm down. The butterflies creeping up at his arrival and my heart pounding a little too harshly. I feel the heat on my cheeks, indicating a blush.

*Dammit!*

"I had a lot to drink." He sits down beside me on the couch, resting his arms on his knees and leaning toward me, so his eyes can fully lock with mine. I know he's being the gentleman, I know it's my fault. I thought of nothing else all night. This is why I ran from Chicago and ran from angry teen Emma ... To reinvent myself and to leave behind all the men, and my mother, who ruined my life.

He looks effortlessly sexy this morning, freshly showered and bright eyed, despite the fact he should have a hangover.

"I hadn't expected you to walk in, I was just getting a drink." I'm rambling, overly bright, and trying to excuse my behavior. Trying to mask my uneasiness, trying to get back to yesterday. He watches me thoughtfully for a moment then changes his gaze to the floor instead.

"When did you start wearing things like that to bed?" his tone drops. His whole demeanor changes slightly, I realize he's never seen me in anything like that before. I always wear my toweling robe when I leave my room.

"Always."

*Maybe that's the issue? I dress like someone who wants sex, even though I don't; maybe that's something I should consider changing.*

*No.*

*Stop thinking like that!*

"I see." He sounds low and brooding and he's watching me again, only this time oddly. I want to know what he's thinking. I want this to be over and the tension gone.

I'm trying to sit perfectly still and calm, but I'm squirming inside. The way he's sitting has his T-shirt straining with tautness over his biceps and pecs, I try to focus on typing. I don't know who I'm even typing to anymore.

"I'm going for a run ... I'll pack when I get back." He makes to move away, but falters, reaching out, he shoves my shoulder so that my laptop slips slightly. I snap my chin up to look at him, surprised, and see the wariness, and the glint of playful. He's trying to make amends, he's trying to smooth it over and get back to yesterday too. I relax, there's my Jake, back to being adolescent, trying to make me smile and it's working. Our stupid juvenile way.

"I'm suing you for sexual harassment." I smile shyly. Making light of it all, hopeful that it'll work. My heart still beating fast, wanting to just let this go.

"I'll blame Jack Daniels for my misdemeanors. I was in no way in control of my faculties last night." He smiles, and I see relief, the tension between us evaporates and he ruffles my hair in his irritating manner.

"Go away and have your run. Stop annoying me." I pout and smile to myself as he wanders off, giving me a backward glance and a grin.

*We're okay. It's done ...*

Back to how we were. Like it never happened.

\* \* \*

# Jake & Emma

I drop my pen several times and feel him frowning at me several more, alerting me to the fact I'm twisting my hair absent-mindedly.

*When the hell did that habit return? That crap stopped months ago, when I relaxed with my new boss.*

I've been so antsy and jumpy on this flight, I think it's the lack of sleep. It's a six-hour flight, give or take, and so far, I've spent most of it rereading the same document in front of me. My focus shot, I slide the laptop closed and check my cell for the twentieth time.

Jake's now asleep in his seat, with headphones on, listening to his playlist before he dropped off. I smile as I hear a song with the lyrics "Cry Baby" playing quietly even from here. Our passing of jokes song.

He looks relaxed and young, a peaceful expression on that flawless face. I've seen him asleep a thousand times, but for some reason, right now, his face fascinates me. I forget that he's still so young. I know he's older than me, but still, it's only by two years at the most. Everything he handles, things he's capable of. I wonder if he will turn out like Carrero senior when he's older, work fueled and commandeering.

*No ... Jake will always be this way. Cool and relaxed like his mother. Effortlessly laid back and smiley.*

That happy look he always has in his eyes, the easy charm and smile he treats everyone too. I watch him for a while longer, finding peace in it, watching him breathe, watching him lay motionless; fully trusting his staff to fly us home. I've rarely slept on any of the flights. I'm not a good flyer; something he teases me about it endlessly. Edgy and tense until we land, having to put my life in someone else's hands doesn't sit well with me, it's not easy.

I stare out of the window and watch parts of a movie that doesn't really capture my attention for an hour. I know I keep adjusting my position and I pick up my pen so many times, just to have something to fiddle with.

"Relax!" His sleepy voice draws me to turn to face him, he's watching me with heavy lids, boyish yet sexy at the same time. My heart melts a little.

"Hey," I say softly. He looks comfortable, still resting in the position he's slept in, but his green eyes focus lazily on me across the aisle. We're sitting in opposite directions.

"I'm trying." I smile.

"I know something that will relax you." He smiles softly, and I feel myself frowning with the ghost of a smile on my lips.

"What?"

He rests his head back in its previous position and closes his eyes.

"Two weeks on a yacht in the Caribbean ... And you don't get to say no!"

# Chapter 12

"I'm home," I yell out into the apartment, dropping my keys on the hall table. There's soft jazz music coming from Sarah's room, the distinct smell of Marcus's aftershave in the sitting room, and a half empty bottle of wine and two glasses on the table. I sigh and ponder showing up at Jake's apartment for the night as he offered. I should have stopped over, instead of the extra car journey home, we'd be watching a movie by now.

There's no response from the closed bedroom, I assume they don't want to be disturbed, so I don't attempt to call out again. I go to my room and dump my luggage by the bed, glad to be home, yet at the same time the familiar pang of missing Jake already washing over me.

We have worked together so much over the last few months, glued side by side, so being apart feels abnormal. Even though we do occasionally spend weekends apart, somehow the recent non-stop chaos of trips and work days, flowing into each other, had meant a long few weeks of barely, rarely, being separated and I guess it's why I feel it more now than ever. I haul open my suitcase and discard some of the dirty laundry into the hamper, plug my technology into the chargers on my desk and begin to change into nightwear.

My cell vibrates across my desk and I see the notification, with Jake's name, lighting the screen, lifting it with a smile I see the familiar notification.

*Jake Carrero has gifted you an iTunes song.*

I swipe open the screen and open the email, smiling stupidly.

*Jake Carrero has sent you "Bryan Adams" - "When You're Gone."*

I feel the grin spread across my face widely and shake my head. I know the song well and laugh at his cuteness, I guess he's feeling the same. Like his right hand has been removed. I laugh at the pun, scrolling iTunes, looking for an appropriate title while listening to the song he's sent me. So very Jake, with his love of crooning rock stars. Despite the love lyrics, most of the song mirrors how I feel. I send him back a gifted song.

*"Are You Missing Me?" by Jim & Jesse McReynolds*

I have never heard it before, but the title makes me smile. I laugh at its cheesy country-ness, knowing he will be amused by it too. I put my cell down and go back to unpacking my bags slowly, again interrupted by the vibration of my cell and another iTunes gift.

*Jake Carrero has sent you—Bon Jovi - "Always".*

I can't help the wave of warmth, followed by the pang of sadness, I really do miss him, despite only leaving him less than an hour ago, he has a way of getting into my head and under my skin. I wouldn't know how to carry on if he ever decided we were no longer to work together. The memory of what that kiss could have ruined shakes me inside.

My cell vibrates in my hand again and my mother's mobile number appears on the screen, instinct causing me to ruffle my brow. I take a deep breath, letting out a sigh. I don't have time for her guilt trips tonight, I'm tired and fed up, and all she ever does is make me feel bad for never coming home. I hesitate, but answer, despite my reservations. That ingrained guilty conscience she has burdened me with.

"Hey, Mom." I say flatly.

"Emma, hi," A strange, young girl's voice answers, making me frown in confusion.

"Is that Emma?"

"Speaking." I reply tightly, unsure as to who she is or why she's using my mother's cell to call me. She sounds young, very young. Early teens young.

"Emma hi, my name's Sophie ... Your mom's been helping me out." She sounds scared, her voice wavering and I feel a trepidation move up my spine. Sixth sense tingling.

"Mmm hmm." I say snappily, aggravation building up; somehow deep inside me I can sense her apprehension and it's raising mine. I can hear the emotion in her voice.

"Your mom's in the hospital ... You need to come home to Chicago ... Someone really hurt her." She all but bursts into tears.

* * *

Twenty minutes after I finally hang up on Sophie, I'm sitting on my bed staring at the cell. Numb and raw at the same time. My heads reeling. Somehow my body and mind are detached.

Someone has beaten my mother to within an inch of her life, left her for dead in her own apartment. My old home.

*Again!*

Sophie found her, a young teen from the homeless shelter. She's taken her under her wing and let the girl stay sometimes, the poor thing had been the one to find her, get her help. Just like I had, so many years ago.

I get up and walk to Sarah's room, desperate to share my internal agony and find some calm in the chaos but find it empty. They're not even home; just the radio playing on low and I snap it off in irritation. I sigh and walk back to my room anxiously. My brain running through a memory of my mother this way once before, and I choke it back down.

*When is she going to stop doing this crap to me? Is it not enough to go through all of this once? No. She has to keep going back, over and over, to the same kind of abusive relationships. Like a moth to a goddamn flame.*

Her choice of men, my whole life, just one long, bad memory of violence and abuse. She has a type and she attracts them, repeatedly. She never, ever, stood in the way of them, never stopped what they did. She chose her men over me so many times, letting them in, letting them hurt us both, and never once did she put my needs first. Not even her own needs, and here she is doing it all over again.

She is caring for a fourteen-year-old girl and has just subjected her to the same sight I had seen at twelve years of age, a sight which led to my being in a children's home for almost a year. Social services invading our life and taking me from an abusive environment, sending me to one that, in my eyes, was far worse—in a children's home; only to return me when she promised that her life was different. That particular lover, long gone, but we both knew a new one was around the corner any day. I learned to lie after that, to help cover up who she really was. That year in care taught me that there are far worse people in the world than my mother when it comes to parenting.

I look at my suitcase and feel the crushing weight come over me.

*I'll have to go back there. I'll have to go home to Chicago after being away for almost six years.*

I want to cry, I want to lay down, open my mind and let it all pour away. I feel desolate and scared. An internal agony, threatening to consume me. I never thought I would be in this place ever again. I'm scared, fear is not something I ever wanted back in my head.

I pick up my cell and call Jake's number. It's impulse, something I do without a thought. He always knows how to make me smile, how to make me feel better. Just his voice on the other end will make me feel calmer. I need to tell him I'll be gone for a few days, maybe he'll let me use the jet, instead of commercial airlines and save me the misery of facing people for this two-hour flight. I just need to speak to him, so badly I can almost taste it.

"Hey," He answers, after only two rings, he sounds cheerful and it tugs my heart into chaos even more, picturing his smiling face and perfect, clear green eyes.

"Jake ... I need to go home ... Back to Chicago." I sound shell shocked and small. I can't pretend right now, I'm too raw to try. I try to control the waiver in my voice, but I fail, unable to contain my emotion at the sound of his deep comforting tone.

"Emma? What's wrong, *Miele?* Are you crying?" his soft, soothing voice causes a solitary tear to slide from my eye and I wipe it away.

*Maybe I shouldn't have called him. He sounds surprised to hear me tearful.*

"No." I lie. "My mom's in the hospital ... an accident." I can't tell him that she's let another abusive man destroy her life and left her half-dead; open that can of worms and confessions.

"Shit ... Do you want me to come with you? I'll call the airfield and get the jet ready." He sounds concerned; my sweet Jake. I want to run into his arms and feel him hug me, like he did in the hotel the morning we fought. What I would give to have him here right now.

"No ... I have to do this alone." I want him to come with me, so badly, but knowing what he would see, the questions he would ask, is unbearable. I don't want him to know that part of my past. Ever!

"If you're sure, *Miele*? I'll call the airfield. I'll send Jefferson to pick you up and take you to the airport. Just pack, okay?"

"Thank you." I know I sound alien, even to myself. I wonder how I sound to him. I hope I'm sounding more in control than I feel. I don't want him to get off the cell and leave me with myself.

"You know, I'll come if you want me to?" his husky statement makes me feel even more overly emotional and vulnerable.

"I know. I just can't, Jake ... there are things ..." I stop myself. I was about to say too much, things he should never know about my past life. He would never see me the same again.

"One day, Emma ... you'll want to tell me ... I'll be here when you do." He sighs on the cell and I'm scared he'll go. I can't let him go just yet, my hands have started trembling and the tears building up in my throat ache so badly.

"Jake?" I panic, not sure how else to stop him from going.

"What, *Bambino*?" his voice is breathy, he's being gentle with me and I feel the rip slowly tearing across my chest. A small ache breaking through. I can't hold it in and I break down completely, unable to hide my sobs down the line.

"That's it, Emma! I'm coming over right now," he says firmly, no hint of backing down in that commandeering tone.

I can't respond, all I can do is try and refuse through tears, but only hysteria comes out.

I hate that she's brought me back to this place, brought down the walls and broken me open wide to the world, to Jake. All it took was the repeat of a buried memory. He says something else, I don't hear over my own tears and the line goes dead. I can't even argue anymore. I curl up on the bed and cry my heart out in despair. Once again broken. I don't have the strength to deal with any of this, it's all too much, all falling apart after years of holding it all in, and I'm so very tired tonight.

I don't know how long I lay on the bed crying into my pillow, I finally calm and realize I should call him back. Stop him from coming over, but I'm too late. I hear the knock on the door and my heart lurches. I want him to leave, never to see me like this, but at the same time I need to see him.

I rush to the door, yanking it open without hesitation, all self-composure gone and replaced with only the need to have him with me. Faced with the only person in the world I want to see right now. He says nothing, just looks like my safe haven, he steps in and wraps his arms around me tightly in the doorway. I fall to pieces, a tidal wave of pent-up tears breaking free, and don't hold back. He holds me, patiently waiting, staying silent and just being my rock, holding me up, arms cradling me, and fingers in my hair keeping me held steady.

Finally, he guides me inside and pulls me to the sofa to sit me down, his face close and arms enveloped around me. I cling onto him as though my life depends on it and let all the tears and heartbreak out with fresh vigor; a million thoughts running through my head. Emma who doesn't cry—forgotten. Emma who never lets anyone see her vulnerable—vacant. Strong Emma—dissipated.

"Jefferson is downstairs," he says. "The jet will be ready by the time we get there." He pulls my chin up to his face and wipes away some of the wetness with his thumb. He knows I don't want to talk, so he's just being here. I want to tell him that he can't come, but I don't have the strength.

I allow him to pull me to my feet, toward my bedroom and he leaves me at my door; pulls my empty suitcase from the floor where I left it, hauls open my wardrobe and starts throwing in random clothes haphazardly. This makes me laugh through my tears. Jake looks hopeless as a domestic and I shake my head at him, pushing him aside gently.

"If you want me dressed in sweats and blouses for the next few days, then you're going about it the right way," I say through a runny nose and hazy vision and start pulling out the clothes and packing my things properly, getting items out I'll actually need. The focus bringing my emotions into check and calming me fully. Tasks always do that. He moves back and stands watching me. Looming close by, hovering as though I may keel over at any moment.

"Might be a sexy fresh look for you, Ems. You're cute enough to pull it off." He smiles at me and I sigh, pulling myself back together and dry my face on my sleeve. I take the gadgets he hands me from my desk and put them in the base of the suitcase, gently wrapping them in the protective sleeves I leave in there. My mind is blocking out any thoughts about my mother lying in a hospital bed right now, I don't even want to process this anymore.

"I can't let you come Jake ... I don't want you to see her like she is." I glance at him nervously.

"Why, Emma? You haven't told me what happened." He moves behind me, taking a strand of my loose hair and tucks it behind my ear, a normal Jake gesture which serves to make me feel fully calm. Safe. His presence and touch like a balm.

"I don't want you to know ... It's too ... There are things about my life before here, that should stay in the past." I look back at him pleadingly and see his frown soften into a gentle smile, he hides his disappointment well.

"Okay, Emma ... I promised I wouldn't push." He sounds defeated in a way.

"But you better call me every night and keep me updated ... If you need me, I'll be there in a heartbeat. Can't leave my number one girl coping alone when she's upset." He brushes another strand of my hair behind my ear gently, his fingers lingering, brushing softly over my cheek bone. His green eyes locked on mine.

"Promise me?"

"I promise." I smile, basking in the caress and turn away to continue packing. Poor Jefferson has been sitting down in the car for long enough already, and I have a two-hour flight to take, minimum. Then after that I must face a sight I already know will be unbearable in so many ways.

When I'm done packing I go into Sarah's room to leave her a note. I don't want to call her and say the actual words in front of Jake. Her bed is a riot of covers and clothes and I can only guess they've gone for a night out on the town, not that it bothers me. We lead separate lives nowadays.

I leave the note on her mirror and close the door as I leave. In a way I'm glad she's not here, not having to explain, with Jake so close by, about what's happened to my mother for the second time in my life. Not having to deal with that knowing look on her face, thinking exactly as I do.

*Will she ever change?*

Jake accompanies me to the airfield and deposits me on the plane personally. Hugging me goodbye he makes me promise that I'll call when I land, and every night that I'm gone. I feel myself torn in two at leaving him, and not wanting him to see who I used to be. I need him far away from that part of me right now.

Reluctantly, I let him go, flanked by the onboard hostess

taking my coat and bag, Jefferson depositing my suitcase on the plane himself. He waves from the tarmac and I head to my seat, shutting out every thought and emotion, holding myself in, to focus on the long flight ahead and all that I'm about to encounter.

# Chapter 13

It's the middle of the night by the time we land in Chicago, and the hired driver takes me to West Englewood. The streets are badly lit, but don't conceal the grubbiness or derelict area from view, the streets, although busy with traffic, seem almost deserted. The aura of poverty and hardship reflected in the brown buildings and scruffy stores. I feel a ripple of trepidation, unease moves through me and that weight of emptiness I used to feel at being here, returns with a vengeance.

I'm to meet Sophie at my old home, the apartment that my mother has lived in since the day she brought me home from the hospital. My mother is stable in St Bernard Hospital, but I won't be able to see her until morning and assess how much damage has been done.

I still feel numb, with a tinge of anger, even thinking about her. I know this isn't natural—she's my mother. I should feel concern, devastation, worry even, but I don't. I feel cold and empty and upset at her. Angry at her, that she just keeps following the same path in life, over and over. She's my mother, yet all she taught me was that the people who are supposed to be there for you, above everyone else, only have their own interests at heart.

She did teach me one valuable lesson: the only way to get through life is to trust no one except yourself, self-reliance is the only way to live, and never let anyone get close enough to damage you irreversibly. She taught me that men will only look to overpower you and abuse you, that she is so weak in her quest to find a man that she accepts any form of control they exert. Any punishments they hand out.

*She disgusts me. I'll never be like her.*

The car pulls up in front of the scruffy convenience store, its lights flickering in the dark, the letters peeling, paint chipped, and exterior ugly. The apartments above are brown and grubby. The windows appear dark and dirty from down here, sending a shiver through me.

*Home sweet home.*

The driver gets out and retrieves my bags from the trunk, but I tell him I'll take them into the apartment myself. I don't want anyone in there, nor do I need his help. He reluctantly hands me the bags and watches me walk around to the side door, concealed by shrubs, into the main foyer of the building before he leaves. It's narrow and stinks of rotten food and urine. I push my way up the stairs, to the top landing and straight to the scratched, blue front door which met me every day of my young life. There's a light on inside, shining through the glass, indicating Sophie is here as planned. I stop and knock on the door.

Sophie opens it quickly, I guess she's been watching for my arrival. She's not what I expected, she appears a lot younger in person than the age she told me on the phone. She's small and wiry with long tawny hair, and vibrant blue eyes. She looks exactly as I did at the same age, even the pouting lips and innocent, naive expression. It tugs at my chest and I wonder if my mother sees me in this girl, and that's why she feels compelled to help her. The thought makes me laugh inside.

My mother was always good at seeking out those in need of help, offering her shoulder and arms, driven to be a good Samaritan. Yet she failed her own child in ways she has no way to fathom. Still, to this day, completely oblivious to the fact she was no mother at all. All her energy at trying to be a better person for other people, to help them. Ironic really.

Sophie is shy and sweet and leads me through to the open plan sitting room. She tells me she's cleaned up the apartment for me, removing all traces of the attack after the police were done in here.

I look around numbly, it's exactly how I remember it. Nothing has changed, not even the paintwork. The bohemian, almost hippy like décor; cushions and throws and mismatched furniture, the odd pieces of art from junk shops hung on the walls. The whole place crammed and cluttered. The smell of cleaners and incense lingering in the air, bring back memories of so many nights locked within these walls, praying for the day I could run far, far away.

A memory of her battered and broken body by the couch when I was twelve years old flits to mind but I push it down with the wave of emotions and anger. I'll not allow myself to think about her until I see her tomorrow.

"If you don't mind, I've been staying in your old room ..." Sophie looks at me shyly, warily, but I give her a warm smile.

"It's fine, I won't be here for long ... couple of days at most ... I'll use my mother's room." I look her up and down again as she heads into the kitchen and makes us coffee. Watching the childish mannerisms and her obvious maturity for her age, contradicting each other, much like I always had. It's late, she should be in bed, but I'm curious about her.

"So, do you know who did this to my mother?" I ask outright, get it over and done with, time to have the talk I've been dreading. She looks up warily and shakes her head. I see apprehension and immediately wonder if she's lying. I used to lie for my mother on a daily basis, I know the signs.

"Does she have a new boyfriend?" I coax, although I know nothing of the men she knows nowadays.

*What does it matter? Do I even really care?*

"Yeah ... I never met him, I don't know his name ..." She can't look me in the eye; I know pushing her will tell me nothing. I had the same look of determination at that age, guarding my mother's secrets as though my life depended on it.

"You found her? How bad is it?" I sit at the table, crossing my hands; she comes over with the mugs, sliding mine before me and sits opposite. There's something so fragile about her, yet so strong and capable. I find it hard to believe she's only fourteen.

*Why are her parents not looking for her? How long has she been here? She looks too young and vulnerable to be alone.*

"Yes ... I came home from school ... she wasn't conscious at the time, she came around when the ambulance got here. I think it looks worse than it is, maybe a broken arm ... ribs ... her face is a mess." She looks at her hands the whole time she talks, and I note that they're trembling. I think the girl may be in minor shock, even still, and feel sorry for her. This is not her burden to bear.

"The man was gone I take it?" I try a different approach.

"She was alone, I have a key, so I let myself in." I see it fully this time, the slight waver in her lip, the darting of her eye. She's hiding the fact that she knows who did this. She doesn't know me, and I know from experience she will never tell me unless I gain her trust.

"Do you want to come to the hospital with me in the morning?" I ask, sipping my coffee and watching her; she moves in her seat uneasily and nods.

"Go to bed, Sophie, I'll get you up in the morning for breakfast." I smile warmly at her and see the look of confusion spread across her face. I want this girl to know I only have her best interests at heart. I'm nothing like my mother. She uses people like Sophie as a balm, self-gratification in helping people in need.

"I normally do breakfast and get your mother up." She blushes, as though she's said something wrong and I feel the anger simmering deep down inside me.

Of course, she's living my old life. Being the caretaker, the cook, the cleaner, the mature responsible one, while my mother is the eternal victim. Nothing changes.

"Not while I'm here, Sophie ... You get to be the kid for a few days." I want to ask her about her life, why she's even here, how she ended up in the homeless shelter—meeting my mother, but I know it's late. I'll have time to talk to this girl, save her from a life she doesn't need with a woman who can barely look after herself, let alone a teen. I won't let Sophie have the childhood with my mother that I endured. That much I can promise.

\* \* \*

After I've cleaned up our mugs and straightened the kitchen a little, I head to my mother's room, pulling out my cell to call Jake, and sprawling across the comforter.

He answers immediately, glad that I'm here and that I sound okay. I've nothing much to tell him, just glad to hear his voice. I tell him that I won't see my mother until tomorrow and don't want to talk about her.

He makes me laugh, talks about how much he's pining in my absence and being silly, usual cheeky Jake, that's what I need right now.

"You know, tiny toots. I don't have anything much going on. Just Daniel's birthday." I hear Daniel's protest in the background, but Jake ignores him.

"I could hop a plane and keep you company?" he sounds serious, despite the casual tone to his voice.

"He's your best friend, you can't bail on his birthday bash." I object.

"I'm sure he won't even notice if I'm not there, he has a new porn star to keep him occupied. This one has even bigger breasts than the last. I swear he's going to die from implant suffocation one of these days." Again, I hear Daniel's voice as he responds to what Jake is saying. Jake's muffled replies to him with a jibe and then a laugh as he tells him to stop eavesdropping like a girl.

*Men!*

I laugh at Jake's joke, trying to picture Daniel with another brainless bimbo. He seems to choose girls who wear underwear as day wear and a collective IQ of four.

"I needed that," I tell him as I wipe moisture from my eyes from laughing. "You always cheer me up, you know?"

"It's my job, *Bambino*. As your official shoulder to cry on." He sounds like he's moving around, and I hear the noise of jangling keys.

"Are you getting ready to go out with him now?" I probe, wishing he was here. That heavy feeling that soon he will need to hang up.

"Sure am, but I can change plans if you say the word. One little word, Ems and I'm on a plane to windy Chicago."

"Jake. Don't ... I'm okay, really." I brush him off, ignoring the sinking feeling in the pit of my stomach. I hear him sigh and his tone loses the humor.

"I just want to be there for you and make sure you're all right, Emma. Is that so wrong?" The pleading tone is so far removed from who he is, it just makes me feel guilty. My heart aching for him even more picturing that wounded face.

"No. It's just complicated with my mother, and I don't want this life to touch on the one I have now." I try to explain, hoping he won't get annoyed.

"Guess I'll just have to get smashed out of my head and drunk call you in the early hours then, *Miele*. Better get prepared for it." He laughs softly, and I just shake my head, making a mock groan sound.

"Please ... Just no asking me to research any fetishes for you. I don't want to know what weird and kinky things you get up to on nights out." I grimace at the thought, pushing that horrid tightness in the pit of my stomach away.

"I could always come and show you some of the weird and kinky ..."

"Jake!" I break in laughing, relieved at his laugh on the other end of the line.

"Can't blame a guy for trying." I hear the smirk in his voice.

"You never stop trying." I point out.

"I need to go, it's getting late and I have to get up early."

"Okay, shorty, call me tomorrow okay? I swear I'll try not to drunk dial you, but I ain't making no promises. For some reason your cute little face comes into my head when I want to have 4.00 a.m. drunken chats about the weather, cats, and weird fetishes." He laughs, a deep, hearty, sexy tumbling noise.

"Go away, Carrero. I'll be silencing my cell, so you can't do that to me again." I laugh and finally feel a pang of sadness at having to hang up.

"Sweet dreams, *Bella*. Dream of your sexy boss, I hear he's a big manly hunk."

I roll my eyes and sigh heavily, shifting on the bed where I have got comfy.

"You know you could bottle all your excess ego and make a killing with it as a new Carrero product. You certainly have enough to spare."

"Good idea, Anderson. I notice you never disagreed that I was your hunky boss though. That'll keep me warm tonight." I can almost hear his winking down the line. "Go to bed. Sleep tight and don't let the bed bugs bite ... That's my job, *Bambino*."

"So many things I could sue you for, boss! I should record our telephone calls, I would make a killing in law suits," I jibe back, my mood definitely lighter with his jokes.

"Baby, you would miss my attempts at sexually harassing you. I don't want you thinking that you're some ugly little pudding that no man wants to bed. I have to keep your self-esteem high, to keep up with mine."

"Jake, I'm hanging up now, I can tell you're already on the vodka." I hear a faint voice behind him that sounds a lot like Daniel Hunter again.

"Whiskey actually! I like my drinks to put hairs on my chest. Goodnight, Emma. I miss you, kiddo." The smile in his voice makes me picture his best Hollywood, sexy smile, and again with the pit in my stomach, aching oddly.

"I miss you too, Jake. Goodnight."

I reluctantly put the cell down, wishing he was here with me. Even just his light carefree banter for ten minutes is enough to put my whole evening in a better mood. Sighing and getting ready for bed, I let nothing but thoughts of him fill my head, keeping the shadows at bay.

Jake & Emma

I find that he's on my mind as I fall asleep, not my return to Chicago and it helps push me to peaceful slumber.

\* \* \*

In the morning light, I tidy up and make breakfast for us both. Scrambled eggs, toast, coffee, and smile as Sophie wanders through, already dressed in jeans and a hoody, with sneakers. Her hair in a boyish ponytail. She's an early riser like me.

She sits awkwardly at the table, as though she feels like she should be helping, but I brush it away with a warm smile and put her plate and mug in front of her. I genuinely like the girl, even in such a brief time, there's something about her. I sit down to face her and let her eat for a few minutes, I can only pick at mine, appetite gone, knowing we're going to see my mother this morning. Teenage anxiety in full force.

"So, Sophie, tell me about you ... How did you end up here in Sunnyside?" I keep my tone bright and easy, if she's as guarded a person as me, then she will never open up if I don't tread carefully.

"I ran away from home ... I had enough money to get on a bus and I just chose the first one ... It brought me here, and I found the homeless shelter." She avoids looking at me while she speaks, and I see the tinge of color high on her cheeks, she's trying to sound nonchalant, but her body language gives her away. Her fork rattles lightly, showing her hands are trembling.

"Who, or what, were you running from?" I coax gently, lifting my mug and sipping slowly. Trying not to stare, trying to act like I'm engrossed in my mug instead. I used to hate coffee, but somehow Jake, like he does with everything else, got me used to it. It reminds me of him.

"My dad ..." She flushes, fully red in the face and shifts in her chair. I bite my lip, holding back the feeling that rises inside of me, a deep heavy pit of sadness for this girl. Showing too much emotion will make her clam up, showing any form of sympathy will only bring her walls up fast.

"Physical or sexual?" I can see into her soul almost instantly, I can't tear my gaze from her. I can sense that she doesn't want to shut me out, even though it's hard for her to say the words, she's offering me a slight insight.

"Both." A single tear edges its way from her eye, and she brushes it away, tightening her face, reigning in the emotion and replacing it with a defiant look. She's like a mirror image to my teen Emma and seeing it on someone else for the first time causes me so much conflict.

*Is this what Jake sees when I let him in, only to close that door? Do I do that? Look hopeless and vulnerable, then shut it down with fire and aggression.*

I sigh, pushing the thought away.

"They haven't tried to find you?" I probe gently, trying to feel out the situation and not pondering on what she wouldn't want to pick at.

"My mother told me to go ... She gave me what money she had, so I could get far away from him." She still can't make eye contact and I feel the rage inside of me on her behalf, a mother just like mine, yet she had the misfortune to fall into the lap of another, who would never protect her.

"What are your plans now that you're here?" I ask, wanting to know if she has tied herself to my mother for the long-term.

"Jocelyn enrolled me in school, we never really decided on how long I would stay; indefinitely, I guess. I don't have anywhere else to go, so until I finish school I will be here." She sips her coffee and comes to look back at me, full of wide-eyed wariness. A deep weight in my stomach, knowing that for the foreseeable future she will be in my mother's life, under her care.

"My mother is no good for you, Sophie ... She's not the protector and carer that she pretends to be ... This ... Incident ... It's not a one-off." I want her to understand that staying here will not benefit her in any way. Her eyes flick up to me quickly, and I see the moment of hesitation and fear; she thinks I'm telling her she needs to go.

"Sophie, I would like to take you back to New York with me when I leave ... I have friends who work with abused children, they can find you a better life than this." I look at her sincerely, I can't let the circle of abuse continue. I can't let this girl have the life I had.

Jake's mother helps run a charity for damaged children, she will know what to do, find her a shelter or foster home, and protect her. Jake would do that for me, I know without hesitation that he would do that for Sophie, if I asked him.

"I can't just leave her ... She needs me to help look after her. She was so kind to me and gave me a room here, instead of at the shelter." She protests with wide eyes, dropping her fork in alarm.

And there I see it, in her determined response. Emma shining through, that need to protect her, make excuses, the guilt at leaving her. She really has woven her pathetic spell over this girl, just as she had done to me all those years. I sigh; I love my mother for the fact that she's my mother, but I don't love who she can be. I shake my head.

"Sophie ... My mother will always be a victim in her own life, because it's the path she chooses over everyone else. She'll do it to you, no matter how much you do for her." I reach out and cover her hand with mine, relieved that she doesn't pull away.

"She maybe won't be the one who hits you, calls you

names, abuses you, but she will stand by and let them and do nothing to protect you. She'll look at you like you're to blame when she loses another precious man who can't keep his hands to himself." I realize as my eyes fill with emotion that this girl is probably the first person in the world that I've opened up to in this way, without coercion. Mini Emma. I'll not leave her here when I go, I'll make her life something I always dreamed of.

"I can promise you, Sophie ... I'm not her, I'm nothing like her ... I'll do everything in my power to change your life and protect you."

*I swear, I will.*

Sophie finally looks up at me and the silent message that passes between us, a bond between kindred souls who recognize each other's pain. Recognize a fellow sufferer who understands. She nods as a tear silently slides down her face, I feel wetness on my own cheek as emotion slides out and it surprises me. She tightens her fingers into mine, that small gesture, an instant bond between young teen Emma and mature adult Emma. I see myself in her eyes, and she sees my genuine concern and conviction. She'll let me take her away from all of this, and at least save one soul from the all-consuming energy that is my mother and her train wreck of a life.

\* \* \*

The hospital is as every other in the state: clinical, white and blue; sterile halls and rooms, and the strong odor of chemicals with a dingy taint in the air. Sophie is holding my hand as we walk, and she looks so very young and afraid. My maternal instinct is to haul her close to my side and place a protective arm about her shoulders and the thought makes me smile. I do exactly that and meet no resistance from her. Jake and his over-familiar, hands-on way of life has turned me into a touchy-feely just like him.

*Does he see me this way? Is this why he's so hands-on?*

That strong urge to protect me, seeing glimpses of unsure, scared Emma, under the mask. The thought warms me inside and I miss him so badly, it aches in the depth of my stomach.

Sophie seems to relax in my embrace and we walk in companionable silence, we may only have just met, but we both sense a deep, instant connection with one another, I've never felt with anyone else. It's almost as though I've just discovered a little sister, with my story to tell.

We finally enter the side room and I get my first glimpse of my mother. I release Sophie and she goes to her bedside and lifts her hand tenderly. I can't deny the genuine love I see in Sophie's face, yet I feel only irritation.

My mother's appearance causes me to take a sharp intake of breath, but I steady myself, I have to be strong for the girl's sake, be her rock, like no one ever was for me.

My mother's face is swollen, bruised, and scraped up, almost beyond recognition. It makes me feel sick to my stomach. Her left arm is in a cast and her body, concealed by covers and sheets, looks thinner and more fragile than I remember. I glance at the clipboard of notes quickly, able to determine that most of her injuries are minor, the broken arm and concussion seem to be most of the worst. I see her move as she awakens and clasps Sophie's hand, an attempt at a smile on her face. She hasn't seen me yet.

"Emma is here." Sophie breathes softly and looks toward me with a smile, her blue eyes cloudy with the strain of trying not to cry. It tugs at my heart. My mother's face follows and breaks into a smile when she sees me.

"Emma! My little girl." She releases Sophie's hand and

reaches out to me, her other one bound in a cast and strapped to her chest. I hesitate, straighten my tailored pants and blouse and walk toward her, bracing myself so that I stay calm and in control.

"Mother." I take her hand, it's cold and smooth but feels like skin and bone and it angers me. She's obviously not eating properly again, so caught up in another affair of the heart, bogged down with infatuation. She was always good at ignoring her own basic needs when wrapped up in another unhealthy relationship.

"It's so good to see you ... You came home to Chicago for me!" her voice is soft and injured, the emotion catches in my throat. Guilt, tears, anger, a chaos of emotions, and I can't look at her in the face, already uncomfortable holding her hand. I glare out the side window over the buildings in Chicago and the dull weather outside, trying to be impassive. Trying to steel against all that she makes me feel. I want her to cut the crap with the over sentimental greeting, it's obviously purely for Sophie's benefit.

"What have you told the police?" I ask, I don't want to do this tear jerking, emotional conversation crap with her. I just want to make sure she's okay, that she's healing, then I want to get the hell out of this place. As soon as earthly possible.

"Emma, please? You know it's never that straightforward," she whines, I bristle and drop her hand coldly. My face snapping around to lock eyes with her in rage. Same old familiar conversation.

"You're kidding me, right?" I snort in disbelief, spinning my head back around to glare at her.

"You have no idea, Emma, you don't know what happened." Her voice seems suddenly stronger, losing all ounce of vulnerability now that I'm peeking anger at her.

"I don't need to, it never changes. Who was it this time?

Another five-minute romance, or is this someone longer term? How often has this one hit you huh?" I snap, my temper getting the better of me and I see Sophie move off to sit in the corner. She looks uncomfortable and wide-eyed and it makes me feel guilty. She doesn't need to see all this.

"That is none of your concern, this is my life and affects only me!" My mother snaps back at me, yanking her hand back to her chest in anger.

"Don't you fucking dare! What about *Sophie*, Mom? ... What about justice? What about *me*? It affects all of us!" The tears blind me, and I feel myself losing it, I storm away, wrapping my arms around myself and glare out of the window.

"I shouldn't have started a fight, Emma ... This was as much my fault." The same pathetic cringey voice, the same pathetic excuses as she drops the attitude and goes on in full blown victim mode. There will be tears soon.

I can't do this, not again; coming back was a mistake and this is just a sad repeat of a dozen conversations. I can't hold it in, hold my anger or the heart break. My mother is once again ripping out my very soul and throwing it to the wolves. She hasn't changed at all and this could be fourteen years ago, all over again.

"This was a mistake ... I can't be here. I was stupid to think this one might have knocked some actual sense into you. I'm taking Sophie to New York with me, away from this bullshit existence that you inflicted on me ... Don't even begin to argue." I swing back around at her, my eyes pouring tears; she looks shocked at my obvious distress. She has never seen me cry, not since I was a very small child.

"You've no idea the chaos that you cause ... This ..." I gesture across her body and injuries. "Is only the tip of the iceberg, Mother! I won't let you subject Sophie to more of the same crap." I can't say anything more, my voice breaking, the tears taking over. I just shake my head aggressively and walk out fast. Unable to say anything else or keep myself in check, not staying to have her argue or try to bully me into changing my mind.

I already agreed to let Sophie stay this morning and get a bus home later, giving her extra money so I don't have to stay and endure this. I have no reason to stay another second and blindly storm out, heading straight for the main exit while internally ranting.

I march across the wet car park, my coat in my hands, shaking and sobbing. The driver that Jake hired standing dutifully to open my door as I approach, and I get in. I can't contain everything going on inside my head.

*I was stupid to come here, I was a fool to think I could handle this. She will never change. She will never see that she's the one who brings this on. She chooses these men, then makes goddamn excuses for what they do.*

It only makes me more determined to take Sophie with me when I leave. I decide it'll be sooner rather than later, I can't stay here much longer, she won't talk to the police, even I know that. She will make Sophie lie to them for her too, like she used to make me.

*Deny she knew her attacker, and then what? He will be back in a heartbeat, until the next time when she ends up back here and then? Maybe one day one of them will kill her. Can she not see how what she does affects me, affects Sophie?*

I calm down as we drive, wiping my face and bringing rational thought back to my head. PA Emma winning over when faced with too much emotion to cope with. My defense mechanism kicking in and numbing it all away, pushing it down until I am nothing but a cool shell once more.

I gulp down air, pull it all back in and focus instead on

getting the hell away from this place. I hate Chicago, I glare out at the passing scenery and just feel like I'm suffocating.

I pull out my cell and see an email from Jake, instantly bringing softness to my face and a lift in my mood. He always brings me back from craziness, even when I think nothing will.

*Jake Carrero has sent you an iTunes gift.*
*"Just Give Me A Reason" by Pink.*

I look at it with confusion, sure I'm missing the message. I press play, listening to the song, trying to decipher the meaning for sending it. I glance at the time of the email and realize he sent it at four in the morning, most likely when he was out with Daniel. This was instead of a drunk dial episode.

It seems to be a love song about learning to love again ... It causes a pain in my chest as I absorb it, it's beautiful and deep, but I can't see the connection. The title confuses me. I've no idea what to send back to him. Maybe I shouldn't send anything because he was obviously drunk when he sent it. I like the fact he was thinking of me at that time though, while surrounded by friends and women. Even if it makes no sense.

*Maybe it was a mistake and he'd meant to send something else? Knowing Jake, it was related to his current thought and probably stupidly obvious at in his drunken state.*

It plagues me as we head back toward my mother's apartment, a welcome distraction. Jake is never usually one to be so cryptic, his songs are either all about the title, or usually at least the song has some obvious message. This time I have no idea.

I slide out of the car and dismiss the driver in front of the shady convenience store, ignoring the two drunk men sprawled on the pavement. It looks as though one of them is laying in a puddle of urine and I grimace as I scoot past and let myself in the side door. I intend to pack and wait for

Sophie to call, we'll be leaving tonight, there's no reason to prolong the agony of this place anymore.

I turn the corner onto the upper landing, the keys in my hands, ready to let myself in. A noise in front of me causes my head to snap up as I see a dark figure standing against the wall in the shadows. I freeze, blood coursing through me at speed, my heart pounding. There's something familiar, yet terrifying, about the figure. I know they see me too and don't move to react. They stand staring back at me.

"Well, well, well." The hoarse, gritty voice comes at me, my body recoiling inside and my brain freezing. Even after all this time I know that voice and it makes my blood run cold.

Ray Vanquis stands five-feet away from me, like a mad man in the shadows, his eyes glinting before he steps into the light. All six feet of tattooed, menacing rage, and muscle. The devil from my nightmares. I gasp, and my body goes into high alert, adrenaline coursing as I begin to tremble. Fear gripping me.

*Oh, my god!*

"What are you doing here?" I snap coldly, bringing my shorter height up to appear more menacing, appear more in control. Ice and hatred in my voice, teen Emma bristling up and getting ready to defend me.

"I came by to see Jocelyn ... To talk to her." He sounds amused, he thinks I'm intimidated by him, but he keeps his distance. I reach into my bag and feel my cell, it's the only thing I have that I can use as a weapon; my body vibrating with nerves. I have nothing else, not even my trusty mace that used to be a constant when I lived here. I think of the baseball bat in my old wardrobe, something I slept with many a night and wonder if I can get inside to get it, to feel safer while in the presence of this monster.

*Would he follow me? Is he going to hurt me?*

"What could my mother have to say to you after all this time?" I spit, edging toward the door, but keeping my gaze firmly on him as I near. Untrusting. He smirks and in that look, a light switch goes on in my head.

*Surely not? She wouldn't do this to me, even the way she is, she wouldn't take back Ray after what he did to me, and have a relationship with him again, would she?*

The confusion, anger, and panic whizzing through my head at a hundred miles an hour, he sees the realization dawn on my face and grins in that lop-sided sneer he has. He's the one she's been with, the one who beat her to a pulp. It flashes like a spark in my head pushing all rational and logical behavior completely out of sight.

"You bastard!" I scream and lunge without thought, my nails and keys slicing at his face as I attempt to kick at him. He's surprised by my fierce, impulsive attack, caught off guard. Trying to shield his face as I rain my fists on his head. It's a stupid, impulsive move. His rage ignites, grabbing my wrists and thrusting me hard against the wall, knocking the breath out of me. He spins me and thrusts me hard into the cold concrete wall with a force hard enough to almost break ribs, I gasp for air, adrenaline spiking. Memories of his attack so many years ago flash through my mind and I fight back with all my might. Pushing myself back hard, using hands and knees so I collide with him. I elbow and stamp as he tries to encircle me, teen Emma in full rage and fight mode.

I started this and I know I have no one to save me this time, he's twice the size of me, multiple times my strength. I'm no match. He lifts me off my feet, squeezing around my pinned body with his huge arms so that I can't breathe. I can't move. I feel nausea rising with the blackness coming around me, terrified I'll pass out; I know what he'll do to me if I do. I'm struggling to take air into my lungs and focus on staying awake, my voice lost in an effort to breathe.

Then, with a thud, he lets me drop on the ground in a lifeless heap and laughs. He kicks me with the tip of his boot, so I fall forward into a slump and walks off laughing. Leaving me broken, devastated and huddled like a child.

I break down and cry, crumpled on the ground. He's achieved the humiliation he desired, satisfied with his little power trip and exertion over me. Showing me who is still boss. He goes on his way, giving himself a high five and I want to die. I want the ground to open up and swallow me whole.

I crawl to my feet, falling against the front door, sobs racking my body painfully as I pull myself up to rest against it and drag air in to my bruised lungs. My face falling against the chipped surface as I try wildly to ground myself and bring some sense of calm back to my devastation. Shame descends over me, shame at my own defeat, my own stupidity. My fingers and hands are splayed across the door trying to keep my body from self-imploding, shaking violently as I stand in the shadows gulping down air.

"Emma?" Jake's voice is suddenly behind me and he's around me, hauling me into the warm protective circle of his arms. His heady scent and warm body enveloping me into safety. It's like being lifted into a bubble of protection, a home coming.

*Why is he here? Where did he come from? Oh, my God. Jake ... My perfect Jake!*

I don't care right now, I just feel like I've been pulled into the warmth of my life, to be comforted and protected. I love that he's around me, I need him around me. Pulling me back from devastation. Concealing me from the world.

*Maybe I'm dreaming. I hope I'm not. I need him so badly right now.*

"*Bambino!* What's happened? Is it your mother?" His

deep smooth voice in my hair by my ear, his warm breath on my cheek, bringing back the calm and sense to my inner world. My sobbing calming at the feel of him. He'll always be my life buoy, my lighthouse in the dark.

I shake my head, allowing my arms to creep around his waist and hold onto him tightly, feel the familiarity of his body and skin against me. I need him more than I need air right now.

*He came, he's here, he ignored me telling him not to come ... "Give Me A Reason". It was about why he shouldn't come.*

It doesn't even surprise me, Jake never follows the rules. I can't even be angry with him right now, because he's everything I want and need, to pull me back from the darkness that almost overtook me moments before.

"Talk to me, Emma ... You're scaring me." He sounds raspy, his voice wavering, I lift my wet face and swallow down my emotion. The genuine concern in his eyes, looking at me in a way I've never had anyone look at me. He has no idea how he makes me feel, no idea how much he has changed every part of me and my world. That I need him, I need his security, his calm reasoning and confidence. His way of making everything okay.

"You just missed the man who tried to rape me at eighteen ... He reminded me that I'll never be able to match him." I reply calmly, unsure why I'm even telling him this. I just need to. Because he's really here. I think it's shock and it just comes out.

"*What?*" His face breaks into something I never expected to see on him, his jaw tightening, he looks terrifying and aggressive.

"Did he hurt you, Emma?" He snarls and the air around us feels immediately charged with electricity, emanating from him. I don't recognize this version of Jake. I nod, unable to say anymore, sure I must look exactly like Sophie did when she admitted her father abused her. Jake curses and lets me go, his body buzzing with tension and rage. He tenses his muscles and paces across the hall. Energy simmering.

"I passed a guy coming in here ... Tall, stocky, and tattooed with a shaved head ... Is that him?" his voice gritted and revealing a rage and venom in him I've never seen. He intimidates me, all I can do is nod.

"Mother Fu ..." he turns and speeds into the stairwell, pursuing my attacker.

*Oh, my God ... No. Jake, no!*

# Chapter 14

All my vulnerable woe fleets away into a panic as I realize what Jake intends to do. Jake boxes and practices martial arts as a fitness regime, he used to be a scrapper in his teens, always fighting. I know he's a fighter, but I'm still terrified. Ray and Jake are equally matched, body size, almost in height and definitely in aggression, there's no telling what the outcome will be, and I can't bear it.

I run after him, yelling his name; he's much faster than me and he's already out of the building, tearing off in the direction of a lone figure walking in the distance. Jake can run like the wind. I can't even begin to catch up, throwing my stilettos off and going barefoot, my body losing its adrenaline fast and I get a cramp in my leg so badly I fall. Panic searing through me as I try to get up, they're too far from me to really see what's happening but the figures have collided. They're a jumble of blurry shapes, a joined mass of movement, arms coming out and throwing back in with force.

*Oh, my god. Jake, no!*

I see one figure step back, holding the other by the throat, throw a punch with a short swing and the other hits the ground. Then the two are joined, rolling around.

I feel sick, I'm trying so hard to get up, dizziness and nausea fighting with my mind to take over, tears pouring down my face.

*God please, don't let him hurt my Jake.*

The cramp begins to fade, I haul myself up and stagger toward them, looking for anything as a weapon to defend him. My bare feet making running almost impossible.

I get closer and see that Jake has Ray by the shoulders, he brings his knee into the man's abdomen twice, contact thudding loudly as Ray snorts out with pain at every collision. Falling into a heap, Jake hauls him back up, delivers perfect blows to his face, head and body three times before Ray crumbles to the ground, lifeless. Jake in a perfect boxer stance, towering over him. Glaring with a fury I've never known from him.

I finally manage to close the gap and throw myself at Jake, my clothes dirty and ripped, but I don't care, I swing myself around his neck enveloping him. Grabbing onto him in despair and relief.

"No more ... Please ... No more." I beg, I can feel his heart pounding through his chest, his breathing shallow, he's perspiring. His arms come around my waist, pulling me in hard against his strong body and he turns me, so I can look down at Ray Vanquis. He's completely out cold, laid out on the damp dirty pavement, looking pathetic. This devil of a man looks almost pitiful.

"Tell me what you want me to do with him, Emma." His voice is husky and breathy, the serious tone terrifying, hinting that he'll literally do whatever I ask, even if that means killing him. I see the rage in his green eyes, making them almost luminescent. This is not my Jake. This is a primal, carnal version of my Jake and I want him to leave. I need my normal

Jake back. I need his face, his voice, and his arms right now.

"Leave him here, leave him to rot in the street." I whisper, burying my face against his neck, his hand comes to cradle my head protectively. He rests his mouth on top of my head and breathes out slowly, some of the tension in his body releasing as he sags against me. Using me to calm down and disperse all the anger and adrenaline coursing through his veins.

We stand silent for agonizingly long minutes as I watch Ray's huddled body on the damp, dark ground. He doesn't stir at all.

"We should call the cops." Jake says flatly, finally. His breathing has calmed to normal and his arms around me is all I can focus on.

"No ... Let him go. My mother blames me for enough already ... This will only send her over the edge." I say drily, his fingers come under my chin to bring my face to his. I see the confusion in those green depths and shake my head.

"Please don't make me tell you ... Not right now ... One day, Jake, I promise." He frowns, pushing his forehead against mine firmly, as though he's trying to reel in the frustration and anger, but still respect my wishes. The fire blazing in his eyes, but he just exhales deeply. His jaw tense, which only adds to that male aggression in his look.

I can't help but think how breathtaking he looks, in protective mode, fighter mode, scariness gone, and just overwhelming masculinity left. He's nothing like the men from my childhood; they were aggressive and cruel, they liked to inflict pain on me, but Jake isn't that way. For all his strength and power, he's the gentlest person I've ever known when it comes to women. A real man.

He hauls me away from the lifeless body on the ground then stops, thinking a moment, he swoops down placing one hand on Ray's throat to check his pulse, his other hand still on my waist. He pauses, taking a count, sneers, then straightens up.

"He'll live ... Unfortunately," he growls, then delivers a swift kick to the man's ribs in passing, extruding a muffled grunt. He pulls me off in the direction of the apartment, his arm tightly around my shoulders, keeping me pressed against him. I can feel the ripple of adrenaline still coursing through him, but we walk in silence.

"Thank you." I smile up at him shyly. I know thanking him for physically beating someone up for me is wrong in so many ways, but somehow, teen Emma, broken and cowering at the hands of that evil man raises her sweet innocent head and smiles. Jake says nothing, just leans down, kissing me tenderly on the forehead, lingering a moment before giving me a gentle squeeze; walking on, pulling me along until he stops to pick up my discarded shoes. Realizing I'm barefoot, he picks me up and carries me the rest of the way. I don't protest, just hold on and curl up within his hold and feel safe.

*Jake my boss. My friend, my protector. The first person in my life who has ever risen to the challenge of being one for me. No one else in my life deemed me worthy of fighting for.*

\* \* \*

In the apartment, we sit drinking coffee, we don't talk about what happened, instead, I tell him about Sophie and that I want to help her. I can't tell him why without explaining about my mother's injuries. I know that if I tell him Ray is the reason she's in the hospital he will go back out and find him, drag him to the police station or worse, and I know it's pointless. My mother will never point a finger at him. I already know that she won't even break up with him after what he's done. She'll be angry at me for letting Jake beat him.

## Jake & Emma

*Such is the twisted logic of my mother.*

"Isn't that what your mother does?" he asks gently, I watch him carefully, realizing I'm still scanning his face and hands for injuries. I've been doing it since we walked into the apartment and I still can't rest at seeing no evidence of any, aside some bruised knuckles. He's indestructible, like a hero should be.

"No ... She runs a homeless charity, she helps adults find shelter and food. Children are not her forte."

*Obviously.*

"Sophie has real abuse issues, she needs a place that will help her heal ... not here." Never here.

"I'll call my mom ... She has places she can put her while she deals with the legal side. Sophie will need protecting, legally. So, her parents can't just come and take her back. My mother has lawyers who deal with all that." He looks at me softly, reaches out and entwines our fingers on the table with one hand; reassurance. It feels so normal and necessary, sending warm rivers up my arm.

"Thank you, Jake, this really means a lot to me." I look down, watching our hands, my small pale fingers in his large, strong, tanned hand; chalk and cheese yet they fit perfectly. They look right together.

"Where is she right now?" I notice he's gazing at our hands too, his expression blank.

"The hospital, still. I stormed out ... I should call her, she gave me her cell number." I see the questions arise in his face, the twitch of an eyebrow as he decides to leave it alone. Thankfully. I reach into my bag, retrieve my cell and text Sophie. I notice the email notification still in the top corner and think back to the song.

"Why did you send me that song?" I ask innocently.

He shifts back in his seat, his arm is at full stretch, so he doesn't need to break the hold of my hand, he looks thoughtful then shrugs.

"It came on in the club and it made me think of you ... I just didn't think you gave me any really good reason not to follow you, you didn't respond, so I figured you still didn't have any good reason. Here I am." His expression gives nothing away, but his eyes darken slightly, his pupils expanding a tiny bit. His gaze is steady on me as I study him, neither of us say anything.

The moment is broken by my cell buzzing on the wooden table top and I pick it up to check the text.

"Sophie is coming back, she got a bus ... Jake, I want to go back to New York tonight." I say it without looking at him, sure the questions will come this time.

"Okay," is all he says as he squeezes my hand a little. I'm confused, this is so non-Jake, but I don't push it, he's being agreeable for once, no questioning, no pushing, just letting me be and I love him all the more for it.

\* \* \*

By the time Sophie walks in I'm cooking dinner for the three of us as Jake watches an action movie in the sitting room. He's lounging on the couch as if he's always lived here, his shoes discarded on the floor and I smile at his ability to just exist in any surrounding that he's put in. He just adapts effortlessly and never questions or criticizes. I'm sure he's on the verge of sleep, I can tell by his relaxed posture. It all seems very domesticated and normal, like this is how we always are.

When Sophie's changed, and returns from my old room, she casts me a timid look, I know she wants to talk about what happened at the hospital, but I shake my head and nod toward Jake on the sofa. He's engrossed in his movie. She smiles softly, an understanding look, and lets me instead introduce them properly.

They seem to get on immediately, he keeps casting looks from Sophie to me throughout the introductions and I know what he's thinking, he can see the resemblance. He's wondering about how deep it goes. I feel apprehensive, but I try and ignore it. Sophie seems awed at his presence at first, but that Carrero charm soon lulls her into relaxation and he has her joking and laughing with him before long. A cute camaraderie developing easily between them. Eventually, she joins me in the kitchen to finish preparing the food while he returns to lazing on the sofa.

I tell Sophie my plan to leave, but it's met with compromise, she wants to stay until my mother is healing and home. To be here to take care of her; she wants to make sure she can cope alone. I think of Ray and shake my head. Sophie shouldn't be here at all; my mother won't throw him out or give him up and it won't be long before he's back. Jocelyn Anderson would never give him up. Not for her, not for me, not for anyone. I try and talk quietly, so Jake doesn't hear the conversation.

"One week?" she says softly, and I see the desperation in her eyes, her affection for my mother strong. I close my eyes and steady the internal war. I need to relinquish a little over this. I don't want to push her away.

"Okay ... But you come to me in one week and we go from there. You call me every night, Sophie, so I know you're okay. And no lies!" She snaps up to look at me and we see each other, deeply. She knows that I know she lied for my mother, she forgets I used to do it too. She nods and bites her lip, another teen Emma trait. I wonder if that's why she keeps her hair tied up, away from fidgeting fingers. I smile at the girl, the shadow of my past, only this one has a chance at being saved.

"Okay." She finally pouts, and I smile at her, she makes me think of everything I was when I first arrived in New York. She has a fire inside of her just like I did, a determination to rise from the ashes. She'll be okay, she's a fighter.

Jake sits up suddenly and fishes his cell from his pocket, putting it to his ear, he says a few words then looks across at me with a glance, it catches my interest.

"When then?" he moves to sit properly and plants his feet on the floor, sounding a tad annoyed.

"Okay, well yeah ... Sure ... First thing ... Keep me updated." He closes the cell and casts me an apologetic look.

"No flight home tonight, Emma ... Jets grounded, there's a storm brewing outside of Chicago and heading this way. New York is already in a full blown blizzard." He shrugs, as if to emphasize that there's nothing he can do, and I curse. The drop of weight in my stomach at the disappointment.

"When's the soonest we can leave?" I ask,, certain he can hear the edge to my voice.

"Maybe in the morning, we have to wait and see." He gets up and comes to stand beside me in the kitchen, tucking a loose strand of my hair behind my ear and then moving to lean on the counter between Sophie and me.

"Need any help?"

I shake my head; Jake is a half-decent cook, his mother taught both her sons at a very young age and he told me he does it occasionally.

"We're about to serve." I smile. Inside I feel deflated, I pinned my hopes on leaving tonight.

"I'll head to my hotel after we eat. After I lock this place up and check there are no snooping assholes. I'll call you in the morning to let you know when the plane is ready to go."

"You're not staying?" I snap my head around, the fear of

Ray still in the back of my mind. Still shaken from earlier, despite pushing it to the depths of my brain. He sees the hesitation in my face and moves close so our noses almost touch. Tilting his head in toward me and stooping slightly to bridge our height difference.

"You just need to ask." He smiles softly and the overwhelming urge to lean forward and rest my face against his grasps me, I move away unsurely.

"I would feel safer." I say instead, in a way asking without having to say the words. I don't know why it's so hard for me to do so.

"Well, if I'm staying, I'm sleeping with you, that couch is a no go." He winks suggestively, grinning at me. I think he's waiting for my refusal, but I say nothing. Sharing a huge king size bed with Jake is hardly a punishment, it's not that much different to sleeping beside him on a plane, or the time he fell asleep on my lap when our flight was delayed for two hours and we had to couch share in a waiting room. I shrug as if to say, "fine by me" and ignore the shiver of anticipation running up inside my stomach. Truth be told, the thought of being alone with only Sophie tonight after what happened with Ray is the last thing I want, having Jake in my bed may actually help me sleep.

*Tomorrow I get to leave here for good. I'm never coming back.*

I think about my mother for a second, how she looked in the hospital and push it away. I know she'll try and call me when she's mobile, she'll try and guilt me about leaving and taking Sophie away, and I don't want to hear it. She's betrayed me for the last time. This one is a huge deal. She let the one man back in her life who could have completely destroyed mine, and it's unforgivable.

## The Carrero Effect ~ The Promotion

\* \* \*

I wake early next morning, completely entangled in Jake's limbs on my side of the bed, lying on my back. He's wrapped around me possessively. One arm around my waist, pulling me into his abdomen so that his face is in the nape of my neck, the other behind my neck, his arm bent so his fingers are entwined in my hair above my head. His legs looped through mine and twisted so I'm immobile in every way. I feel stiflingly hot because he's so naturally warm and I try to maneuver out of his grasp but my efforts only cause him to pull me tighter to him, making it near impossible to get out.

*Who knew Jake was a cuddler in bed? More like a squeezer; suffocates all life out of you.*

Although part of my brain isn't surprised, he's so hands-on and touchy-feely in every part of waking life that I guess being this way in sleep is a given. I lay still, staring at the dark ceiling for a moment, listening to the heaviness of his deep breathing, he sounds so peaceful and being held this way is comforting. I feel cherished and safe. I have never slept with a man, even my ex-boyfriends never spent the night. This is new and strangely nice.

It dawns on me slowly that my usual night terrors have not woken me today, the sound of car alarms outside have instead. Having Jake sleep with me has kept them at bay, despite the events yesterday with Ray Vanquis. A little rush of affection swamps me at the thought he can keep me safe, even from my own dreams.

I look across at the alarm clock on my mother's side table, it's only 5.00 .am. I don't need to get up anytime soon but now I'm wide awake. I try to wriggle to my side to get comfier, managing it very slowly before Jake shifts in his sleep, releasing me for a second. I quickly turn before he's hauling me back into him in a spoon hold. His body behind me, both arms coming around me tightly, one leg lifting over mine and pulling them against his, so I am literally pulled in tight once more.

*For the love of god, Jake!*

I wonder how many poor teddy bears in his childhood died this way. I can barely move again, he's managed to pin my arms against my chest, his face against the back of my neck so his breath tickles down my spine, below the neck of my oversized night shirt. I wonder at this position, how I feel completely relaxed, no warning signals going off in my brain. No fear or awkwardness. No nerves; because it's Jake, and with Jake it all stopped a long time ago.

"Emma ..." Jake breathes in his sleep and I still to listen, I wonder what he's dreaming about, I wonder if it's a dream that has him gripping onto me for dear life. It would explain the death grip. I gasp as his grip tightens a tad too much.

"... I'll kill him!" He growls into my neck and his body tenses, my heart constricts. I feel that wave of fear wash over me. He's dreaming about Vanquis, I know he is; maybe that's why he has been wrapped about me all night, holding me close, protecting me. More affected by it than I am, evidently.

I wriggle my arms free of his vice like grip and try to pull them loose so I can breathe, it really is like being squeezed by an octopus with limbs wrapped all around you. Trying to expel the air from my body. I pull at his naked arms, managing to expand the space around my ribs, just enough to take a breath. Holding his wrists, I pull some more, releasing me just enough to sag away from his body a little. I glance back at his sleeping face, his T-shirt has ridden up, showing off the sculpted abdomen and the start of his tattoos on the side of his ribs. He really is the perfect specimen of man. In every detail.

# The Carrero Effect ~ The Promotion

I turn completely around to face him, still held firmly in his arms. I study his face, the shadow of his ever-present stubble and the chiseled features that grace magazines frequently. He has the face of perfection, in every line and curve. Perfect eyebrows and eyelashes, so dark they're almost black. The urge to reach up and trace his sleeping face with my fingers gnaws at me. I feel embarrassed by it and try to move away to give myself some breathing space.

Somehow, my movement away from him triggers another sleepy move, he reaches out to me, his eyes still closed, his face still relaxed in slumber. His hand grazes my breast on its way to my throat, he cups my jaw and pulls me forward so we're nose to nose. Our mouths only millimeters apart, his forehead against mine and inhaling from the same air. My body jumps into high alert, my breath held from the moment his fingers grazed the intimate parts of my chest. I'm tingling with so many sensations that I can't explain what I'm feeling.

The fact that his action was innocent has quelled any fear, no panic in my response, no fluttering stomach. Instead the intimacy is sending me haywire.

Without thought I lean up gently and kiss his mouth. A slight touching of the lips, almost a chaste kiss. I don't know what makes me do it. I've no reasoning or thought in my head, only this need to feel his mouth on mine. His soft, warm, full lips enticing me, for just a moment, to see how it felt again, pushed on by the proximity and gentle warmth of his breath against my own. I feel my body react low down inside me, spreading heat through my groin.

I'm playing with danger, and fear is beginning to rise within me, fear at my own reaction to him. He smells amazing, his mouth too alluring. I kiss him again, only slightly firmer this time. Pushed by something inside of me, but this time he responds, his mouth parting lightly and he kisses me back.

I freeze. My heart rate escalates into a frenzy and I hold still, very, very still. He doesn't open his eyes or move, just inhales heavily indicating he's still asleep.

*Crap. What the hell am I doing?*

I make to move away, no longer able to trust myself, but his hand on my jaw tenses, pulls my face forward and he sinks his lips to mine. It's tender at first, my heart pounding, my head spinning, but every part of my body responds with a vengeance. I open my mouth to his kiss, his hand slides down to my breast once more, laying over it and cupping it; my body sizzles under his palm. His lips move against me seductively, kissing me—not tongues—but it feels like the most erotic thing in the world.

Jake kisses exactly as I expected him too. Mind-blowing and perfect. His mouth matching mine in soft grazing movement; my head light and breathing shallow. I allow my hands to wander up to his face and trace his jawline softly, bringing us closer together. He feels so good, his face firm, I want this more than I should, and I allow myself to move into the kiss and let it continue. Lost in how he feels and tastes.

His hand moves down, curling behind my butt and pulls me into his groin, making it clear he's aroused, his hard body pressing into my pelvis. I groan involuntarily, closing my eyes tighter, letting him take control, ignoring the little voices in my head trying to pull me away. I feel his lips part more, pressing into mine further and his tongue slides into my mouth, kissing me more passionately. Deepening it. It's erotic and feels intense, the sensation causing my stomach to flutter and flip, he tastes like heaven and for minutes I'm lost to what we are doing, all reason floating away. His tongue feels divine and I respond with a longing I never knew I was capable of; his arms come around me tightly. Breath hitching between us.

# The Carrero Effect ~ The Promotion

One hand releases me to grab my thigh and pull me up the bed so it's around his waist, grinding our pelvises together. He maneuvers over me, his body weight pressing down on me, and our pelvises rammed hard against one another. I can feel everything, my body sizzling with the sensations and my breathing shallow and fast. Passion, his hands and arms caging my head and my hands, cupping his jaw, pulling him close. Mouths fully intertwined. His stubble grazing my soft face.

*Hell!*

I know where this will head, in the darkness, escalating the way it is. Our bodies moving against each other in the first throes of foreplay. I know I won't have the strength to say no or stop it. He's causing cravings I have never experienced, a low, deep, throbbing heat and the desire to have him satisfy my hunger. His kiss too addictive to want to stop. I instinctively know that these urges are a longing to have sex, something I've never felt before. Something so new and so over powering. The apex of my thighs hard against him is almost on fire and waves of desire pulsing up to my stomach.

He moves against me breathing heavily, his kiss more urgent. Upping the gear from erotic passion into searing lust. Our tongues caressing one another in a more intense motion; he knows how to seduce my mouth in ways that has me gasping for more, the taste of him exquisite. It's like we just know instinctively how to come together, how to kiss each other. A perfect fit. The first man I have ever wanted to ever kiss me and lets me lose myself in him. My first French kiss ever and it's beyond perfection. I moan out softly, lost in this. My hands in his hair and nails raking down the back of his neck and over his shoulders.

Every alarm bell in my brain starts going crazy as the realization dawns on me and the lust fueled haze subsides a little. I'm on the verge of complete surrender or complete panic, body ready to self-combust, starting to realize what the hell I am doing; when he just stops. He moves back off me, rolling to his side, resting his face against me, his body relaxing fully. He mumbles something incoherent and returns to deep heavy breathing while I pause and wait, scared to move or breath and realize he has been asleep this whole time. I'm laid panting and heaving and he's just, well, he's sleeping!

*It wasn't real!*

He's dreaming and acting out in his sleep, sleep walking in a way. I feel confused, but relieved, disappointed, conflicted. He'll never know what we did, he'll have no memory of it. I'm not sure if I want this or not. I have no clue what the hell I'm doing, or even thinking.

I think about kissing him again, trying to rouse him properly, but don't. Instead, I slide free and get out of bed, aware of how close I just was to screwing everything up with him. Despite being completely lost in how kissing him felt, I feel as though I've broken some line of trust, that I abused him in his sleep and it makes me feel disgusting and vile. No better than my mother's perverted lovers and what they did to me. I slide out of bed and get up quickly, in a rush to put distance between us and cool my overheated senses.

I wander to the sitting room, shaking. Unsure what to feel, I'm angry and so confused.

*Why would I kiss him like that? It's Jake! I have no excuse. I wasn't drunk, I wasn't half asleep; maybe it was the shock? But that kiss ... Oh, my god ... that kiss!*

It must be shock; yesterday, from the episode with my mother, with Vanquis, and here he is, my savior, my protector, the hunk of the Carrero empire. I am a woman after all! I can see why my body would respond to him that way. He is gorgeous in every way and despite my issues with my past, I am still capable of being turned on. By him anyway. And that kiss is something no woman can deny.

*I shouldn't have touched him that way. I crossed the line and I'm glad he never woke up to realize what we were doing.*

I could forget it ever happened if my brain would stop turning it over and over in my mind. I can still feel his mouth on mine, the taste of him, the way his tongue slid against mine, urging my body to tingle and sizzle.

The feel of his strong body caging me in, pressing down on me ...

*Stop it!.*

I shiver and reach for the throw on the couch, wrapping myself in it; standing by the window, looking out over dark Chicago to distract myself. The rough down-trodden area looks worse by moonlight and I'm counting the hours until I get out of here. It's a distraction anyway. Something I so need right now, instead of obsessing over the highly erotic episode a few minutes ago. My skin is still tingling from it.

"Hey," Jake's husky voice startles me, and I turn quickly, my face flushing with heat and shame. Embarrassment oozing from every pore, there's a possibility he did know what we were doing after all, if he's awake so soon.

"I woke up in a bed alone ... Thought you'd run off." He smiles lazily, still looking sleepy with messed-up hair, in his T-shirt and jeans. Poster boy for ultimate sexiness. I swallow the urge to groan with desire.

*Crap. Don't go there.*

"Hey," I say quickly, looking back to the window, unable to make eye contact with him, the memory of his mouth still on mine. My body going insane with a thousand confused sensations. On high alert at his nearness.

"I'll call the air field in a bit ... You want to go see your mom before we leave?" he yawns, and I catch him in the corner of my eye stretching out, elongating his body and showing off naked midriff in the motion. I inwardly tense. Sculpted perfect abdominal muscles, memories of his body pressed on top of mine, the way I reacted to him. The heat in my body refuses to simmer down with so much of him on show right now.

"No ... I don't need to see her, she's fine, her injuries are minor." I say quickly, flippantly, tension in my voice giving away my emotion, but he doesn't pick up on it and if he does, he ignores it. He comes up behind me, wraps his arms around my shoulders casually, resting his chin on my head, he has no clue. He's acting as though nothing has happened and I tense inside even more. I shrug out of his arms, unable to control the longings I'm feeling. Leaving the throw to slide off onto the floor at his feet, I duck toward the kitchen. I catch sight of him frowning at me.

"Something wrong?" he asks while studying my face, I put my head down and head into the kitchen, switching on the kettle, avoiding him. Willing my heated face to cool down; I know I'm probably blushing like mad.

"No." I say overly brightly and focus on getting the mugs ready.

"You're acting weird, shorty ... What gives?" he's frowning. I can see him in the corner of my eye, I carry on with what I'm doing, the blood has rushed to my face even more so now.

"I'm just making coffee." I shrug, trying to appear normal.

*Jesus, Jake, leave me be. Stay back.*

"Look at me then," he commands, I tense and glance up, pasting a fake smile on my lips. Raising eyebrows before returning to what I'm doing, I can feel the heat radiating all over me and return quickly to looking at anything but him, but that is so hard to do in a space this small.

"Okay ... What did I do?" he crosses his arms menacingly, his biceps bulging, the stubborn Carrero look pasted on his face. I think I may faint.

"Nothing." I laugh nervously. I drop the spoon and spill coffee granules everywhere.

*Shit.*

"Spill, Anderson ... I'll torture it out of you. You know I will." He walks toward me with a look on his face that means business and I cave, if I let him get too close I may self-combust. I may actually pass out right in front of him.

*I need to calm my hormones down.*

"We kissed," I squeak as he gets dangerously close to touching me. Then I hide my face behind my loose hair as heat envelopes me tenfold. I can't tell him that I practically molested him in his sleep. That we were dry humping and I know what he feels like turned on and pushed against me.

"I've been known to do more than kiss in my sleep." He laughs.

"They call it Sexsomnia. It happens very rarely. It's like a form of sleepwalking." He shrugs it off, obviously in acceptance of this quirk of his.

*Only Jake would have a manly sex related sleeping disorder. Well, that explains a lot!*

He comes to stand beside me.

"Are you mad at me?" his breath warms my neck, indicating how close he is. I tense and move away to get coffee from the cupboard, glad of the reason to move away. He has no idea that internally my body is acting like a pubescent teen after her first sexual experience.

"No ... it was ...you were asleep." I have no idea what to say.

*Do I admit that I was the one who started it? That I liked it.*

My heart's pounding through my chest, his proximity making breathing difficult suddenly, in a way I have never reacted to him.

"Well, that's not fair ... You get to have a memory, but I have none ... I demand a re-enactment." There's humor in his voice as his hand catches my shirt from behind, pulling me back against him softly, his mouth by my ear.

"How about a replay, Anderson? Literally make my dreams come true." I swat him away, pulling myself free, my skin burning and shame swamping me. I should have known he would react this way. Casanova Carrero! He makes a joke about everything, so why not this?

I can't help myself. I laugh, relieving some of the tension at his playfulness, the usual flirty Jake, but still trying to twist free from the body I'm a little too sensitive to right now.

"Go away." I giggle as he tries to capture me again, this time holding my wrists in front of me, so I can't get away from him. My body held tight, his mouth by my ear, he has my back pressed to his abdomen.

*God!*

"I want a second take, so I can at least say I remember that time I made out with you in my sleep." His husky voice sends tremors down my stomach. I wriggle free and he lets me go, grinning wildly. He tilts his head.

"At least this time you're smiling about it, *Bella*." I turn to look at him, feeling my face is probably red from top to bottom and see the relaxed easy look on his face. I shake my head and tilt it to the side to match his. His mentioning the kitchen kiss in such a blasé way, making me feel calmer. I wish I had his ability to brush things like this off so easily. Make it all out to be nothing, forgettable misdemeanors. I guess when you've had more bedroom romps than hot dinners, it is easy. This really is nothing to him at all.

"I can't be mad about things you do while unconscious." I lie, fully mindful that this is all on me. A secret I'll never tell him. He stops for a moment, taking in my face, his smile slipping as something registers in his mind.

"You said "We" kissed? Not that I kissed you ... So, you kissed me back?" he moves forward, closing the gap between us, his face now serious. All humor gone. I gulp and hesitate, unsure how to answer.

*Crap. Fuck. Shit.*

I look down at what I'm doing, gulping quietly, thoughts scrambling in panic at how to answer him now.

*Please don't, Jake! Don't go there.*

"Morning," Sophie's tired voice comes out from behind Jake's all-consuming stance, and she wanders into view, dressed in a fluffy onesie with rabbit ears on the hood. Her presence makes me sag with relief. I have never been so happy to have a third person show up in my life and save me from Jake's burning gaze.

"What time is it?" she yawns loudly, I see the opportunity and dive away from Jake toward the toaster as his attention is diverted.

"Just after six" Jake answers, turned toward her. I catch his eye as he turns back and see the moment pass between us. I know that look, it's his "we'll come back to that" look, before he fully turns his attention to Sophie.

"Why you up this early?" he goes on. I sigh, feeling a knot of apprehension rise inside of me that I haven't dodged the bullet fully.

"Nightmares," she says softly, and we connect eyes, kindred in so many ways. I throw her an understanding smile and she smiles back acknowledging it. Jake seems to notice the look, but says nothing, just a hint of narrowed eyes and thoughtful lip chewing before it fleets away. His sharp, keen focus, never misses a beat.

"So, we're all up at the crack of dawn it seems." I say overly brightly. I finish making three mugs of coffee and slide two toward them on the counter.

"Looks that way," Sophie sighs as they both lift cups.

"Are you going to see your mom today, before you go?" she asks innocently but I throw her a warning look that equates to "not in front of Jake".

"No. Sophie. I said everything I had to say to her yesterday ... I wish you would reconsider coming with me today," I plead. I don't like the thought of leaving her here alone at such a young age.

"Your mom's going to be discharged in a day or two, Emma, I'll be okay." She looks determined. Jake looks to me, then her, confusion on his face. I hadn't yet told him of Sophie's plan to stay here another week.

"She's following us in seven days." I point out to him and see the twitch in the corner of his eye briefly, he doesn't like this idea but knows it's not his place to say anything. His jaw tenses, he gets up, and leaves the room for a few minutes. I know him too well, he's walking off, so he doesn't say exactly what he's thinking.

"Sophie ... Yesterday a man called Ray Vanquis came here. I know he's the one who did this. He was very aggressive, he may come back." I tell her, scared to divulge the full story in case it makes her afraid. Maybe I should, so that she'll come with us today after all. I see her swallow hard, her eyes shifting to the window, she looks nervous.

"Your mom told me not to tell you it was him," she says softly, and I nod, indicating I already guessed that.

"He won't come here until she gets out," she adds hastily. I want to point out that he already did, but her face hushes me. For a moment, she looks so young and vulnerable that my throat catches with emotion. I can't leave her here alone. The thought of him coming back when she's here by herself makes me tense up. I hadn't thought about this fact. I realize she's staring at me and I assume my expression is betraying me.

"I don't want to go until you come too, Sophie." I sound uptight. Suddenly unsure about what to do.

"I know, Emma ... But I can't just leave her like that. Helpless and injured." She tries a smile, but I just stare at her impassively.

"Is that the issue?" Jake's voice breaks in, he's at the door with his cell in his hand, as though he's just used it. Walking back in at the opportune time.

"She has no one else," Sophie answers him, glancing at me warily. I feel a pang of guilt but push it down. She has no clue how complicated my relationship with my mother is. I watch as Jake frowns, his eyes losing focus for a second as he thinks something through. Even standing like that, I feel the heat surge through me still and push it away.

"If I arrange for someone to care for her, until she's well, Sophie. Will you come with us? ... Today?" he's in negotiation mode. Mr. Business. Watching him lifts my heart. I knew from the second he met Sophie that he had taken an instant like to her, I knew he would help her. Jake is that kind of person.

"Maybe," she says quietly, I see her mulling it over in her mind.

"If I can go see her and tell her myself," she adds softly. My heart lifts, hopeful and satisfied, the sooner I detach this girl from this situation the better. I could kiss him right now, he is just too perfect sometimes.

"It's a deal then, Sophs." He smiles at her.

"I'll call an agency this morning and hire a live-in nurse

until she's fully recovered ... On me." He looks at me as though asking for my permission, but I just shrug, a smile creeping over my face. At this moment, I could not love him anymore, he is amazing.

# Chapter 15

Sophie spends a half hour in the room with my mother as we wait in the hall. Jake has asked me a dozen times if I'm sure about not going in and I glare at him coldly. He clamps his mouth shut and looks away. I see his jaw tense in agitation, but he leaves it alone.

He just doesn't get it at all, he has no way to understand my relationship with her, his own mother is everything you could want in a parent. Kind, caring, protective, and loyal. She would move mountains for her sons and is an advocate for abused children across all states.

My mother is the polar opposite. I spent my childhood being her carer, protector, and mother. Fighting off aggressive men she brought home. I bought my baseball bat with money from a paper round at eleven, I used it more than once to shield her from an overly violent argument with her current beau, even at such an early age; my fire and rage uncontrollable. It saved me from advances so many times. Men pushing the line into perversion, but I fought back, said no, and erupted. I had been hit so many times, but for each strike, I would lash back. It was never worth their while to pursue it. A crazy little fireball of spitting rage, wielding fists at them. Ray, on the other hand, was truly a monster, the fighting back only turned him on. He pushed the boundaries and showed me that, at the end of the day, I was still a weak little girl.

Sophie finally emerges, her eyes wet and her nose running. I feel the bite of anger. My mother always knows how to break you down and make you feel guilty. It is just one of the many reasons I can't walk into that room today, or ever again.

"She's asking to see you," Sophie says softly to me, touching my hand gently. I say nothing, only shake my head and turn on my heel, indicating they should both follow. Jake doesn't, he stands his ground, looks at me with narrowed eyes before he turns and walks into my mother's room with a frown. I freeze, my breath catching in my throat.

I snap around and run after him at speed, ready to haul him back out. He knows nothing about why she's in here, one look will tell him everything and he has that stubborn air on, the one which means he isn't going to take no for an answer. I'm too late, his long strides have him past the curtain and around her bed as I enter the room. My mother has the good grace to at least sit up and fix her hair at his presence.

*Well, who wouldn't? Look at him!*

I see her confusion as she takes in his appearance. Casual in jeans and a leather jacket, trademark tight T-shirt and his shades nestled in that spiked hair. Definitely not a doctor, although he looks like he would make a really hot doctor. He's appraising her face, his eyes moving to her broken arm, the bruised swollen chaos. I slide up beside him glaring coldly, but he only raises an eyebrow at me and I know what he's thinking. He knows this was no accident, he knows I've been keeping this from him and somewhere in that quick brain, he's wondering if Ray is involved. I can bet he's already figured it is Ray who did this. I feel myself crumble under his scrutiny as my mother grabs at my hand, taking full advantage of my distraction.

"Emma, I'm so glad you changed your mind," she wells up, sounding pitiful and childish. I force down the wave of guilt and emotion. I won't let her get under my skin this time.

"I never had a choice." I glare at Jake again, who at least has the sense to step back and shove his hands in his pockets. His eyes resting on me, but his face is blank.

"Hey, Mrs. ... Ummm, Jocelyn?" he pulls a hand free again and waves awkwardly at her.

"I'm Jake Carrero ... Emma's ... Boss." His eyebrows twitch as though he feels stupid introducing himself that way. I feel my anger simmer, I don't see shy and awkward from him very often, in fact, I've never seen shy. It's so at odds with who he is.

"It's lovely to meet you, Jake ... I'm sure Emma told you about my car accident," she lies, and I feel myself roll my eyes and clench my teeth.

*Mother, he's not a fucking moron.*

She's still gripping my hand, but I tug it free and move away from her so she can't try to touch me again. My mother never really did affection in the form of touching as I grew up, she never cuddled me or sat me on her knee. This little scene is for Jake's benefit, I guess, much like yesterday was for Sophie's.

"I came to say goodbye, mother, the doctors informed me your injuries are not life threatening. You'll be home in a couple of days." I sound cool and distant. I can feel Jake's gaze on me, studying my tone of voice and controlled manner. I know he's trying to analyze the relationship; I wish he would stop watching us so closely.

"I will be, yes ... I hoped you would stay a few days," she

says wistfully, big eyes blinking up at me childishly, trying to give me her most needy look through swelling and bruises. I turn my face away to inspect the tubes hanging by her bedside. Avoidance always works a treat.

"I have work ... A life." I mumble, there are a minefield of emotions and thoughts rushing through me. I hate how she always reduces me to this over-emotional, erratic mess so that I never know which way is up. I made the best decision years ago, when I walked out on her. I needed my mind free of this trauma and tugging to find myself and gain some inner peace. I need it again now.

"Emma ... you're my child ..." She whines quietly, putting on a show for Jake. I snort involuntarily, causing Jake to narrow his eyes at me. My mother carries on unhindered, used to aggressive, insolent Emma, used to my coldness toward her.

"Regardless as to how you behave, I know you love me. Somewhere deep inside the icy exterior. It's why you came at all." I feel the tear tug at my eye involuntarily and storm away from the bed. I won't do this again, every time she's near me, this is how she gets to me.

"We have a plane to catch, Mother ... Jake's arranged for a home help until you're healed, she'll be here for your release and won't leave until the cast comes off," I say flatly. "Appreciate it, sort your life out." I stalk out of the cubicle, my heart pounding with so many sensations, my hands trembling. I walk past Sophie who's staring out of a window in the stark hall and she turns and follows as we start heading out toward the main floor exit. Jake catches up in a jog moments later, coming to walk beside me. He reaches down, taking my hand in his, entwining our fingers softly. He opens his mouth to say something, but my cold, "back off", glare makes him clamp it shut again, so he looks away and I see that familiar

# The Carrero Effect ~ The Promotion

tense of his jaw as he quells his anger. We know each other too well.

I feel his arm against mine as he thinks better of pursing it, body relaxing and the calming effect he always has over me. Grateful that he's here after all and enjoying his hand enveloping mine securely. Grateful that he says nothing and just holds my hand. We leave the hospital wordlessly.

\* \* \*

Everything Sophie owns is in the car with our bags, which isn't much. She is, after all, a runaway from a poor town and impoverished parents. One grubby and torn rucksack, that's so full the zipper is coming undone.

The trip to the airfield is short and silent as we all mull things over in our heads. Jake has glanced down at his cell a ton of times and I know he's been waiting for his mother to call back with more definite plans for Sophie. In the meantime, we have agreed that we'll both stay at his Manhattan apartment with her until she's placed in a safe environment through the proper channels. He has more than enough rooms for all of us. Jake feels she needs me there to feel safe, having her with him alone just doesn't feel right to him, considering her back story.

Sophie is sitting with eyes as wide as saucers, all of this so overwhelming to her and I think, realization, is finally dawning that this is the start of her new beginning. I remember feeling that way on the coach out of Chicago with Sarah by my side. Finally free, running far away from all of it. Running from the influence of my mother. Running from a lifetime of terror and fear.

She reaches out to me and takes my hand, she's sitting between Jake and I on the rear seat and this small motion brings up an internal feeling. Maternal protective instinct. This girl will have the chance I should have had at her age. I'll make sure she has a life that is so far removed from where she has come. In a way, I know partially my reasons are for myself, as though adult Emma is somehow reaching into the past and pulling teen Emma to freedom, saving her in a way I could not so many years ago.

\* \* \*

Sophie looks around the apartment with the same huge eyes and gaping mouth as she did at entering his private jet. This whole thing, like a fairy tale dream to her. I know the feeling well; first time faced with the glamour of the Carrero empire so many years ago, when entering Executive House to be interviewed. Girls like us, so unused to refinery and wealth, a completely different life from where we had come.

It is amazing how in the years that followed, I have stopped noticing it at all. Become so un-phased by the expensive surroundings and more recently, with the way Jake is always surrounded by it. I stopped seeing his expensive clothes and accessories. Stopped looking at the five-star hotels and luxuries as anything abnormal. They are just a part of who Jake is; he never makes a show of it, or makes you feel in awe of it, to him it is normal.

I show her to the guest room that's never used, it's right beside the room I use when I stay here; Jake thought she may like my closeness. I guide her in. It's like a modern hotel room, but the bed is laden with bags and boxes. I frown and walk over to open one and feel the tug of warmth as Donna's perfume rises from the bag, her scent over everything. Inside are clothes, shoes, toiletries; everything a fourteen-year-old girl would ever need to start a new life. Jake and his ever-attentive nature surpassing my expectations again.

"These are all for you ... courtesy of Jake." I smile, nodding to the door. "When you go, you'll take all this with you." I pull a bag toward the edge of the bed and nod again, this time giving her permission to look through them. Her eyes are almost popping out of her head.

"I'll leave you to get adjusted, your bathroom is through that door." I point at the inner white door of the room.

"If you want a bath or shower, go ahead. Jake is having Nora, his housekeeper, cook for us, so you've an hour before we eat, okay?" I smile widely at her, her face displaying her overwhelming gratitude and shock. She looks like she needs to pinch herself and get back to reality. Time alone to adjust is exactly what she needs right now. Processing time.

"It's all too much." A tear rolls down her cheek and I give her a quick embrace. Her eyes huge and damp, her cheeks flushed.

"We all deserve better lives, Sophie ... This is just your beginning." She hugs me tightly before I leave her to absorb all of this and get herself acquainted with her temporary room. A swelling of happiness inside me now that we have her here, away from Chicago, away from the likes of Ray Vanquis. Away from my mother.

Jake's in the large, open plan sitting room, using his cell, when he sees me approach he grins and motions me to come over. I obey and close the gap between us smoothly.

"That's great, Mamma ... Yep ... Completely ... *Tiamo anch'io* ... until tomorrow then ... Uhuh." He says his goodbyes and hangs up, beaming at me like a child.

"My mother has found Sophie a place to stay, a friend of the family. Someone she trusts, I trust too ... Long-term foster arrangement while it goes through the legal process, then a forever home if she likes life with them." He's beaming at me in a way that makes me feel excited for her; the Carreros work fast.

"That's amazing, Jake, really brilliant news! ... So, what happens now?" I smile and throw myself into him for a quick celebratory squeeze, he hugs me briefly then releases me, sighing lightly. Keeping a hand on my shoulder as we face each other, so I am held closer than before.

"Sophie will need to be interviewed, she'll have to tell the child services her story. Everything will be video documented, so they can put her under the protective services umbrella ... My mom is taking special interest in this, so she'll be helped at every step, Emma."

I frown and look away; that will be agony for her. If she's anything like me, the thought of telling people everything will be the hardest thing she will ever do. She's strong and if I explain that this will help her secure a happy future, I'm sure, I can assure her it's the best thing to do.

"She'll do it ... She wants to start over again so badly." I look back at him with determination, already formulating my speech for Sophie in my head when I break this news.

"That's what she'll get ... The Huntsbergers are a lovely family, they have grown children, all of whom they adopted. They have experience with troubled kids. She'll get a loving home and a good education with them." He's watching me closely, his green eyes sparkling with happiness.

"You know them well?" I ask nervously, suddenly afraid that this won't be a right fit for my precious little Sophie. I don't want her life to be out of her control, unable to break free if it's not right for her.

"Very ... My friend, Leila, is their youngest daughter, she's been my friend since she arrived at age seven; when they adopted her too. They live relatively close to my parents, so my mother will be able to keep tabs for both of us, Emma."

He rests his forehead on mine, bringing both his hands to my shoulders reassuringly.

"It's the fairy tale ending she deserves ... I promise, this is a good thing. Trust me on this, trust that I know these people well enough." He brings his focus to me and moves closer, intimately closer. I feel the fluttering in my stomach again.

*Damn. I thought I had this under control.*

"If you think so, then I trust you, Jake ... I just want her to be safe."

"I promise you, Emma ... This is the best outcome I could have ever hoped for." He places a gentle kiss on my forehead, leaving his mouth against me as we stand motionless, lost in thought. My skin warms and my stomach flips at his touch. I feel my inner worries and stress drain way.

Jake would move mountains to make things right when it's something he's invested emotion in. I know Sophie will never want for anything again and he'll have the best legal team he can buy to guide her through the process of cutting all ties with her real parents. He'll bring her perverted father to justice and I want to be there to hold her hand through it all, watch her rise like a phoenix from the flames.

# Chapter 16

The day is tiring, and my hair has endlessly stuck to my face in this humidity. Vegas is hot and dusty and I'm still grumpy and tired. We flew out here right after Sophie was taken away by the care worker and Jake's mother, Sylvana Carrero. The beautiful, kind goddess, who looks so alarmingly like her son, but in a very feminine way. I love her in every way, anytime I meet her, she has this easy charm and stunning green eyes and the ability to put you at ease, much like he does.

I fought tears when hugging Sophie goodbye, our time together so short, yet she has come to mean so much to me. Jake bought her a new cell and pre-set both of our numbers and emails into it as a parting gift, that way we can always stay in touch and she knows we will be there if she needs us. We are to be her eternal guardians in life, and I know that from this day on, I will always be in Sophie's life. We have a bond like no other. We understand each other.

"Want to try the casinos, tiny?" his voice comes up behind me as I empty out my suitcase onto my bed, looking for a change of clothes, anything to relieve the stickiness of my suit. We arrived in such a rush that neither of us have unpacked yet, normally housekeeping do such things in our absence but this time they haven't. I hate incompetence in one's job.

"I'm still tired, I think I'll have a bubble bath and go to bed." I sigh.

"First time in Vegas, and you want to go to bed? *Bambino*, No! You gotta live a little." He sounds frustrated with me, it's been a hell of a long week by normal standards, I feel like I've been free falling for days. I can't keep up the pace like he can. Jake has no sense of exhaustion—Ever!

"Would you rather I stay out late with you, then pout for the entire morning like I did on the plane?" I was probably the most irritated, grumpy person I have ever been on that flight, reeling with emotions about Sophie, my mother, Ray Vanquis. Trying to ignore memories of kissing my boss and going pie-eyed over him on that brief trip. Thankfully, I seem to have normalized a little in his presence again. The kiss not such a bright burning memory as it has been and allowing me to detach a little from it.

"I'm sure I can have the hotel bring me a bag for your head, so I don't have to see it." He grins, raising a cheeky eyebrow. Everyone back to normal.

"Nice ... Charming. As understanding as always Jacob!" I pout again, sighing.

"Less of the Jacob or I'll put you over my knee. Come out with me." He's in boyish pleading mode now. Tugging at my hair in a bid to annoy me into a yes.

*Bored, Jake, darling?*

I don't know where he gets his boundless energy, it's after nine at night and we've had a day of grueling appointments, boring meetings, a late business dinner, and now he wants to go play. Has he no clue of how much of an emotional roller coaster I have been on lately.

"Don't you have any Vegas hotties lined up yet?" I smile

demurely; of the vast number of women he has tucked at every port, I often wonder in awe that he manages to find half of them with very little effort. I guess being drop dead gorgeous, built like an underwear model, and rich, has its own perks.

My own suggestion for him to find a date grates on my nerves, rattling me inside. A little jealousy raising its head and I bite it back down. I have no idea why I even suggested it.

"I don't want a Vegas hottie tonight. I want my pouty PA to let her hair down and come kick back with me." He moves in closer, I can feel his warmth on the back of my neck and it makes my skin tingle. His familiar aftershave surrounding me in a very disturbing way.

"I was under the impression I already did." I ruffle my loose hair to make the point, lately I've been too tired to tie it up at all. Its length has been annoying me too, I keep thinking I may get it cut shorter, maybe shoulder length.

"You know what I mean, sassy pants." He mock chucks me on the chin with a smile.

"You pay me to be bright and chipper at your meetings." I try a wavering smile, turning to look at him over my shoulder as he walks away to lift his cell from the charging dock. I'm trying to express my tiredness as I look at him coquettishly.

"I pay you to do what I say ... And right now, it's to come out with me. I want to go play. Get drunk and feel up my sexy PA." He throws his charming wink over at me and walks back, cell in hand, moving closer in behind me and I can feel his presence through the thin material of my blouse. He's almost touching me, his heat radiating through me alarmingly. I have been way more sensitive to him since our sleep kiss and it's throwing me all out of whack these past few days, his touchy-feely hands-on self seems a lot more so.

"We both know that's not on the cards, besides, I didn't

bring anything to wear to a casino, Jake." I lie, I know there's a black cocktail dress in the suitcase. I'm always under order to carry a dress for an impromptu dinner or party when we travel. He leans past me, pulling my dress out, like an eagle with his eye on prey at a distance. Lifting it up to let it roll loose and hang in the air between us accusingly.

*Hmmm, busted!*

"Perfect! Sexy dress, for little sexy Emma." He drapes it over my shoulder and slaps my behind with a swift sharp smack. I squeak in protest and throw him a haughty look.

"Put it on, I'll be five minutes max."

I sigh heavily. Ordered about by him again! In Jake terms, he will be more like twenty minutes. I can't even argue. I sigh again, more defeatedly this time and sag, knowing that he's in his delightful stubborn mode and I'll get no say; arguing is pointless. I really am tired, and I want to go to bed; the last thing I need is a tight dress, alcohol mixed with the proximity of my boss when he's in flirt mode and I'm struggling to control my hormones around him. I make a habit of avoiding him in drunk mode, ever since the kitchen kiss. Drunk Jake just makes me wary, he loses even more of his inhibitions, if that is even possible and I have no idea how to deal with him if he gets a little amorous. Or I do.

\* \* \*

I grimace as I catch sight of myself in the mirror; once again Donna has excelled herself and I chastise myself for not trying this dress on before this trip. It's tight and short and revealing. My stilettos do wonders for my legs, but I feel a little naked. It has no sleeves, just thin straps and a fitted bust, leading down to a tight figure hugging knee-length skirt. It's mainly made of lace with an under layer retaining my modesty, but the result is sexy, in a non-slut way. Well, maybe a little slutty.

I brush my hair and leave it down in a bid to try to cover some of my exposed shoulders and cleavage. It waves naturally, coming down to my elbow. Make-up is darkened and smoky. I'm ready unusually fast, still with a deep knot of anxiety in my lower stomach.

Jake strolls back in wearing his favorite black shirt, open at the neck and black trousers. Effortlessly suave. He always looks amazing in black. His eyes practically glow with green coolness. He seems to falter as he catches sight of me, frowns, and adjusts his cuff, averting his eyes. He says nothing at first, before setting a normal smile on his face and looking me over once again.

This is a bad idea, I can feel it already, I want my suit, my hair tied up and my cool and in control mask back in place.

"You look stunning, Emma ... May have to beat off a few men tonight on your behalf. Pee on you and mark my territory." He grins at me as I blanch in disgust.

"Ewww, hell no!"

He checks his hair in the mirror over the mantle one more time, before reaching a hand out to me. His eyes still skimming me with a look that he never throws my way—appreciation. Not flirty Jake eyefuls, like he normally does, but serious, eye skimming, checking me out. I swallow down the nerves, no idea why I feel this nervous and accept it. He takes my hand and pulls me toward the door before I can argue, always so overbearing when his minds made up.

\* \* \*

The casino is everything I imagined it would be; I've watched enough episodes of *CSI* to not be awed at the splendor of the vast red carpeted room, filled with machines and tables and noise. He tries his luck at a few tables and soon looks bored.

He's never been much of a gambler, he likes to have situations laid out in a way that he controls the players and always wins. It's why he's his father's second in command, his inherited skills. Although after the Hunter merger, I'm beginning to think his skills surpass that of Senior, he knew how to play him well.

"You want to hit a club instead of this?" he's close to me and I can already tell he's fed up with the casino, I glance at a couple of women looking him up and down and feel mildly irritated. Maybe I should point him in the direction of the two leggy blondes and go back to the room. Have my quiet night after all. Seeing them look him over like fresh meat I pout; I feel irritated again and I'm aware it's unattractive. I glare and turn my attention back to him.

"Sure." I decide defiantly as I catch blonde girl licking her lips and thrusting her boobs forward, readying herself to approach him from the corner of my eye.

*No doubt the slutty pair don't mind group sex.*

He grins widely, unaware of the female attention he's receiving. Impulsively, I slide my arm through his possessively, throwing back my hair and sending the "hoes" a signal.

*Back off, he's not interested.*

\* \* \*

The nightclub is dark and booming and we get in easily, they know who he is, even though we're far away from home; a common Carrero curse. I spot some well-known faces and gush when I realize there are some celebrities here and even more so when a couple of them wave his way. He's holding my hand and pulling me through the crowds. Jake is never wary of unfamiliar places, and new crowds, he feels at ease wherever we go.

I'm trying to go easy on the alcohol, but Jake's a seasoned-drinker and frequents the bar for top ups faster than I can drink. He has me half-drunk already and I don't know how many times he's pulled me onto the dance floor, everything bumping and thumping around me. He's a good dancer and even though we have danced close at times, I get the impression he's trying to keep a gentlemanly distance. He's still flirty and having the usual banter with me, but there's a definite distance in him now we're here. He is also staying pretty sober, considering the way I have seen him fall into hotel rooms after a night out.

We're dancing to a high-tempo song and people he knows are around us, he seems to find acquaintances everywhere we go. The upside to having a famous face and travelers blood I guess. We sit with them and share a few drinks before I get up to dance with a girl named Lolly, who can't keep her eyes off Jake; it's irritating as hell. It only makes me snarky and I find I have no warmth for the girl at all. I cut in a few times to dance in front of her in a sexy shimmy, in the name of saving him from her wandering hands, anytime she gets too close to him. Jake seems amused and just pulls me close to let me dance against him.

*He came out to have fun, not get mauled by some overbearing red head in a Wonderbra.*

Jake doesn't even seem to acknowledge it at all. Maybe this is why I avoid going out with him? This need to have women leave him be and let him enjoy his night. I suppose it's the opposite of what he wants, but right now I don't care. I'm not playing third wheel.

He leaves to go to the bar with one of the men that we have started to party with, I'm pretty sure I've seen him on the big screen, but I'm too shy to ask and his posse all look a tad familiar. I'm wildly outside my comfort zone.

I feel hands around me as a shady, sleazy, familiar face slides in behind me and tries some sexy dancing. I remove his hands icily, feeling that rise of bile in my stomach at a male touch, and stumble to the bar feeling thoroughly cringe; looking for the one guy I feel safe with. I don't want this creep's hands on me, his breath on my neck; I want Jake's presence and the security it offers from overly handy men.

Jake's being served and hands me a colorful cocktail as soon as I appear beside him. It has a sparkly straw and umbrella and he grins as he places it in my hands. I'm sure there's some sort of joke in it, but I'm thirsty and it tastes amazing, it reminds me of the drink he gave me in his office the first time I ever met him. He looks at me weirdly and shakes his head in amusement, looking at the drink in my hand. I guess it's the fact I'm holding a pink sparkly drink with a ménage of decorations that's amusing, without argument, and obviously liking it, it's not me. I kind of like it and I like that it amuses him. That smile always makes me smile, looking down at my pretty drink.

I feel a hand slide slowly over my ass, copping a feel with a firm squeeze, and I jerk my head up in shock.

*What the hell is he doing?*

Except, Jake is standing in front of me with a beer in one hand and his cell in the other, staring down at the illuminated screen, he clocks my reaction and looks past me, frowning.

"Hey, buddy ... Hands off." He glares, and the shady familiar face lifts his hands in mock apology. Still towering behind me a little too closely. I move closer to Jake in a bid to put distance behind me.

"Jake, mate ... You said she was just a friend," he's slurring, almost in my ear, he's so close.

"I know what I said." Jake moves forward, pulling me aside with a strong hand and placing himself between me and sleazy. I'm not sure how to react so I sip my drink nervously. Glad of his powerful body shielding me, in this state I may just curl up and cry.

*Where is feisty Emma?*

The rear-view of Jake's body towers in front of me and I can feel the tension emanating from him. I guess this is a hint at angry Jake coming out to play. He's always quicker to temper tantrums when he's drunk, or so Daniel implied when regaling drunken tales last time he stayed over. His stiff body and electric sparks crackling in the air, even from back here. Angry Jake is not much fun. Whatever sleazy is saying to him, he doesn't seem to like it at all. I can't hear their mumbled conversation over the music, so I look him up and down instead, feeling the waves of drunkenness calming and pulling me into a unreal euphoria.

I like his back, it's strong and sexy, especially in black tailored shirts; and those ass hugging black jeans, he has the perfect ass. He has the perfect male body if I'm being honest, no matter what he wears. He's still so cool and in control, regardless of his stance.

"Buddy" displays defeat, says something quietly and moves off with a frown. I can tell, even from behind, that Jake's glowering at him, I saw his ears move. I had to suppress the giggle it pulls out of me, some vague, drunken memory about his ears. I don't know why that's funny. I can only blame the copious amount of alcohol that Jake has kept throwing at me since our arrival.

"Jake?" I'm feeling tipsy and a bit unsteady on four-inch heels.

*Damn Donna and her love of high shoes, and my weakness at seeing them. Damn me for not keeping track of how much I've drunk and letting him fuel me on cocktails this way.*

I realize how much things are swaying around me, or maybe it's me that's swaying? He turns to me and there's a look on his face I've never seen before, scary in a sexy way. Possessive. A tad dangerous, but then it's gone and he's all Mr. Smooth smiles again and asking what's wrong, with a look of concern.

*I love his looks of concern, they make me warm inside, sexiness personified when he looks that way. I just love all of Jake's looks, heck I love Jake's face. I just love Jake.*

"I think I'm too drunk." I giggle and realize I just sloshed my drink over the glass and barely missed both of our shoes. He frowns down at where it went before a smile breaks across that charming face.

*How the hell did that happen?*

"I think you're right, lightweight; I forgot how intolerant you are to liquor." He takes the glass from me carefully and places it on the bar as I sway around. I can't help but watch the way his upper arm bulges when he bends it.

*Why does he have to be so muscly and hunky?*

He always buys fitted clothes that only add to the effect and it's really soul destroying. He should wear sack's from now on, maybe that would help. I can picture him in a sack, it's still sexy and that alarms me. Life isn't fair in any way.

"Dance with me, Jake." The slurring, flirty, female voice sounds loud.

*Who said that? I think that was my voice, wasn't it? Damn, maybe.*

I guess by the way he smiles at me in response, it was. I feel merry. I like being merry, it feels kind of light and warm. I'm completely aware that my internal dialog is that of a very drunk person. He says nothing just puts his beer down, slides me toward him with a very hot hand, and pulls me toward the dance floor with ease.

*He's smooth. Why would I expect any less from Casanova Carrero?*

He manhandles women effortlessly on a daily basis. Lots of practice at it. Well, not so much lately, he seems to be cooling his jets on the women front. There hasn't been a girl on the scene for a couple of weeks at least, maybe longer, but I hadn't noticed at first.

It's a slower song and he moves in close to me as we join the throng of dancers, it's hard to dance when you're this drunk and in very high heels on jelly legs. I'm swaying, but I don't think it's in time to the music. I trip, stumble into Jake's nice strong arms, he knows just how to catch me, and I catch my breath a little. He's good at pulling my body into his in a hurry.

*God, he smells good! My hero! Who would have thought hot boss Carrero was my sexy hero? Sexy and hot—yes! Hero. Most definitely!*

"Maybe we should go, tiny?" he seems nervous and puts me back on my feet, at arm's length.

*Except that can't be right because my boss is never nervous. He's always Mr. Confident.*

"I want to stay and ... Let my hair down." I giggle and fall into him again as I lose my footing for the second time, my shoe moving into a right angle that should have broken my ankle ordinarily. He catches me and my nose grazes his collar bone and I get a full lungful of Carrero scent. It's pretty heady, his aftershave and his personal scent, an intoxicating mixture. I could breathe it in, over and over. He feels good, strong, powerful and safe ...

*Crap, what am I doing?*

If I keep at this I know I'm going to do something stupid, like the kiss in my mother's bed. I've entwined my hands around his neck and I'm nuzzling my face into his chest without even being aware of my own body's actions. I'm too drunk, this is a bad idea. I feel as brazen as I did the night I kissed him in his sleep.

"Okay. Time to go, tootsie." He unwraps my arms from his neck, leans down and picks me up, lifting me up in a fireman's hold, so my face is behind him. His hot hands around my thighs, holding them tight against his muscular chest. I wonder if this is a safety precaution, so I can't attempt to kiss him. I'm too drunk to react and am kind of glad to be off those shoes; my ankle is tingling. I feel dizzy and I don't think I should stay and explore what I was trying to do.

*Good save, Mr. Carrero. I can't trust myself, but I can trust you to look after me.*

I hang down his back limply, sliding my arms around his sides, so they come around his waist to the front. I can feel his taut stomach muscles under my flattened palms and have to quell the urge to slide my hand inside his shirt for a better feel. I lay my cheek against his back, closing my eyes at the feel of him instead. Giving in to the motion of his walk as he takes me out of the pumping club. There are a lot of glances our way, but Jake doesn't seem to care. I guess a Neanderthal carrying a drunk woman out of a club in Vegas is a normal occurrence.

* * *

In the car, he lays me down flat on my back and pulls off my shoes, cradling my feet in his lap with warm sensual hands kneading them softly, avoiding conversation or eye contact; I nestle my head against the door.

His hands are exquisite on my ankles and feet, it feels better than nice, no one's ever taken my shoes off like this. No one has ever just run soft fingers over my feet at all, the way he's doing now. He's gentle and attentive, something most people would not expect of Jake Carrero. Handsy, but not in a sleazy way, not really, despite all his jokes and sexual innuendos. He just always makes you feel safe.

"Why are you stealing my shoes?" I mumble playfully, trying not to squirm in case he stops.

"I like those shoes." I'm angling for humorous Jake, flirty Jake. I like arguing with him, he's always funny; I don't like this silent, pondering version, even though he's drunk as much as me, he looks so serious.

"I'm taking you home, Emma. You're going to bed and you don't need your shoes for that. I'm satisfying my foot fetish instead." He smiles, but it doesn't reach his eyes. He sounds tired; maybe he really hasn't got boundless, eternal energy, after all.

"You don't have a foot fetish, silly! I need to walk up the stairs." I argue with a smile. Stifling the urge to giggle.

"I don't think you could, even without your shoes, Emma, I'll carry you. How do you know I don't have a serious thing for feet?"

A memory of the shoulder lift to the car pops into my head and it's not altogether unpleasant. In fact, I almost feel myself looking forward to it, Neanderthal carrying from Jake has its upside. I get to feel those shoulders for a start.

"Okay ... And you don't. You check out women's boobs, occasionally an ass, not their feet." My eyes are closed, my arm is laid across my head as I try to get comfy. The car is spinning, and my hair is tickling my face; I feel too heavy to move it away, so I try and blow it out of my face instead, childishly, and making a lot of noise. I'm blowing, but it's still in my mouth, irritatingly so.

"You're a hopeless drunk, you know that?" his voice is warm. I think he's laughing at me, but I'm a little too comfy to reply. I feel him move the hair off my face, he lifts my arm to untangle the strand caught in my bracelet. It feels nice, relieved to have the tickling removed as he pulls my arm straight toward him and lays it on the cool leather seat. The sway of the moving car lulls me into a calm, relaxed mode, with closed eyes, I could fall asleep easily.

"I'm just hopeless in general," I giggle again. He says nothing, and I feel a tug of outrage that he may agree, but I let it slide over me the same way these waves and warm tides are doing. I realize my arm is still warm, I think he still has his hand on it. I open one eye and look down, his fingers are tracing my bracelet and he looks lost in thought, a tug of a frown crossing his beautiful face.

"What are you thinking about?" I ask, like a child, no filter. Alcohol taking away my normal inhibitions.

"You ... Me ..." He sounds distant. Something cold in his voice and I don't like it, he looks away from me, toward the window and gazes at the passing night scenery and bright lights of Vegas. His perfect profile looking very much like a magazine cover, outlined in the dark window. I feel saddened by his mood and expression.

"Are you mad at me for being this drunk, and making you bring me home?" I ask, trying to understand his somber look. My voice is almost childlike.

"No ... I like this side of you. I just wasn't feeling it anymore, figured it was a good time to leave." He throws me a small quick smile, and looks away again. His eyes so dark with emotion. I hate seeing him like this.

"Then why so glum, Mr. Cartierro?" my joke again, raising from my last drunken bout.

*How funny.*

I giggle and hear him laugh softly. He remembers my joke too.

*I love his laugh.*

"There's so much about you that you keep from me ... Your mother ... Nightmares." He releases my arm and leans away, shoving his shoulder against the door, resting his head against the frame. I wonder why this is going through his head now, after a great night.

Why now?

"My mom's a Pandora's box, Jake ... I wouldn't know where to begin with her. Yes, I have dreams about what Ray did to me. I didn't think it was something I had to share ... Are you upset with me?" I sit up a little, trying to read his expression, his hand has come up to the side of his face, cushioning it from the door frame and he's glaring outside. He doesn't reply. I know he's mulling over Vanquis, both the past, in my teens, and more recently in Chicago.

"Physical pain goes away, Jake ... Don't focus on injuries that healed in weeks." I flop back down, the irritation rising to strangle out my mellow drunkenness, I don't need this right now.

"What do you mean?" I sense his shift in position, so he's looking at me.

*Does he really have no clue?*

The physical side means nothing in the grand scheme of things, it's the emotional mess left inside of me that I don't want Jake to see.

"He broke my arm and ribs, he almost broke my nose and he gave me a concussion that had me in hospital for days. But it all healed in time."

*Why am I telling him this? Alcohol is like a lubricant for my goddamn mouth.*

I'm drunk and somehow it doesn't feel as bad saying it out loud when I feel this detached from normal Emma. It's like I'm talking about someone else, sad little Emma back home in Chicago, so far away. He needed to understand that none of it meant anything anymore.

Jake makes an odd noise; I think it's a grunt, a snort—maybe a moan. I don't know, but it's not a good noise, it's a reaction to what I have said, and I talk fast to cover it.

"I mean, I don't remember the physical pain. You should forget it too," I say it so matter of factly, yet so softly, it makes me feel sick and I feel tears sting my eyes.

"How can I forget it?" he looks at me as though I have two heads and I suddenly feel over-emotional. Anytime we broach this subject, we fight. I don't want that right now. I can't handle this tonight.

"Same way I do, push it out of your head. Ignore it. Lock it away deep down and don't talk about what he did to me." I try for a shrug, but at this angle it's more of a squirm.

"He raped you?" his voice is quiet and unsteady, he sounds different—afraid. I guess he has been trying to figure this out for a while. How far Ray had gone.

*Oh, Jake, don't sound that way.*

"No ... He didn't ... He tried ... I fought back ... My mom came home." I stare at the ceiling of the car, listening to another version of Emma, talking out loud, detached from the secrets she's telling and trying to quell the low pain building up inside.

"Jesus, Emma." His voice breathy, talking as he exhales, he sounds relieved, but also sad for me, and I don't like it. I pull myself up and glare at him angrily.

"Don't do that!" I snap angrily, emotion from deep down suddenly jumping out. He spins his head to look me in the eye, shocked, confused.

"Don't do what?" he frowns defensively.

"Don't you dare feel sorry for me," I spit, pulling myself up and trying to force away the spinning sensation.

"Don't look at me in that way, like I'm some sort of damaged broken glass who is too fragile for life." My feet have been in his lap this whole time and I pull them away fast. Sitting up, I sway, and realize I've got a seatbelt clipped over my waist. Safety Jake. I un-clip it and pull myself to sit properly and face him.

"Emma, how can I not feel something when you tell me that asshole beat the shit out of you and tried to rape you?" he looks angry, it's unexpected. I wasn't prepared for angry Jake, but maybe that's better than sad, sorry Jake. I don't want sad sorry. I hate people looking that way at me.

"Well just don't ... I don't need sympathy. I fought back ... Hard ... He broke my bones for it, but you know what? He didn't manage to rape me, he didn't do what he wanted ... I won!" I yell out loud, not at Jake, but at the world in general. Anger spewing out in every direction.

"And what if your mom hadn't shown up, Emma? What if I hadn't shown up in Chicago and he had come back?" he retorts, I don't even know why He's angry, I'm the one who has the right to be mad. Not him!

"I would have kept fighting ... I wouldn't have let him do that to me. He wasn't the first of her creep boyfriends to try." My face is wet, I ignore it, barely noticing the tears running down my cheeks. I'm angry and I'm yelling, but I don't even know why I'm yelling at Jake, he's not the one who did it. Sleazy Ray is the one who did it, my mom's creepy ass boyfriends and their wandering hands. I'm shaking with emotion, my body has betrayed me and heaving with tears in my drunken stupor seems to let all this mess out.

"Emma," he breaths. Jake hauls me toward him, trying to wrap his arms around me, but I don't like it. I'm in memory mode and men's unwelcome hands firing through my brain. I don't want him to see me cry over this, not over these memories and those men. Not over that shit, Ray Vanquis.

"Stop it ... Stop it ..." I'm fighting him, but he's stronger and faster and I'm still drunk with slow reactions, the racking sobs making me weak. He's determined to hold me.

"Shhh. Shhhh. Emma. Shhh." He holds me, cradling my head against his cheek; even though I'm still fighting, but I'm losing. I don't like the noises coming from deep within me, like I'm spiraling out of control. I hate this. I'm not weak. I'm not vulnerable. The sounds don't sound like they're coming from me. I push his hands off me again and again, but he's relentless and his grip tightens. He pulls me hard onto him, so he can get better control of me.

I'm in his lap and he's all around me. Strong, tight arms and firm hands, trying to calm me; I finally give in.

Ray wasn't the first to try and touch me inappropriately, there had been many hands and each one had met my sheer fire and fury. Ray hadn't been the first man to hit me either, despite all of it, I never allowed myself to be a victim. I'm not a victim now. I'm stronger than all of them.

"You'll never look at me the same way, will you?" I choke; it's what I always fear about people knowing. It's one of the reasons I left Chicago. I hated people knowing what happened, looking at me that way. My friends knowing that my mother never protected me against the myriad of perverted fucks she brought home, refused to acknowledge it instead. Why she couldn't be stronger and protect me? Sarah never looked at me that way, she knew, even then, that I was made of stronger stuff. I look after Sarah now, it's my way of proving I'm stronger and somehow showing myself how my mother should have been for me.

"Emma ... You don't know how I look at you ... Even before this ... This won't change any of it." His voice sincere, I'm confused; I don't know what he means, but I'm too distraught to think straight. The tears still rolling down my face, his forehead against mine, his hand cupping my face and thumb trailing across my cheek softly. His arm around me so tightly, keeping me against his warm, strong body.

*My eternal protector. He always brings these emotions out of me, they struggle to the surface somehow.*

"I'm not broken ... I'm not ... I'm strong and this means nothing." I pull myself out of his embrace, off his lap, and move away; he doesn't stop me. I have to show him that I don't need him to feel sorry, or sad for me, that my past doesn't change who I am now.

"I know you're not, Emma ... Is that what you think?" his voice is low and husky, as full of emotion as mine is.

"Do I think I'm broken?"

*No, did I say that? I don't think I did. God why did I get so drunk?*

Everything is spinning wildly. My mind a mess.

"No, Emma ... Do you think I would look at you any differently?"

*That's what he meant. Well, now he mentions it. Yes, I did actually. Why wouldn't he?*

I let men think I want them to touch me, I somehow attract it. I must do something to deserve it, for it to have happened over and over. Even coming here, men at Carrero House still targeted me.

"Why wouldn't you?" I reply flatly, staring out of the window absently, back in control of my tears and tired from the exertion.

"Emma ... You did nothing wrong." It's breathy and tense, I think he's having trouble believing I would feel that way. He has no idea. He's probably never been in a situation anything like my past.

"I'm supposed to be strong and cool and capable. I mean,

you rely on me for everything. I can't just fall apart and whimper like some broken China, because I have a shitty past." I stare away from him. Trying to fully regain my cool. He's looking at me with such an odd expression, and I realize we've been driving for an age.

*How far from the hotel did we stray? Seems like an eternity.*

I need to get out of this stifling car. Take deep breaths to both cool and calm myself.

"You're all of those things, Emma, and I think partly, because of the shit you endured." He sighs heavily. He doesn't know what he's talking about.

"You're also allowed to be human and ... vulnerable ... You're allowed to let someone in. Let me in!" Almost pleading at me.

"Not with my job, Mr. Carrero." I smile finally, voice lighter and trying to sound normal, wishing to end the tension between us. Even though he doesn't reciprocate, I see his eyes soften. I wipe away my tears; turning to him once again. Calm and in control once more.

"Even with your job," he says softly, reaching out and taking my fingers in his gently, entwining them with mine and leaving our hands on the leather seat between us. I don't look down, but the warmth of his touch sends a small reassurance through me.

"I think the boss would soon have something to say if I reverted to some feeble, emotional victim who wept over old scars, don't you?" I smile, hoping to turn this conversation back to our usual banter. Release this heavy tension around us.

"The boss would be an idiot if he did." He looks over at me, a hint of a sad smile. No fun and flirty from Jake, he's still in serious mode.

"My boss is sometimes an idiot." I smile at him shyly. "He gets me drunk, irrationally drunk and lets me fall apart when he should know better."

"Maybe getting you drunk is the only time you're truly yourself around him. That, and it's easier to seduce you when you can't see straight." Finally, I see that glint of cheeky in his eye.

"So, you planned on getting me drunk, Mr. Smooth? To take advantage of me!" I shake my head, mood fully restored to tipsy mellow, everything fading away, and I'm glad that we've steered away from emotional topics. This weird habit we have of going from fire to soft lapping waves in a flash.

"No ... Maybe ... Yes. Damn, you caught me!" he's smiling, but it doesn't reach his eyes and I know he's still digesting what he's learned about me. I didn't want him to know any of that stuff. I want to take it all back.

*What does he see now? Damaged goods ... Some pathetic little girl that men tried to molest. A slutty girl who encouraged it maybe? Her own father couldn't even look at her, was too disgusted to want her.*

That inner shame and self-loathing rising out from the fiery depths.

"I don't want to do this, Jake." I say softly. Looking down at our hands, held together.

"What? Snuggle in the cab? Let me take advantage of you?" he looks at me a little unsurely. Humor evident, but not quite hitting the mark.

"This whole bonding over shitty childhood experiences ... I want to take it all back, so you don't know any of it." I say honestly, still holding his hand, still taking comfort from his touch.

"Why?"

"Because it's ... Shameful. I'm ashamed of it." It's the first time I've ever said it out loud; I sigh, steadying my inner turmoil. This is harder than I thought it could be. He shakes his head and pulls me close to him across the seat, releasing my hand to bring an arm around me tightly, his forehead resting against mine as he pulls my face back to him. His hand along my jawline.

"Emma, you never did anything wrong ... You didn't ask for any of it." His green eyes lock on mine, dark with emotion.

"I must have ... Why did they keep trying?" it comes out from somewhere inside of me, causing a sharp pain in my heart. I hate that alcohol causes this verbal diarrhea. Anytime I think I have a handle on it, teen Emma blurts out the dark secrets and insecurities to Jake. He has a way of making it happen.

"Because you're beautiful, and they wanted you ... It makes them the sick fucks. I would destroy every single one of them to prove to you that this isn't your fault." The conviction and fire in his voice and eyes makes me want to curl up in his lap again. I know that he means it, that he's capable of it. I can't let things slide so far into personal in this way, it would affect our relationship in so many ways. I look up at him, with what I hope, is a grateful look and a soft smile.

"I don't want to talk about this anymore." And this time I mean it. I've never opened up about this, never cried about it to anyone, except him and I feel sick at the thought that Jake just saw all of that. I want to recoil and hide in shame and take it all back. I move his hand from my face and pull away, still sitting close but gazing away from him, out of the window.

"Emma ...?" I can tell by his tone that he's going to push this further. I feel myself stiffen.

"No," I say with determination.

"You can't open a door to let me in, then shut it in my

face." He pleads, his hand coming to trace my jawline tenderly. His touch making me lose some resolve for a second. His touch always makes my body sag hopelessly.

"Yes, I can ..." I stay, calm and emotionless, wanting to remove his fingers from my skin but needing his touch more. Taking solace in it.

"I won't let you, Emma ... This isn't the last time we talk about this, next time you won't be drunk," he sounds determined. A tension heavy between us.

"There will never be a next time, Jake, just let it go." I'm back in PA mode. Emotion pushed down and voice steady. I know he's frowning at me. I can tell by the tone of his voice, but I don't care, the alcohol is numbing things again, but I'm starting to feel overwhelmingly sick.

The car stops as we pull into the hotel garage, finally, the endless journey comes to a halt. I slide out as soon as we stop, moving from his lap and feel him tug me by the wrist back to him, he follows me out into the dark electric lit basement. He has my shoes in one hand and he stoops to scoop me up in princess carrying fashion. My arm sliding easily behind his neck.

"I can walk," I protest weakly.

"There's broken glass and all sorts of crap down here ... Be quiet and just hold on. Enjoy being the damsel for once, woman!" he's in boss mode and I know argument is pointless. In a way, I'm glad because I'm still swaying, and everything keeps sliding around me. I hold on around his neck and rest my temple against his jaw, inhaling him. He feels good, he smells amazing, safe, strong and warm. I glance up, trying to gauge how drunk he is, in the hopes he'll forget our entire conversation, but he seems normal. His focus intent on where he's heading. His green eyes clear.

*Was I the only one to get plastered?*

He catches my eye and gives me a genuine smile, a soft and warm look. The urge to trace his chiseled lips with my fingers shocks me and I rest my face back down into the hollow of his neck, inhaling him while I can and taking away the temptation. He carries me into the elevator and back to our rooms.

# Chapter 17

I spend the meeting the next day wearing Jake's sunglasses. My eyes are puffy and sore and my head's banging.

He put me to bed last night and left me alone until our first meeting this morning, he didn't even push at me to eat breakfast or jog with him for a change. I know he's walking on eggshells waiting to see how I am. He's giving me distance, or maybe he's just looking at me and thinking I'm probably mentally broken, and could fall apart any day now so he should handle with care.

I'm in cool and grumpy mode and I'm really excelling at it. Covering my inner turmoil and regrets; so far, I think I've snapped at every person I've met in triplicate and Jake's met my **PMS** face with a vengeance. He's said nothing about it, no funny comments or sarcastic telling off's, just frowned at me. He's tugged my hand out of my hair repeatedly, which is down because I couldn't bear to stand doing it this morning and I've finally decided it's going to get cut short. So, done with all the fussing and styling it.

He's being unusually patient and steady, despite the endless raised eyebrows and cool glares. I think he's allowing me to behave badly because he feels guilty; guilty at getting me drunk and urging some shocking truths from me. Guilty that I'm suffering a hangover at his request and alcohol fueling.

I feel angry at him today, angry at everyone. I'm not sure if it's because I feel rough or that I had some sort of emotional breakdown which dredged it all up to the surface for me. Either way, a bear with a sore head hasn't anything on my mood and the day is dragging endlessly.

The flight back to New York isn't as bad, I sleep a lot and feel better for it. I sit in one of the rear seats, away from Jake, amazed that for the first time in my life I manage to sleep on a flight. I guess a hangover really is a cure for fear of flying.

Maybe, I'm finally learning to trust his pilot. I have my own space to just get a grip on myself. I thought things would be awkward with him after I let all that horrendous crap slip out in the car, but he seems the same; if anything, he seems more normal than normal. Effortlessly Jake.

Finally, I wake and move to a seat beside him. Sliding in easily and meeting his smile with my own. Within moments I'm staring out onto the clouds in the beautiful blue sky, Jake has papers in front of him with his cell on top.

"Emma, for the love of god." I look up confused and frown as he tugs my fingers out of my hair. I roll my eyes, both at him and myself. I've literally given up trying to counteract this annoying habit when it surfaces, half the time I am oblivious to it.

"I swear, I'm going to insist on tying that back up." He seems narky now. Whatever has transpired while I slept has him in a grumpy mood.

"So, first you get on at me to wear it down all the time, and now you want it tied back up?" I pout, a little annoyed at his new mood.

"I didn't think you would pull and twirl your hair like a

child every time you got stressed." He tenses his shoulder and moves in his seat a little. He looks agitated, hands raking over the paper he's dropped in his lap. A quick glance shows it's a contract that has been causing headaches lately.

"Maybe it's endearing to your clients ... I'm not stressed." I lie. Lately my head never stops obsessing over how Sophie is getting on. Whether my mother is home yet, and whether Ray has crawled back into a dark hole after Jake's beating. Stressed would be an understatement and probably the cause of the hair twirling. He gives me a strange look and frowns.

"I don't care if my PA is endearing to my clients, I just want her to do the job I ask of her," he sighs, he's on edge too, he seems distracted. Moody Carrero on full show.

"Which I do ... Hair twisting and all. Grumpy!" I sigh too, he looks at me for a moment, a brief flicker across his face as he gives up this pointless bickering. We're both so touchy today it seems. No idea where all this came from. Possibly his delayed hangover.

"Have you got any info on this dance my father has conned us into? Eternally pimping me out to yet another glitzy affair," he says instead, softening his frown. I slide the file out of my bag and give it to him, a dance and auction for some vague charity. We received his father's request that we should make an appearance at this event. Luckily, I managed to print off the details before getting on the plane. It's not unlike Senior to make such requests.

He flips through the file and I go back to gazing out at the clouds floating by. I feel his eyes on me and I realize I'm doing it again, I release my hair and tuck my hand under the side of my leg. I can't help it. Everything that's happened in under a week has me on edge, even when I'm not thinking of anything. I've been uptight constantly. I seem to be unable to stop fidgeting lately, I can't even begin to trace back when it started again; subtle and mild fidgeting. I'm sure he started chastising me after ... The kiss—in the kitchen. I gulp.

"We may have to get really drunk to get through this one," he sighs dramatically.

"I think we should give the booze a rest for tonight. I don't think my poor body can handle a new hangover when it's still suffering with one." I grimace.

"Never heard of 'hair of the dog', tiny?" Jake smiles at me.

"Drink to kill a hangover and worry about it later."

"Is that a Jake Carrero hangover cure?" I roll my eyes.

"Tried and tested. I'll happily let you try it."

"I'll pass. I don't want to spend my first weekend off dying in bed with a hangover, thank you very much."

"You can stay in my bed, and I promise I'll distract you from any nasty hangovers. Second tried and tested method, is to sweat it out of you, with some vigorous acrobatics." He winks at me with a grin and gets another heavy sigh in response as I battle the urge to laugh. Jake never tires of the sexual references. I wonder if I'll ever tire of laughing at them. If it was anyone else, I don't think I would find them funny at all.

\* \* \*

The dance is nice, very grand with an awesome Asian feel. There are lots of authentic looking costumes, drinks, and lots of sparkly things to eye up. There's a whole host of speeches and droning before the dance gets underway, and as usual, the flashing of a million cameras. I'm so used to them nowadays I never really notice anymore.

"Dance, Miss. Anderson?" Jake's back in charming and happy mode and dazzles me with a sexy smile.

"Certainly, Mr. Carrero." I take his hand and follow him through the crowd to join other dancers, it's a slow song and he moves me expertly. Dancing with Jake is fast becoming one of my favorite past times. Like everything he does, it's with a smooth, confident capability that seems annoyingly easy for him.

"It's a good thing you got a young female PA." I smile up at him, feeling relaxed in his embrace.

"Why is that?"

"Saves you having to wine and dine leggy blondes on short notice, when you can't be bothered or have a hangover." I smirk. Inwardly glad he has no date with him tonight.

"I guess. Although that stiff double whiskey sorted me right out." He's smiling, he seems relaxed tonight despite his earlier weirdness.

"What's with that anyway?" I ask curiously.

"What's with what?" he looks over my head and smiles at someone trying to catch his attention, ever sociable Carrero. Back to swaying with me to the music. He seems distracted, but I know he's trying to avoid my gestapo questioning.

"The lack of leggy bosoms lately?" It's been in the back of my mind, his lack of playmates and sleep overs.

He shrugs and spins me around, pulls me back into his arm playfully and lightly smacks me on the butt. I throw him a mock alarmed look; the tug of his smile is not lost on me and I get a warm fuzzy feeling in the pit of my stomach at his good mood. He's so much more mellow since we landed.

"Lost your sex drive or merely misplaced it?"

"Nope." He's smiling, but that guarded look is back, he's being deliberately evasive, and I feel that tug of irritation at him.

*Oh, so we're playing the one word answer game, are we?*

He looks amused at my dry expression.

"Bored?" I press.

"So, so ... Just taking a break." He shrugs and looks over me again, this time nodding at another attention grabber.

*For goodness sake.*

"You do that, do you?" I cock my head to the side, studying his perfect jawline, the sparkle of his green eyes in this light. He looks particularly gorgeous tonight.

"Sometimes."

I doubt it very much. I'm pretty sure in all the years I researched his social endeavors, I have never seen a break in the flow of women, but maybe some of them were just stand in dates, like me. PA and assistants, when he couldn't be bothered.

"Are you sick?" I know I'm prying but I live with him and I know how much he likes to roll in the sheets, and by my calculations it's been a while since the last one. A long while.

"Not that I'm aware." He throws me a look with raised eyebrows that says, "Where are you going with this?", but he's still smiling. He catches my hand and holds it to his forehead with a furrowed brow.

"Do I feel sick?"

I pull my hand free and shake my head at him. We go back to dancing, but my head is still mulling it over.

"You're not? ... You know?" I hesitate, feeling the blush run up my cheeks.

"What?" he's laughing now, I think he knows what I'm going to ask. He has that amused look on his face; the all-knowing eye.

*How does he do that?*

"Having man problems?" I blush furiously.

*Why am I even asking this; god? I've become as nosey as him! And as inappropriate!*

"No ... No "man problems", Emma. Don't worry, my libido is still intact and waiting for you to name the place. Why are you so interested in my lack of sexual partners?" He shakes his head, locking eyes with mine finally.

"It's just ... I've worked for you for a while now and it's the first time there's been a lull in ... playtime." I answer, my face hot and I suddenly wish I never started this line of interrogation. I am practically squirming with awkwardness.

*Why do I care so much anyway?*

"You're keeping tabs? Little bit jealous, maybe?" he smirks at me.

"No!" I flush and realize my cheeks are flaming now, I must be bright red. He's smiling at me hopelessly as he moves me around again, in time to the music and pulls me against his jaw so we're resting easily, giving me a break from his eyes and instead enjoying his warmth against my face. He moves my body against his in the slow dance expertly.

"I just need a little break from demanding, stroppy women ... even casual sex can be a hassle." He shrugs, flatly.

"I see. So, am I just the stand in date from now on then?" I say seriously.

"Never! You're always my number one girl." He throws me a mock shocked look, as though I've offended him.

"I don't know why you're complaining. I don't think I've seen you warm to a single female I've dated," he states matter of factly, then spins me again and brings me back to his face, tipping his chin down so his nose grazes my shoulder. I can feel his breath on my naked skin, this dress is strapless, and it makes me tingle. It's a little red number and far too molded to my body for my liking. He presses his ear against my ear. It feels intimate, the new position meaning my face is almost buried in his shoulder and neck, closer than moments before. I feel a tad breathless and to anyone watching, this is not a platonic pose. Especially as this dress is all cleavage, and Jake's looking directly into it, inches from it.

"I didn't know I was meant to?" I breathe the words, conscious of the fact I'm suddenly feeling light-headed. Overly aware of how well our bodies fit together and how intimate this feels.

"You're not ... It's up to you ... Either you like them, or you don't, it doesn't matter ... not one of them is permanent." He moves back to his previous hold, giving me some breathing room again. He lifts his hand from my waist and waves at someone behind me then returns it back to its warm spot on my body. Pulling me in a little closer, if that is possible.

"What do you see in them?" I've mulled over this every time I met one, never seeing the connection. He raises his eyebrow, followed by a smile which says "really?" at me, and I feel stupid.

*Okay, so he's a man! And they're all drop dead gorgeous, with scantily covered, perfect bodies, and huge boobs; every one has been stunning, in that fake, plastic over-manicured way.*

"I mean besides that?" I falter drily.

"Nothing ... hence why they're all temporary. None have your cute little face, perfect figure, or sexy little personality." He throws me another flirty grin. I think eye rolling has become my most used facial expression since meeting him.

"So, another deliberate move by smooth Mr. Carrero then?" Another premeditated game play. Maybe we're not so different after all, both control our lives so fluidly.

"Pretty much." The music tempo changes slightly, but it's still a slow song, he lifts my hand in his, a tad higher, checks his watch and puts his arm back to its previous position. He's getting bored being here, all the Jake signs coming out. We'll be leaving soon at this rate, but I want to know.

"So, you avoid people you might actually want to make more permanent?" I press on.

"Mmm-hmmm ... makes sure I don't get too involved ... Waiting on you to hurry up and confess undying love, *Bambino*." He smiles at me, flexing his eyebrows knowingly.

"You're exhausting, you know that?" I sigh again.

"So? What is your type, if it's not leggy boobs with perfect nails?" I push, smiling shyly. He looks at me seriously for a moment, then shrugs.

"Someone more real. Maybe short, blonde, blue eyes with a name like Emma." His grin is over the top, full on charming Carrero and I resist the urge to bop him on the head. He's never serious about this stuff. Ever!

"More real than fake boobs and Botox you mean?" I ignore the comments about me, despite the little elevated heartbeat it has erupted.

"Something like that." His short answers are starting to drive me slowly insane, I think he's deliberately trying to be obtuse.

"You're not giving much away," I pout, a little huffily.

"What do you want to know exactly? I thought I already described the perfect woman ... did I forget pushy and nosy?" he spins me again and now I'm back in his arms, but able to see his face better.

"If I believed you for one minute, Carrero! What's your type, if you wanted more than just sex? Brunette ... red head, short ... curvy? What?"

He frowns down at me, spins me under his arm and pecks me on the cheek with a quick kiss.

"It's not so much about looks, Emma ... It would be someone I can hang out with, who doesn't bore me ... Someone with an IQ larger than her bust size."

*Well, that's a revelation, and it's kind of sweet. I grin at him.*

"Someone smart ... and normal?"

"Pretty much." For once he doesn't add in a flirty comment, finally being serious. I figure so many women in the world would gush over this tidbit of information right now, giving hope to the millions of adoring women.

"Someone like me?" I laugh.

"I already told you, *Bambino*. Confess how crazy you are for me and I'll marry you before dawn. We both know you've the serious hots for your sexy boss." That face is nothing but sheer cheek and smiles. I shake my head, eye roll and sigh all at the same time.

"You're infuriating," I scold gently.

"That's why you're crazy in love with me, shorty. Drink?" He leads me to the table, but I shake my head; I guess he's signaled the end of conversation. Something we're both good at.

"Maybe best if I don't," I grin, I'm still not fully recovered. He studies me for a second then smiles.

"One won't hurt. Live a little."

"I think you like getting me drunk, Jake."

"I like loosening you up, starchy pants. Makes it easier to get you naked." He winks at me and that devilish smile reappears, a nearby waitress gawps at what she has overheard and moves away fast. I can only sigh.

"You pay me to keep my pants starched remember, and on! If I was, Miss. Loose and lively, I would be a shitty PA." We move to sit at an empty table.

"I don't know, might be fun having a drunk PA. A naked one would be even better. Would love to see you endure a stuffy meeting in full blown drunk Emma mode. Not sure I would let others see you naked though." He smiles again,

# Jake & Emma

pulling out my chair and seating me at the table. He gestures for a waiter seeing as our server as taken off.

"I probably wouldn't be a hit ... naked or not. Especially with the stuffed shirts you have meetings with."

"I can agree with that." He's still smiling and hands me a champagne glass.

"I like drunk Emma, might ask her to be my temporary girlfriend. You know, anytime we're both drunk—we're in a relationship." Despite my protests, I take the glass and throw him an indulgent look.

"So, you've mentioned many times before." I'm feeling edgy suddenly, I don't like where this is heading.

"I'd like to see you really let go, Emma." He watches me carefully as though examining something under a microscope.

"In what way?" I'm not sure I like that look on his face.

"No work ... just chilled and loose and free to have a good time."

"I work for you remember ... if I'm around you, then it's usually a good sign that I'm meant to be working." I raise my eyebrows at him and sip my champagne, seeing his look of approval.

"Maybe I need to take you on holiday then." I see the spark of determination fleet across his face. His body sliding down into the chair, a la casual Carrero posture.

"This again?" my gut tightens.

"We go away together a lot ... maybe we both need a trip for pleasure? Lots and lots of pleasure." He's off on negotiation mode and I sigh.

"Jake ...?" I warn.

"Listen to me ... after Chicago ... everything that went on, please ... We both need this; it's only two weeks, Emma ... you'll have your own room. No hanky panky, I swear. I will be the perfect gentleman. My dad's yacht ... the Caribbean ... just picture it."

"I agree, Jake, but it's still not right to take me on some romantic getaway." I try to refuse.

"Is that the issue? You think a tropical beach on a boat is too romantic? Worried I may make good on some of my promises?" An edge to his tone indicates he's getting annoyed with me.

*Why am I so reluctant?*

"No, it's just ..."

*I don't actually know what it's just ...*

"Just?"

I'm lost for words, and he sees me flounder.

"It's agreed then?" he looks smug.

"What is?" my voice tight. Knowing him only too well and how overbearing he can be.

"We go on a trip," he says.

"I didn't say yes." Jake is in steam rolling mode, he always does this to me. I've never known anyone with this ability to maneuver me into his way of thinking. Or just bullying me into it.

"You didn't have a reason to say no either ... I'll just make you come with me and call it a business trip ... I'll fire you if you refuse." He drinks some of his champagne, his eyes never leaving mine.

"That's not fair," I sigh, knowing I'm losing.

"You're the only girl I know who would turn down two weeks in the sun, Emma ... I'll still be paying you, regardless." He shrugs at me.

"I'm not worried about the money." I glare at him haughtily, but it only gets me a smile in return.

"You're worried about being alone with me? Worried I'll

get you naked and you can't refuse me? We're alone most of the time ... we've shared a million hotel rooms ... you've stayed in my apartment too."

"It's not that, it's just ..." I falter and sigh.

"It's not work and you're unsure how to navigate it?" he frowns down at me, a softness to his expression.

"Maybe." I shrug, perplexed.

"Relax and trust me, for once in your life, woman." He sighs, a look of irritation in his eye; he's starting to get annoyed with my refusals.

"I do trust you and stop calling me that." I shove his foot with mine, hard. It's in its usual close position, almost welded next to mine.

"Do you?" he looks at me seriously and I see the hint of hurt.

*Wow, when did that happen, when did Jake start doubting that I trust him?*

I feel a wave of guilt run through me, I want to smooth away his frown, on his perfect face.

"Yes, I do ... I don't know why you're looking at me that way. Who else would get away with half the crap you say and do to me?" I try a softer tone, but he just looks across the crowded room sulkily. He sighs and indicates we should go.

*Jake my sulker.*

I glance at my watch and smile tightly, it's not too late, but he's right. I'm tired and I don't like the way this is going. It's no fun here anymore. We only needed to show face, and we have done. Jake seems agitated.

I sigh and look away from him, knowing he's right, he's never mentioned what he did to Ray after we walked away from his lifeless body, but I know he's been thinking about it. We do need a break. To clear the air, to reset the button. All this irritation and tension between us lately, maybe he has a point. I don't want this to be something we bicker over endlessly.

*What harm could it do?*

"When do you want to go?" I finally breathe out.

"You're serious?" he catches my chin with his fingers and forces me to look at him. I shrug in answer, knowing when I'm defeated and his face breaks into adolescent happiness. He swoops down with a kiss on my head and I can't help but smile as he beams at me. Like a kid who found a lollipop.

*This is the man worth billions of dollars, who runs an empire. Yes. This childish pain in my ass is meant to be my boss!*

# Chapter 18

We're finally home and I'm standing in my apartment. Sarah isn't here, as usual, only this time it vexes me. There's a crap load of male things infused throughout the apartment, and that rank smell of Marcus's aftershave is over everything. I'm also aware that in the whole time I've been gone, I have only heard from her via text, asking about my mother briefly. I know I shouldn't be upset. I barely touch base with her either, but I assumed I would have at least one call. Seeing as I haven't been home in a week or more.

I go to my room and throw my suitcase down in agitation. I have two whole days at home for a change. Jake is shooting off to see his mamma for her birthday, and for once, I'm not being dragged along for the occasion. I know Jake loves his mother and he wants some alone time with her, he has plans to take her on a shopping and spa day, her and her two sons.

My room looks depressing, after the weeks of jumping from grand hotels and Jake's apartment for quick changes and flight stop overs. I kind of miss it, the view from his comfy ivory tower and the city lights stretching below. My room feels claustrophobic, it doesn't help that there's a mountain of clothes piled on three surfaces, from my coming home to throw out the contents of one suitcase, and pack another before leaving again.

My cell beeps and I open the text, surprised to see Jake's name already. We've barely left one another. I'm still wearing my dress from the dance. Red satin and floor length, all boobs and shoulders on show.

*What are you doing?*

I guess he's bored already, maybe like me he's feeling listless and unsettled. I've been home less than an hour and already I'm itching to get out of these four walls. He's supposed to be getting an early night for his trip home tomorrow. I send a reply with a smile on my face.

*Staring at a sea of pointless clothes, and wondering how I'm going to wrestle Donna's gold card away from those itchy fingers.*

*Can I come stare with you?*

His reply makes me smile.

*My poor boss is really losing the ability to socialize with normal people, beyond me ... What am I doing to him?*

It's still early, so I guess he isn't ready for sleep. I know I'm not.

*What's the matter, Mr. Carrero, are you lonely in your ivory tower without me?*

*Maybe.*

His reply is instant. I stifle a giggle; he's impossible at times, like a child who needs my constant attention. Unable to satisfy his own boredom. He's never actually been in this apartment, not that he's had reason. I wonder where all his buddies and play things are tonight? Surely, he can't only have me to hang out with.

*If you're that bored, how can I deny you my sparkling company?*

I have to admit, I miss him already, I'm so used to his constant presence that standing here alone feels alien.

*Are you home alone?*

His replies are swift, and I can't help but smile.

*Aren't I always?*

He knows about Sarah's almost constant absence, he knows that Marcus hangs around, even when she isn't here.

*I'll be there in 20 minutes.*

I close my cell and look around.

*Should I clear up? It's only Jake.*

I laugh.

*When did I start thinking that way, it's only Jake? How many weeks ago would I have had a meltdown at the thought of Jake Carrero in my apartment?*

I hear the door and I'm surprised he's here already, that's been less than five minutes. I'm pretty sure he won't have been hanging about outside waiting, he's not that kind of creepy at all. It can't be him, he's not rude enough to just walk in, he has impeccable manners.

I wander out of my room and see the sleazy Marcus, all floppy curly brown hair and sulky brown eyes, in that unshaven face, carrying a brown grocery bag.

*Great. So now he has a key.*

"Marcus," I say drily. He seems to get a little shock at my arrival and throws me a nervous grin. His lanky frame meandering into the kitchen to dump the bags.

"Emma, you're home for once ... started to think you were never coming back." He grins with his lop-sided, toothy mouth. Eyes appraising me openly.

"I'm guessing you're living here now? If my whereabouts has become your concern?" I say flatly, anger simmering low down inside of me. Sarah has no right. I despise this guy on normal terms but him living here is worse. She should have at least asked me if I minded.

"Sarah and I decided to give it another go, and as she works a lot, we figured this would give us our best chance at working it out"

*Great ... thanks Sarah.*

I grind internally.

"She didn't think I should know?" my voice thinly veils the venom; I can't stand this wiry, curly headed, out of work actor. Free riding from my friend in our home. My voice is tight and haughty.

"Why?" he blanches at me, and I push down the urge to throw something at his head.

"Because it's half my apartment, and I pay half the bills." I retort angrily.

"We kinda figured you would be moving out, seeing as you're shacked up with your boss." He smirks at me. His eyes doing the usual route from my cleavage down to my ankles and slowly back up. He makes me sick. I'm beyond livid, and Sarah knows that nothing is going on with Jake and me. I swallow the urge to slap him across his messy head, tightening my fingers into fists by my side.

*Smarmy prick.*

"I'm not shacked up with my boss! I work for him, that's all." I keep my teeth clenched, my voice is full of hatred.

"Yeah sure." He's eyeing me in that "know it all", sleazy manner of his, that makes my skin crawl, his eyes saying, "I can imagine you screwing him in all those fancy hotels"

"Fuck you, Marcus! ... You know nothing." I turn on my heel and stalk back into my room, anger threatening to burst out, and I just cannot be bothered with him or a fight.

*Asshole. I can't stand that weaselly little prick. What the hell is Sarah thinking?*

He has the good grace to disappear into Sarah's room and I'm left to change quickly, glad I have a lock on my door. I just don't trust men like him. Men who undress me with their eyes, they always make my skin crawl.

I opt for jeans and a T-shirt and leave my hair in a ponytail loose,. I push thoughts of Marcus away as a minor irritation, and focus on the task at hand. If I'm going to be clearing out a mountain of clothes then I would rather be comfy. It's not lost on me that a few months ago I didn't even own jeans, Jake mentioned that fact in sarcasm right at the beginning.

*What has Jake Carrero done to me?*

I haul a pile of clothes from the top of my dresser and dump it on my floor, followed by subsequent piles around my room and open my door so I can listen for Jake's arrival.

*Jesus, that's a lot of clothes!*

It's almost half as tall as me. I really need to clamp down on this excessive buying from Donna, it really is abusing the company assets, spending so much on stuff I don't need. I haven't even worn half of the things she sends my way. I'm like her own dress up doll.

I put the iPad in my docking station and turn on some music, it's the random mix of popular songs that I like, and the ones Jake has sent me over the months. Our weird form of communication. I smile at some of the titles as I scroll through, able to pinpoint the memory of the reason he sent each one.

I don't hear Jake arrive, but Marcus lets him in and next thing he's standing in my bedroom doorway, looking hot in a red T-shirt, and jeans over sneakers. His presence, as always, makes me feel instantly happier.

"Hey." He smiles but throws a wary look and thrusts his thumb over his shoulder, indicating he's asking about Marcus. I shake my head and shrug, he knows I don't like him. He frowns in response as I turn my attention back to the piles on the floor of my neglected bedroom.

"You weren't wrong ... I think Donna has dressed you for a year." He exclaims, coming to sit on the floor beside me, sprawling out casually. It just looks odd on him, sitting among a sea of girl's clothes on the floor in a girly bedroom.

"Whose fault is that? Mr, Oh, buy her an outfit for this, that and the next thing, every time you see her." I poke at him with a smile.

"Maybe I should tell her to ask you from now on, when you need something?" he holds his hands up in mock apology."

*Too much money and not enough sense.*

"That would be an idea." I smirk.

"Get rid of what you don't want." He pulls a dress from the pile and holds it up to admire it, thrusting it down to pick up lingerie instead, with a smile and wink.

"Most of it still has tags, Jake, she should return them." I snatch the bustier from him and throw it toward my dresser where my lingerie lives. His raised eyebrow look is not lost on me and yet, I ignore it, not really wanting Jake to ogle my lingerie.

"Just give them away, Emma, they're already paid for." He shrugs.

"Jake, there's thousands of dollars worth of stuff here." I look at him in frustration, he has no concept of money sometimes.

"And?" he says as if to prove my point. I forget that he probably spends more than that on one piece of jewelry for a passing date. He's always been generous in that way.

"So, I should just donate it? What I don't need?" I ask sardonically.

"They're your clothes, *Mio Amore*." He shifts on the floor, picking up another dress, this time having a closer look at it and looking at me. He's trying to remember if I've ever worn it. I throw him a disdainful look and start throwing items to the door for donating, this feels so wasteful. I don't even want to tally up the costs of half of this and, apart from Sarah, I don't know anyone I can give them too.

"You've never worn this?" he raises an eyebrow at me. I look over at what he's holding.

"Nope."

"Why not? It's nice, kind of cute, yet sexy." He's still admiring it.

"Where would I wear it?" I look at it, it's not exactly formal, but it's not exactly casual. It's a sort of romantic floaty dress, in a short, flirty style, and a lovely deep red.

"Take it with us on our trip. Parade around on deck for me in it." He puts the dress on the bed as though he's decided it's coming on the trip, regardless of my view on the matter; sometimes Jake can be exasperating. I can't argue though, it's a lovely dress and perfect for a holiday.

"Just the two of us?" I ask warily, I've been wondering about this since I agreed.

"Not if that makes you uncomfortable ... I have friends we could invite; my father's boat has six double cabins if you want a crowd." He's still looking through the clothes on the floor, with a little too much dedication.

"Who would you invite?" Maybe it's the thought of just the two of us alone for two weeks, on a beach, that's bothering me. No work to converse over, nothing to distract me from my own mind. I think he's hit the nail on the head, no boundaries and rules to keep things in check.

"Daniel; a couple of the guys I sometimes take trips with, and whoever they want with them ... I was thinking Leila Huntsberger, that way you could meet Sophie's new sister." He looks at me and I smile gratefully. I would really like that a lot.

"So, they're going to be couples?" I ask warily, not sure how this will work.

*What if Jake wants to hook up while we're there?*

"Really, Emma?" he sighs. "What do you think I'm going to do? Try and seduce my PA, because we're surrounded by couples and I'm incapable of abstaining from sex? I may always be trying to chat you up, but I'm not an idiot. I know where the boundaries are, *Bambino*." He looks exasperated for a moment.

I'm not sure that would be a reason to refuse, if I am being completely honest. I'm just anxious about all the possible outcomes, not having the control or planning.

"No, it's just ... It will be awkward." I don't look at him, just keep sorting random clothes from the pile. Jake has stopped and is leaning against my bed watching me.

"Why?"

"They might think we're ..." I hesitate and catch his eye. His relaxed pose accentuates that upper body mass and I glance away quickly. Always caught off guard by my own hormones.

"Who cares what they think? I don't give a shit what anyone thinks, Emma ... I need a break and so do you. Stop overthinking and just agree; besides, they're my friends, they'll know right away that we're not screwing." He slides his hands behind his head, frowning at me and shrugs, a little angrily.

"Okay, for god's sake." I put my hands up in defeat, he's so grouchy tonight. I throw him an apologetic look.

"Don't laugh, Jake, but I don't own anything I could wear on a beach, or a boat." His face breaks into the biggest smile I've ever seen.

# Chapter 19

In great Jake fashion, the trip is organized in lightning speed. A matter of days at most, which pass in a flurry of a busy schedule, and before long, we're heading to the sunny deck of Jake's father's boat.

The boat is huge, we're anchored a half a mile from the shore of the most luscious, secluded beach I've ever seen. I'm completely overwhelmed at the beauty of this place; the sun's beating down, I'm surrounded by a gentle breeze and salty air. It's truly a paradise haven, complete with palms and white sandy shores.

The crew is formal and walks around in white uniforms, the captain even wears a hat and everything we desire is brought to us by these magical servants who stay out of sight until needed. It's beyond my wildest dreams, and for a minute I wonder what it would be like to be married to someone like Jake, having this life all the time.

He seems so much more chilled out and carefree, a smile never far from that handsome face. Jake's friends seem okay. Daniel is keeping his distance and I wonder if Jake has warned him off.

There are six of them with us. Daniel and two other men called Vincent and Richard, twins with white blonde hair, gray eyes, all American good looks and square shoulders. Jake has an alarming amount of good-looking friends. They have brought hot, leggy women on board who are completely topless, bar the one called Leila, and wandering about on deck having some sort of bitchy glaring competition with one another.

Marissa, Vincent's date, is small and tawny haired like me, although hers is browner with highlights; she's curvy, and has an almost exotic look to her, a bit like Jennifer Lopez, only sulkier and with a lot more curve. There's something I really dislike about her immediately, she's superior and icy toward me, from the second Jake arrived hand in hand with me at the airport.

Leila, Richard's date, is amazing, she's small and blonde and like a little hurricane in a teapot. I fell in love with her spirit and hyper energy as soon as she blew on deck, always smiling and the center of fun and hilarity. She introduced herself with a hug and a giggle and then poked fun at Jake mercilessly, highlighting a real friendship there.

The other girl, obviously Daniel's lady of the moment, is a mirror image to most of the women Daniel has dated in the past; her name is Miracle. I assume it's a porn name, as she's hanging over Daniel's arm, practically licking him. She's tall, slim, and seems to be all brown hair, boobs, and legs.

It has not been lost on me that two of the women swoon and pout whenever Jake appears. Leila seems oblivious to his charm, and spends her time crooning over Richard, adoringly.

Jake's looking as hot as always, he's wearing long shorts to just above his knees, he's topless, showcasing perfect physique, bad boy tattoos and tanned skin, his usual cool shades and ruffled hair. I admit that not staring at him half-naked has been hard, awkward at first, considering he's my boss and I have never actually seen him minus T-shirts before, except on Internet pictures. He is a lot sexier in the flesh.

He's been swimming with Daniel in the ocean, topping up that Italian tan and he is looking jaw-dropping hot. We've been here almost two days and I've managed to relax a lot and start on my tan.

I was met by Donna before our trip, laden with bags of clothes suitable for a tropical getaway and threw Jake an accusatory glare. He's since promised to limit Donna's gold card to a budget, under my direction, and promised to stop reaching for her number anytime he has an obsession to dress me up like a Barbie doll. Wasn't hard to figure out that he was behind the non-stop purchasing.

I'm wearing a bikini that's a nice shade of coral and a matching sarong around my waist in a pale print, I'm not really a bikini wearer, but I don't feel so self-conscious, now two women's breasts are jaunting around on deck before me. The men must be used to the spectacle as none of them seem to pay any attention to the naked boobs. This surprises me, in fact, Jake seems to avoid looking that way at all. Totally un-Carrero of him.

I'm leaning against the rail near the front of the boat, absent-mindedly watching the gentle waves, aware of his presence as soon as he comes close. It gives me a warm tingling feeling whenever he's around, a feeling of safety and familiarity, and even a couple of feet away, my skin tingles at his presence.

"Here." He hands me a bottle of cold, flavored water, with a smile, his eyes shielded from view by his Ray Bans.

"Thanks." I open it and take a long drink. I didn't realize how hot I was, maybe a little too heated with his topless body so close.

"You look nice." He appraises me through tinted lenses. I wait for the sexual banter or joking come-on, but it doesn't come. I noticed since our arrival that flirty, always giving me the charm, Jake, has relaxed back.

"Thanks." I blush. He's skimming my swimsuit, appraising me with his eyes and I turn away, so he doesn't see how awkward it's making me feel. Bikini wearing is a new sensation, I have to acclimatize to it. I also don't want to stare at his expanse of naked torso, it's an understatement to say he looks hotter than hot. Up close it's hard not to admire what being a fitness freak has done to that chiseled body.

"We're going to the shore tonight for dinner ... You want to come?" He's looking across the calm water now. Stretching out lightly and distracting me.

"Sure." I smile at him, as I shield my eyes from the sun, he automatically swipes his shades from his face to my mine, it sends a little shimmer of warmth through me, like it always does. My attentive Jake. I can't help but smile at him. I feel like I'm always smiling at Jake nowadays.

"I really should carry a pair of these." I laugh, but he just shrugs.

"They look better on you than they do on me. Your cuteness just goes with my shades." He winks.

That's doubtful, he has a knack for buying things that just increase the level of sexiness he exudes.

"Where are we going for dinner?" I try to direct conversation away from staring at his face, his shoulders, his chest, his abdomen ...

*Oh lord.*

"Some little seafood place Marissa knows."

"I want to get my hair cut while we're here ... Do you think there are any hairdressers on the mainland?" I regret asking as he turns toward the topless women, sunning themselves on towels, two of them watching him studiously.

"Leila will know ... She comes here a lot." He nods toward the only one wearing a top. I resist the urge to ask him if he's slept with any of the three women, but I know it's probably inevitable. I know how these rich men pass around the beauties between them, like some sort of guy's club; the women only too eager to please.

I notice Marissa watching him coolly, a strange expression on her face. He catches her eye, his jaw flexes and turns away quickly; a sudden sharp pain in my chest pushes me to ask before thinking, impulsive observation.

"You know Marissa well?" I blink toward him and see him pause for a second.

"Once." There's a coolness to his voice and he's staring off toward the distant horizon, it sends trepidation through me. This is a side to him that mystifies me, when he clams up and doesn't speak. It doesn't happen often, but it makes me feel anxious, he's usually always so forthcoming. Jake never has weirdness over women he used to date either, normally they know they will always be temporary and most stay friendly after. I glance at her again, watching her biting her lip and staring at his powerful body.

*I hate her already.*

"Want to come for a swim with me?" his voice slices through my wandering thoughts, visions of him and her passionately entangle.

*Stop it, Emma! What the hell?*

"Now?" I blink.

"Why not?" he smiles at me, watching me closely, I'm pretty sure he's waiting on the magical moment I unwind and chill out that he's expecting to see on this trip, and I'm really trying to relax. Hard to do when two of your holiday mates are mentally undressing your date, openly; well, escort – because we are *not* dating, not that we ever would, of course. I'm regretting not coming alone.

*Maybe it would have been easier without the playboy bunnies over there, trying to eye screw him.*

"Sure." It beats watching them writhing on deck suggestively as their men folk slug back Martinis, listening to bass pounding dance music, while snorting lines of cocaine. I'm glad that's not something Jake has done around me or has ever admitted to anyway. He's never mentioned Daniel's frequent use of drugs or that he's ever joined in when with him.

We wander to the open area of railing and I strip off my sarong, watching Jake expertly dive in and follow after him.

\* \* \*

The water feels amazing and Jake is an amazingly powerful swimmer, he looks as good in, as he does out of the water, and has tried to push me under twice now. I swim toward the beach, but I'm too slow and he's caught my ankle for the third time, dunking me under. This game isn't so fun now, he's too fast.

"Stop ... it." I splutter to the surface, coughing and choking, pushing the water out of my eyes again. I'm met with his grin.

"Only if you ask me nicely, tiny tots." He wipes the water from his face and I can't help but notice his hair gel must be water proof, apart from looking a little ruffled, it's still pretty much spiked to the center in his trademark style. Carrero products really were worth the high price tag.

He swims to me and comes dangerously close.

*Whoa there, sexy boss. My bikini is virtually underwear*

*here, and you're only half dressed.*

It seems a little more inappropriate somehow. To me, it really is like frolicking in underwear.

"Will you please stop trying to drown me, Mr. Carrero." I beg, the cheeky glint in his eye only makes my heart sink, he's in full blown play mode. This will not bode well for me, it never does.

"Seeing as you ask so sweetly, Miss. Anderson." He pushes me under again, this time he catches me under the water and I'm pulled back up against him, hard. We're nose to nose and it doesn't seem so right anymore, now it's a little too much like being naked. It's closer than I think even he expected and he releases me quickly; I'm more than conscious that my naked stomach just had an undeniable graze with his groin and now I can't shake the feeling from my skin. Maybe this is a bad idea after all. There's a strange atmosphere between us.

He swims away from me, toward the shore and all I can do is follow. The beach isn't that far, but it's exhausting. I manage the swim behind him in the crystal depths and the reward is worth it.

The beach is gloriously hot, with swaying palms and soft white sands. I can hear the distant hum of music from the boat behind us and watching Jake lazily walk across the shore line is breathtaking. I'm lucky that my boss makes for a gorgeous view in all terrain, keeps things interesting.

*Can't ever deny a good bit of eye candy.*

I realize I've left my sarong on the boat and now I'm walking around in bikini bottoms, showing the full length of my naked legs. It's nerve racking, considering I'm someone who rarely wears short skirts, or dresses and now here I am, skimpy beachwear in public, in front of Jake, with a body like his. This is enough to give anyone a complex.

My hair feels heavy in its ponytail so I pull it free, ringing out the water and leave it to hang down my back in a bid to cover some skin, it's got way too long lately, and I should look at a new style. My minds made up, it's time for a change.

*Maybe a sleek bob? Maybe not; all that loose hair to twirl will send Jake crazy, he'll probably shave my head.*

He stops to look back at me and pauses, his gaze on me as I close the gap slowly. It's hard to ignore his eyes doing that same sweep over me he did on deck. Male eyeballing, taking in the amount of exposed skin and how my boobs look in a bikini. I squirm under that gaze yet feel nothing of my usual revulsion when men check me out. He takes my hand to drag me with him and thankfully turns away, looking toward our destination.

It's not long before the sun dries me off, and I'm feeling the glistening heat on my shoulders, warming me through, making me feel lazy and forgetting all about his smoldering looks. We walk a fair bit and skim pebbles on the waves; easy, quiet companionship. I find so many beautiful shells to take home for Sarah and we pass the time with small talk, about Sophie, about work. I never realized how easily we blend when we're just chilling out. It's natural, unforced, and we talk about everything from current events, and movies, to what we think is happening on the boat in our absence. I like it; I think he's right. We needed this. We needed this time to chill and relax with each other again, remove all the pent-up frustration and agitation. Rebuild our easy friendship. I needed this to let go of all the Chicago crap.

"Here, Emma." I look back and he hands me his shades again, now the sun has moved higher in the sky. I was shielding my eyes without even realizing. I smile and put them on, they have a crazy rubber band thing across the back that holds them to your head when swimming. I guess that's how he kept them on his head on the swim over here. I give him a grateful smile.

"Thanks." I say as he throws another pebble into the water, looking at me oddly. I can't help but notice the expression.

"What is it?" I tilt my head to watch him.

"You seem a bit more relaxed now we're over here." That is an understatement; being away from over-sexed women with lusty looks certainly takes the edge off the atmosphere. I am regretting not coming on this trip as just the two of us. I would have liked it more.

"I feel more relaxed," I say lightly, without explanation.

"You look it." He skims another stone, like an expert. I glance at him, catch his smile, returning it.

"I'm glad you made me come." Hard to admit.

"I'm glad I didn't have to force you." His smile turns cheeky and that little eyebrow raises as dimples appear.

"Technically, you gave me no choice." I frown back at him.

"You always have a choice with me, Emma, you know that." His voice is gentle. Irony without meaning it. He has no clue how overbearing he can be sometimes. I laugh and shake my head in exasperation.

*Sure, I do, Carrero.*

"We should be getting back; the others will think we don't like them." He's watching me, and I can't help but notice the way the sun glistens on his skin, shadows falling under prominent muscles, making him look all the more chiseled.

*Yes, we should.*

"Sure, I'm kinda hungry too." I pull off his shades to hand them over. Following him to the shore to wade out until the water lifts our feet from the bottom and break into a swim behind him.

We swim back leisurely, and he stays close to me, I think he's worried I won't have the stamina to do it, but I prove him wrong. It's exhausting, but all those sessions in the gym lately, the early morning jogging, has been doing me wonders. I'm glad that I prepared my beach body ahead of time, without knowing I needed it. It makes lounging with Jake, in barely any clothes, less mortifying.

\* \* \*

We spend lunch on deck with the rest of the party, eating chicken Caesar salad and drinking wine; relaxing on the padded double loungers on the main deck. Jake's beside me, leaning toward Daniel's bed, his strong back covered in a pale gray T-shirt, in the mid-day sun. They're talking about the New York Giant's game they recently went to at the Metlife Stadium, while I'm leaning toward the bed with Leila and Richard, girl talk and making plans. Leila agrees to take me to the mainland for some girly shopping, and to source a salon to cut my hair.

I catch Jake looking back at me as she picks up strands of my hair, talking about cutting it short; he frowns when she mentions a real short pixie style, but I shrug it off. I wonder what he's thinking. He seems only half tuned to what Daniel is saying, and more interested in how much of my tawny locks are to be shorn off.

"I think you would suit maybe shoulder length." Leila's sweet little voice breaks into my thoughts. The girl is the dictionary definition of a perky blonde. All smiles and cuteness, ample boobs, and gentle curves.

"Maybe." I pick up a strand too, twirling it as I look at it. I catch Jake watching me again and this time lock eyes. I want to know what he thinks but I don't want to openly ask his opinion.

"What's wrong with how it is?" he breaks in with a frown, creasing that pretty face.

"Jake ... Men have no clue. Woman like a drastic change every so often." Leila quips at him, with a beaming smile.

"If it's not broke, then don't fix it." Jake raises eyebrows in reply and his eyes skim my hair.

"Maybe it's not broken but can definitely be revamped. Women do like to shake it up every so often. Try on a new look." This has a comedy battle of two obviously good friends written all over it.

"It's my hair!" I point out, putting my hands up between the two of them. Jake reaches out, takes a strand and tucks it behind my ear, his eyes skimming it again as though he's thinking about something.

"I like it how it is. If you want to change it, then fine, it can always grow back."

Leila smirks, and I just laugh at him. He sounds like a boyfriend and definitely not a boss.

"Worried your girlfriend won't get you all hot and bothered with short hair, Jacob?" Leila leans over me to prod her finger in Jake's shoulder. I open my mouth to right her on the fact we're most definitely not in a relationship, but Jake leans over me, shoving Leila back.

"Shut up, wench. Emma has more sense than to let me be her boyfriend." He sounds a little more serious than I think he means too.

"Oh right, I forgot. You're just friends." The honey like way she says it, makes both Jake and I throw her agreeable fake smiles.

"I can see that," she adds sarcastically.

"Really, we are." My feeble attempt is almost ignored by her. She smiles and sighs loudly, throwing herself back on her lounger.

"Well then, you won't care if I take her to get it all shorn off then, will you?"

Jake just casts her a look that's somewhere between a frown and a glare, before turning to me, a little friendlier.

"Emma can do whatever she wants with her hair. She'll always look beautiful." He gets up and walks off, following Daniel, who has left his seat to go to the table, laden with lunch, and turns his back on us.

"Someone is not a happy little playboy today!" Leila grins and throws me a charming, feigned innocent, smile. I feel that little lurch in my stomach at his calling me "beautiful" and push it down quickly. I don't bother replying to Leila. I don't even know how to.

# Chapter 20

After lunch, Jake takes us ashore on the speedboat which is moored to the back of the yacht. He doesn't say anything again about my hair, whether I should cut it or not, and I don't bring it up. He has a car and driver waiting on land to take us anywhere we desire, and leaves us with a goodbye at the port, and orders to call him when we're returning.

He hands me a credit card which I try to push back at him but meet his death glare. I know better than to argue with that look. I slide it in my bag, knowing better than to push, he made it clear before we came here that this was all on him. That if I even mentioned paying for a single thing he would tie me up and dump me in the ocean. Jake's funny about very few things, but women paying is a strong dislike. He likes to be the traditional, chivalrous gentleman. Some may think it chauvinist, and maybe it is, but it's a Jake characteristic. Brought up in an old-fashioned Italian family paying for everything when a girl is with him is natural to him. There's no arguing with it.

I feel excited and apprehensive about a shopping spree, spending time alone with this girl I just met. I don't really hang out with women, apart from Sarah, and even then, it's been so long since we did. I don't do social outings and girly shopping days. I never did. Sarah was always more of a tomboy type; movies and baseball games.

Leila soon puts me at ease with her never-ending chatter. She catches my heart with talk of Sophie almost immediately, she only met her briefly, but I can tell that Leila will be a good, protective, older sister.

Her mother sounds amazing. A woman who adopted five children from varying backgrounds, loves and raises them all like her own, and is the motherliest woman you will ever meet, according to Leila. It is obvious she adores her.

She drags me into a couple of boutiques, swanning over rails of high price tag dresses. I don't need any more clothes, Donna has made sure of that and I already know most of the items she bought me carry tags higher in price than anything here. Jake is rather indulgent on that front.

I wonder what he'll be like as a husband, should he ever find the inclination to marry. I can see him as a spoiler of his wife, money no object and the inability to say, "No" to what she wants. The thought leaves a bitter taste in my mouth. I don't like the idea of Jake marrying some woman and doting on her with gifts and clothes.

"Here we are." Leila announces proudly as we stand in front of a classy looking building with tinted windows and potted bushes at either side of the door. It's a bit Mediterranean-twee.

"Where?" I ask, confused, looking around.

"Best salon in the Caribbean ... come and meet Andre." She smiles, a huge bright flash of perfect teeth and charm, and drags me inside the cool, air-conditioned building.

Our sandals echo on the tiled floor and there's a strong chemical smell in the air. We're greeted by a round man in a

Hawaiian shirt and bald, shaved head, he waves his arms around energetically at the sight of her before they embrace excitedly amid air kisses. It's obvious they have met before. Many times. The cooing and crooning which follow make it abundantly clear that Andre is very gay, and his personality is just infectious.

\* \* \*

An hour later I'm staring at my reflection in the mirror, unsure how to feel as Leila and Andre gush over my new hair. It is cut to shoulder length, but the natural wave of my hair has pulled it up by a couple of inches, the weight which had pulled it straighter now gone. It's lying in natural beachy waves, framing my face, he has lightened my tawny color with some sheer highlights and I look so transformed. Younger, softer, blonder.

I shake my hair, feeling it move around my face freely, it's different. So un-me. This is a huge step; cutting away my security, so that it has to hang loose around me at all times, too short to really tie up in the way, as I always did. I wonder how often I'll have Jake pull my hands out of my hair now, when I fidget.

*This was such a dumb idea.*

My face is all big eyes and pouty lips now, I look more like a vulnerable child.

"I love it ... You look super sexy yet, adorable still!" Leila grins at me in the mirror, and Andre nods in agreement. I grimace but show nothing in my face. Instead I plaster on a bright, fake smile as though I agree.

"I guess, I'll get used to it." I try for a bright sounding tone with a smile. Completely torn about what I really think as I stare back at the stranger in the mirror.

"Jake will go pie-eyed for it, trust me. You look sexy!" Leila giggles and catches my eye in the mirror, catches my blush and I try to push it away.

"Yesss, beautiful girl, now has beautiful hair. You look so very sassy." Andre cuts in with his two pennies worth and over-dramatic hand waving as he returns to fluffing my layers.

"Sassy and sexy!" Leila giggles.

"Seductive, sassy, and sexy!" Andre quips in, not to be outdone.

"Okay, we should go." I bust the little "S" word competition they've started and slide out of the chair. I stand and let him remove the cape, now seeing it with my floaty beach dress and tanned skin, it doesn't look so bad. I can see why she thinks it's cute, I mean sexy. I guess it is a little bit.

A lot more than my long locks were. I can see why they would say it's sassy, whenever I move my head it moves around in a very sassy way. It certainly suits my face, I'm just not sure. I've not cut my hair in over ten years, letting it grow out so I could always tie it up, this feels terrifying and new. The girl staring back at me is nothing like the manicured PA that graces Carrero Tower. This girl with short, wild hair and floaty dresses looks romantic and soft, and a little bit flirty. She looks like a girl I never have the courage to let anyone see. I don't know if I like it at all and my stomach is in knots with what Jake will say.

As we walk out into the sunshine, Leila fusses with my hair, fluffing it out with her fingers as I pull my head away.

"I really do love it; your hair is so nice. I love your natural curl, it's to die for."

"I just feel weird," I say tensely and look away stupidly; I feel like a child admitting it.

"Why?" she laughs. Leila is too easy to be around, she's like Jake in that she can make me lower my defenses and feel more relaxed. Maybe it's not her, maybe this is his effect on me, carrying through, even when he's not around.

"I've worn it tied up for years, to keep it neat and feel more professional ... Like this, I feel more relaxed and less precise." I laugh nervously.

*Yes, it sounds more dumb verbalizing it.*

"And that's a bad thing, because?" she giggles at me.

"I'm not used to being so casual, and laid back." I shrug, my cheeks warming with mild embarrassment.

"Jake kinda has that effect on everyone." She winks. I see genuine affection in her eyes and it makes me smile, then frown, wondering what way she thinks of him.

"He's the master of making people lower their guard." I see the look in her eye and the hidden meaning behind it. A moment of uncertainty fleeting through me. Little green-eyed monster poking out again.

"You?" I ask cautiously, an inner pang of worry that maybe Jake and she dated in the past. I really hope not.

"I didn't have a good start ... I was adopted when I was seven, my mother was a drunk and she didn't look after me too well." Leila says matter of factly. I see no shame or embarrassment in her eye, and it surprises me. She's completely open about her past, you would never know from how she is now that she even had a bad start in life.

"You, were guarded?" I laugh, unable to believe it.

"Jake's a really good friend, he's like a big brother, in so many ways to me ... He's known me since I was just an angry and troubled little girl and he made me laugh, pulled me out of myself." She links her arm through mine casually, her eyes wide and bright. I get the distinct impression Jake has never been romantic with her. I don't know how I know, but it's obvious. I sigh a little with relief.

"So, you two ... You never ...?" I stumble over my words.

Just need to be sure.

"Eww, hell no. That's gross. Jake is like a brother to me, there's literally nothing there at all. No spark—there never was. I mean; I appreciate he's good to look at, but I just don't get any butterflies from it, from him. He's just Jake, and he knows how to annoy me on so many levels, just like my brothers." She squeezes my arm, as though trying to reassure me.

"You've nothing to worry about from over here! I'm all like eww, no. Jake is not someone I would ever go there with ... And I'm like, totally hot for Richard right now." She grins, and I bat her away playfully.

"You know that's not how it is with him. He told you that already." I try and defend our relationship.

"I know, so did you ... Three times already. Thou doth protest too much." She bursts into a childish, but adorable giggle and I try for a subject change instead.

"I can't imagine you being anything other than you are now." I say, trying to steer back to our pre-Jake conversation.

"Jake introduced me to all his friends, he would let me hang out with them and come away on trips. He really took me under his wing ... I see him doing it with you, and I guess, Sophie, because my mom says she raves about both of you." Leila's smile is infectious. This makes me stop and take note.

*Is that what Jake does with me? Protects me like a little sister? No! He kissed me ... He touches me in ways that would be odd if I was his sister ...*

"Jake and I are just friends, and co-workers ... He doesn't need to take me under his wing." I say brightly, but she gives me a knowing look.

"Whether he does or doesn't, I know him. He's very protective of you. It's really kind of sweet."

"We have a weird relationship ... forced together, I guess,

and it's made us really close." I know I'm trying to sound nonchalant, but truth is, I'm beaming from her observations.

"It's more than that. You forget, I've known him since I was seven. His flirty little remarks, his almost aggressive protectiveness of you, and the way he just had to butt in over your hair. Jake doesn't do stuff like that with girls he isn't invested in." Leila stops me with a hand on my arm, turning me to face her. Even though I'm small, I stand taller than her curvy little frame.

"You're reading too much into things. I've been his PA for a year now, we really are completely platonic in every way." I can't help but feel a blush at the little white lie, platonic didn't involve sleep kissing in the slightest.

"He flirts with every girl he meets, he can't help himself. It doesn't mean anything."

"No, he doesn't. He doesn't have to make any verbal effort at all. Girls tend to throw themselves at him, literally. Jake is all about the hot looks and quick smiles, he never has to try; it's boring to witness. He rarely breaks out the cheesy come ons, or fast lines, for any girl. Until you ... with you he uses so many cringe worthy lines, he's so obvious. Emma, I think the boy has it bad. You gotta trust me on this." Leila can't stop giggling, but I shake my head.

"I know Jake better than you think, he's funny and he's over-sexed. The flirty lines are just his humor at play, because he seriously does not look at me that way. It's our banter, our friendly to and fro." I sound a little sterner than I intend.

*Who am I trying to convince—her or myself?*

She needs to stop with this crazy notion already.

"When you guys finally get over this weird denial you're both going through, I want to be maid of honor." She grins at me and wraps an arm around my waist, ushering me onward again.

"Leila, it's never going to happen." Even though the words sound true, a little thud in my heart betrays me.

"Jake will figure it out, or you will. Then we'll see." She winks cheekily.

My cell vibrates and it's a welcome distraction. I don't like how this conversation is going anymore and would love an end to it. The text is from Jake, informing us that they're heading to the mainland and to meet them at the bistro for dinner. Leila knows where we're going, so we go off in pursuit of our driver and car.

\* \* \*

Leila chatters non-stop while touching up her make-up in the car, the journey is short, and before we know it we're stepping out onto a scene from the movie *Cocktail*.

The restaurant is nice and private, it has a beach theme and little palm roofs over each table which spill out onto the sand, near the shore and are strung with fairy lights, which are twinkling now that the light is fading.

As we approach from the entrance, we spot our party immediately and make our way across the crowded sands of the outer part of the bistro. Jake has picked us an almost shore-side table. He stands up as we approach, unaware that we've arrived.

He's looking gorgeous in a white shirt and blue designer jeans over sneakers. He's talking to Daniel in a rather animated way as Daniel hops about beside his chair, demonstrating something ridiculous. They're both laughing heartily, Richard shaking his head at whatever they're talking about and his twin blushing with sheer embarrassment. It doesn't take a genius to figure out that he's the source of the joke.

Jake glances our way absent-mindedly, then does a double take, his eyes coming to lock with mine in recognition. His mouth almost drops open as he runs his eyes over my hair then back to my face.

*Holy hell.*

He's never looked at me in that way before and it sends a shiver through my abdomen, heating my pelvic floor instantly.

*Jesus, Emma.*

He smiles and walks toward me, his hand going straight to my hair and pushing a strand back off my face gently. Runs his fingers through it lightly, the motion tingling my scalp seductively; his face is close enough to feel him breathing on my low neckline of my dress, and I almost stop breathing. He knows how to command attention anyway, I can see why he doesn't need to make much verbal effort.

"I like this. A lot," he says softly, his green eyes look heavy, his pupils dilated. I guess they've already been drinking before coming to the mainland, he looks intoxicated. The overall effect is devastating.

My body is on high alert to him, like it has been since Chicago and I breathe in slowly, trying to not to openly react to his proximity. Every part of me trembling at his contact.

"Thank you." I smile and pull the hair from his hand, tucking it back with the rest of my short waves, shyly. He leans down, planting a gentle kiss on my cheek, a sensation of warmth and stomach fluttering. I quell the urge to moan at the contact.

*What the hell is going on? Leila planted seeds in my head, and now I'm all out going cuckoo.*

Grasping my hand, he breathes, "Come on," and leads me back to the table, Leila throws me a wink and grin. She looks mighty pleased with herself. All I can do is follow weakly, momentarily knocked limp with his reaction to my hair. I'm over analyzing everything, from the reaction, the cheek kiss, hand holding, and the way I'm almost falling over myself; to the look in his eyes as he turns to me to guide me to a chair. Leila has messed with my head big time and I'm uber aware of him, and I try to shake it off as I sit down.

\* \* \*

We sit outside under palm frond umbrellas and the food is amazing; we're drinking cocktails and it's helping me unwind and relax. Fruity, decorated drinks that taste like fruit juice and soda.

All three of his male friends have whistled and complimented my hair and I keep catching him looking at me as though he's seeing me for the first time. I try to ignore the frequency in which I catch his eyes on me. A small ripple running through me, with both warning, and thrill.

*Why does Jake have to be so good-looking, with eyes that can strip you bare?*

It's unnerving.

I'm starting to warm a little to Daniel Hunter now he's stopped leering at me, that is. Well, in such a sleazy way, now it's more of a male flirty look every now and then.

"What motivated this?" Daniel reaches out, scooping a strand of my hair and Jake bats his hand away.

"No touching." The scowl is somewhere between funny, and serious; Daniel just raises an eyebrow and grins.

"Sorreeeee, big man. You have to admit though, your girl does look extra hot with this new do." He winks at me.

"Ummm, thanks." I cut in blandly, watching the way Jake frowns at Daniel, then punches him lightly in the shoulder.

"She's not going to sleep with you, so you can cut out the

compliments, and the flirty crap." Huffy tone, alpha male stance going on.

"Oh, I don't know. I reckon I could charm Miss. Ander ... OWWW." Daniel squawks like an injured animal as Jake's shoulder punch is applied with a lot more aggression.

"Calm your pants, Jake. God! You'll be pissing on me next." He huffs and swipes his beer from the table.

"Don't tempt me." Jake's joke seems drier than humor and he swipes his own beer. Both men throwing a look at one another, before taking what looks like a precision planned swigs of their drinks.

"Jeez, testosterone flying, much?" Leila laughs, pulling some of the tension away.

"Men!" I offer as in way of answer, and we both raise eyebrows at one another.

"Needless to say, I was right!" Leila grins.

"About what?" Marissa cuts in with a pinched tone that makes us both look toward her with cool indulgence. She's sprawled at the table, with full cleavage on show, right in Jake's eyeline. Miracle is picking her nails at the right of her, in a similar pose.

*Ughhh.*

"That Jake would be enamored with her new short do ... That she would look sexy as hell!" Leila's triumphant tone earns her a roll of the eyes from Marissa.

"Jake's a man. He appreciates it when women try really hard to get a reaction from him," she says icily with a flick of her hair. Jake and her exchange harsh glares. I simmer, holding my tongue.

"You would know." Leila's scathing comment comes with a new tone for her. Disdain. I glance over at her and catch sight of the twins moving uneasily in their chairs as they lift their drinks to focus on that instead. Miracle lifts her head in interest, eyes gleaming with the possibility of drama.

"Emma doesn't need to vie for my attention, she already has it, and her hair is a knockout. Much like her." Jake cuts in smoothly, his cold glare fixed on Marissa, and everyone hushes up, eyes averting and a lot of fidgeting. Leila smirks.

"Man did it just get cold in here?" Daniel jumps up from his perch on the edge of the table and slaps Jake on the back.

"We need a new topic and way more booze, man."

"Couldn't agree more." Jake relaxes back, leaning to peck me on the cheek, before he turns to gesture a waiter. I feel that inward surge of smugness to match Leila's. He cut Marissa down easily. My champion.

* * *

Having Jake keeping the conversation light and funny helps a lot, he's a great socializer. He knows how to keep the chatter flowing, he's attentive and quick witted and draws everyone in, even the dreaded Marissa. All previous tension forgotten.

He revels in company and I can imagine what he was like in his teens, hanging out with friends. I wish I'd met him then and seen what adolescent Jake was like. I imagine he wouldn't be very different, only younger, maybe with a less powerful physique, less stubble. I doubt he would have liked teenage Emma, though.

The cocktails come regularly and soon I'm feeling warm and floaty, I've even managed to carry out a coherent conversation with Leila and Richard, despite the swaying, we've talked books and movies and the more time I spend with this girl, the more I like her.

I see Jake watching us and he smiles, a hint of affection in his eyes. He likes that I like Leila, I guess. For him, I realize, it's a first, he's never seen me warm to women, in general, especially not around him, he must think I don't like my own gender.

Marissa watches me coolly from the other side of the table, flanked by Miracle, who looks bored, both only talking when the men direct conversation their way. I get the impression they don't like Leila, me, or each other.

*Suits me fine. I don't like her in the slightest, or the hawk eye way she watches Jake's every move.*

Jake hauls me up to dance when the band comes out and it's then I'm fully aware of how drunk I am. I'm giggling as I try to dance with him, a lot of him holding me up, keeping me from falling into other people. He's laughing and picks me up several times to place me back on my wedge sandals, persevering with my atrocious dance partnering. Flirty Jake is back, now he's relaxed with way too much alcohol.

"Your moves are terrible when you're plastered, shorty." He spins me around, catching me from the back and pulls me against him. Our hips swaying in time and his arms firmly around me. It feels sexy yet still safe. Cuddling, yet in tune to music.

"Shhhh. I'm doing just fine." I slur playfully.

"Sure, you are. The second I let go, you'll face palm the deck. I'm all that's keeping you upright," he laughs softly.

"I'm sure I wouldn't ... You're exaggerating my drunkenness." I purr demurely, turning in his arms and giving him a gentle chest shove.

"Let me go and see."

Jake lifts his hands with a shrug, and a smile, and steps back. That look of "know it all" all over his face. I attempt a dance sway and stumble dramatically.

*Crap.*

His quick reflexes mean he catches me before I kiss ground and he laughs at me instead. Hauling me back to that chiseled chest and hard abdomen.

"You were saying?"

"Shut up." I warn, leaning back to throw a threatening finger his way.

"Not another word, Carrero."

He motions the locking of a key over his lips, and pretends to throw it away, before casting me a wink and then he pulls me back in for another slow groove. Another bout of my terrible balancing act.

After another song, he gives up on us dancing and leads me back with a grin. I throw that warning look and almost challenge him to mention my drunkenness again. He just laughs, tugging me along by the hand and pulls me closer, so he can put an arm around me instead.

Back at the table, Jake practically carrying me with the arm round my waist, the men are in the middle of some heated story. Daniel is sitting up on the back of the chair with his feet up on the seat. They're laughing and joking about something mid-conversation when we approach, and don't stop to acknowledge us at all. Jake slides his arm from around my waist and throws it casually around my shoulders instead, as we stand to listen. Resting on me like it's the most normal thing in the world.

He hands me my drink from the table, before taking his beer and turning his full attention to the men. All on their feet now and crowded by one side of the table; Leila is resting in the crook of Richard's arm, gazing up at him adoringly.

I can't help but stare at Jake's profile as he listens intently, of all the men here, he's by far the best looking and most sexually appealing of the group. In fact, the whole restaurant.

*I need to stop thinking this way. Bad alcohol, bad!*

"Yeah, so Jake's like, I'm sure we can make it ... and he goes speeding off on his fucking jet ski, right in ... Doesn't give a fuck." They all burst out laughing and look toward him as Daniel pats his back. I can't focus on anything except the way Marissa is watching him. She's zoned in on his every feature, biting her lip sensually, and trying to seduce him with her eyes.

*What the hell? Whore.*

It's obvious she's a lot more drunk now than she was prior to our going to the dance floor. He seems to be avoiding her gaze, but every so often I catch them connect and he looks away. I feel him tense every time, and it alarms me on so many levels.

*I want to know what's going on, if these looks mean anything, if it's just irritation on his part or if he has reason to be mad at her. Earlier, I got the distinct impression that he didn't much like her. But now?*

Vincent, her man of the moment, seems oblivious. I resign myself to the fact I'm imagining it, that he's merely willing her to stop eye raping him. I'm being paranoid and stupidly jealous, even though I have no right, but it still causes me to watch them a little too closely.

"What choice did I have?" Jake cuts in.

"Daniel would have had us sleep out there at that rate, not that he would have minded. Daniel's always trying to get in the sack with me, the boy's still trying to deny his feelings." He jests and swigs at his beer.

"It's kind of heartbreaking to watch him suffer ... Unrequited love." Richard breaks in, stifling a grimace as Daniel slaps his back.

"Fuck you. Both of you."

"You know when you know ... Right?" Vincent throws a wink at Daniel and three of the four men burst out laughing, Daniel rolls his eyes and gives them the finger.

"Tried so damn hard to let him down gently, he's just too

sensitive." Jake ruffles Daniels hair.

"I've caught him sobbing into his Hagen Das a few times when you stood him up, Jakey." Richard shoves Daniel in the ribs playfully.

"He stole my *Endless Love* CD when you missed his birthday bash last year. Perfect crying anthems on there." Leila quips in, throwing a huge smile at Jake, yet avoiding Hunter completely.

"I swear to god, you guys better stop with this shit. Even if I was that way inclined, I wouldn't jump Carrero's bones. I know where he's been, I have standards." All three men look at Jake with eyebrow wiggles, and he only sneers at them.

"Umm, I think I've way higher standards than any of you three." He defends himself with a frown.

"Questionable." Leila throws him a disbelieving look.

"But you've improved a lot." She then smiles at me, concealing nothing. A big hearty, wink type of smile.

"Leave her out of this." Jake warns, squeezing me a little too tightly. I haven't been able to help laughing along with all of them, but things just shifted tone and Jake feels suddenly tense.

"You know when you know, right?" Vincent smirks Jake's way. I try and ignore the way all three men seem to look at Jake for a split, perfectly timed moment, all three with raised eyebrows and smirking expressions.

"Daniel certainly seems to think so." Jake makes kissing noises, releases me to haul his friend into a head lock and plaster his cheek with wet, noisy kisses.

"Fuck off, you creep." Daniel fights as everyone laughs. Everyone except Marissa. Her straight faced, bitchy eyes have been watching with nothing but boredom this whole time, she seems to change tactic as soon as the men settle down and Jake comes back and puts his arm back around me.

## Jake & Emma

Marissa pouts at Jake sexily, and I feel myself bristle. *Back off, Señorita, get a grip and take a hint!*

"Admit it, you've been planning the Hunter-Carrero wedding since you were just a little girl. It's kind of sweet really." Jake prods Daniel with his beer bottle and receives two fingers on one hand and one on the other as a response.

"You're riding dangerously close to a Hunter free existence. Then we'll see which dude is crying into his Hagen Das. We all know that Mr. Smooth Carrero has the biggest man crush on me." Daniel picks up a beer, mock throws his hair back like a woman and flutters his eyelashes.

"In your dreams, pretty boy. I'm hoping for a threesome with the twins." Jake winks at Vincent and Richard who throw on matching "Eww" faces. Everyone laughs, even Marissa this time. Then she goes and ruins the atmosphere by biting on her lip suggestively and making direct eye contact with Jake. She's practically screaming, "Take me."

I lay my head into his chest softly, unsure why I feel like I should be sending her messages. Jake just seems to adjust his hold, so I can move closer and lay my head against his neck more comfortably. His arm coming further around me, he switches his beer bottle to his left hand, so it hangs in front of me. His other takes my empty cocktail glass from me and lays it down. He doesn't falter, just continues talking to his men folk as though my snuggling closer is the most natural thing in the world for us. I listen to the steady thud of his heart under his shirt and the way he feels under my cheek. None of the group seems to even acknowledge the way we are cuddled up together or the way he slides his arm lower to make me get even closer.

Now they're talking about some trip last summer I've not got any interest in, as soon as I realize that Marissa had been there too and not with a beau in tow, in the story version.

Again, a look on her face aimed at Jake, and I assume it's meaning is sexual.

*Had she been his hook up on that trip? God please, tell me no.*

I shake the thought away.

The waitress comes with a tray, laying down another round of drinks on the canopied table. Jake hands me a fresh cocktail with his free hand, his mouth lingers close to my temple a little longer than necessary as though he's watching me, or simply feeling my hair against his face. Maybe I'm imagining it.

The cocktail tastes amazing; I've no idea what he ordered for me this time, but it has a tropical coconut taste and I could drink it like juice, he has a knack for buying me drinks that I really like, always varying them so I don't get sick of the taste. He knows me a little too well.

He lets go of me as he bends down to look at a picture on Hunter's cell, that he's holding out, some past memory they're all discussing, and I feel strangely lost. His sudden departure from my body and the realization that I was only happily listening into this group the way I was because of him. He always grounds me, makes me comfortable, wherever we are.

I tense as I see Marissa look up at him with doe-eyed innocence and a suggestive part of the lips. She's seriously ruining my calm. I see him pause and catch her eye, before he turns his head to me with a quick smile and straightens back up, returns his arm around my shoulders, this time, though, he pulls me in firmly and kisses me on the side of my face quickly and gently. I feel the instant rush of warmth and satisfaction at his touch and equally at Marissa's frosty look. I guess he's sending her a message, telling her to back off and I'm reaping the rewards. I can't say I mind. Glad to be back in his arms, back to safe and warm.

"You're very quiet ... Want to go back to the boat?" he asks softly, for my ears only. He locks eyes with me, the restaurant around us fading away.

"Yes, please, I'm so tired, it's been a long day." I smile, but I know it should be, "I'm actually really drunk and I'm probably going to fall over or pass out." Truth is, I just want to get far away from Marissa and her silent messages across the table. She's like a thorn I can't pull out.

"Oooh, party on the boat." Leila chants and jumps up, impressively bouncing her boobs, all male eyes immediately follow, and it causes me to dig Jake in the ribs. He gives me an apologetic shrug and wink.

*Casanova Carrero, what will I do with you?*

Men and the inability to watch a decent cleavage, pass them by.

# Chapter 21

As much as I wanted to go to bed, or lay down, the full sway of my drunkenness hits me, fueling my desire to join the party. The lights on the deck glow beautifully in the dark and the thrum of music from speakers give it a romantic vibe. Leila has a tray of cocktails and they look good. It's then I find out she spent one summer here as a barmaid and has a wealth of knowledge on tasty drinks; despite a super-rich family, it seems Leila is pretty self-sufficient at times. She loves nothing more than sharing anecdotes of her past experiences and she has a humorous way of reliving the past.

"I should stop, I think I've had enough." I try to reject Leila's push of another drink, now that I'm barely upright anymore, and should probably sit down. I've overdone it way more than I intended and now it's dark and the boat is moving all around me.

"Hush now, we're on vacation ... Party, party, party!" She grins and tries once more.

"End up comatose, or throwing up in my own shoes, you mean?" I sigh and sway, grabbing the rail for support.

"Your loss, sweet cheeks." She turns to swing her

impressive booty across toward Richard, with drinks in hand.

Jake is sprawled over one of the loungers and he's been hitting the booze, lazily watching us dance and chatter, occasionally joining in the conversation. His manner is slightly more relaxed than normal, if that is even possible, and despite seeming mostly okay, I can tell he's in the top limits of his drunkenness.

I wonder who'll be putting whom to bed tonight, and it makes me giggle; he looks inviting on the double lounger and I have the urge to curl up beside him and sleep right there.

"Come, *Bambino*!" Jake's eyes meet mine with a beckoning finger wiggle before he pats the lounger beside him suggestively. I try to walk demurely to the lounger next to him, but end up sprawled over the top of him after connecting with a chair leg. Falling in the most ungraceful manner.

"Crap." I breathe as I feel his arms move around me, he shifts so my weight ends up beside him on the lounger, instead of on top of him, keeping me in his arm and laying us both back. The lounger is comfy and warm from his body heat in the now cooler night air.

"Bit drunk there, Miss. Anderson?" he's laughing at me, sounding boyish.

Just charming. "Sof course not"

*What?*

Okay, so maybe, I'm a lot drunk.

He laughs into my hair, his mouth against my temple as he slides his other arm across my neck and shoulder and pulls me against him. Cuddling me in easily.

"Glad to see you letting go." He smiles, almost nose to nose with me. His warm breath on my face, heavy scent of alcohol; it gives me the overwhelming sense of intimacy and I feel my body tingle.

"I think falling on top of your boss is more than letting

go." I laugh, relaxing to the sensation and surrendering to the sway around me, regaining the control on my vocabulary, even if it's slurring.

"I'm not your boss for the next two weeks." He winks. That handsome face close enough to touch.

"Okay, I shall rephrase ... Falling on top of your temporary not boss, is overdoing it." I giggle again, I feel so light and free and a little bit silly. My hair blows gently across my face, yet he strokes it back, lingering, playing with its new short waves. I think he's more than a little obsessed with the haircut, and it makes me grin. The sensation of having my hair played with is addictive.

"Do you need me to put you to bed?" he asks, still focusing on twirling my hair, his face so close I can almost lick him without moving.

*Stop it, Emma!*

"Do I not need to put *you* to bed?" I slur again and bask in his laughter, he finds that highly amusing. I want to wrap myself up in that laugh, it's so inviting.

"I'm sure I can handle way more alcohol than you, tiny."

"I'm not so sure, I haven't seen you walk yet." I point at him with a drunk air jab. Being drunk can be pretty amazing.

"I'm sure after seeing you try that, it proves you're worse than me." He stays smiling down at me, finally letting my hair go. Shifting his body weight and making the bed dip lightly. The chatter of the others nearby has droned down to a background hum and I'm barely even aware of them anymore. It feels like it's just the two of us.

"I like your dimples when you smile." I prod his face. Focusing on his features a little too closely, distracted by them.

"And there she is." He grins at me.

"There who is?" I ask in confusion, a frown creasing my

forehead.

"Drunk Emma ... How are you doing? ... I missed you, baby." His dimples indent with the huge smile he's giving me.

"You missed drunken Emma?" I ask blinking suspiciously.

"I did."

"Why? Do you like her more than me?" I pout with sad eyes, not even smiling when he laughs at me and shakes his head. A childish surly mood instantly brewing.

"You are drunken Emma ..."

"No. I'm not ... I'm just Emma ... Drunken Emma is ..." I'm confused and I've no idea what I'm saying, he's laughing at me again and it's infuriating.

"Why are you laughing? I'm being serious!" I scowl at him and pull my hands down to cross over my chest. He prods my nose playfully.

"Both Emmas are you, they just choose to come out at different times. You're cute when you pout." He prods me in the face lightly again, before pinching my nose, like I'm some sort of juvenile.

"Why do you like her more?" I slap his hand away. I'm being sulky, and I can tell by the humorous glint in his eyes he's finding me amusing. It does nothing to help my somber state of mind on this topic. If anything, it just adds to it.

"How can you not love this version of you?" He wraps his arms tighter around me, pulling me closer and planting a kiss on my cheek. Snuggling his head into the crook of my neck and maneuveeuvring my body to mold into his a little better.

"Pffft ... I don't love her then." I try and wriggle free.

"Because I do?" he has a permanent smile on his face now, as alluring as it is, I'm still frowning.

"Yes!"

"That makes no sense."

"Yes, it does ... If you like her so much, she must be a leggy bimbo." I huff.

"I already told you, I don't actually like leggy bimbos, Emma." He stares at me, nose to nose. His smile vanishes, his eyes becoming serious and dark. His focus moves across my face and rests on my mouth for a moment. A slight frown, a chew of his bottom lip and he looks back at my eyes with a sigh.

"I don't believe you." I almost gulp at the nervous reaction I'm having to the closeness.

"Well, that's your prerogative." He smiles softly this time, his mouth moving dangerously close to me, achingly close; there's a noise on deck and we glance over to see Daniel stripping off Miracle's clothes in a rather smutty fashion. Jake frowns and pulls me up quickly to his side by the lounger, breaking that moment of tension.

"Time for bed ... I know what Daniel's like. Show-time equals go time!" his voice sounds grim, tight, all humor gone as he hurries me.

"What's he like? What do you mean, "Show-time"?" I honestly don't know and as I'm being pulled up like a child, I can't help but stare at the group.

"He likes kinky sex, he's an exhibitionist, doesn't matter if you're male or female; he'll try and pull you in, he has no qualms about fucking in front of an audience." He hauls me to my feet as I inhale sharply, staring over at the man and his bimbo porn star, in shock.

*That's so gross. I hope Leila has the sense to get out quick.*

I see Richard and Leila get up and move to loungers, away from Daniel. Thank goodness.

"Will you join in?" I squeak in surprise, a sudden swift knock inside my stomach. I don't like the thought of Jake doing that, with them, with anyone.

"No, it's not my thing, Emma." Jake narrows his eyes at me, a deep frown on his forehead. I feel that relief wash over me as he pulls me by the hand, a small tug to break my focus on Daniel.

"You said you did it on your dad's boat when you were younger ... group ... stuff." I accuse shyly, thinking back to an old conversation a long while ago.

"Who do you think was at the root of that?" he raises an eyebrow toward Daniel and pulls me with him toward the stairs leading to lower deck. I don't argue, just follow.

"So, you liked it then?" I ask, looking back once more as Marissa gets up and begins a slow strip tease, her eyes following us. Jake ignores her, and I feel a wave of happiness at this fact; he shrugs and puts his arm around me as he leads me down the stairs slowly and carefully, so I don't fall to the next floor. On the second to bottom step, he pulls tight and lifts me off my feet to the floor.

"I was young, it's just sex. I was pretty much partying and pissing my dad off at every turn." I stumble on the carpeted floor and he rights me, pulling me close. I notice him sway a little as we head through the door to the internal hall of the boat. I'm glad he's leaning against me, I'm finding it so much harder to walk than I realized.

"You don't do group sex anymore?" I hiccup.

*Why the hell am I so obsessed with this topic? I don't even want to know any of this.*

He smiles at me, showing those perfect white teeth and devastating smile and I'm instantly distracted.

"I like your smile." I say, alcohol very effectively removing my internal filter again.

"No, I don't, and I like that you like my smile, shorty." He stops and pushes me against the wall to steady me, he pulls his cell from his pocket, swipes the screen, checks who's calling and pushes it back from where he produced it.

"I like when you laugh like that." He glances up at me and it's then I realize I've been giggling.

*Where did that come from?*

"Like what?" I ask innocently, still unable to stop grinning. Maybe it has something to do with the fact he has my body pressed to the wall with his and he feels every bit like my idea of a good dream.

"Unguarded ... I like drunk Emma." He pulls me back off the wall and leads me to my room, disappointment flitting through me.

"I like drunk Emma too." I sigh, following him as he opens the door, his hand still grasping mine. She gets to touch Jake in ways sober Emma doesn't.

"I thought you said you didn't?" he frowns at me with a confused smile. Pulling me through my bedroom door.

"I was jealous ... You like her way too much." Now he's laughing at me again, only this time it's deep and heartfelt as though I've said the most hilarious thing. I pout at him, annoyed that he finds everything I say so funny.

"You're the same Emma ... No reason to be jealous, *Bambino*." He calms his laughing, pulls me to the base of my bed, letting me go, sits me down, and pulls my sandals off my feet easily. I like when he takes care of me like this, as though I'm something more to him than just his PA.

"Nooo, you like one more than the other." I sigh. He smiles up at me and moves closer so we're nose to nose, him bent down at my knees, his hand comes to my hair and ruffles it, toying with its new shortness.

*He really is infatuated with my new haircut. Best idea ever!*

"I like both versions of you, in different ways, equally." He sighs, keeping close. The lights are off in the room and the only light is from the moon shining in the porthole window beside us. It's so intimate and romantic.

"What do you mean 'different ways'?" I'm inquisitive, being drunk seems to make me crave for knowledge. He sighs, running a hand across my face lightly and moving my hair to tuck behind my ear, sending a million tingles across my skin. He chews his lip in that childish way he has when he's trying to think out an answer before he speaks. He has no idea how much it makes me ache to bite his lip too.

"PA Emma is cool and capable, and she's the best assistant I've ever had, she's funny and sharp and she's good at what she does. I like PA Emma." He nods to himself as though rattling off a tick list. Finished with my shoes, he kneels up, so even though he's still on the floor his head is towering over me.

"You like her in an employee-employer way?" I reach up and toy with his spiky hair, seeing as he keeps messing mine up, he raises his eyebrows in surprise, but only smiles and lets me continue.

"Yes and no ... I just like her, because she's *her*." His eyes come to rest on mine, distracting me from his hair. It feels good.

"And drunk Emma?"

"I'm a little infatuated with drunk Emma, if I'm being honest." He pulls my hand down and straightens up.

"You are? Why?" I sulk at both his answer and his removal of my fingers.

"Because she's fun ... She doesn't guard what she says ... or does." He nods toward my fingers.

"She giggles and lets her hair down."

"So do most of your leggy boobs." I sulk at being compared to one of them.

*Except am I not the one doing the comparing?*

I'm confused.

"They're not the same. Not even close, *Bella*. They don't have the other side to her ... That's what I mean by "I like you both". One can't exist without the other. I wouldn't like there to be only one and not the other."

"So, you like my split personality? A lover of the cray cray." I grin playfully, motioning in circles at my temples and cross my eyes. He smiles and moves another hair from my face. Seems short hair equals messy hair that clings to your face at every opportunity. Not that having him stroke it away is a bad thing, it's a very, very good thing.

"It's not split though, there's glimpses of both versions all the time, just one chooses to dominate ... I see drunk Emma sometimes in PA Emma, when she occasionally relaxes too."

"Maybe she doesn't know how to relax all the time." I confess, with a conspiratorial wink.

"I think she's scared." He answers thoughtfully.

"Why?" I watch him carefully, I want to know why he thinks this third person me is scared. I'm curious as to how he sees her. Me.

He stands up, his hands move across his chest, he looks too sexy standing like that, touchable and I look away. I'm conscious of the fact my head is now level with his crotch. I'll definitely not look. Well, not for long, so that he doesn't notice.

"Because letting her guard down means she lets go of a little bit of control, and she likes to hold it all together. Letting go makes her vulnerable, leaves her exposed, and that's worse than death for her." His voice is steady and low. My breath catches in my throat, I feel a tug in my chest of surprise and a little emotion that he really seems to know me.

"If I'm vulnerable, people can hurt me ... Men can hurt me." I whisper into the darkness of my room, a little too

# Jake & Emma

honest in my drunken stupor. I feel his eyes on me as he bends so his forehead meets mine and presses our noses together, an awkward position for him but the cutest move I've ever seen him make; there's something insanely tender about it. I glance up at him.

"I'd never let anyone hurt you, Emma." He breathes against me. His hands coming down to hold his weight on the mattress at either side of my thighs. It brings his mouth so close to mine, we're sharing air.

"What if you couldn't stop them?" I sound young and scared, suddenly serious.

"I'd always stop them." He promises, with conviction in his voice. I sink forward wanting to feel the safety in his arms that I get when he's around me. Reaching up so I can wrap my arms around his neck and press us together more firmly.

"You won't always be around." I say quietly.

"I'm always around, if you haven't noticed." The breathlessness of his tone urges me to pull my face away and stay level with his eyes.

"I guess."

"Let go, Emma ... Trust me to look after you ... If not long-term then for these two weeks at least. Trust me to protect you."

"I'll try," I whisper. Not wanting to part from this intimate position. My heart bursting with the tenderness I feel for him right now, the sensual way this feels.

"Good girl." His arms come around me, pulling me up to him slightly, for a gentle embrace, lifting me from the bed.

"Don't say that to me." I pause mid-hold, causing him to halt. My voice childish as it hits me somewhere in the gut.

"Why?"

*I don't know.*

Jake called me it before, and I felt like he was talking to a puppy. Maybe it's calling me "girl" ... Ray called me girl. Stupid, slutty, cock teasing, little girl. I always hated it.

"Just don't ..." I say as he smiles and slowly pulls me the rest of the way to cuddle me; I'm on my feet against him. It's unexpected and so gentle and I'm instantly sagging into his body greedily. When he loosens his hold to let me go, I stumble backward, grabbing onto him, but the sheer suddenness of it catches him off guard. His own drunken stupor causing a loss of balance. He leans forward to steady me, losing his footing too.

Somehow, we both end up falling flat on the bed. Him on top of me, nose to nose, and laughing like fools at the awkwardness of our ungraceful collapse. His face so close, like the night we shared a bed, his mouth too inviting. Everything within me clenching tight and hungry for him now that his body is fully connected to mine in such an intimate pose. His lips too perfect to be ignored.

I'm drunk and I'm going to regret it so badly when I sober up, but in the mind of a drunken, wanton female, what I'm doing seems totally fine. I throw my mouth against his in a rather satisfying manner, soft lips hungrily connecting, suddenly on fire. Aching to feel his lips on mine, like that night in Chicago.

My mouth and his are entwined in seconds, he doesn't hesitate. Our tongues are most certainly finding pleasure at meeting once again with his hands in my hair and around my throat, softly holding me still. I'm rejoicing in the feel of his muscular body on top of mine, a little wave of smug pride. It feels right in every kind of way, male hardness and soft feminine curves entangling.

This feels good, too good, and the fact he's just as into this as I am has me ravenous. Panting as my heart pounds from my chest, this feels better than good.

*I should really listen to him more when he says let go.*

His hands find mine and he presses them against the mattress beside my head, pulling away to catch his breath momentarily, his eyes dark with dilated pupils, so close.

*Don't stop please, don't stop.*

He looks at me for a millisecond, his face in shadow so I can't read his expression clearly, pondering what we're doing, then drops to kiss me harder. I'm breathing hard and fast, this could go one of two ways. Right now, that giddy head is throwing the sensible option off the boat.

I don't care about the consequences, I want him more than I've ever wanted anyone in my life. Inhibitions gone, mind fuzzy with alcohol, for once just following instinct and ignoring my brain. He pulls away and kisses me again, this time, sucking my bottom lip seductively. I almost lose all control right then. His hands around my face, he's putting all effort into kissing me, and caressing my tongue with a fire that could wipe out cities.

Jake knows how to kiss, he kisses like a guy who has learned the art of making a woman pliable under his skilled attentions. I am no different, body and soul screaming for more. He tastes like alcohol and tropical juice, mouth soft yet agonizingly sensual. I can't help but tremble with every movement he's making. Every slight tensing of his muscles, and lines of his body against mine, is beyond sexy. My hands are exploring his upper torso, those hard, taut muscles.

I'm probably the most inexperienced girl he's ever had under him, he makes me crave him. His mouth on mine feels like every good thing I've ever known, his taste, his caress, his smell; it's intoxicating, the best kind of drug. He's making love to my mouth, pulling me further into erotica, my body aching for more. I'm clinging to him and trying to pull him further into me.

He responds with equal fervor, his hands moving to skim the side of my breast. Holding his weight up so he can shift against me harder, bringing his groin to my pelvis and parting my legs, never breaking contact with his mouth; his body all over me in the most satisfying way. I'm almost on fire with the longing I feel in every cell of my body; I'm so ready to let him take me in every way. We just fit so perfectly, everything coming together easily and in unison.

There's a mass bang in the hall behind us, we had left the door wide open. There's lots of hysterical screaming as the door fills with the dark looming figure of a man and Jake pulls away to turn and look.

"What the f—?" Jake sounds shocked, yet angry, maybe like me he's not so happy about the interruption. He's still on top of me, braced on his arms, but our bodies are still entangled.

"Jake? Jake?" The voice at the door sounds hysterical. I think it's one of the twins.

"What is it?" He snaps.

"It's Daniel ... He fell off the boat ... We can't find him."

# Chapter 22

I'm grasping the rail and leaning over, scanning the dark sea. The ship's crew are out on small boats searching the water and Jake's already dove in and swam back twice. I'm feeling hysterical about the fact he's this drunk and yet swimming to find his friend in an almost pitch-black ocean. Watching the water with fear in my throat, holding my breath with every dive he takes and willing them to find him so Jake will get out of the water. I've never been so terrified in my life.

"He's here, Mr. Carrero." Yells one of the crew from the boat, and I see them with flash lights hauling a lifeless body into the boat under the moonlight.

*Oh my god.*

\* \* \*

I'm sitting in my room and I'm tired and cold, I haven't slept. Last night was hell, Daniel was airlifted to a hospital on the mainland, he's okay but it gave all of us a huge scare and the atmosphere left behind is silent and tense.

Jake has been gone most of the night and I'm left reeling

from what happened.

Daniel being given CPR by Jake, then his coughing up tons of water and coming around. The drama at thinking Jake was going to drown every time he dove under, all I could think was how drunk he was. How terrified I was, counting the seconds until I would see him surface again, and the fear whenever he went back down.

The craziness when he left in a flurry of paramedics, and helicopter turbulence hovering over the yacht; I barely got to say two words to him, or even check how he was.

Finally, what we were doing when Vincent raised the alarm that Hunter was in the water. What Jake and I had been doing! Where that had been leading, and just how far down that road to having sex with him I had been. I can't bear thinking about it.

I'm sobering up, and it's hard to digest how close I came to ruining all of this.

*How could I contemplate even doing it?*

I need to get off this boat and get some distance between us. I need to claw some perspective back and sort my head out. This is getting ridiculous, my inability to separate my hormones from rational thought when he is in proximity. I did this! I'm the one who made a move and kissed him, we were both drunk, but I'm the one who initiated it. Hunter maybe did a dumb thing and almost got himself killed, but he inadvertently stopped me from making the biggest mistake of my life. Jake doesn't look at sex as any big deal, but I do. I've only slept with two people in my life and that was years ago, and I was pushed into it.

*He would have been able to brush it off to a drunken night, but would I?*

I have a feeling that would have killed me more than being fired.

*What's wrong with me?*

I get up and head to the boat deck in a bid to stop thinking. In the early morning sun it's warm but not overly so, and I'm still wearing last night's dress. I like the fact it still smells of him and right now I miss him so much. I can't stop obsessing over him: how he is, when he's coming back. This is exactly why I need to get my head together, this kind of stupid thinking. I'm seriously losing it over my boss.

I lay down on the double sun lounger on deck, sinking into the softness of the cushioned mattress, the sun has warmed it enough to give me some much-needed heat. I'm beyond exhausted, fatigue washing over me and leaving me feeling detached.

*Why haven't I slept?*

I know why. Jake left with Daniel, wet and ruffled hair, in sweats and a T-shirt, a towel round his shoulders. He looked— primal. Devastated. I never really understood the bond between him and Daniel Hunter, but it exists; they're like oil and vinegar, yet they really are best friends. I guess, in his past, he was more like Hunter than I want to admit, I'm glad Jake is nothing like him now.

It was that inability to touch him, stop him, and check he was okay that has left me pacing and restless.

I doze, finally, warmed by the rising sun, listening to the noise of a boat returning across the soft lapping waves and it makes me glance up. Startling me from the first stages of slumber.

*Is it? Oh my god, it's them ... He's coming back.*

I feel my heart lurch and I'm suddenly shy and afraid, despite my longing to see him back and safe.

We kissed last night. I mean properly kissed, a two-way, no objections, and taking it further than just a moment of madness, kind of kiss.

A real make-out session. I've never been kissed like that before Jake. I had never really been kissed by someone I wanted to kiss me. I never wanted to be kissed, yet with him it's like a primal urge. I almost lost control, I have never known a man could ignite such flame, with something so simple.

*Do I get up and greet him, or do I stay here and hope he bypasses me?*

I don't want him to bypass me. I don't know if I want to face him either. I feel ashamed, embarrassed, and uneasy. He'll be sober now.

*What will he say? What will he think about last night?*

I stay still as I hear him get on the boat, sensitive to every tiny noise and movement. His low voice as he quietly converses with the men, even that simple sound, making my heart pound through my chest. I hear the engine thrum as it moves away; I feel like my heart is going to explode through my chest and for a second, I waver, wondering if he will even come up here or head straight to his room. I wonder if he's even thought about what we were doing last night at all.

*God, this is agony!*

"Emma?" his voice pulls my gaze to him, he sounds husky and exhausted and my stomach lurches.

*I guess that answered my questions.*

"Hey." I smile shyly from my position on the lounger as he walks toward me intently, he doesn't hesitate but slides down beside me and lays down with a tremendous sigh. His body taking up a vast amount of room beside me. He's close enough that our bodies touch delicately in places, but not deliberately. He smells good, of sea and sun and him. If I could bottle that smell and keep it forever, I would. My body is tingling at the proximity, but I'm holding my breath, waiting. He's on his front and he's buried his face in the crook of his arms.

I glance over at his profile and see how exhausted he really is. For once, his hair has nothing in it, and it's the first time I've seen it au natural. It's ruffled like he has a hint of curl in it and looks boyish and sexy. I like that he keeps a short back and sides, it showcases his neck and jaw, but there's enough hair on top to run your fingers through.

*Not that I should.*

It's thick hair; dark and unruly, a bit like him and the temptation to touch it is overwhelming.

I watch him for a minute, wondering what he's thinking. His eyes are closed, and he seems like he's fallen asleep, maybe he has. I don't blame him. He was up all night, in a cold sterile hospital after the drama of diving into the ocean, frantically searching for his friend and being whisked away in a helicopter ambulance, in a flurry of chaos before dawn.

"I'm still awake." It's as if he's listening to my thoughts. I feel my eyes widen and I glance away, I don't respond.

*Crap. How does he do that?*

Maybe he could feel me staring, I know that I'm always aware of his eyes on me. He reaches out an arm, shifting his position slightly, and drapes it across my waist loosely. He pulls me closer so our bodies mold in the best way they can and brings his face closer to my shoulder. Still, his eyes are closed, I've literally stopped breathing and I think my heart skips at least three beats. The touch is beyond good, but the fear inside of me is notching up into frantic worry.

"You smell good." His nose is against the naked skin at my shoulder, where my dress strap stops, his touch burning through me, igniting some of last night's flame. I need to push it down and shove it away fast, before I make another stupid mistake.

"Thanks," I mutter, really trying to calm my racing thoughts. I'm tense as hell. I need to relax. I must be emanating all sorts of crazy anxiety, but he smiles against my shoulder and I cannot only see it, but feel it, the delicate, soft brush of his face as it moves. The slight scratch of the stubble of his jaw on my soft skin.

*God!*

"Are you ever going to just learn to let go when you're sober, Miss. Anderson?" His voice is lazy from tiredness, the change in its normally clear tone is devastatingly sexy.

"What do you mean?" I blanch.

"I can feel you ... Stiffer than a board ...Why so formal after last night?" He smiles again, tickling the skin at my shoulder with his mouth. I wasn't expecting this kind of conversation, especially after the kitchen kiss. I want the kitchen kiss conversation, the "sorry we were drunk, it never happened" speech. I've no clue what to say, so I swallow and chew my lip, I'm twisting my hair; practically ripping the strand from my scalp. He reaches up, still with closed eyes and tugs my hand out of hair. He has that annoying habit perfected nowadays, he can even do it when not looking.

"Relax, I only want to sleep," he mumbles, returning his arm to its previous throw across my waist.

"Stop thinking and sleep with me ... You look tired." He sounds gruff.

I glare at the side of his face, hating his ability to read me.

*Why did I ever let my boss get so goddamned close?*

I know, because since I took this damn job he's practically forced me to live with him. I'm at his side every second of my waking life, and now it seems he wants me there unawakened too. The betrayal of my own body, reacting to his, has set me off in a weird mood, irritation rising.

"I'm not tired," I huff and slide out of his grasp, diving off the lounger.

"I'm going for a swim." To cool myself off and put some

much-needed distance between us. I catch his movement from the corner of my eye, he lifts his head and looks at me walking to the stairs, then lays back down.

"Don't drown ... I don't have the energy for a repeat of last night." He's already making jokes about Daniel, I guess that means Hunter really is going to be fine after all. I feel guilty for not even asking him, but right now I feel pissed off. I don't even know why. I throw him a shady look and head to my room for a bikini.

\* \* \*

The water feels amazing, it's cooler than yesterday, because of the early hour and even though I'm tired, I feel a little rejuvenated. I love the ocean, the peace it brings over me is unparalleled to anything I've ever felt, maybe because there are no oceans in my past. No childhood traumas in the sea.

I eventually haul myself back onto the boat, along the lower floor and to my bedroom, to dry and get dressed. I notice as I pass, Jake's room, which is next door to mine, has his door ajar. It was closed this morning, he must have come inside. I peek into the darkened room. I can make out his still form in the bed, the heavy, calm breathing indicating he's asleep and I suddenly feel emotional.

*My Sexy Jake, my hot friend, stroke, whatever he is; he ignites some maternal urge in my belly when he looks so still and peaceful.*

I can almost make out his face in the dark; he's just so damned cute when he's asleep like this. Irresistible in a completely different way to his wakened self, vulnerable and young. He sleeps in a way I would expect him to; sexily sprawled over the whole bed, taking ownership, cushions strewn, and sheets tangled in his limbs. No wonder he wrapped himself around me in Chicago. He's a bed hogger. He's face down and his arms are sprawled, letting his fingers hang over the edge of the mattress, laid diagonally from corner to corner. He's in his sweats and T-shirt, despite the heat and I feel a tug of disappointment at not glimpsing some naked flesh. Something childish about that spectacle as though he came in and literally flopped down to sleep in any way he landed. I close the door gently and head to my room to get changed.

\* \* \*

Breakfast on deck is amazing after the swim, pancakes and syrup, with a fruit cocktail. We have a cook on the ship's crew, who's only too willing to throw food our way whenever we beckon. I like this perk of being with a super-rich guy, being with Jake. Wherever we go, I'm always well fed and never have to cook or clean up. Definitely a perk!

I cast my mind back over yesterday and inwardly hope the next two weeks are not as eventful as our first couple of days here, I may need a holiday to recover from my holiday.

I dig out a book and return to the lounger when I'm full, trying to put it all down in one file labeled "crazy drunken night", to stow away in the recess of my brain. I'm sure most people have those kinds of nights and manage to get past them quickly.

I don't expect to see any of the others up at this hour, most of them stayed up long after the chopper left and I'm not sure when they finally went to bed. It had been a traumatic night.

I manage a few pages of my book before I feel my eyes getting heavy and lay it across my face to shield myself from the sun, a nap would be good. Five minutes of shut eye.

Exhaustion finally catching up with me. I don't need to try as I feel myself slide away.

\* \* \*

I'm vaguely conscious of the fact that the shadowing warmth on my face has been slid away, but I'm still sleepy and don't want to open my eyes and face the glaring brightness. A warm sensation runs across my face and removes the tickling hair which has been bothering me in the mild breeze. Now my sun screen has been taken from me, I'm starting to waken fully and register that my book has been removed. I blink my eyes open sleepily and see a dark figure leaning over me, with the sun behind its head, I know without focusing it's Jake.

"Hey," he sounds husky, like he's not long woken up.

"Hey." So do I, except, I really have just woken up.

"You shouldn't sleep in the sun," he scolds gently, I blink up at him, trying to make out his face, but it's cast in shadow with the sun behind his head.

"I didn't intend to." I know that's not entirely true, truth be told, I didn't think about it. It annoys me that I can't make out his face, as it's so cast in darkness, in contrast to the blazing circle of light behind him. I squint and feel the smooth movement as he slides his sunglasses on me.

I smile involuntarily, like I always do when he does this.

*Oh, Jake.*

"Want to go somewhere?" His voice is uncharacteristically quiet, and I see he's looking off to the side at something, he seems distracted. It makes my heart expand with a pang, I hate seeing him so—deflated.

"Such as?"

I see him shrug and he tilts his head up, looking away

from the direction which first caught his attention, to across the water. He's sitting on the lounger, that's why he's towering over me, one arm across my body holding his weight, so he can look down at me directly.

"Anywhere but here."

I bite my lip, he sounds tense; maybe I was wrong about Daniel. Maybe he's not okay and Jake's mulling over it.

"How's Hunter?" I ask gently. I don't like Jake this way. He turns back to me and I see him relax a little.

"He's fine ... He will be. They just need to monitor him ... Secondary drowning is a risk when you swallow as much as he did." He says it lightly, I see no untruth in his face, he really isn't worried about Hunter's recovery. His mood is unexplainable, maybe he's just tired still.

"Secondary drowning?" I query. I have never heard of it.

"You can drown long after you come out of the water ... It's in your lungs still." He tenses, and I know he doesn't want to talk. I vaguely remember a conversation where he told me one of his friends, in their teens, drowned after a boat party. I wonder if it still hurts him. The thought makes me long to wrap my arms around him and squeeze it away. Take away this somber mood he's in.

"So, where will we go?" I change the subject instead.

"We could drive somewhere." He's back to watching the horizon, he's tense and distracted. I don't think there's any chance that he's going to bring up last night, he seems preoccupied.

"Okay." I just want to get him out of this funk, and maybe going out will do that. I move to sit up and he gets out of my way.

"Shall I get changed?"

He shakes his head, looking over my floaty dress and sandals with no hint of a facial response.

"No ... You look perfect." His eyes flicker down the length of me again, I smile and indicate I'm going to put my book in my room, sliding off and quickly leaving.

* * *

I look at my reflection, I've caught the sun majorly during my time here. I look glowy and tanned and my hair has developed some new light highlights, among my chemical ones, which catch the light, giving me a blonder look. I grab my bag and chuck in the normal essentials; cell, book, sun cream, sunglasses, despite Jake's being on the dresser. I put them back on my face instead of my own, I like feeling them on my face, a reminder of how well he looks after me.

I'm ready and I meet him back on deck. Now I can see him standing and not cast in shadow; I see he's in jeans and a T-shirt, with that perfect superman body and his hair is damp. He's had a shower or been for a swim before he woke me. He looks relaxed and casually hot, as always. I'm always in awe of the way his clothes sculpt his powerful body, it should be illegal to look that hot.

He smiles as I close the gap between us, he automatically ruffles my hair, lingering to twirl a strand, and smile before he makes me follow him down to the lower floor behind him silently. We head to the back of the boat and I see the small speed boat anchored to the back ready and waiting.

* * *

He's as good at driving the low grumbling sports car his father keeps ashore for mainland visits as he is the speedboat, effortlessly confident and capable, and it's kind of seductive. Seeing a man capable of driving an expensive, powerful machine is a turn on. He drives fast, but I don't feel unsafe; he molds to the curves and the roads like a pro, while I'm left to ogle the surroundings in awe. The scenery is breathtaking, and we don't talk much as music blares from the speakers, wind in my hair from the open roof.

We don't need to talk, we long ago mastered this companionable silence through forced proximity and I'm glad of it now. Scatterings of meaningless small talk and mostly quiet. I glance at his profile and watch the concentration etched on his face, he's too perfect to be real.

I can't help but linger on his mouth and get lost for a moment in the memory of how his kiss had felt last night, of how it had made me feel. Allowing myself the brief memories before guilt and shame push them away. He glances at me, catching my eye and smiles, it's soft and relaxed and I can't help but smile back shyly. Sometimes he just looks so young, welcoming, and I forget that he's my boss. That this is beyond complicated.

We still haven't spoken about last night and I'm not sure I want to; in fact, I don't. I want to forget it happened, forget what it felt like and act like everything is the same. I need this job, I need my mental faculties to deal with this job, and I feel that going to bed with Jake would probably have altered that for an eternity. He's watching the road again, I relax back in my seat, sighing. This is so very complicated.

Friendship, career, fear of being used and hurt.

Just fear.

Inability to let a man in, trust ... There's no simple solution when it comes to Jake and me. He's the poster child for casual sex, and commitment phobia. Complicating everything last night with drunkenness was stupid. I try and focus out on the scenery to clear my mind. He hasn't even told me where we're going.

"So, are we literally just driving then?" I ask brightly, he's uber focused on the road and giving off a weird vibe.

"Nope." He's obviously still in that weird mood. Preoccupied and tetchy, monosyllabic.

"No clues?" I try, feeling irritation rise, I hate vagueness and surprises. Jake doesn't do vague very often and when he does I really don't like it.

"None!"

*Hmmm.*

"How do you know I'll like it?" I try a different approach, shoving down the surge of annoyance in the pit of my stomach. He only shrugs.

*For God's sake, why is he being so ... So pissy and closed off?*

"It's not fun is it?" There's a tightness to his voice, but he's keeping his focus steady on the road still.

"What?" I snap back around, catching his face turned to me for a second, his eyes narrowed, he looks minorly pissed off.

*What the hell? Where did that come from?*

"Being closed out." He has a hint of humor in his eye, but I know he's being serious, sardonic, and not in a friendly way. I frown at him and go back to my sight-seeing, confused at his manner. Trying hard not to rise to it.

"What does it take, Emma?" That edgy tone in his voice betrays a pissed mood looming up.

*Why today?*

I curse inwardly. Jake's bad moods are the worst thing ever, maybe he's hungover and obviously still tired. He shifts gear as we round a rather craggy coastal road; his focus on the road, his brows furrowed, and a tightness to his jaw that screams of tension.

"Jake, please ... What are you talking about?" I move in my seat and adjust my clothes to distract the awkwardness in my pose.

*How have I closed him out? He's seen more of me, knows more of me, than anyone on the planet, does he not see that?*

"You're not even going to mention last night? Is that another conversation over?" he snaps at me and I feel myself bristle.

"You didn't mention it either." I spit, a little too aggressively. Riled by the up by his mood, it's like he's getting his period.

"I was waiting to see if you would." Eyes cool green and face tense, he's in difficult and stubborn mode.

*Great!*

"Why?" I snap. He shrugs again.

*Oh my god.*

He can be so infuriating. I think he's still tired for sure, and he's being crabby as hell. I don't want to fight, I want to go back to playful, fun Jake. This is not the little outing I was expecting.

"Jake ... It shouldn't have happened, we crossed a line." I plead, trying to make him see sense, trying to stop this tense conversation and get back to something lighter.

"And there she is! Right back to square one." The sarcasm thick in his tone. His body stiffening in his seat.

"What's that supposed to mean?" I turn at him angrily.

"Anytime you get close, Emma, even a hint of letting go, you snap right back in and shut the door. No conversation. No acknowledgment of it, just wham. Over!" He barks at me, all hope of not fighting out the window.

"What?" I hiss with a sardonic laugh. "Because I won't

sleep with my boss? I'm not letting myself go? That's being closed off?" I turn away, anger flaming my face.

*Fuck you, Carrero. Why is it always about sex with him?*

"I don't think there was any doubt about it last night ... It's not the issue ... It's the afterwards, Emma." His voice is laced with venom, anger seething from every pore, his body tense. I stay silent, anger prickling my scalp. I'm as tense as him now.

"I was drunk ... being stupid, anyone can make a mistake." I huff.

*Stop being an asshole and ruining this.*

I shift in my seat to turn away from him further, trying to fully face out of the side window. I'm thrust forward as he slams on the brakes and we screech to a halt, kicking up dust and stone around the car, throwing everything loose in the car toward the front with a clatter.

*What the hell?*

I snap my head around at him shocked. He's gripping the wheel aggressively and staring straight ahead, taking a calming breath. I notice he's swerved us into the side of the road, out of the non-existent traffic. He unbuckles and gets out of the car and stalks off toward the side of the high edged road, overlooking the vast drop off the cliff. Every muscle in his body tense and flinching with rage.

*What should I do? What the actual hell? Where did this even come from?*

I've never actually been the focus of this version of angry Jake, not like this, not with this kind of rage. I feel sick. I feel emotional and I reel it back in, taking smooth easy breaths, trying to still my hands. Trying to not let him get to me while my stomach ties itself in knots.

He comes back to the car and slides in stiffly; he's making me jumpy and nervy. He's not looking at me and he doesn't try to put his belt back on. I really don't know what to say.

Angry, aggressive men as big as Jake are my worst nightmare.
*Why is he reacting this way?*

I've no clue what goes on in his head sometimes as I watch him tensely, every nerve end of my body on high alert.

"It's not about sex, Emma." He's quiet and pensive and his hands move back to the wheel, but he doesn't start the car. "It's about this eternal need in you to stay in full control ... Never letting anyone in, never letting yourself enjoy anything, and letting your guard down. Always keeping me at arm's length." His voice is gruff and edgy with an undertone of aggression.

"That's not true." I do enjoy things in my life, he has no idea. He's the closest person to me in the world.

"Really? Emma, I've been with you for months now, I've seen just about every version of you there is ... Tired, grumpy, bossy, happy, PMSing like fuck." He's calmer, but his voice is still strained, that edge to his tone. I sit tersely, watching his hands grip and un-grip the wheel as he talks. His body language speaking volumes.

"I've seen vulnerable only briefly." He glances at me and I look away, hating that he's even seen it at all.

"I get it, Emma ... You're strong, you want everyone to see that. You don't need anyone ... But it's not who you are ... And it's not true."

"Yes, it is ... Do you ever think that maybe you overthink it and try to see stuff that isn't there?" I spit angrily, I hate him analyzing me, trying to make out that I don't know myself inside out. He has no clue what goes on inside of my head.

"I think I know you better than most people."

I think of my mom and Sarah, and push both images away, I don't think I've cried in front of either of them since I went through puberty. He's right. He does, but it doesn't mean he knows all of me.

"What if I don't know how else to be, Jake?" I turn to him accusingly.

"You keep pushing ... Keep telling me to let go, and what if I can't? What if this is me? This is all I know. I'm not capable of doing it any other way, or needing other people, because I don't know how." I'm shouting.

*Why am I shouting?*

Because he's hit a nerve and it hurts, and I hate him for it, hate him for stripping me bare. He bridges the gap in an instant and his mouth is on mine, completely unexpected.

His lips are hot and soft and swiftly open mine. His tongue in my mouth and it feels good, instantly crushing my defenses and melting my armor. His hands burying themselves in my loose hair and I kiss him back, tangling my fingers in the collar of his shirt so I can pull him closer, instinct taking over. Breathing heavily and getting lost in the sensation of his kiss, that perfect mouth which does amazing things to my very soul. We both moan lightly as the kiss deepens, my stomach lurching with desire.

My head reels around full circle as though trying to slap some sense into me. I can't do this; I can't. I can't stop, it's addictive, he's pulling me closer and I've literally no defenses. I feel my belt slide loose as he unclips it and I'm against him, his arm around my waist and pulling me hard into his body; awkwardness of the car's confined space forgotten.

I fear he will drag me onto his lap and then what?

This will change everything, this could ruin my career, my life, my mental state, our relationship. What if we cross the line and I start to feel more for him ... I don't think I can trust him not to hurt me, it's what he does. Sex and casual affairs, meaningless hook ups. I'm just a challenge to him, a new toy that holds his interest, because I've been evasive and once he has me. What then?

*I can't, I just can't.*

I feel myself recoiling from him, the passion in me burning out, replaced with fear, suffocating terror, my hands sagging and start pushing against him. He feels the change in me and lets me go, coldly. Both of us breathing heavily; he sits back in his seat harshly, glaring at me.

"That's exactly what I mean." His voice is cold and angry.

"This is your biggest enemy, Emma ... Not me." He taps my temple with a finger, rage in the depths of his green eyes.

"Why did you do that?" I spit, my body still reeling and out of whack from the assault on my senses. Lungs struggling to self-regulate.

"To prove a point." He snarls and turns away.

"What point?" I almost cry at him. I'm so overwrought with emotion. So confused. He scrubs his hands through his ruffled hair and exhales; for a moment I think he's going to jump out of the car again and walk off, but he just sits and sighs, grasping the wheel and pulling himself to sit properly.

"What does it matter?" his voice is deflated, and he avoids looking at me.

*So? What? He's decided, screw it, we're not talking anymore? How can he assault me with a kiss then just say forget it? What the hell?*

I'm angry, I'm really goddamn, seething, angry.

*How dare he!*

"Fuck you." It's out of my mouth before I even really contemplate screaming at my boss, and I'm out of the car too. I'm raging. My eyes are stinging and blurry. I hate that he makes me fall apart like this. He knows how to rip my head open and I hate him for it, hate the way he strips me of the control I've built up over the years.

His hands pull me into him and spin me around, he was fast out after me. I try to fight, but he envelopes me and buries his face in my hair, holding me in a vice like grip so that I can't struggle free.

"I'm sorry ... Emma, stop ... Emma. I'm sorry." His voice is raw and strained. I'm fighting but losing, he knows how to hold me so that I can't move, my body wrapped in his, almost suffocating me. He pulls me tighter and I slump, anger dissipating when held to him this way. He's breathing into my hair and I can feel the warmth on my scalp, I feel overwhelmed, tears running down my cheek.

"I don't want to fight with you." His voice is quiet now, close to my ear, his crazy mood taking a new direction again. I relax into his hold, no longer struggling, unable to hate him when he's this close to me, sounding this way.

"I don't want to fight either." I swallow a sob. Slumping into him.

"Maybe we should go back to the boat?" he sounds tired, I don't know how to navigate this version of Jake; more moods than I'm used to. It's exhausting. I put it down to the scene with Hunter and the after effects of too much alcohol, lack of sleep, stress. This isn't him.

"Maybe," I whisper; at least there I can go to my room and get some distance, get some perspective. Let him alone to get a grip of his roller coaster mood swings.

"No," he snaps, surprising me again with a U-turn in attitude. The way he says it causes me to bristle and look up. Mood shift suddenly ... again?

*What the hell is going on with him?*

He pulls away and stalks back to the car, stops at the hood, leaning down to tense his arms against it, broody and aggressive in his stance.

"I can't do this, Emma." He snaps, his gaze steady on the hood of the low sleek car. For a moment, I think he may even hit it.

"Do what?" I'm beyond confused, I think Jake has been invaded by a body snatcher. He's all over the place and I just can't keep up.

"This! ... Us!" He waves his hand in an exasperated motion and I'm dumbfounded, I blink at him. I don't actually know what else to do. There's no us! He looks at me haughtily, most likely because I'm still silent and frowns.

"You drive me crazy ... and not in a good way." He sighs, facing the car again. His body emanating all kinds of crazy, manic, signals.

"I do?" my voice is tiny and unsure, I feel like I'm walking on eggshells with him right now, yet he's accusing me of driving *him* crazy!

*Well, it's goddamn mutual.*

He sighs again and his face tenses.

"You frustrate me on so many levels." He carries on, although he's lost all conviction in his tone.

*Likewise.*

"Sorry," I murmur sarcastically. Rolling my eyes at his back and trying to simmer everything I am feeling.

*Yes, Jake, I can do moody and sardonic too.*

He throws me an unamused look over his shoulder, I look down to twiddle my fingers. He's sighing again, I can hear him kicking the wheel of the car, funneling some of his rage onto the rubber, and it makes me flinch.

"Why do you never talk about your childhood?" his tone changes again, a new tactic or a new mood? My head's dizzy with this swing door version of him.

"What?" I pale, I feel my face sweep with cold and my hand's pause. Nerves fluttering from low down at a topic I do not want to follow.

"There's nothing to talk about ... You have knowledge of

## Jake & Emma

the highlights." I say drily, the urge to clamp down and stop this direction of conversation kicks in, there's a mild warning in the back of my brain.

"I know bits and pieces, Emma, mostly from getting you drunk." He glares at me and it's almost like an accusation.

*Jesus!*

"Where is this going?" I plead, I don't want to do this, I don't want to have this type of psycho babbling conversation with Jake. Especially when he's being so weird, so **PMS**.

*How did we even get to this? Why is he so obsessed over this? Freaking Jekyll Jake and his neck breaking mood swings.*

"It hurt you." His eyes come to rest on me, his face endearing and open. All anger gone, but it only makes me want to cry, so I look away, crossing my arms around my body protectively. The look on his face claws at my heart.

"It's the past and it should stay there." I can feel the sting in my eyes, he won't make me cry again. My heart aching with everything he is trying to pull out of me.

*What's wrong with him? Is this what he's after? Tears, confessions?*

I move away and turn my back on him, it's better when I can't see him. Can't see that look in his eye.

"Your mom? You don't talk about her much either." He pushes, his voice gentle. Every part of me screaming, leave me alone, let me be. I hold it all in, closing my eyes. Insides clawing desperately.

*Just hold it together, Emma. Take deep calming breaths.*

"She's my mom ... What else is there to say?" I say it coldly, hoping he understands that he should back off.

"Tell me about her." He obviously ignores the silent plea and decides to just go in for the kill.

*Thanks, Jake.*

I'm wary of his crazy mood swings, I don't want angry and irrational Jake back. I grit my teeth against the urge to tell him to mind his own business and try to appease his curiosity instead.

"My mom is a sucker for a sob story." My voice grates every word out painfully, laced with anger and warning. "That's about all there is to her."

*So back off.*

"She has bad taste in men?" his voice sounds closer, I walk further off, putting the distance back between us a little. Every part of me on high alert; my anger simmering to something more heart wrenching. I hate these kinds of conversations, someone trying to lay you bare and uncover your pain.

"That's an understatement," I snap, shielding my despair with anger.

*Control ... Emma!*

"Her boyfriends hurt you?" his question catches me off guard, his voice closer again, despite my moving away; I feel his fingers move into my hair near my ear. Flexing his fingers into my scalp, making me lean into his touch, closing my eyes. I've no defenses when he touches me. So much pleasure from such a simple motion, dispersing my anger. His other hand sliding over my shoulder on the other side and sliding down my arm a little. I feel his breath on the back of my neck, between my shoulder blades before his mouth comes to rest on the back of my head and he sighs. It surrenders me to him, body and soul, my rage draining away. Jake knows how to get under my skin with so little effort. Just a touch.

"Some ... Some just wanted to ..." I can't say it. I swallow hard. His hand leaves my arm, snakes around my waist, and pulls me into his body smoothly. His mouth moving to my neck gently, his hair against my face, pulling me tight and close to him.

"She didn't protect you," he whispers against my collar bone, the gentle flutter of his mouth on my skin and the heat from his breath sending a thousand electric tingles through my body. I know I should pull away from him, but I'm memorized by the way he's holding me, the way my body is sagging into him, losing all control. Floating away on a warm breeze. The memories of last night pulling me back and unable to resist the way he makes me yearn to be connected to him.

"She did what she could," I mumble, even though I know that's a lie. I'm too lost in the way his nose is skimming my shoulder and neck, my skin erupting with goosebumps. The hand that was in my hair now trailing down my naked arm and wrist and back up, he's a clever one with all his seductive ways. Lulling me into a sense of soft security, teasing my body so I'll open up to him. I don't have the energy to fight it. I'm his captive when he touches me this way.

"She didn't stop bringing men around her child, *Miele*." His voice takes on a hoarseness and I stiffen, I've told myself this, a million times over and over. He's not telling me anything I don't already know. Yet, it still hurts like he's thrust a knife into my chest, to hear someone else say it.

"Why did you leave Chicago? Leave her?" his voice has deepened, his hands trailing down my arms and up again, gentle tingles on the surface. His face back in my hair, releasing me a little. I want to melt into him, let him do with my body as he pleases. His touch sending searing pleasure wherever it lands, my eyes still closed and lost in sensation. For once the doubts sliding away. He's bewitching me to open up and I'm completely lost to it.

"I needed to walk away from all of it ... I needed to save myself, because no one else was going to." I feel the tear course down my cheek, saying it out loud for the first time is bittersweet, yet I sound so pathetic. Heart gnawing with pain.

"I think you need to talk to someone about all of this, Emma ... a counselor ... I could ..."

My eyes snap open and I jerk away instantly, spinning to glare at him angrily. My mood changing with those simple words that wound me deeply.

"Not a goddamn chance." I spit, all venom returned defensive and lashing out.

"I'm not fucking crazy!"

"Emma, that isn't what I said," his voice is one of surprise at my reaction, he attempts to put his arms around me again, but I hold out a hand, stopping him. Brimming with rage. He stays back, wariness in his perfect eyes, my anger spilling out.

"Don't, okay ... You wanted to know ... Now you know, and that's the end of it." The strength is back in my voice ... PA Emma has returned, and I stalk past him toward the car. I can't look at him, my eyes are drying now, and I can feel that steel wall building back up, I'm gaining control again.

To be looked at like some broken mental case is too much. I don't need a shrink. I need him to stop prying.

"Don't do that," he snaps accusingly, following me back to the car, close on my heels; he grabs my arm to turn me, but I yank it away.

*He thinks I need therapy! He thinks I'm some broken, pathetic girl with emotional issues, and he's wondering why I'm pissed. I knew this was a bad idea, I knew he would see me differently the more he knew.*

"Do what?" I yell, deliberately looking anywhere but him to get away. He grabs my arm again and tugs me around to face him harshly, this time succeeding.

"Don't shut me out again ... Clamp down like you always do ... Not after everything ... I'm sick to death of this never-ending fucking circle." He rages at me.

## Jake & Emma

"I didn't want to tell you ... You just keep pushing." I wrench my arm away, and I'm back in fight mode, ready to push it all back into the black box in my head and act like it never happened.

"Let's go back to the boat. I'm hungry and I'm tired." I spit. I didn't know I could sound so cool, amid the sea of emotions swirling around my head. Sending a very loud and clear message that this conversation is over. He lifts his hands as if he's going to choke me and grits his teeth, his eyes burn, and he paces away from me again, cursing and raging into the open air. I ignore him. I walk to the car and get in, slamming my door and buckling up in stony-faced silence.

Eventually, he angrily slides in to the car and I can tell he's given up, he knows it's pointless. My mask is well and truly back in place and even though his mood is coming off him in aggressive droves, he doesn't look my way.

"Conversation fucking over," he mutters to himself and thins his lips, he's angry. He's sulking. I don't care; I don't want to do this. I glare at him then turn away, to stare out of the window as he turns the car in the road and heads back to where we came from at a neck breaking speed that makes me uneasy, but I bite my tongue and say nothing.

We don't talk as we drive, he turns up the stereo loud, indicating he won't attempt it and I try and relax into my seat. Pretend to anyway. Hard to do when you're being driven around winding cliffs by a maniac in a temper, with a sports car at his command.

I feel his hand tug mine out of my hair angrily and throw him another furious glare.

"Stop fucking doing that!" he barks over the music, eyes glinting.

*Nice.*

"That hurt." I snap, reaching out to turn it down again. I

touch my head where I yanked my own hair painfully almost out at the root.

"I didn't mean to hurt you." He's talking through gritted teeth, glaring even though he's apologizing.

"I'm sorry."

"I don't know why it bothers you so much." I spit at him childishly. "I don't know I'm doing it."

"It bothers me because it's a sign that you're anxious ... That you're nervous or upset ... I don't like it." He retorts with that same pissed tone.

"Oh, so you want me to unleash vulnerable Emma, but only if she doesn't act nervous or anxious ... Makes so much sense." I seethe. He glares at me, his jaw tensing, fire meeting fire. The sizzle of electric between us causing the air to crackle. He looks away and focuses on the road, gripping the wheel so hard I'm sure it's going to come off.

*I hope it hits him square in the face.*

The journey back to the boat is silent and quick.

*Helps when your driver thinks he's Schumacher.*

# Chapter 23

The others are up on deck, lazing around and eating a cold buffet that has been set out on a long, low table by the loungers; it looks amazing and I feel my stomach rumble, despite the anxious tension between Jake and me. It's a welcome distraction and I head straight for it to pile myself a plate, deliberately ignoring Jake behind me.

"Oh, the love birds have returned." Leila squeals and almost throws herself into my arms for a hug. I throw her a warning look, but she doesn't seem to notice.

"We went for a drive." Jake's broody tone comes from far behind me, as though he's still standing at the top of the stairs to the deck, I ignore him. I see Leila cast a worried look behind me, then back at me, but she keeps her mouth closed. I hear his footsteps as he leaves and heads down to the second floor and feel relieved. We could do with some time apart to get over whatever this is between us; I can't even begin to dissect the past twenty-four hours of this trip. So much for a holiday break that would relax us!

Leila, sensing something is up, goes into overdrive in a bid to distract me. She is infectious, and she soon has me laughing, some of the tension easing and I'm good at pretending every is okay on the surface, that Jake isn't at the forefront of my mind every second. I just want Jake to come back up as relaxed and normal and join in. Put this mess away, but he doesn't re-appear.

I'm cool toward the other girls ... Marissa has been watching me with a sour expression on her face since I arrived, and Miracle is lying topless, facing me, pouting and applying her third layer of lip gloss.

*Jesus, put them away.*

The men are huddled together over one of the double loungers, listening to some game coming from Richard's cell and making male grunts and moans when something isn't going well. I assume it's baseball.

Jake reappears half an hour later, changed into a black fitted shirt and jeans, his usual clubbing look. I love that on him and it cuts me inside, I just need us to be okay again. He has his shades on, hair spiked, and looks casual as always; even when I'm still mad at him, he makes me ache inside.

"Emma, I need you a second." He sounds like boss Carrero and not Jake, I feel myself prickle inside, but get up dutifully.

*Well, at least I know where I stand with boss Carrero.*

I follow and we walk down to the lower floor of the boat, I can sense his tension and stiffness, even at a distance, he's emanating anger. It makes my stomach drop down to my knees, but I only stand taller and maintain a look of disinterest. Clasping my hands behind my back to hide the trembling.

"I'm leaving for a couple of days ... I've left you a credit card in your room in case you want to go out; there's a car on shore that will take you anywhere you want to go." His voice is flat, he avoids looking at me directly.

## Jake & Emma

*Wait, what?*

I feel the panic rise in a tidal wave of emotion.

"Where are you going? We cleared your schedule for two weeks, so you wouldn't need to go anywhere." I react in panic, my voice slightly higher and faster than normal. I'm practically hyperventilating, this was never part of the plan.

"Change of plan ... Try and relax and have fun. If you can." He almost spits the last words, sarcasm oozing from him and it cuts me like a knife.

*So, we're still at this, are we?*

"Do you need me to come?" I reply coolly, in my best PA tone. Pushing everything down and bringing that mask into play. I won't let him see how much he's wounding me.

"No, I don't!" he's closed off, face devoid of expression, only his eyes betray him, with anger seething in the glittering green depths.

"Jake, you pay me to be at your beck and call and go with you at a moment's notice." I'm indignant, I don't want him to leave, I want to know what's going on. I want to be with him. Know what he's thinking. I want us to go back to before, and behave like we normally do, like we used to do.

"I don't pay you to watch me fuck other women, Emma." He snarls at me and I feel myself recoil as though I've been slapped. The knife slicing into my heart, causing my body to reel back slightly. He knows how to deliver a low blow. He stalks away from me, toward his room, but I follow angrily.

"What? ... Why are you being an asshole?"

*Why are you going to fuck other women suddenly? You don't need other women, what happened to your sabbatical?*

I want to grab him and shake him, bile rising in my throat at the thought of him with someone else. Pushing it down, trying to fight the urge to cry.

"I'm redefining the boundaries of our relationship ...

Uncrossing the line. That's what you called it, right?" He tosses back casually. I reel back, but I steel myself. Swallowing my sobs and forcing my face to stay as impassive as I can muster. My body retching inside in agony.

*Isn't this what I wanted? Him to go back to him and his women and I return to being just his PA? No! Yes! ... I don't know anymore.*

"You think going off to screw someone will uncross that line?" The words catch in my throat like steel wool, I feel sick with the pain in my heart.

"It's a start." He turns into his room and pulls a suitcase from the cupboard, I notice he's already packed a flight bag on the bed, his passport lying beside it.

"Got over your little break, I see." I sound cold. The reality is that I'm dying inside, and I want to yell at him. Hold onto him.

*You kissed me, Jake ... twice. No three times. You kissed me and now you're going to have sex with someone else.*

"I think that's probably the reason for the latest tension ... I need to go let off steam." He smirks icily, I don't know this Jake. I hate this Jake. I want my normal Jake to come back, the one who would never talk to me this way, hurt me this way. My Jake would never abandon me to go off and be a lothario!

*So, kissing me was "recent tension"?*

I've never known him this way, this cold and cool angry Carrero. I don't like it, I don't like it at all; I want to throw myself at his feet and cry and hold him back from going, but I don't. I pull my chin up defiantly and push down the hurt, replace it with anger and glare, let that trained part of me take over, in all her icy maiden coolness. That old reliable self-preservation kicking in.

Pride!

# Jake & Emma

"Enjoy yourself." I turn on my heel, close to tears inside I'm a chaos of emotions and trauma, but my exterior is calm and controlled.

"Don't miss me while I'm gone, *Tesoro Mio*." His voice is oozing with charm. It only stabs at my heart more. Unbearable pain.

"I won't," I say icily. Holding myself tall.

*Fuck you, Jake ... Fuck you, Mr. Carrero.*

"I'm sure you'll find something exciting to do." He's focusing on packing, but his voice is flat and emotionless, the cruel and harsh side of him, the first time I've ever seen his father within him. I want to slap his smug, angry face, with all my strength.

"When shall I expect you back, Mr. Carrero?" I'm in full PA mode now, I'm making a point, a "you don't affect me" point. If he's trying to get a reaction out of me with this shocking move, then I won't let him enjoy it. I won't let him see that it's affecting me at all.

"When I'm done ... hard to say ... It's been a while." He sneers without looking up. I see him clearly, twisting the knife harder in my chest.

*Fuck you—fuck you—fuck you.*

I smile graciously, ten out of ten for acting ability and still the need to clench my teeth. His cell vibrates and he slides it out, answering it despite my presence.

"Hi ... I'll be leaving soon ... Yeah, I missed you too, Honey ... I'll meet you there." He sounds like Casanova Jake of old.

*Oh my god.*

I want to throw up, but I steel myself against the door frame.

*Why, Jake, why?*

"Who?" It's out before I can monitor it, cursing at myself for asking, showing an ounce of emotion over this. Giving him the satisfaction of knowing he's got to me.

"No one you know. Old flame." He closes his suitcase, throwing me a fiery look, warning me to keep going with this, he wants to torture me with details. I can't bear this. My self-preservation kicks in even more viciously and I smile coldly.

"If that will be all, Mr. Carrero ... I'll leave you to it. Enjoy your trip." I'm using the door frame as a crutch, but I can't stand watching this painful scene unfold; he's going away with some brainless boobs legs on to screw her for at least two days ... maybe longer. I don't want him to. I don't think I can bear the pain.

*When did this happen? When did my feelings spill beyond friendship this badly?*

I've seen him with other women ...

*He's always been this way, when did I start reacting like this? Breaking my heart over him being his Casanova self.*

"Tell the others, after I'm gone, I had to go away for a couple of days." He's picking up his suitcase, his body stiff with tension.

"What reason shall I give?" I sound alien. This fake politeness between us, thick in the stifling air. We're both exceptionally good at cold and polite.

"I don't give a shit, Emma ... The truth for all I care." He flexes his eyebrows sardonically.

That was a blow ... it hurt, it knocked the wind out of my sails. I move back as he stalks out with suitcase in hand, he slides his shades on, despite it being duller in here and he doesn't even look at me, he looks beyond pissed.

*Should I follow him? Should I stay here?*

*Stop hovering, Emma, it's pathetic.*

I don't know what to do, this isn't me, not anymore. He's

up the hall and out the door in the blink of an eye, obviously determined to leave. I hesitate and follow, I'm not sure why, but I suddenly need to cling to his presence, the last moments of him. I just want him to stop this, he's making me feel so alone. So, broken.

I lose him at the top of the stairs, the sun hurting my eyes. I blink and shield them from view and suddenly I want him to slide his glasses over my eyes, the way he always does. I want him to brush my hair back and take care of me. I want the Jake I know and care about, not this cruel cold man who doesn't give a shit about me.

I want to cry. I catch sight of him near the rear of the boat, he's following one of the crew down to the awaiting speed boat.

*Oh my god. He really is going, it's not a ruse. He really wants to hurt me.*

I want to scream out and run after him, but I'm rooted to the spot as I watch him descend into the waiting boat. I can't bear to watch him leave, so I turn on my heel and run back to my room at full speed. I run like my ass is on fire and don't stop until I slam down onto my bed and sob every bottled up, hysterical emotion, right up from the tips of my toes in a spewing out of desperate agony.

I don't know how long I'm there, but I can't stop, it's like a damn has opened and the floodgates break. Everything I've ever held back, slips out with the pain I've always avoided. I can't breathe, it's suffocating and unbearable. It's excruciating.

*Jake's breaking my heart.*

# Chapter 24

I'm lying in the dark watching the shadows of the water on my ceiling, calm and numb. I feel like I'm floating on the ocean directly, but I'm still laid on my bed. It's night ... I haven't left, and I don't want to.

I've cried so much that I feel ravaged and weak. I didn't know that crying could do this to me ... release so much ... doubt ... insecurity ... pain. I haven't cried properly since I was five years old; back then you didn't cry over heartache, I only knew the tears from physical pain and illness. This is so much worse.

Crying over Jake has to be the worst pain I have ever known, it leads to crying over the way my life has turned out. The way I am. I think of my mom and wonder if she cried like this over the men she dated.

*Did she cry this way over Ray Vanquis when he left?*

Except Jake never dated me, he never left me in that way. I never experienced her kind of heartache. Ray inflicted more than heartbreak on her. I have no clue what to call this.

The thought makes me feel sick.

*Did she cry when he beat her to a pulp and left her half-*

## Jake & Emma

*dead on her own floor? Why am I even thinking about this?*

I never dwell on this, I don't want to, it's a thought that makes me feel ill. I can't stop though, in my emotional state, the walls in my head have been broken and I'm not in control of the thoughts and memories flooding in. The memories flashing into my mind like a stop motion movie and I've lost control.

Ray and his ugly, screwed up face towering over my mother, her body broken and bruised after he had raped her, yet again, for making him angry. I witnessed so much cruelty and perversion when she was in a relationship with him, powerless to stop him and afraid to try.

My mind like an open door, without any ability to stop it, he's in my head and she's there, crying on the floor; but then it's not her ... it's me and I'm eighteen ... memories I've tried so hard to push down, for an eternity, breaking through my broken walls and fatigue.

The first hit was a punch, a reaction to my self-defense slap when he tried to force a kiss on me, right in the face. It knocked me down, made me groan and my head spin. It wasn't the first time I'd been punched. I tasted the blood in my mouth, fueling my rage, and tried to get back up, but he hauled me up by the hair and threw me against the wall.

He was a big man ... strong and cruel. I had seen the bruises on my mom from being with him, she would laugh them away uneasily and say he was just a rough lover. Rough was true, he tried to push his tongue in my mouth and I fought with all my might but he grabbed my clothes and started to tear at them. My jeans at the waist, bursting the button off, trying to thrust his hand down there. I kicked and bit, clawed until I felt the floor hard against my face with another jarring punch.

He yanked my jeans down when I was reeling, hunched

over onto the wooden floor. He knocked the sense out of me and I knew what he was going to do, I had seen him hold my mom down this way more than once; she didn't know I came home and saw it many times. I had hidden in the shadows and slunk away quickly, afraid to intervene. Ray was a devil and he instilled so much fear with his aggression and bulk.

My jeans were around my ankles and he pulled my underwear to follow. I flipped, in panic and rage, turned and twisted and thrust about, trying to save myself from him, his grip was strong, but I had a renewed strength as adrenaline coursed through me. I managed to gauge his face and it angered him, getting up to rain more cruel kicks on my body.

I remember chanting internally, "I'm not going to crumble, I'm not going to pass out, I'm going to fight," in a bid to stay conscious. I grabbed for the table nearby and it fell, the vase smashing over the top of me; scrambling desperately to grab a piece of the glass, but he grabbed my ankles and hauled me backward, my arm dragged through the broken mess until I saw my blood smear the floor, my arms warm with the thick liquid. I kicked with my restrained ankles, knocking him over into the couch and it gave me time to yank my pants back up and scramble to my feet.

I tried to run, but he was on me with a fury that I'd never known, beating me and pushing me into a corner, blackness wrapping around me. Then there was a thud ... a low, empty thud, and he stopped. His face went blank and he crumbled to the floor to reveal my mother standing over him with a huge, twisted, wooden sculpture from the wall unit, above her head. She looked at me, her eyes red rimmed and her face white; it's what I saw in that look that will always haunt me, worse than what he had done, what he had been attempting to do that had finally ripped my heart right out. The anguish in her face, the accusation in her eyes as all I could see was—

*"What did you do, Emma?"*

I close my eyes against the fresh torrent of tears, I try to push that memory away again and again, but her face stays insistent. My mother always blamed me for Ray leaving. I was eighteen by then, no longer a child. No longer her sweet innocent little girl, but she saw me as a capable woman who must have given him some sign that I wanted it. She felt betrayed by me; it's the one thing I've never been able to admit to myself. If she believed that of me, then, why wouldn't I?

*All of this with Jake ... Has it been because of me? Because I led him to believe I wanted these things from him?*

How can I remember these things and feel like I asked for them? I didn't ask for them ... I didn't ask him to try to rape me, but deep down, somewhere inside, that child is nodding at me and she's saying: "Yes, Emma, yes you did. Why else would these men, one after the other, try to touch you? Try to take you? You must have done something, Emma. Your own mother believed it."

It's the guilt that I forever shy away from, the shame and misery of my internal battle.

*Is this what I do to Jake? Do I make him want to push things further between us? Like them, will he take what he wants, then leave me broken on the floor, the way my mother was left. I was left?*

Jake isn't capable of such things, but I must be doing something for it to turn out this way.

*What has Jake done to me? Why is he doing this to me now?*

My mind is a messy scramble of thoughts and emotions, half of which make no sense.

I didn't drink before Jake Carrero, I didn't like how it made me feel. Like I lost control. I never kissed men ever, because all it did was bring back memories that make me feel ill. Never wanted anyone sexually, or even felt turned on by anyone before Jake.

I never opened up and told anyone the things I've told him. I never kicked back and just let go, relaxed and had fun, before him. Never took my hair down, let alone cut it. I never cried, and now I can't seem to stop.

Jake has slowly unraveled me, and he has no clue. He has no idea the depth in which he has infected me, changed me.

I keep people at arm's length, even Sarah ... She's my best friend, yet I've never told her anything that would justify that title. I don't blame her for drifting away, because I've never given her a reason not to. I know everything about her, yet she knows very little about me. Only what she witnessed at being around me.

We drifted apart, and I was glad. She was my focus, my person to protect and care for, in place of the mother I was leaving behind. She gave me a purpose, someone to take care of, and when she no longer needed me I pulled away. I didn't want her looking at me and remembering who I was.

It suited me that I got a job that required devoting all my time and attention to organizing someone else's life. It's what I needed; control, calm, organization, safety, and security. Independence and self-reliance. I could focus on someone else's existence and deny my own. Sarah never really knew the real me, she'd always seen the facade. Everyone has always seen the facade.

Everyone except Jake.

Men have always made me nervous ... despite moving away and starting over. Men have a way of making that wall go up. I don't trust them, I never have. I don't trust anyone except myself. Well, I didn't.

Until Jake.

*Do I trust Jake? I did ... In my own way, but now?*

Knowing what he's gone to do, I don't know anymore. I deserve it. He's been patient and he tries; in a way no one has ever tried, to see through my brave facade. He saw it right from the start, he said as much. I don't want him to see through it, because if he did and he found this Emma, what would he see?

*Insecure, troubled, and emotionally all over the place. What would he do?*

She's a broken little girl who flinches when men raise their hands, even though she's practiced to remain cool. She's scared of getting so close to anyone, even a friend, in case they rip her heart out like her own parents did. Her first start in life, learning that she could rely on no one.

I can't even relax and let anyone else look after me, I'm the only one I can rely on. But I let Jake ... so many times, he's taken care of me. It hurts to remember the countless ways he's taken care of me over the past months, but that Jake has just walked out on me, gone to hurt me in the cruelest way.

Letting people in just takes away your defenses and they learn how to wound you deeper, like Jake has done now. People say they love you, but they don't ... it's the ones who apparently love you, that cut the deepest.

*So why let anyone love you at all? Why care about him leaving you now? Stop caring, stop crying. Go back to numb, it was always better that way. Loving no one, letting no one in.*

* * *

I finally emerge, like an exhausted shell, hours before dawn. I watch the ocean lap up and down on the distant beach in the moonlight, the boat is still and quiet and I feel alone. I wonder where he is, and it slices across my heart cruelly; I wonder who "she" is.

*Don't do this to yourself, this isn't worth it.*

I push it away and try not to dwell anymore. I create a new little black box in the recess of my mind and push everything in there ... I'll label this one "Jake" and file every single hurtful memory in there. Every kiss, every touch, every tear.

Then I won't just close the lid; I'll lock it tight and throw it into the deepest part of my crazy mind. That's what I do when life throws me so much pain and misery. I move on. I stop myself from caring anymore, and that is exactly what I will do to him.

He wants to uncross the line, well I will change the line and build a fucking steel wall, to keep us on either side. He wants PA Emma back, that's what he will get.

# Chapter 25

He's been gone more than two days, and I've tried his cell so many times. He's monitoring his calls and I get voicemail almost immediately. I know he's declining my number and it hurts more than I can bear. I don't want to email or text, so I don't, I don't know what to say, I only want to hear him and know he's still there. I want to know what the hell is going on in that head of his, to know why he's being this way, and what the hell happens when we go back to work together.

I've been swimming and reading a lot and eating with the others; I'm getting used to them and although Marissa and I give each other a wide berth, I'm starting to warm to the rest of them.

Leila, as always, is a joy to be around, but I feel melancholy and would rather my own company. We went shopping on the mainland and I loved what having a girly friend felt like again. I made sure I abused Jake's credit card shamelessly, somehow it felt a bit like payback, not that he would care. More money than sense; he would not even blink at it.

She showed me how she does her beachy look make-up

and gave me some tips on how to wear my hair, she's the girly girlfriend I've never had before, and she's a good distraction. Sarah was never much into girly things and shopping.

Daniel seems to have changed somewhat, in that he's treating me respectfully now he's back on board and fully recovered. I don't know where the shift happened, but I'm warming to him. We have had many an enjoyable conversation about movies, books, and politics, which surprised me. He seems to have heard from Jake, seems to be in the know, and gave me a knowing look over dinner last night when Marissa continued to press about his absence.

Daniel is an odd one. The playboy, sleazy persona, all round party guy, seems to have slipped a little after his near drowning. He's been more reserved, less laid back. I wonder if this is a Jake-less Daniel, or if the near-death experience has maybe given him something to ponder. He seems somehow, sad. Pensive.

I miss Jake in a way I've never really evaluated until now. Even when I'm not working and have time off, he's always on the other end of the cell, sending me frustrating texts and pointless jokes. Sending me songs that make me laugh or have some vague meaning in the title or lyrics. His presence has always been looming, until now.

I'm getting the cold shoulder. He's freezing me out and it really hurts; I know he's punishing me, but I don't understand why. I can't stop thinking about him, my mind wandering over memories of him; his face, his body, his mouth on mine. It's only been days, but the inability to talk to him is making it feel like weeks. I'm so done with crying in bed over him. He's supposed to be my friend, yet he's acting like a prize "A" prick.

Margo has emailed me asking about my trip and I feel myself break as I read it. She's enjoying retirement, only not as much as she thought she would, and she enquires about Jake; I think she misses him. I think she misses being part of the sixty fifth, and her husband has a newfound love of golf, which she hates. She asks a dozen questions about her golden boy, obviously suffering from lack of Carrero charm.

*I know how she feels.*

I reply as breezily as I can, being vague and not mentioning that he's left me here. Not mentioning that we have ceased to communicate and send it on into the depths of the interweb. I hover over Jake's personal email address in my contacts list and then close my laptop.

*No, I won't lower myself to that.*

\* \* \*

It's now been six days and I'm pretty much done with this boat. I'm done with the people, and the sea, and the silence, I'm going out of my mind. The others like to party every night, and even joining in, I can't really get in the mood. I don't drink much without him here, I don't want to let my guard down and get in that state with no one to put me to bed. No one to watch over me. I smile sardonically at that.

Who knew the reason that I felt able to get that drunk and let go a little was because he was around. Ironic really.

The one thing he accused me of not being able to do and I did it because he was here.

I check my cell for the millionth time, I guess he really needed to let off a lot of steam ... I wonder how many women it's taken exactly. It isn't like Jake to spend six full days with just one ... he doesn't like any of them that much. In six days he's probably seen at least three women, if not more. It's a sobering thought and I try to squash it back down.

I've trawled my iTunes list so many times, considered

sending him a song and picked more than a dozen, ranging from deep and meaningful, to witty, then angry. I discarded them all, knowing I should leave him alone to simmer, sulk through whatever is wrong with him. This is sheer agony, slow torture. But I have my pride, and he's bruised it.

*Pounded the crap out of it, more likes.*

\* \* \*

"Are you sure?" Leila is pouting at me and I give her a quick squeeze, she cuddles me back. It's like being hugged by a child; she's so small, and cute, and adorable. I feel a tug in my chest at leaving her, but I can't stay here anymore.

"Yes, I think I just need to head home." I sigh. I'll genuinely miss her. She's the friend I never knew I needed. Infectious and sweet. Like Jake, she has a way of getting under my skin.

"Was it a bad fight?" she throws her doe-eyed expression up at me, petting her lip, which only makes me smile.

"What do you mean?" I grin and bat her on the head playfully, trying to play it cool. She moves herself to perch on the rail of the boat, we're standing on deck, watching the early morning water.

"You and Jake? Asshole is not answering calls, so I can hardly ask him." She's blinking at me innocently, not fooled at all.

"I told you, he had to go leave for business, I wasn't needed so he left me here." I lie expertly, PA mask perfectly in place, despite my wild wavy hair. I reconnected with feeling less Emma, somewhere along the past six days.

"I think you had a fight and he's off sulking ... Men sulk! Jake not so much, but he's still capable." She blinks at me.

"There was no fight, we're not together ... I'm his assistant, that's all." I feel the warmth in my face and hope she doesn't see it rising, I turn back to my bag and push my cell inside, to hide the blush. My luggage is already packed and on deck as I wait for the speed boat to come for me. One of the crew has gone ashore for supplies and is due back any minute.

"Men only bring assistants on holiday that they're screwing, Emma, or if they're in relationships." Her tone is serious. Honestly forward, one of her cute qualities.

"I'm not screwing my boss, Leila. We're just friends." I feel irritated at how close to a lie that statement had come; I need to go, I have a plane to catch and still need to get ashore.

"Are you in love with him?" she looks up at me with fluttering lashes and a wispy half-smile. I blink at her.

"No, I'm not."

*Am I?*

I don't know how I feel anymore, and I don't want to examine that possibility.

"I think you are ... I think he's maybe in love with you too." She pouts sweetly, her eyes wide with possibility. I shake my head sadly. Well, I know for a fact that's not true. The fact he's somewhere, doing god knows what, to other women, is proof of that.

"Jake doesn't do love, Leila ... He likes things casual." I point out matter of factly. A fact I know only too well.

*Hasn't he even admitted it?*

"I've seen him in love once," she says wistfully and looks away from me shadily, as though she's let a secret out.

"You have?" I blink hard and feel my cheeks flush. That stomach lurch of pain at her admission.

"Just friends huh?" she watches me with a little smirk on her face. I stay silent and just frown.

"I've known Jake since I was seven ... Our parents are

friends." She's avoiding my gaze. I wonder why she's never been on his bed list, if he's known her all that time. She's adorable and sexy. I look her up and down and try not to dwell on that tit bit.

"I can't imagine him being with just one woman." I smirk, my insides pounding erratically.

*Do I really want to hear this?*

"He was very young ... I think he was maybe fifteen or sixteen ... She was his first real girlfriend ... We don't get on much." She smiles at me shyly, a wicked look in her eye as though she wants to reveal more. I don't want to know, I don't like this feeling burning inside of me and I want this conversation to end.

"Leila, I really have to go. Don't forget I told you to keep my number and we could meet up sometime." I kiss her on the forehead affectionately and lift my bag.

"Yes, yes, I love New York. Just try and keep me away, sassy Ems. Give that boy a good talking to when you get home." She gushes and kisses my cheek, over excited and energetic, a Leila trait. The subject change is something she does, flitting from one thing to another in a blink of an eye.

I really am sad to be leaving Leila behind, I never imagined I would let someone in as my friend the way I've let her. Sarah would be shocked at seeing us together these past few days, and I feel a pang of guilt about it, though Sarah dwells on my mind a little lingeringly.

\* \* \*

The plane ride is going to be long. I pull out my laptop, drink my glass of water, and try not to dwell on the fact I've cut my vacation in the sun short, to go home to New York and Sarah's sleazy boyfriend in my apartment. I should tell

Jake somehow, maybe a text or email, but I don't want to. If he wanted to hear from me he would answer my calls.

I answer some emails briefly, sort some minor issues out for Rosalie. Now she knows I'm back in work mode I tell her to relieve the temporary PA on my return.

I can't concentrate. I dwell on Leila's last conversation and find myself pulling up Google images of Jake in his early teens, trying to see if I can find this mysterious first love. There are so many images of him with women, it brings a pain to my chest and I can't look anymore. Can't bear to see the endless pictures of him with endless bimbos. I don't want to see some ethereal looking woman child that he once fell in love with, I can almost bet that she wasn't one of the leggy boobs and would stand out a mile.

It mustn't have been serious because she no longer exists. He's never mentioned her. Not once.

Or maybe she is the one that got away and that's why he never brings her up. Why he never commits to women.

*Way to ruin your mood, Emma.*

\* \* \*

My apartment looks depressing after living on a luxury yacht for a week and I can smell Marcus in everything, even the air around the front entrance. It makes me cringe. There's no one home and I'm grateful for that; it's late, Sarah will be at work and Marcus, god knows where. I leave Sarah a note on the fridge, not to disturb me because I'm jet lagged and head to bed. I just want to lay down and get lost in a book or movie, anything to keep my head empty and unfocused.

I need to wait until my boss decides to finally show face or contact me, to know what the hell is going on. I dwell over the fact he might fire me, for the hundredth time, and shrug.

# The Carrero Effect ~ The Promotion

Maybe I'll quit ... With this job on my resumé I'm sure I'll get another PA job quickly.

*Do I want that? I don't know anymore. It might be for the best.*

\* \* \*

It's after midnight when I'm woken by the buzz of my cell sliding across my night stand. I reach out to it, fuzzy from fatigue and blurry eyed, disorientated.

"Emma Anderson." I breathe huskily without opening my eyes. I'm on auto pilot.

"Where are you?" That bark has me sit up with a start.

*Crap. Jake.*

He sounds pissed and I'm too frazzled with sleep for this, shocked awake with his final contact.

"New York," I gulp, suddenly reeling by the fact He's finally calling me.

*Is he back on the boat?*

I feel a tinge of regret at leaving.

"You're at your apartment?" he sounds grumpy and coldly distant.

"Yes." Is the only reply I can give; I sound so vulnerable and young it annoys me. There's a silence and a tension crackling on the line. I rub my eyes in a bid to feel less zombie like, pinch my cheek to waken me up more.

"You cut your vacation short?" he starts, his voice softer, but still tinged with irritation.

"Yes ... I wasn't in the mood for any more surf and sun, Mr. Carrero." I hope he hears the sarcasm in my voice. Did he really think I would stay out there without him and hang out with his friends for a full two weeks? Again, another agonizing silence.

"Good, because we need to be back at it ... The Hunter merger has encountered issues. I need you at the office tomorrow." He's in business Carrero mode, all affection and humor devoid.

"Will you be there?" I'm trying to sound as cool as him, but I feel that rising warmth of hope lift its head and scold it back down.

*Get a grip, Emma, stop being pathetic.*

"No ... I'm still elsewhere ... You can handle things for a couple of days." A curt response. I want to cry.

"Yes, sir." I hate that it sounds young and feeble ... He's caught me off guard. I'm half asleep and crumbling at the way he's being, still aching for some of my normal Jake to shine through, but it's completely gone.

"I'll be back Friday. I want a full report on my return." His tone is still cold and flat. I miss my Jake. It's obvious that whatever he left for, is still in his head. That despite the distance, he isn't going to talk about it. He's making it clear that now our relationship is all business, no hints of friendly, or friendship, anymore.

"Very good, Mr. Carrero." PA Emma raises a haughty head and pushes feeble out of the way.

*Well fuck you very much, Mr. Cold and Moody, Yes, sure, I shall jump, because you've demanded it.*

"Enjoy the rest of your trip." I smile coyly, knowing that will only piss him off more.

"I intend to." It's raspy and almost threatening, but it has the desired effect and I'm glad he hangs up before the sob surfaces. Leaving me alone with a silent line and not even a goodbye.

*I fucking hate you ... Bastard!*

I throw my cell across the room.

*Screw you! Maybe I'll resign. I don't want to work for an ego maniac with a constant fucking hard on anymore.*

# Chapter 26

The office is a welcome sight, my assistant, Rosalie, greets me warmly and compliments my hair, tan, and natural highlights. She gushes a little too much at how I look, and I'm forced to coolly look her down, to get her to return to a professional manner.

The issues with the merger are nothing and could have been handled by anyone involved, there is no need for me to be here at all. The lawyers have handled mostly everything, and the minor details are rectified in half a morning. I walk through to Jake's office and dump the files on his desk, I like that they scatter messily, and I don't bother straightening them. I quell the urge to push over his desk tidy beside them.

"Fix them yourself," I mutter and toss his pen on top. It's fair to say I'm still as pissed as ever and right now, the thought of resignation is swirling in my mind rather childishly.

*No, if I'm going to do that I'd rather say it to his face. I wouldn't want to miss the reaction.*

I have a business lunch with a client that's been waiting to discuss some points with Jake and assure them that at Mr. Carrero's earliest convenience, he will arrange another meeting. I smooth over the fine particulars and swell with satisfaction that I'm more than capable of doing his job for him when he's not around.

*What do I need him for anyway? To pander to his ego and swat away sexual innuendos all day. Pffft!*

"Where is my son?" the booming voice rips me from my reverie at my desk, as I snap up to see the force that is Carrero senior, stalking in. I stand quickly.

*Hell.*

This guy is like all of Jake's worst traits, amplified tenfold, and stuck in a far moodier exterior. Less attractive exterior.

"He's away for a few days, Mr. Carrero, sir, he returns on Friday." I smile brightly and smooth down my skirt impulsively, he always makes me feel so nervous. He's very commandeering in a superior way.

"I'm guessing if you're here, then it's not on business." He balks at me, and I smile tightly. The urge to stick my fingers up almost choking me.

"I presume it's a personal trip, yes, sir." I fold my hands gently across my waist and smile brightly, the urge to fidget is strong in his presence, must be a family trait, having that sort of intimidation over me.

"He's ignoring my calls." He rages at me.

*Well, at least I'm not the only one. He was ignoring Leila too apparently, and now Senior.*

"You tell him I want to hear from him today," he snaps.

*Well, that might be hard considering he's also ignoring me.*

I sulk inwardly.

"Yes, sir." I answer, fake brightly.

"I'm sick of this goddamn sulking fucking distance he's put between us these past few weeks. He got his fucking merger, so he can fucking talk to me." He rages at me. Slamming a hand on my desk and makes me jump.

*Wow, Carrero is a swearer!*

I remain impassive, my insides turning to jelly at his booming voice and aggressive manner.

"Very good, sir." I smile sweetly and try not to crumble when he throws me that intense glare. I see the family resemblance. That scary, intimidating glare and furrowed brows. He storms back out and I realize my hands are shaking. He's not a Carrero you want to piss off at all; Jake but with a much worse temper and I am aware that my blood has run icy cold.

I reach for the office cell and dial in Jake's number, hand still trembling ... talking to me or not, he has to call his father. I would rather not have a repeat of that little meeting. My nerves would rather not have a repeat.

"Jake Carrero," he says smoothly, and I know he's aware it's his own office calling him ... he has caller ID, yet he's in Mr. Business mode. Maybe that's why.

"Jake. Your father requests a call from you before the close of business today," I say smoothly, that inner dance in my chest bounding out to remind me that I miss him. Achingly so.

"Does he now?" flat toned and disinterested. He doesn't even question why I used the office cell to call him and not my cell.

*Hmmmm.*

I hate that the tension between us is still as thick. I'm trembling, and I have to sit down, his voice, even like this, is causing me to break inside. I just want it back to how it was.

"He was rather verbal about it, so I suggest you call him sooner rather than later," I say quietly, praying he just calls him, my nerves can't deal with anymore visits.

He scares me so much.

"He yelled at you?" there's a hint of annoyance in his voice this time, a slight hope lifting in me.

"Not directly," I reply softly. "He yelled ... about you ... in my general direction." There's a tense silence.

"I'll call him." His tone is even softer; a hint of Jake in there somewhere. I feel emotion rise in my throat at the slight show of someone I love ... I can't bear this.

"Thank you." My voice is softer too, I push down the urge to sigh heavily and try to think of something else to say, to change how this is between us. I open my mouth to say something, but I'm cut off by him.

"Well if that's all." With that he hangs up. No goodbye, no thank you. Nothing. Just click and the line is dead.

*Fuck you very much, Carrero. Asshole.*

# Chapter 27

I get bogged down with work and end up with the headache from hell, before heading home; it's been a stressful first day back, and now, more than ever, I'm hating his absence. We're a team ... We work on all this crap together and we do it well. I've never had to single-handedly take over and I don't like it. I'm angry at him for making me do this. Angry at the way my emotions are up and down, and I can't stick on hating him or missing him.

I know it's part of my job and I know I'm capable but still ... I hate it. I know more about the Carrero empire than I could have ever imagined, I've so many staff at my fingertips it's terrifying. I converse with lawyers, security, HR, and other crazily titled employees constantly, and sometimes I wonder how my head hasn't self-imploded. I'm only twenty-six and to have so much resting on my shoulders at this age, is a huge achievement. I know I'm good at what I do. But still.

*Why the hell did I have to find my calling at the side of a complete asshole named Jake, who makes me feel completely lost without him?*

\* \* \*

"Miss Anderson?"

I look up at Rosalie as she stands in my office doorway, I was lost in this spreadsheet, my thoughts, and never heard her approach. It's Thursday afternoon and I'm feeling the strain of another busy day.

"Yes?"

"There's someone at the reception desk who's asking for you." She seems nervous.

*Do I make her nervous?*

I don't like the fact that I do.

"Send them in." I smile brightly, trying to put her at ease. I never used to care about the effect I had on her, but I don't like the way she's hovering, or the unsure aura she has about her.

*Am I that bad to work for?*

"Not up here, Miss ... down at main reception ... security doesn't want to send them up." She hesitates. I frown and glance at my watch, I've no meetings planned for another two hours so this confuses me.

"I'll go down." I smile and wave her away. Seeing her relief at my calm response.

\* \* \*

I check over my appearance in the elevator mirror, smooth down my pencil skirt and jacket. I'm back in PA mode with tailored perfection, the only difference being my hair, which softens all of it. I'm getting used to it now, even though it throws off my whole style and often, I catch people staring at me.

I move through the building and out toward the main desk at reception.

"You've someone here to see me?" I smile at the faceless red head as she looks me over blankly.

"I'm Emma Anderson."

She balks, obviously realizing who I am and fumbles; I've had this a lot since I returned with new hair. I sigh heavily in irritation.

"Of course, Miss. Anderson, yes. They're right over there in the waiting area ... The gentleman in the green coat." She points toward the seated area, seemingly flustered.

*Jeez, do I just have that effect on all of them? How have I never noticed this before?*

"Thank you. His name?"

"Ummm, he didn't leave one, he said you would know him, Ma'am." She looks away quickly, she's just peeved me off further. I frown and nod, feeling a little irritated at her lack of capability.

I move toward the large seated waiting area and run my eyes along the people lurking around waiting for appointments. The green coat has his back to me and does seem vaguely familiar. I hesitate, then move forward, and tap his shoulder gently.

It feels like the world stops spinning when he turns, and I'm faced with the familiar blue eyes that resemble my own, that faded gray stubbly face, and crooked mouth, aged but still recognizable. The shifty eyes and awkward posture of that creep from my teen memory.

My father.

I inhale sharply and step back, trying to conceal my revulsion.

"Emma." He grins at me as though we're old friends and I just openly stare at him, speechless.

"I know I shouldn't have just shown up but ..." he starts.

"Why are you here?" I sound as cold and shocked as I feel, cutting him off with a glare and raspy voice.

"I haven't been able to call you or contact you. I tried before, a few times, but you're never here. Your cell says it's cut off." He actually has the nerve to grin again, I think he's mentally unstable.

*What the hell?*

"Why are you here?" I snap. Not even taking a moment to point out that I changed my cell number because of him.

"You're my kid, Emma ..." He shrugs, as if that's all the excuse he needs; my anger simmering under my skin.

"I'm surprised you're aware of that." I realize surrounding eyes have looked up in interest and we are drawing attention to us.

*Crap. I can't do this here, too public and we have an audience.*

PA Emma takes control over shocked and emotional Emma.

"Please come with me, we can talk somewhere private." I turn on my heel, holding my fingers together harshly, I can feel my nails biting my flesh and ignore it. I want to throw up, my skin bristles as I feel him move behind me into the elevator and I take my stance as far away as I can.

"You don't know what it means to me, to actually have you see me." He slurs, a lop-sided grin on his face.

"Stop talking," I hiss as the doors close on us and face him aggressively, now that we're concealed.

"You can fuck off back to whatever hole you climbed out of, you hear. When I get off this elevator I'm going to have security remove you." I spit, venom thick and pure in my voice, barely concealing my rage. My body barely concealing the anger running through me, or the revulsion at his presence.

"Emma, please, I'm your dad," he whines, defensively lifting his hands. His eyes widening in disbelief at my sudden change in demeanor.

"No, you're fucking not!"

*It takes more than a sperm donation to be a father!*

He steps back blinking, but I feel nothing but seething rage and anger growing from deep within, hatred consuming me.

"You think I don't know why you're here?" I laugh sarcastically. "You think I've lucked out and got myself a rich man in Jake Carrero ... He's my fucking boss, okay? So, boo on you ... I get paid a wage, like everyone else. A normal fucking wage, that doesn't even touch on any sort of lavish lifestyle. I am nothing to him except his assistant." I sneer at him. The urge to shake him coming over me and tears hitting the backs of my eyes.

"No, no ... I'm not here for that, really." He scrambles, his eyes darting anywhere but on mine, he looks confused. Dare I say it ... Disappointed.

*Yes, that's right, asshole, squirm!*

"Really?" my voice is dripping with sarcasm, unconcealed disbelief.

"I just want to get to know you ... I missed so much." He's flailing, he knows he's dive bombing, his voice lacking conviction. His eyes searching the elevator for a point to focus on.

"You're a fucking liar ... You had your chance when I was fourteen ... Where were you for the last twenty odd years?" I bite. Emotion stinging my eyes, heart aching badly.

"I was, uummm, ehhh." He's raking his hand through his hair evasively. Probably shocked that I'm nothing like my mother. If I was, I would be lying in a bed beside her in Chicago, thanks to Ray Vanquis. The elevator pings and the doors opens, but no one's there to walk in. I turn on him again.

"What do you really want? Be honest ... I might actually give it to you, if you are." I test him. He has the grace to look uncomfortable at least, and shiftily looks away. I can smell booze on him at this distance and it's the first time I notice the yellow stained whites in his eyes. Maybe he's a drunk.

"I could do with a little help out ... Get back on my feet, you know?" he answers sheepishly, barely able to look at me.

"You mean money?" I grit my teeth. His face flushes and he nods.

"What's my middle name?" I snap suddenly. My frayed emotions kicking in.

"Ummm." He moves back, blinking hard.

"What's my birth date?" I yell, this time loudly, voice shaking. He gulps and tries to look anywhere except me.

"Do you even know what age I am?" I scream in his face and he looks like he's going to run. I throw my hands up in exasperation and turn away.

"How much money do you need to get the fuck away from me?" I am so angry I can barely think straight, heart pounding through my chest and head aching badly. I just want to curl up and cry right now.

"If it's like that, then as much as you can spare." He whispers, there's a hint of success in his tone that acts like a spear in my chest.

I'm floored. I can't even formulate a response, I feel it rise up inside me like a volcano about to erupt. All-consuming, pushing down any rational thought, after the week I've had, the month I've had.

I turn and slap him hard across the face, with the force of all my pent-up emotions of the last week. The strength of it stings my hand and I recoil, gasping in shock.

*What the hell did I just do?*

His eyes are huge, and he's fallen into the corner of the elevator with the sheer force of my smack. I've never actually lashed out and hit anyone like that, with unprovoked sheer violence. I can't talk. I'm in as much shock as he is. I just shake my head, words catching in my throat as I sob and run for an escape. The doors are still open, and I blindly move with speed.

I head for the stairs, kicking off my shoes and hurtling past a couple of shocked women in suits, in passing. I hit the stairwell in its gloomy darkness, tumble clumsily down a few steps, sink down onto the cold metal and let loose. My chest is caving in, and I'm struggling for breath. My head is a jumbled mess of confusion, adrenaline coursing through me savagely.

I clutch at my head.

*I just assaulted a man in the elevator of my high-profile workplace!*

I'm pretty sure security have cameras in there and I've probably just broken about ten laws. I can't get up. I can't make my legs work. My breathing is labored as the sheer panic at what I have done sets in.

*Why did he have to come here? Why did he have to ask me for money? Why couldn't he just leave me alone?*

My head spirals out of control, my body falling into a mass of trembles and shivers, the realization dawning on me like hitting a brick wall. The tears start to fall thick and fast, that I have literally, single-handedly destroyed my career, over someone who is supposed to love me.

*Why did he have to do that? Could he not pretend, even for one minute, that I was worth more than money? Genuinely want to know me?*

As much as I hate him, it still hurts to know that the only

value I have, to my own biological father, is in how much cash I can give him. I break down, howling, and falling to pieces. I can't breathe, this pain is too much and now to top it off, I'll be fired for sure. The only worthwhile thing in my life, and I go and do something that is sure to get me sacked.

Blinded by tears, I pull my cell out of my jacket, without thinking, I dial Jake's number; the tears are coursing down my face and my nose is running wildly. I can't think, I just need to feel grounded again, to feel safe. I need to hear his voice. I need my Jake to do what he always does and bring me back from the brink of hysteria.

It rings twice, and he answers ...

"Hello."

*Oh my god—he answered.*

I pull the cell tighter, stifling my sobs. The wave of relief hitting me hard like a punch and I am momentarily stunned.

"Emma?" he sounds concerned before I even speak, he must be able to hear my heavy breathing and pathetic sobs and sniffs.

"Jake I ... I." I don't know what I'm doing, I can't get the words out. I don't want him to be mad at me anymore, I need my friend, I need my Jake. I'm so desperate for it that it physically hurts. I have no idea what to say, or that I should even be calling him, but it was automatic; like breathing.

"Are you crying?" that shocked tone.

"Please don't fire me." I sob, it's the only rational thing which forms in my head. I'm wiping my face with my sleeve, but it's pointless as the tears are falling fast and hard.

*There goes my make-up.*

"I'm not going to fire you ... Emma. Is that why you're crying? Is that what you think? Where are you? What's wrong?" He has my Jake's normal voice, his tone concerned; a little more than concerned. He sounds worried. It makes me break down even more; I miss him so much, it's killing me.

"I hit him ..." I whisper painfully, ignoring his questions. I'm ashamed.

"In the elevator." I know I'm barely coherent. I need to calm down, take some deep breaths, bring the hysteria to a more manageable level.

"Hit who? Emma has someone hurt you?" his voice is panicked, he sounds odd, angry; but not at me. The same anger he had before he beat Ray to a pulp. I wonder if he thinks Ray's come back.

"Yes ... No ... Yes." I'm so confused. He hurt me, just not physically. But it hurts so much.

"Emma?" his voice becomes strained, he's trying to keep his emotions in check, he's trying to get me to talk sense. "Where are you exactly?"

"I'm in the stairwell of Carrero H..H..House," I stutter and sniff loudly. "I don't know." I break down again, absolutely gone to pieces and completely useless. He has no idea how it feels to have him talking to me again. The way my heart has lifted, pushing a ton of weight away. He sounds like *my* Jake.

"Listen to me, *Miele*," he says gently, soothingly. "Look around, there should be a sign with the floor number, at every entrance." He sounds tense and I'm glad ... I want him concerned. I don't want mad, cold and cruel. I want my Jake to come back, my real Jake. The one who takes care of me.

Just his voice is calming me down and the tears have stopped spilling. I take a deep breath, wipe my face on my sleeve, not caring about the mess that it leaves. I look above me, up the small flight of stairs I'm sitting on and see a white sign high on the wall.

"Floor thirteen," I sniff and swallow back the tears that are lingering, gaining some control and wiping moisture from my chin.

"I'm going to send security to get you, stay on the line Emma, I'll be one-second. I promise. I won't leave you," he pleads gently.

I cradle the cell to my ear as though my life depends on it, the only contact I have with him, and the version of him that I have been pining for. My cell goes quiet; I'm calmer, but I can't stop the fresh tears pouring down my face. This time they're tears of relief, tears because he's come back to me. Jake is being Jake.

"Emma?" He finally comes back, and I let my breath out, unaware I have been holding it.

"I'm still here." I'm quiet and weak. I guess opening up this damn of tears has caused considerable damage, I can't seem to stop them nowadays.

"Who hurt you, *Bella*?" his voice is soft and gentle. His pet name causes another tear to roll down my cheek.

"You need to tell me who he is, so I can have them sweep the building." He coaxes gently and firmly, sounding so warm and safe to me right now.

"I hate him ..." I whisper softly, the child in me making herself known. I sit in silence for a moment. My throat constricting painfully.

"Talk to me, Emma ... Please. I can't stand this." Pleading and gentle. Jake's irresistible to me right now, I wouldn't deny him anything when he is back to being the man I miss so very much.

"My father ... He came here." I sniff, wiping away more tears, starting to gain control over them, he just calms me effortlessly and he has absolutely no idea. He's my lifeboat in a storming sea.

"To the offices?"

"Reception, on the ground floor." I swallow and sit up,

able to take a steadying breath, my voice getting stronger.

"What did he do, *Bella*?" his voice is barely above a whisper.

*God, Jake, I need you so much.*

"He asked me for money ... To stay away from me." I smirk through wet eyes, laugh sardonically. I sound heartbroken. Maybe I am. There's a deathly silence and I hear him curse quietly, calling my biological an awful name. Jake at least gets it.

"I slapped him in the face ... My hand hurts." I look down at the bright red skin of my hand and feel the throb emanating. It was worth it.

"I would have broken his neck," he snarls. "Emma, you need to calm down, okay. I'm getting on the first flight back, *Bambino* ... I'll be home as soon as I can get there." The genuine care in his voice causes a fresh wave of tears, more relief. I want him home more than anything in the world.

"Why did you leave me?" it comes out before I can stop it, emotion fueled. Desperation at finally having normal Jake back.

"Don't talk about this now ... When I'm home." He breathes, as I hear men come into the stairwell, feet clanking on the floor and door creaking; they call my name.

"Security is here." I whisper. I hear him sigh with relief.

"Go with them ... show them what he looks like on the security footage, then I want you to go home ... to my apartment. Stay there until I'm back, wait for me." Bossy Carrero is back, but I won't argue, this is who I need. I won't even argue about going to his place, I want to be there when he gets back.

"Okay."

"Emma?" he adds as an afterthought.

"What, Jake?" I pause.

"You won't get fired for slapping that fucker in the elevator. The tapes will be wiped ... I'll deal with him myself." The gruffness of his voice is reassuring; I sigh, sniffing and finally calm my tears. Relief that he will take care of everything, like he always does.

The man above me on the stairs is holding my shoes out to me and I accept gratefully, the other offers a hand to help me up. I'm suddenly aware of the mess I'm in, a little self-conscious now.

"I need to go now," I whisper into the cell reluctantly. I don't want him to go.

"Put one of them on," he commands gently. I hand the cell to the one holding my shoes.

"He wants to talk to you." I hold it out and he accepts, and promptly puts it to his ear.

"Yes, Mr. Carrero?"

"Yes, sir." He glances at me and away again.

"Right away, sir."

"As soon as she identifies him."

"Understood!"

"Yes, sir, She's ... She's calming down." He looks me over again, this time I frown at him. Fully calm and back in control of my faculties, but I just feel drained.

"Okay, sir." He hands the cell back to me and I notice it's still in call mode, I put it back to my ear.

"It's me," I say softly.

"Go with them, do as they say ... I'll be back as soon as I can. Try not to think about this until I'm home."

I tell him I need to go, calmer and grounded. Commandeering Carrero has taken control and suddenly I feel nothing but fatigue. I say goodbye before I hang up; a wash of warmth, relief, and calmness overtaking me.

*My Jake is coming back ... He's coming back for me. He's going to make it okay again. He makes everything okay.*

\* \* \*

I'm laid in bed in my room at Jake's apartment and have dozed in and out of sleep, listening to distant sirens and noises from afar. The calming hustle and bustle of Manhattan. It's late, I'm tired yet I'm not. I'm somewhere between dosing, and over thinking.

The housekeeper has retired to bed and the apartment security is out wandering the outer halls again. I hear the faint sound of a crackling radio occasionally, they never really venture inside the main part of the apartment, but I like knowing they're out there. Jake isn't one for much security, but his father insists. He doesn't see the need for it when he's home, he rarely uses it when we're on business either. I guess he knows he's capable of beating the crap out of most assailants, seeing as boxing and martial arts are some of his past times.

I'm uneasy and antsy, I know he's coming home, and I'm afraid about how we left things.

*Will he look different to me now? Knowing that he's been ...? I don't want to think about what he's been doing.*

I hear voices in the apartment. Distant, but they're coming in. I'm not sure why they would be ...

*Oh wait! It's Jake's voice, he's home!*

I don't know what time it is, but he's really home. I can't control the wave of euphoria or buzz of energy this gives me. I sit up in bed and wait, I'm not sure if I should go see him or stay in here; I'm suddenly shy and nervous.

*Don't be stupid.*

I scold myself. I ignore the little voice trying to remind me of how things were the last time I saw him but squash it. I let myself out of my room quietly and pad along the hall toward the voices, it's one of the security men and ... I freeze.

There's a leggy red head standing a couple of feet away from Jake, looking bored, but I recognize her instantly. She's one of "his" Leggy Bimbos and it hits me like a sucker punch.

I hadn't expected this ... It causes a heavy pain in my chest, that I immediately push down and have to gulp down the sudden nausea.

*What the hell? Is that who he's been?*

I don't want to know. I don't want to see. I lean against the wall in the shadows and take a steadying breath, my heart shredding to pieces. He's Jake Carrero. This is how he is, this is how he always is. I need to forget all that crap on the boat and get a grip, put the mask back on ...

*Please put it back on!*

*I can't!*

Its fallen on the floor and broken into a million pieces today and I can't find any crazy glue to piece it back together. I feel vulnerable and I hate it. This isn't me. I stare at my hands in the dark and see them tremble. Feel my body follow suit.

"Is she asleep?" his deep voice rumbles through the pain in my heart.

*Jake ... Why do you have to sound that way? Why did you get a voice that can ravage me with only a few words?*

I've missed it, he sounds so clear, and close, and touchable.

"Yes, sir. She went to bed almost as soon as she appeared." One of the men reply.

"How did she seem?" Jake sounds tired. My arms ache to be wrapped around that voice.

"Upset, sir."

## Jake & Emma

"How did she look?" Jake sounds apprehensive.

"Unlike her normal self, Mr. Carrero." I realize he's talking to Mathews, his head of security. I like him, he always smiles and greets me with a warm look. A man who looks a little George Clooney, yet completely capable of snapping necks.

"Was she still crying?" Jake sounds like he cares, maybe he does, except he brought home a play mate, so he doesn't care that much, I think sadly.

"No, sir. She just looked exhausted." Mathews is certainly observant.

"Did she eat?"

"No, sir, Nora said she skipped dinner and went straight to bed." It feels weird listening to people talking about me in that way. As if I'm a broken child and not really here.

"That's all ... Thank you." He dismisses him. I slide back along the hall to my room and stand by the door; my room is at the opposite end of the apartment to his, he won't come here, so I'm sure I'm safe. I lean my head back against the cool door and close my eyes. I want to wrap myself around him and forget everything but the feel of him, close out everything else including the red head. I remember how that feels. I need it more than I ever imagined I would. I miss his touch.

"Emma?" Jake's voice is alarmingly close. I snap up and see him standing a few feet away.

*Shit.*

He never ventures down here.

"Uhuh" I answer nervously, my heart pounding from the fright at being caught like this.

"I came to see if you were still asleep ... Why are you standing there?" There's only normal Jake in his voice. Jake my friend. As though the past week hasn't happened.

"I wasn't sure if I wanted to come through or not."

*So, I'm Miss. Honesty now, am I?*
I'm too tired to pretend.

"How are you feeling?" he coaxes gently, coming to stand only two feet from me. His closeness suddenly making me nervous and we both seem awkward. My nerves prising up inside, now that he is really here.

"Detached," I say shyly; he frowns in the shadowy hall and I look away and sigh. This is harder than I thought.

"You look tired ... Go back to bed."

"I've slept enough. I can't sleep anymore." I sound tired and soft, I pull my hair across my cheek and twirl it absent-mindedly, the soft touch on my skin comforting me. Partly trying to conceal the awkwardness I feel, now he's here.

"I was worried about you, *Miele*." He moves closer, narrows his eyes and gently pulls my hand from my hair, keeping his fingers around my closed fist and pulling it down between us. His skin on mine feels like coming home. It breaks my heart. He has no idea that he can do this to me.

"You would have been impressed ... I think I left a permanent hand print on his face." I say quietly, covering the way his touch has made me feel, sobering melancholy.

"How's your hand?" he turns over my hand in his grasp, using his other to flatten my fingers open while he examines it, I see nothing there. His thumb crosses the skin of my palm gently, achingly soft. His touch like a balm.

"Sore."

He glances up at me. It does throb still. A burning reminder, yet there are no marks.

"Do you want painkillers?"

"Not that sore." I attempt a smile.

"Do you want to talk about it?" his brows narrow, a small, encouraging smile tugging his mouth.

"Not really. I just want to forget." I let out a slow sigh and shrug.

"Do you want a hug?" his eyes never leave mine. I glance up, startled at his question and smile shyly; I shrug awkwardly, amazed that he would even offer, after everything; days of being that way toward me and yet here he is. As though nothing has happened.

He pulls me to him by my wrist and wraps me in his arms solidly, molding me to him. He rests his mouth against my temple as I sag into him. This feels good, too good. This is what I need, this is what I've missed. I snake my arms around his waist, being fully enveloped in one of the best hugs I've ever felt in my life. I could stay this way forever, inhaling him, feeling his warmth around me like a security blanket. It just makes all the anger, pain and chaos drift away like a dream. Forgotten.

We both sigh.

"I hate fighting with you, Emma." He breathes into my hair, I feel that tug of tears come back.

*Oh, no you don't! No more, I'm done with all that. I've poured enough emotion out this week and I don't think I can handle anymore tonight.*

I mentally shake myself.

"I hate it too." I breathe and feel him tighten around me reassuringly. I feel him inhale slowly.

"How was your vacation? Even though you bailed a week early?" His voice is low and husky, it does things to my insides and I bury my head further into his chest. My hair falling over my face.

"Lonely." I admit and feel him sigh again.

"You weren't alone though." I hear the tinge of regret and I can't stay mad at him anymore. He's always had this ability to make me forgive him. No matter what.

The curse of Carrero.

"I guess ... I like Leila." I admit with a smile.

"Me too ... We've been friends since forever ... She's probably one of my few female friends." He admits.

"You have lots of female friends." I tease, finally lifting my head to look at him properly, our eyes meet as all the awkwardness slowly disperses.

"No. I have dates ... I have very few female friends, and no, I haven't slept with Leila ... She's my friend, nothing else." He moves his forehead to mine, resting easily against me, it feels so natural. Natural, yet agony.

"You don't sleep with your friends?" I'm surprised, considering we almost ...

"No, I don't, Leila is like a kid sister to me. She was around a lot when I was young ... It wouldn't feel right." He shrugs.

*Did that mean that sleeping with me might have felt right?*
I push it out of my head.

"She said you had a proper girlfriend, when you were young ... fifteen?" I don't know why I'm even bringing this up ...

Somehow, I want to hear it from him. I want to know if he had ever loved. Despite the warning pain in my stomach.

"Good old loose mouthed Leila! ... I did ..." He looks at me warily and I see evasive Jake. I was right, the times I thought I imagined this, he was hiding this little piece of history.

*Why?*

"You don't want to elaborate?" I coax gently.

"There's nothing to elaborate on ... I had a first love ... We dated for a year, she wasn't my first sexual encounter, and then it was over." He shrugs, still holding me, but loosely now.

## Jake & Emma

"So, it was love though?" My heart constricts painfully.

"I guess ... maybe." He shrugs again, his hand coming up to my hair and plays with a wavy strand. Distraction as focus, he's uncomfortable talking about this.

"So why didn't it last?" I hate that I'm asking, that his evasiveness is making me question him, but something in me needs to know.

"I was sixteen ... she was fifteen ... do the math. Kids playing at relationships." He slides his fingers down the length of hair he's playing with, rubbing its softness between his fingers. I wonder if he's doing it to distract himself, or me.

"Do you still talk to her?"

*Why do I even care?*

I guess knowing there has been someone he loved bothers me more than it should.

"Can we not do this, Emma?" he inhales deeply, and I feel the tension in him again.

"Go to bed ... We have a busy day, if you're up to it?"

"I'm sorry," I mutter, but he pulls me closer again, hugging me tightly and taking a deep breath. His arms around my shoulders now, a squeeze then he relaxes. Kissing me lightly on the top of the head, the way a sibling would. He turns me and shoves me back into my room gently. Reluctance across his face, replaced with that sudden cheeky Carrero grin.

"Hey!" I yelp and swat at his hands.

"Feisty." He grins at me.

"Slap one shithead out, and suddenly you're karate kid?" He's laughing at me and it sounds like the best noise in the world. I mock glare at him, but he just tweaks my face and pushes me further into my room, he pushes his head around the door, pulling it against him.

"I'm glad you're okay ... I didn't know what I was coming

back to ... You sounded ... Not like you." I see the apprehension as he speaks and smiles reassuringly. If only he knew that I have been that way in his absence, on the boat, that whole time.

"I'm made of tougher stuff, Carrero." I bow lightly.

"I never doubted that, Miss. Anderson ... now go back to bed. We have work tomorrow, if you're sure you're okay?"

I smile, but then I remember leggy red head and it's sobering ... He wants rid of me, so he can go play. We're back to old Jake once more, all the happy bubbles inside of me pop and dissipate as I realize that this is how it is always going to be.

# Chapter 28

It's amazing what the human heart can endure when you have a will like mine. It's amazing how you can bounce back, like you were, no matter what life throws at you. It's amazing how many masks I must keep in my back pocket for when one gets smashed into a thousand pieces.

We're on a plane already, and I'm cool and controlled and acting like yesterday never happened. Red head is gone, thank god, and Jake seems like the normal good old Jake from before our vacation. The past week or so erased from memory. Just like that!

All is almost right with the world, if I can just ignore all of that. Forget all the tears, and ignore the crazy way he makes me feel, that I can no longer honestly say is platonic. He's on his cell, despite me glaring at him about using it on the plane.

"Yes, that's right." He waves his hand at my expression, dismissing me as I picture us crashing into the ocean. "No, it doesn't need his permission, it's my money." He sounds a tad annoyed with whoever he is talking to.

"Exactly as I sent you." He frowns into space and I go back to working on my laptop.

"As soon as."

"Let me know if there's any more contact."

He slides his cell off and chucks it down, giving me a wary glance, yet saying nothing. I'm working through a document and go back to being absorbed. I hate flying ... It's boring, stressful, and I've done enough of it to last a lifetime these past few months. Life has just reverted to complete normalcy overnight. I'm not sure how to feel, but it's better than his absence.

"You look serious." He's looking at my profile as I stare at my screen.

"I'm working." I try and ignore that probing gaze.

"So, it's your serious work face?" I hear the smile and squint up at him ... He's in playful mode.

*Great, that's all I need; he can be irritating in this mood, when we're stuck on a long ass flight. Think bored child without any toys, and only me to occupy them.*

"Aren't all work faces serious, Mr. Carrero?" I ask sassily. Still not completely back to normal with him but trying.

"Yours is especially serious this morning," he teases, pinching my cheek.

*Lord help me.*

"Perhaps it's having me up and on a plane before sunrise, boss." I'm trying my hardest to stay focused on my screen and ignore his distracting hands.

"Perhaps." He's smiling, I can see from the corner of my eye. He leans out and closes my laptop almost on my fingers. I flinch, pulling them away quickly, glaring at him.

"I haven't saved that!" I point out.

"It saves automatically." He grins knowingly, and I pout at him as I go to open it again, but he lays a hand on it firmly.

"Leave it ... We have a long flight ... I want you to relax."

# Jake & Emma

He slides down in his chair as though demonstrating what relaxed looks like.

"It's important," I stress.

*Only I could have a boss who doesn't deem his own company's business as important.*

"It will keep." His tone gets firm, I see the flicker of irritation and back down. Still touchy under the surface.

"Okay, fine ... You're the boss ... How shall I relax, Mr. Carrero?" I sulk as he lifts a hand to the attendant and she comes over with the tray of champagne, he takes two and hands me one.

"Why is it always alcohol with you?" I sigh and sip it anyway.

"Proven method. I stick with what works." He raises his eyebrows cheekily. All hints of annoyance gone.

"The resurface of drunken Emma?" I'm still pouting as I say it and I can feel his grin without looking.

*Ass!*

"Maybe just tipsy Emma ... She's nice too." He winks my way naughtily.

"Hmmm." I'm unimpressed.

"Or just Emma ... I like that Emma just as much."

I glance at him and look away, unsure how to read the distant look in his eyes. He's being unusually nice.

*Guilty conscience?*

"Maybe Emma and her other Emmas don't like you much anymore." I say quietly, looking down at the bubbles popping in my liquid refreshment. Sometimes my brain has this amazing habit of saying out loud the most random of little thoughts, hiding in the back of my head. It really is the worst habit. I bite my own tongue.

"And why is that?" he laughs at me, looking at me steadily.

"Because ..." I pout childishly. I don't really want to follow this line of conversation.

"Just because?" he probes, his eyes burning a hole in my face.

"Do I need a reason not to like you anymore?" I know I'm being stupid, but a small part of me has still not forgiven him for leaving me on that yacht and closing me out for days while he ... never mind. This is why I should never have said it.

"I guess not ... would be nice to have one though. Can't have random acts of boss hating being thrown about." He grins, adjusting his casual lounging in his chair and making it creak.

I stifle a laugh, despite myself; he can be funny sometimes, if not a little obtuse. I frown, trying to bring back my pout.

"You could always just boss me into liking you again ... bossy." I tease solemnly, still trying to retain my upset look and failing miserably. He's too good at always bringing me around.

"I might do that." He watches me for a second then frowns deeply.

"Is it because I fucked off and left you?" there's an edge to his voice with this one and a wary look. I guess he's decided now is the time to talk. We haven't, not about this.

*Shit.*

"Maybe." My voice is inordinately tight. I can feel his frown, even though I'm not looking at him directly anymore, he takes the glass out of my hand, he lays both on the table before us.

"We need to talk about this, Emma ... Right now. Get it out of the way."

*Yup, this is what I feared. Boss Carrero tone, this is all I need.*

I turn slightly to glance up at him, my heart stilling and my breathing pausing. I guess we had to do this sometime. What better place than a private jet, thousands of miles high in the sky, where I have zero escape.

"I had to leave." His focus on me is almost uncomfortable.

"Of course, you did," I say quickly, a little too sharply and chastise myself inwardly.

"Stop it," he warns. "Look at me, and stop fiddling with the laptop, it's staying closed."

I roll my eyes and catch him watching me coldly. He takes my laptop and slides it on the floor between his feet.

"I left for both our sakes, Emma," he continues, still looking at me intensely.

"If I remember rightly, you left for your own ... needs." At least he has the grace to look away and sigh, my face is flushing, and my cheeks are hot. Talking about this is making me feel uptight. This was never going to be a good conversation. It just hurts me irreversibly.

"Yeah, well, we had started to overstep the mark a little too frequently, as you kept reminding me." He points out calmly.

"Is that what we're calling it nowadays?" I sound pathetic, huffy and immature.

"What would you rather we call it ... gross misconduct? Sexual advances from your boss?" There's a slight tone to his voice, but overall, he sounds calm. His face almost expressionless, although his green eyes have darkened.

"Um, no. Drunken antics that got out of hand ... twice." I say nervously, trying to lighten the mood a little.

"Three times," he corrects.

"I'm sure you weren't drunk in the car," I add.

"Maybe I should have been." He shrugs with one shoulder and shifts in his seat.

"Well, that would have been safe ... Driving the way you were." I sound more than immature now, I sound sarcastic and confrontational.

*Why am I trying to antagonize him? Does he just bring this need out in me, to fight with him lately?*

"I'm an excellent driver, Emma ... I've driven with some of the best racing instructors in the world." He ignores my tone.

"Is that the direction we're taking now ... squabbling over your driving accomplishments?" I pout, crossing my hands in my lap and sigh deeply. He frowns at me and looks out over the aisle at the empty seats, shifting in his chair for the second time.

"I left because if I didn't, it was going to go one of two ways ... either I ended up fucking you or strangling you."

I'm rendered gob smacked. There's really no other word for it.

*I'm sure I should read my contract under the section about appropriate conversation topics with your boss, and maybe check the sexual harassment clauses.*

He looks at my burning face, accepting my silence.

"It's clear that parts of our relationship sometimes blur the lines ... We work closely, we live in each other's pockets, and sometimes I forget that you are my PA above everything else."

"What exactly do you confuse me with?" I snort, because that would be nice to know.

*What else would you call what I do?*

He throws me a pained and disdainful look.

"You're younger than any assistant I've ever had; we get on, and we're friends ... I forget sometimes that I need to act a certain way with you." He goes back to staring at the side of my face and I resist the urge to meet his gaze.

"So, you never kissed any of your other PAs?" I sulk.

Margo flashes across my mind and I immediately shake it away with disgust.

*Eeww, she's like a mom to him.*

"No, Emma, I haven't. Before Margo took over full time for me, I went through a few assistants and they never lasted any more than a couple of months. I've tried male and female assistants and I lacked interest, and trust, in all of them."

"I see." News to me.

"Working the way we do requires both ...and being this close means, sometimes I forget there would be consequences in trying to fuck you." He's still watching me closely, I'm dying under his scrutiny and the blatant way he's talking about sex between us. I think I'm also upset by the fact he's making it pretty clear it would only be that ... Nothing deeper. I forget that sex for him doesn't carry consequences, maybe that's the issue. He's too used to meaningless screws and has to remind himself that he would still have to work with me after. And I'm too hung up on what sex with him would do to my heart afterwards.

"So, the red head?" I ask, smarting at this conversation.

"What about her?"

"She's the one you ran off with for a week?" I'm back to immature Emma. Half pouting. Heart twisting in my chest, broken inside. He frowns at me and shakes his head.

"No ... I picked her up before I flew home." He avoids my eyes this time.

*Nice ... Picked her up ... like you pick up a quart of milk on the way home from work, at your own convenience.*

"Back on form then?" I spit, feeling the temper return at the way I've maneuvered the topic, I'm such an idiot.

"Completely." I sense the coolness return to his voice too, he's reacting to my anger and my snippiness.

"Got to the root of the issue?" I ask sardonically.

*Try and keep calm, Emma.*
I scold inwardly.

"Yes ... Isn't an issue anymore." He grunts. I swallow hard, I'm close to crying and paste a smile on my face instead.

"Good ... Can't have you incapable and suffering now, can we? Carrero losing his edge is worse than death for you right?" I smile with the most fake smile I've ever given. He looks at me coolly and hands me back my champagne.

"Maybe we should clink to that," I say drily, hating him in this moment.

"Maybe we should." He clinks his glass against mine and I see the sarcasm on his face. He seems angry now too. I smile icily.

*Are we fighting? It feels like we are, but it's laced in uber cool and polite, and I can't read him at all.*

I'm smarting, I feel emotional and I want to throw my drink at him. He's acting like this is all some cool, casual joke, maybe it would have been two weeks ago but not now, not ever again. I lay my head back, irritation clouding my mind.

"Maybe I should follow your example." I pout loudly, I hadn't meant to say it out loud.

*Crap.*

"What example would that be?" he pulls out his cell and starts typing in response to a text, I wonder which leggy woman has his attention this time. I don't even want to know.

"I should get a string of fuck buddies to go visit for a week, rid myself of the tension." I sigh heavily and stare straight ahead.

I see his hands falter, and pause, his body tenses and it gives me a moment of satisfaction. His thumbs hover over the cell, out of the corner of my eye, I see him put it down instead, leaving the text unanswered.

"If you want to be that sort of girl?" he sounds different, tight-lipped and kind of annoyed.

*Hypocrite!*

I think he's mad.

*Hmmmm, well, if it's good enough for the gander, or whatever that saying is.*

"Well, I work as hard as you do, maybe I should follow your lead and play hard too. Seems to work wonders for you?" I'm fluttering my lashes innocently and I can see his shoulders tense up. I'm enjoying his reaction a little too much, in a way it feels like payback. His jaw is tensing, and I see his ear move as a result.

"I don't think it would make you happy, Emma ... Sleeping around ... Fucking strangers." There's definitely an edge to his voice. His frown has deepened and he's gripping the arm of his seat a little aggressively.

"You seem happy enough?" I push on, feeling brighter.

*See, Jake? Two can play at being assholes.*

"We're nothing alike ... I don't get hung up on the emotions of it." He's glaring out of his window now, avoiding me, his voice still laced with annoyance. He's trying to keep his cool. I know him too well. Seems I got to him, the mighty Jake!

"You don't know that I would. I don't think I would." I know only too well that I can't. I know how I feel when it gets close to having sex, hence my boyfriends not lasting long. But Jake doesn't know that. His hand drops onto my thigh, and he squeezes it rather harshly.

*Ouch.*

Now that's gross misconduct and sexual harassment rolled into one.

"End of conversation, Emma." He looks at me darkly and I can see he's raging mad, his eyes have turned the darkest green I've ever seen, almost terrifyingly so, maybe he does care after all.

*Is this as close to jealousy as I'll ever get with him?*

"You're the one who wanted to talk." I smile sweetly.

"Not anymore ... Drink your champagne and shut up."

*Charming! Loss of Carrero charm in one fell swoop. Seems I've more power than I realized. Huffy and seething.*

Well, I feel better at least, a little tick on my imaginary clipboard.

One–nil to me, Mr. Casanova, who fucks women like it's going out of fashion. I guess we were fighting after all and looks like I won.

# Chapter 29

I catch Jake glaring at me across the table and stop twisting my hair for the fiftieth time, he's been touchy this entire trip.

Who would have thought a week's worth of screwing leggy bimbos actually made him more goddamn sulky?

*I thought sex was meant to put men in a great mood, it must have been awful sex.*

I look him up and down.

I'm sure he couldn't do bad sex, if I'm being honest. He has more stamina than most humans I know and he's an attentive man naturally, I wonder if women can make sex shitty, even if they're being bedded by a "sexpert". Even though I don't have carnal knowledge of his bed hopping habits, I am pretty sure his confidence is a great hint that he doesn't have complaints in the bedroom.

He's barking orders over the cell and I'm glad it's not me on the receiving end. Bear with a sore head certainly suits his mood this past forty-eight hours. The lawyers are moaning and whining in the next room over his absence, and I'm sitting here waiting with pen in hand for the notes he wants me to take.

It's after lunch and I'm hungry. We haven't stopped to eat yet and my hair is sticking to my face in the heat. I regret not being able to tie it up.

We're back in Vegas, same business, second time round and I wasn't prepared for the soaring temperatures. I move in my jacket uncomfortably and catch another glare.

*God's sake!*

He's been all over me these past two days, tugging my hands out of my hair, slapping my fingers when I play with my pen, now I'm getting the eye assault for moving in my chair.

*What's eating grouchy?*

I'm the model of professionalism ninety-nine percent of the time, he can't be pissed over the one percent which fidgets under duress. Especially when he's the cause of it.

"Emma?" He barks and snaps my attention up.

"What?" I sound equally narky, he's been a bastard since the flight, he can have some nark back at him. He glowers at my tone of voice.

"I need those memos resent to Walters in New York, the idiot's lost them on the system." He's still glaring.

*Great!*

I sigh heavily and pull out my tablet, he kicks my foot under the table, making me jump.

"Ouch!" I react more from the fright than any actual pain, he didn't actually hurt me.

He's glaring again.

*What the actual hell?*

"What was that for?" I snap angrily.

"Stop pouting ... and rolling your fucking eyes when I tell you to do something." He snaps angrily.

*Wow. Jake has a whole new level of pissed off, it seems. Fuck off.*

This is how the last forty-eight hours have been, my once hot boss is now my asshole, irritating as shit, prick of a boss who's been riding my back about everything. He's made me redo a million menial tasks that my assistant could have dealt with and he's snarked at me incessantly. If anyone has a **PMS** issue it is him, not me.

*For the love of god.*

Even for Jake, the moods of the last two days have been completely out of character.

"I'm pretty sure kicking me breaks all sorts of employment rules," I hiss.

"I'm sure rolling your eyes and scowling at the boss will get your resumé chucked at you."

He's also not been in any flirty or fun jokey moods. If there wasn't a room of stuffed shirts five-feet away through a glass door right now, I would have chucked my pen at him, square in the face. And I would have enjoyed it!

Instead, I give him a sickly-sweet smile and mouth "Whatever you command!" I resist the urge to stick my fingers up at him. Once again, he's back giving someone else a hard time on the cell, I feel my own vibrate and haul it out.

"Emma Anderson."

"Emma, it's Rosalie ... I need your help with some of Mr. Carrero's requests."

*She's been getting it too, has she? What the hell is with him?*

"Go ahead."

"It's just some of the documents he's sent down, I'm not sure what I'm meant to do with them." She sounds nervous. I ask her to go through what she has and tell her they've to be filed. I go through her concerns about some other matters and sign off. I like Rosalie, she's sweet, although she lacks initiative and confidence. If Jake has been bitching at that little cloud of sweetness, then he really is in the foulest of moods.

I wonder why he sent them to her directly and never went through me, I normally do all of that.

*I guess because he can barely talk to me without fucking moaning lately.*

"Emma. Here." He slides his cell at me across the desk sharply.

"Stay here and take any calls. I need to wrap this up." He gives me a dark look, devoid of any pleasantries.

*Prick.*

"Yes, Mr. Carrero." I watch him stalk into the board room and shut the door. He's in aggressive boss mode, he's probably going to bark at all the suits and have this meeting finished pronto. I shake my head at his back and concentrate on not sticking my tongue out. He really is trying my very last nerve, and it's taking all my will power not to tell him to go shove his job.

His cell immediately vibrates, and I swipe it open. I flinch at the name which appears on screen.

*Marissa Hartley.*

*Crap.*

That was not expected. I glance over at him, through the glass door, trying to decide if I should ignore it. I decide against it and then answer, my nosiness getting the better of me.

"Mr. Carrero's cell ... Emma Anderson speaking." I say icily.

"Oh! Emma?" she sounds shocked.

*I don't know why? I'm his assistant after all, I sometimes do man his cell for him. Bimbo!*

"Marissa?" I try and sound friendly, but just sound pissed.

*Oh well.*

"Ummm, I need to talk to Jake ... is he there?"

*Would I be answering his cell if he was? I mean really, Marissa, it's called common sense.*

I bristle. I can picture her doe-eyed face and have the urge to poke a Biro in one of her eyes.

*I actually hate you!*

"He's in a meeting, Marissa, can I help you?" My clipped tone almost betrays my inner thoughts.

"No ... I just need to speak to him urgently." She whines, her voice grates on my nerves. I don't like the tone. I glance again at him through the door, he's in full CEO mode, commanding the room. Somewhat angrily. I hesitate; his bad mood is enough to put me off.

"Look, he's actually in a really important meeting, all I can do is take a message." I say drily, she's just adding to my irritation today.

"Just tell him to call me back as soon as he can," she snaps at me haughtily. The rich kid attitude toward menial employees. The urge to swear at her is strong, but I bite my tongue.

"Is there any other message, besides calling you back?" I'm trying to ignore the creep of suspicion up my spine.

*Choke on your own tongue, Marissa.*

"Just tell him it's urgent, that we need to talk. Today ... As soon as he can." Venom in her voice, intended for me. Seems the feeling is mutual between us.

"Okay ... I shall, bye then." I say coolly and end the call before she gets a chance to say another word.

*Bitch!*

My fingers hover over the screen with temptation.

*Don't do it ... Don't look, Emma.*

My curiosity gets the better of me, and I swipe and go to

his text inbox, the passcode comes up and I falter. I know the codes to his cell, he gave me them ... I've never needed to check his texts before though. Most business-related enquiries come as calls.

I punch it in quickly before I change my mind and I see a list of names. Marissa is near the top, he's been texting her recently.

*What am I doing?*

I notice a couple of other female names and feel sick.

*Why am I doing this?*

I hesitate again and click Marissa's name ... The last text is from her to him. I pale as I scan it, knowing how stupid this is, but now I can't unsee it.

*I still love you Jake ... We can make this work, I'm so glad this happened between us, a new beginning. xxx*

It's from two days ago and I feel physically sick. I close the screen, my hands shaking, and I slide it back on the desk.

*Shit. I shouldn't have looked, I shouldn't have pried.*

He's sleeping with Marissa again. The tone suggests she was a past conquest. Maybe more.

The thought bothers me so much more than red head, or any other female I've ever known him with. Although that didn't sound like nothing ... That sounds like more than just sex. She told him she loves him ... Jake never does love, he moves on quickly, so it never gets to that point.

*How long has he been seeing Marissa, for love to be involved? Was that why she was being that way on the boat? Was he seeing her even then, behind Richard's back? Even while kissing me?*

I rub my face and realize my cheeks are flaming. I feel dizzy and nauseous. I shouldn't have done that. I need to eat ... Maybe it will make me feel less faint. I'm hot, stifling; maybe I need a glass of water. I get up to move from the table

and the swirling dizziness hits me out of nowhere.
*Crap.*
I reach out to grab the table and miss.

* * *

"Emma? ... Emma?" Jake's voice comes at me from far away. I flutter my eyes open and realize there are several faces above me.
*What the hell?*
Jake's holding my face with one hand and pulls me slowly to sit, a hand sliding behind my back.

"Are you okay?" He looks pale and stressed. I realize I'm lying on the floor of the office I was in, my head still spinning, and the scratchy carpet is irritating my skin. Some of the suits move back as I sit up, held by Jake's strong arm as he kneels over me.

"I just felt a little light-headed." I try, but sound childlike, trying to make excuses. I feel so odd. I feel like this is all some weird dream. I don't think I've ever fainted before and it feels so surreal. I can only assume that's what happened and why I'm on the floor with no memory of how.

"Emma, you full blown passed out." Jake studies my face with a scrutinizing frown.

"I missed lunch," I say, feeling confused by what's going on, I don't remember even falling. I don't feel so good, I'm shaking inside. Someone passes Jake a glass of water and he holds it to my mouth like I'm incapable.

"Drink," he commands. Bossy pants is back; I don't argue and take a sip. I can feel heat radiating from my face, this is so embarrassing.

He's still holding me like fine China and I'm conscious of

the many faces and quiet whispers all around, watching me, watching us.

"We're going back to the hotel right now. I want a doctor to look at you." Jake is oblivious to anything but the marching orders he's issuing me.

"No ... No, Jake, honest. I'm fine. I just need to eat." My voice is wavering and weak, I don't feel right at all, sleepy almost. I take a breath and feel the creep of heat over me, maybe that's got something to do with this too.

"I'm just too hot," I stammer as he leans forward and starts unbuttoning my jacket with one hand, easing it off me. Someone hands him a damp paper towel, and he holds it behind my neck; it feels good, it helps a little to clear the fogginess.

The swimming head is starting to pass. I notice there's still an audience and frown, he follows my gaze and looks up as though for the first time noticing the men in suits.

"Can you all give us a few minutes ... Give her some space," he says. There's a mutter of chatter and they all file back through to the other room. Except it's a glass wall and I'm aware of the eyes still being cast this way.

*Crap—that's never going to go away now, I bet everyone in the building hears how Carrero's PA flaked out over a simple contracts brief.*

"I can get up." I try, but he stops me.

"Stay ... for a few minutes." He's trying to make me sip again, but I take the glass from him and drink myself. His eyes on me.

"You gave me a fucking scare, shorty." He sighs.

*Oh well, he's still sweary anyway.*

"I'm sorry," I murmur.

"Next time I'll be more considerate with my fainting spells." I say drily, and he frowns at me, but says nothing.

"I can get up, I feel better." He watches me intently for a second then moves to pull me up. He keeps his hands on my hips as I waver, holding me still.

"I'm good ... I'm just a tad unsteady." My voice is still shaking. My body feels cold despite the heat.

"We're leaving," Jake says without hesitation. Full commandeering mode.

"No, honest ... Go finish ... I'll sit ... I just needed to ..." I wave my hands airily.

*Okay, maybe I'm still a bit scatterbrained.*

"No ... we're going and you're seeing a doctor." He's in "no argument" mode, bossy and frowning. I sigh heavily, I know this mood and even in my strongest moods. I'm no match.

"Don't, Jake ... I'm fine ... make them order lunch instead, then I'll be perfect." I try a smile and fail. I feel weak.

"Emma, I've seen you skip lunch before, you've never keeled over on me." He has a dark look on his face, I'm too fuzzy to even begin to decipher it and too tired for this to continue.

"It's the heat, Jake ... hot and hungry are not a good combo." He slides me closer to him with both hands on my waist and steadies me against him, so he can let go with one hand, he moves his hand to my head and takes a temperature guess.

Really? Like I'm a child with a fever?

It's so at odds with his serious, frowning facial expression, it makes me giggle. I see him break a smile.

"Just checking." He shrugs, bad mood dissipating. Boyish Carrero shining through finally.

"I'm okay ... I'm not sick, Carrero." I smile, all aggravation of the last two days forgotten so easily.

"Promise?" he looks suddenly so very young, I think it's relief. I can't ever stay mad at this version of him. That face could melt icebergs.

"Promise." I hold up my attempt at a girl guide oath as proof, and he smiles.

"I'm still making you come back to the hotel, Emma ... Enough for today." The tone is still stubborn and serious.

"Yes, sir." I feel very tired and maybe the hotel won't be such a bad idea. I mean, I'm hungry after all, room service is pretty tasty. I could use a lay down.

"You're not arguing?" he seems surprised.

"No."

"Okay, then you're definitely seeing the doctor. I think you're terminally ill." He's being funny, nice to see flirty face is back on form once more. I missed him.

*Very good, ha ha, Jake.*

I waver again, and he pulls me back against him, maybe I should feign fainting in the future if this is the result. Falling into his arms seems to be far too easy and satisfying a habit nowadays. Talking of falling.

*Crap.*

My mind slaps me.

"Marissa!" I say suddenly, remembering what had first caused my dizziness.

"What?" he looks at me with confusion. A frown creasing his face almost instantly.

*Crap. Did I say that out loud?*

"She called ... she needs to speak to you." I cover, hiding the tremor in my voice. He looks annoyed and something else. Wary.

"When?" The dark look is back, I hope that means he's not happy about her call and not that I forgot to tell him. Not that I could be blamed. I was unconscious after all.

"Before I ... dramatically met the floor." I try a small smile, but he doesn't look pleased, he's glowering, at me.

*No ... Too soon?*

I think he's displeased in general. He frowns and picks his cell up from the table, slides it open. I have a moment of panic, wondering if I exited his text box, he doesn't react, so I guess I did.

*That was close! Stupid, Emma, really stupid.*

He's still holding me with one hand, keeping me upright, he sits me down in the seat nearby and presses his cell screen.

*He's going to call her right now! ... Right here, with me sitting there?*

I squirm, sure I don't want to witness this.

"Marissa ... You called?"

There's a long pause as he listens. I don't want to be here. I want the ground to open up and swallow me whole. He may think we're back to just PA and boss, but my heart says differently.

"I told you," he snarls.

He sounds different. I've never heard him in lover mode, he actually sounds annoyed, and in asshole Carrero mode, but hey ho.

"No ... Don't bother. I'll call you," he snaps at her.

*Well, I'm glad I've never met him in lover mode, because he's being quite pissy with her.*

If this is what his dates get, then why the hell do they still date him?

He sighs dramatically, I see him tense as he paces back and forth listening.

"Okay, okay ... Don't fucking cry ... I'll call you back when I'm done."

Now that made me shut up and take note. Confusion all over my face. I try to feign ignorance and look like I'm engrossed in the edge of the table, picking at it. His voice had been hushed, but not enough, so maybe he doesn't know how much I heard. He looks at me warily and comes over to help me up when he hangs up on her.

"We're going ... Now." He's back in pissed and grumpy mode. Boss Carrero calling the shots. I don't even react, just follow and stay quiet. My head whirling with the little snippet of conversation between Marissa and him. Completely clueless as to how to feel.

# Chapter 30

At the hotel, he dumped me graciously in my room.

He ordered me to lay down and there's a tray of eaten food by the bed. He has a doctor coming, despite my protests and has left me to stare at the quiet TV.

He's being distant and as soon as I was settled he pulled his cell out and stalked off, closing himself in his own room. I know he's calling her and despite his manner with her earlier, it still makes my heart constrict painfully. I hate the fact he's calling her. I don't know why, but from the moment I met her, I had this weird, gutsy inkling that I really didn't like her at all. Far more potently than any of his other bimbos and I can't explain it. It's some female thing going off inside of me, that makes me hate her more than the others.

On top of that I just hate that he's calling a woman, completely unable to control my jealous pain inside.

\* \* \*

He's back thirty minutes later as the doctor is wrapping up her stethoscope after examining me.

"What's the verdict?" he sounds concerned. Well, maybe ... Bossy mainly.

"She's fine, Mr. Carrero ... A little rest and she'll make a full recovery." The doctor smiles at him confidently, her swathe figure in a nice fitted gray suit and she has a lovely face. I like this doctor, she has gentle hands and an easy manner that makes me relax under her care, she also seems immune to Jake's charms. I'm glad, because she's hot for a doctor and most definitely someone I could see him bedding.

"Why did she pass out then?" he doesn't seem convinced and doesn't seem to notice how attractive she is either. All eyes on me and frowning.

"Miss. Anderson informed me she'd skipped meals and was overheated, I'm guessing she wasn't drinking enough fluids either, and she became a little overwhelmed. We need to take care of our bodies ... She needs to acclimatize to Vegas weather, I think." She throws me a wide smile and I smile back; how could you not, she's lovely.

He's frowning with his arms crossed and watching me closely. He doesn't look convinced, I know he's inwardly cursing me about how many times he's told me I need to drink more water too. The man should have shares in Evian, the amount he goes through in a day.

"She's going to get enough rest, she's hotel bound until tomorrow, when we fly home," he points out a tad rudely. The doctor smiles and nods. She approves.

*What? This is news ... Since when?*

We're due to stay here for a week. I keep quiet as he shows the doctor out, then slide up from the bed and march through to the sitting area purposefully, to find him. To confront him.

"What do you mean we're flying home?" I accuse angrily as soon as she departs.

"Tomorrow morning ... It's already arranged." He has an air of irritation, his green eyes simmering with warning, but I ignore it.

"Why? Because I fainted? ... We have shit to do here, Jake." I strop at him in sheer agitation.

"Yes ... No ... Because of that, and because of shit I need to deal with, okay?" I pale as I take in the agitated tone and manner. He doesn't need to spell it out, I know him well enough. "Shit" being Marissa?

"You're going to blow out this week's schedules?" I say with a dead pan expression. This is not how he normally operates, this is a crappy way to run an empire if you ask me.

"Sometimes life does get in the way of work, Emma." He glares at me sarcastically.

Actually, now I think of it, this is exactly what he does. He takes off on personal time, or holidays or blows out work for a week to go off and sulk.

"What's that supposed to mean?" I snap at him furiously.

*Why am I so goddamn angry with him? I should be happy ... I hate Vegas and I want to go home. I should be dancing my happy dance and getting out of this place early. But I just feel pissed!*

"It means what it means ..." He stalks off away from me and it only makes me angrier.

*Oh, so we're fighting again? What happened to happy go lucky PA and hot boss? When we used to flirt more than we fought?*

I liked them ... I wish they would come back and replace the constant arguments and anger between us lately. The constant sizzling tension and instant flare ups of bad mood and hurt feelings.

*What the hell happened to us?*

"You think I'm all about my work and I don't what? ... Let

life ever interfere?" I snap accusingly.

"Take from it whatever you will." He's pouring himself a drink. Being cryptic as per usual. For no reason whatsoever, his motion makes me more pissed with him, his chilling and kicking back with booze whenever things get serious.

*Screw him.*

"I know how to have a life ... I choose to work more than I fuck about with sex and parties." I know that isn't fair. He works harder than he plays, more than most in his business, that's why I'm always by his side and flying across continents. I've seen it. I'm being a bitch for the sake of being a bitch.

"Do you, Emma? ... I'm pretty sure that stick up your ass is well and truly lodged."

*What the hell? Why is this attack Emma suddenly and how did we get so goddamn angry at one another, over nothing?*

We're literally yelling at each other, tension crackling in the air again. This constant goddamn weird, uptight air is always around us now.

"What the actual fuck? ... You chose me as your PA because of how I work ... Now what? You're saying I'm too what? Anal? You want a party buddy instead?" I yell at him. My body tense and I'm waving my hands around in frustration, steel glare on his face.

"I want a fucking normal assistant! One who doesn't fucking make me feel like I want to beat the shit out of her one minute and screw her the next! This sexual tension between us all the fucking time, is absolutely killing me!" he spits, looking me dead in the eye angrily and it completely floors me.

*Wow.*

I'm literally frozen ...

*I mean what? That's what this is?*

I gawk at him, wide-eyed and speechless, mouth slightly open with surprise.

"Fuck this shit!" he snaps and throws his glass across at the sink rather dramatically. It smashes across the tiles sending shards everywhere, making me jump. Without another word he stalks toward me, looking dark and crazy, sending a shiver of fear down my spine, immobilizing me.

*I've no clue what he's doing.*

He pushes me hard against the wall behind me and kisses me like our lives depend on it. His mouth rams against mine with such force it takes my breath away and I'm too stunned to stop him. My head is still in the middle of the floor, miles behind me, floundering at his statement, and hasn't yet caught up.

I take a minute to pull in my breath. I respond in a way that shocks me to the core; some primal inner me, taking advantage of the few seconds of shock. I latch to his mouth purposefully, opening my lips to feel his tongue and mine entwine. A groan coming from deep inside me. Hot and wanton. Nothing about this is right, but I can't stop it, I've never known this surge coursing through my body. I wrap myself around him, his hands in my hair and mine are around his neck. He's kissing me with all the passion and pent-up frustration of weeks of weird vibes between us. Making love to me with his mouth while his hands run over me and pin me to him.

This sudden overpowering need to have every inch of him joined with mine overtakes. A release from all the anger and fighting and heartbreak, bursting over me like a damn. The urge to let him devour me and take it all away.

He lifts me up smoothly, so I'm against the wall and pulling me hard against him, my legs moving automatically around his waist and my skirt riding up and exposing my thighs.

The strength emanating from him only pushes me further into this feeling of raging desire. I want this ... I need this ... I feel that little inner voice of fear and panic trying to wheedle in and I push her down harshly.

*No! You won't stop it this time.*

Everything that's happened, everything I've felt these past few weeks in his absence and feeling like we let a gulf open between us. I don't care about the consequences anymore. I want to lose myself in everything that's him and let my control, for once, subside.

He pulls me off the wall and we're on the floor, the carpet soft under my back, and mouths still deliciously molded together. His kiss wakening up that deepest desire in me and his body weight making me feel sexy and crazy, turned on.

He's over the top of me, pulling each other's clothes without thought, every hard curve of his body pushed against mine. I can feel he wants me as much as I want him. His mouth knows no limits and he's kissing me with all the expertise of a seasoned pro; he could make me tip over the edge with his kiss alone.

*Why have I never wanted to be kissed like this? This is every fantasy come true.*

There's nothing terrifying or repulsive about this, its drawing me in, opening me up, and making my head go blank with desire. I mold my mouth to his more firmly, extracting a moan from him that pushes my fire higher. His hands on my body exploring and ravaging me, feeling out my breasts, my waist and my thighs as he maneuvers me into exactly how he wants my body. I'm breathless and burning hot. I've never felt this way or wanted it more.

I feel the rip across my chest, he's yanked my blouse open, tearing it. I'm surprised, but yet I've never been so turned on in my life, my hands reach for his buttons instinctively. I try to get them open. I'm not as smooth as him with his Hulk-like clothes ripping ability, and I'm fumbling. His hands are over me, caressing my curves and pulling me into him. His mouth running over every inch of skin he can find while exposing more. We're frantic and panting and lost in passionate heat.

I'm lost under his roaming hands and I'm burning up inside with desire, my body is clenching in ways I never knew it could.

It's really going to happen this time and I'm not going to stop it, it seems neither is he. He's intent on tasting every piece of me and returning to my mouth with every few kisses, to capture me again, push my surrender to him.

*This is what it feels like to be Jake's focus and desire, and it's amazing.*

He rips my skirt open.

*Jesus ... Does he really have to do that?*

It's making me crazy hot and I'm sure they unbutton easily. It used to be my favorite skirt, I reflect fleetingly.

*Who am I kidding? It's hot, it's searing hot ... It's crazy erotic and primal and I love the fact he's literally tearing my clothes off with impatience.*

I've never felt desired this way. I follow suit and yank his shirt, feeling the overwhelming satisfaction of ripping cloth, buttons popping off, revealing his perfect physique. He smiles against my mouth mid-kiss and I almost spasm with pleasure.

*How can one man be so sexy, with so little effort?*

His hands come up and cradle the side of my face, trying to calm the pace, pulling my hands up beside my head and holding them down. I feel the urgency pull back in him, but I squirm under him, pushing against him hard.

"Slow down, Emma." He breathes against my face.

*No, no, no. Don't stop, don't let me slow down and let my mind take over ... Don't let me start thinking this through.*

If I let the memories and doubts creep in, then I won't let go. I won't let this happen. I need this to happen.

He shifts his position on me slightly, pushing harder between my thighs and I know he's not going to stop. He's turned on too, majorly so, and even with my inexperience I can feel the full hardness of him against my pelvis.

I feel my cheeks flush with the knowledge and embarrassment at the evidence, my innocence and naivety showing. My hands wriggle free, roaming over his body and arms hungrily in response, trying to feel every forbidden part of him. He's teasing my mouth, kissing and nibbling my lips. Driving me insane with desire, I can almost feel my body building to self-implode, yet he's still trying to slow the pace.

*No! I want the passion and the hunger, the fast clothes ripping and heated motion of seconds ago. I want him to lose control in the way I am.*

I groan and pull him down harder on top of me, trying to make that clear. Forcing the inner voices away in a surge of stubborn passion. I've never known the intensity of this burning longing and it over powers me, he goes for my throat, kissing and trailing hot breath, making me writhe and squirm under him in desperation. He pulls what's left of my skirt free and casually tosses it aside. Confident in what he's doing, a sign of his "sexpertease" and experience. His hands are at the lace of my panties, and I mentally thank Donna for her love of buying me sexy lingerie.

*Or not!*

Now that he's literally just ripped it off, the thin lace disintegrating under strong fingers. I squeak in surprise as he smiles again, this time against my throat. I feel his teeth against me and the movement of his face, his stubble gently scraping my delicate skin and it makes me arch under him.

I love how that feels, how he feels. He's teasing me, he knows how to drag this out, so I'm literally begging for more and it's all so new to me. If only he knew how big a deal this was. Sex is easy for him, and he has no idea how broken I really am inside. How, even getting this far is a massive leap for me.

He lifts his body to one side and shrugs out of his shirt over me, I can't help but lock eyes with him, caught in his steady gaze. No hesitation. His pupils dilated, a look of sheer lust. He's still as seductive as the first time I ever laid eyes on him. No niggling doubts anymore; I don't care if he fires me after this. I want this more than I want my job.

I yank at the button of his trousers at his waist, impatient to feel him inside of me, to quell this ache, but he stills my hand. He moves down my body trailing kisses across my naked stomach and lower down to my ...

*Oh fuck!*

I writhe back into an arch as his mouth connects with my core and I moan out. I grasp at the floor. I hadn't expected that at all. He probes again, and I moan loudly, unraveling ... I've never felt anything like this in my life and I'm so close to the edge of a precipice, it's terrifying. No one's ever kissed me down there. It feels warm and engulfing, sensations so purely divine that I literally roll my eyes back and lose all control of my limbs. I writhe beneath his attention; I can feel hot waves building inside of me and I'm trying to hold still, squirming and moving and aching. I try grabbing his shoulder, to haul him up. Scared that the sensation will overpower me. I want more than his mouth, but he pins my hands down, holding me in place.

He continues his erotic assault and I can't hold it ... I can't let go, I can't release like this. I've never known this sensation

... I've never orgasmed before, but I know that's what this building inside of me is, and the growing tension is terrifying me. I have heard enough about what orgasms are to figure this is happening.

*No. No, no ... Yes ... No.*

"Let go, Emma," he growls at me, but I can't, I'm trying ... I'm trying, but my head's spiraling with confusion.

*What happens if I let it happen? What happens if I let him push me over the edge?*

I don't want to fall, I don't want to reach that pinnacle and drop down, free falling. I like control ... I need control ... I don't want this to end, because I'm scared of what happens next. It's too much. It's terrifying. I don't know what's on the other side.

He shifts over me, bringing my hands above my head, pinning them down. His eyes heavy with desire, his mouth parted and breathing hard. I want him so badly it physically hurts.

"Fine ... Have it your way." He raises his eyebrows.

*Was that a threat?*

He's at my mouth again and he's kissing me hard, I can taste myself on him, I know it should repulse me, but it doesn't, because it's "his" mouth. It's on me once more and feeding a fire inside, taking my mind once more and pushing all sense away. I feel him push down his clothes with one hand, while the other cups my face.

*Oh god ... He's naked ...*

He presses against me and his manhood is ...

*Oh god.*

I groan. I lurch myself back against the floor in ecstasy at the touch of warm skin against me ... The sensation overwhelming. I'm so responsive to his body, it's taking me over like I'm a virginal teen with zero experience.

## Jake & Emma

I hear the rip of foil, a condom packet. I guess he keeps them handy and he moves for a moment ... He's back over and in one slow easing movement he's inside me, softly, gently pushing in, as I exhale with pleasure and grip his shoulders ... The sensation overwhelms. Sheer ecstasy and fulfillment. I gasp and grip his upper arms, grinding into him, hungering for more. The feeling unlike any sex I have ever had before. Overtaken with an insane hunger for him; he begins moving slowly, bracing himself over me on his muscular arms, caging me in as I grab and pull him down. The movements sending extreme waves of pleasure and ache through me.

His mouth moves next to my ear, breathing heavily. It's too much ... I'm feeling that build again as he's thrusting slowly and surely, his mouth on my neck. He shifts to pin my hands down again, so his torso presses against my body deliciously.

*It's actually happening, Jake's making love to me. We're having sex!*

Slow and sensual and building into a faster harder frenzy, with a rhythmic stroke, he knows exactly what he's doing and is barely breaking a sweat, while I claw, grip and try to hold myself together from rippling waves of pleasure. I feel full and stretched and yearning, I'm climbing higher and higher.

*Oh my god, oh my god.*

It's all I can chant, not sure if it's internal or out loud as the lapping waves of extreme pleasure wash over me with every thrust. My body moaning and groaning.

It feels beyond good ... It feels like everything I ever wanted it to feel like. Could only imagine it would be. The heaviness of that reality slaps me in the face so suddenly, like an ice bucket of water and I start trying to fight for control against the waves running through me ...

*What are we doing? We can't ... We shouldn't be doing this.*

I struggle with my mind, my biggest nemesis, unaware that my body is responding to the doubts it's pushing to the forefront and pulling away from him. Reality clawing at me like a ravaged animal, trying to force my mind back to attention.

"Stop over thinking, Emma." He grunts into my ear, he sounds hoarse and his mouth is now running over my throat, kissing my naked shoulder. I turn my face to his and breathe him in, trying to get back to the lost abandon of moments ago. To get lost in how good this feels. How good he feels. Desperate to join him again.

He's changing the angle and he thrusts harder. I moan out and arch against him as a spasm of pleasure courses through me again. I can't hold on for much longer. He's managed to pull me back so effortlessly.

I've never had sex like this ... I've never felt this kind of all embodying sensation, and it's terrifying.

*What about when he stops? What happens to me once I'm done being ravaged by my boss?*

I feel the tears stinging my eyes unexpectedly, and try to bite them back ...

*What about Marissa? ... What does she mean to him?*

I grasp at his shoulders and try to turn my face away, afraid he'll see the fear and doubt. Overwhelmed by emotions again, fighting the building tension within my body as it nears a greater height. I'm still clinging to him, still pushing my body against his, despite my emotional turmoil, and it only confuses me more. My body wants something my brain does not, and all I can do is move in motion with his thrusts, groaning and clawing to make him push harder.

*I'm so confused.*

"Stop it, Emma," he hisses ... He grabs my chin in one hand and forces me back toward his assault of kisses.

*Stop what?*

I'm doing what he's making me do, my body moving in time to his, held captive by his mouth and hands. It's climbing again, only so intently I know I'm going to rip apart. I don't know how to react. How to stop it.

I don't want to stop it ... but I have to ... I'm scared that it'll overwhelm me ... Marissa invading my mind, what we're doing, ripping doubt through me. It's too much, it's too intense. I'm writhing under him, trying to keep control, but he grabs my wrists roughly as I try to push him off, holding them down to the floor making my senses reel back to him.

"I'll stop, Emma ... Do you want me to stop?" his tone is serious and dark, but his eyes are wary and pleading with me. It's like he drags my focus back in from all the messy over thinking that is pushing in and I shake my head ... I don't want to face the after ... It can't stop. I don't want him to stop.

"Don't," I pant, scared of the intensity in his look, just how overcome with lust he is and how sexy he is to me right now. He visibly relaxes and starts moving hard and fast inside me, as though he knows I may change my mind, his hands pulling my thighs up for leverage and holding me more firmly with every thrust. His desire drowning out sense.

I can feel every part of him against me, his mouth at mine again and I'm lost as his tongue finds mine. I relinquish all control. That last piece of him entwined with me, drowning out the last of the voices in my head. His kiss, my savior from myself.

It sends me off the edge and I erupt so suddenly; I can't even prepare. It's like nothing I've ever felt before. I cry out, spasms exploding inside, causing a million sensations to ignite at once. My brain spinning in ecstasy ... It's devastating ... It's amazing and overwhelming all at once. He thrusts hard into me once more, causing another explosion of stars and I'm completely spent. Spiraling out of control up and over the building waves, and free falling; crying out and clutching at nothing.

Jake stills, falling on top of me, panting as much as I am, and I guess he found his own climax inside of me.

"Emma ... *Merda*." He breathes and groans into my neck, laying heavily over me after his own completion. I lay sated and breathless as the world slows around me and my senses start to calm.

My body is tingling all over, and I feel suddenly exhausted. Suddenly emotional and all too aware. I feel my self-consciousness roll over me. I'm semi-naked and entwined with him on the floor of our suite. This is more than an "oh shit" moment ... That's a massive understatement. This is more of a "I've lost my fucking mind" moment.

I shrug out from under him, suddenly cold, terrified, ashamed, unsure, panicking, and he rolls away reluctantly. Kicking his pants and underwear from around his ankles. I'm starting to tremble as this hits me.

*What we have done?*

I can feel my face burning and my legs are like jelly ... I can't breathe, my body still basking in the after effects, yet also panic swooping in. I try to get away, but he hauls me back to him, against his naked body; I feel myself stiffen all over.

"Emma, don't."

"Don't what?" I sound small and terrified and I hate that voice, it's betraying the overwhelming panic growing up inside of me like a tornado, about to engulf my entire world.

"Don't close that door ... not after this." He's lying beside me on the floor, his voice deep and sexy. I want to die with the shame of what I have just allowed him to do with me. No better than all the whores he beds.

*I can't ... I can't do this. What the hell have I done? I've just destroyed my relationship with Jake and my entire career in one fell swoop. I've just opened Pandora's box on a whole host of chaos I can't deal with.*

My mind's running at a hundred miles an hour. I'm seeing everything we are, and I've worked for, crumbling away to dust. He can do casual sex and brush stuff like this off, but me? I just completely surrendered what was left of my heart to the one man who would never want it, and I can't go back.

"We crossed the line, Jake ... we can't go back from this." There are tears in my eyes, because I know this changes everything. He swears under his breath and rolls back to me, leaning over me and trying to bring me back to him, but I resist. His eyes searching my face, trying to gain contact. Caging me in with his muscular arms.

"Emma, don't do this ... It's sex ... Don't over think it." His words feel like a slap in the face. This is the problem right here! This was just another meaningless screw to him ... Another faceless woman. But it wasn't. It was me ... Emma! And now everything is ruined.

"I'm not you," I spit angrily, and I can feel the emotion bubbling up, ready to burst forth. That inner self-doubt and fear flooding through.

"I can't just have sex then shrug it off meaninglessly."

*Why did he have to say it like that? Like this is nothing. This is why I should have never let it get this far.*

"You think that's what I'm going to do?" he looks hurt, then angry, all at the same time, his arms tensing over me, keeping us apart. His face a picture of rage and betrayal.

"Maybe I should ask Marissa!" I spit at him, I'm close to breaking down. Jealousy ripping through me at saying her name. Heart wrenching pain hitting me hard. I can feel my eyes smarting.

*Is that what he does? Screws and then forgets it ... Is this who he is? Why am I shocked at this? ... I know that's who he is ... I've seen it a million times.*

"Fuuuck ... Emma." He groans, dropping his face into a hand, rolling onto his back, away from me once more. It sounds like he's asking god for strength, he pushes up and moves away completely, jumping to his feet and stalking off toward the bathroom. I turn away, I don't want to see him naked. Not now ... Not ever again.

I jump up, fully emerged in emotional madness and panic, and run to my room. I slam the door, locking it behind me and stand behind it panting, unable to reel in the chaos inside of me. The beginning of a panic attack overwhelming me.

*I let him kiss me ... I let him have sex with me ... I let him touch me in places with his mouth no one ever has ... How can I go back to normal after this? How can I just rewind and delete what happened? It's monumental. It changes everything between us; how I feel about him.*

He pounds the door behind me violently, causing me to jump and hold the handle tightly. My heart racing in sudden fear.

"Emma, open the fucking door." He sounds livid.

"No." If I do I'll break, and I can't break, I have to stay strong. I need to put distance between us, until I can get a grip on what we've done.

"You're being childish ... We need to talk about this." He sounds enraged.

"Why?" I spit. So, he can inform me that it's casual sex, and I'm making a mountain out of a molehill.

*Is this the chat he has with every woman he fucks?*

"For fuck's sake ... This is the fucking problem with you, Emma. You're like a fucking swing door." He raps the door with a slap and I jump, still clinging to the handle.

*What the hell does that mean? He's the one with the crazy moods and bad temper.*

I glare at the door and jump away when he pounds on it again.

*God's sake, Jake!*

"Open the door or I'll fucking kick it in." He sounds beyond mad, he sounds terrifying ... I'm scared, I've never known him this mad; Jake has never scared me before in this way. Maybe the night he beat Ray, but now I'm shaking so badly I think I may throw up or pass out. I believe him, that he will kick the door in, he's strong enough. Angry enough. And it makes me pale. Memories of a thousand angry men.

"Jake, you're frightening me," I cry, my voice over taken with emotion. Tears stinging my eyes. My body trembling as I revert to teen Emma.

"Open the door. Please," he switches to talking through gritted teeth, as though he's trying to quell his temper and soften his voice, but he's still so angry. I hear the buzzer of the hotel room door and he curses again, only quieter, as though he's turned his face away from the door.

*Go away, Jake.*

I silently pray.

"Emma, open the door ... For the love of god." He returns, his voice calmer, yet still booming through at me.

"Someone's at the door, Jake ..."

*Go answer it and leave me alone to freak out. Leave me to calm down and stop shaking like a leaf.*

I'm trying to sound cold and cool, but I'm terrified.

"I don't give a fuck, now open the door ... Why are you hiding?" he sounds exasperated, hurt.

*Why am I hiding? Because I'm scared ... The*

*overwhelming realization of what I've just done is drowning me. Jake's anger and aggression is scaring me. I'm suffocating, and I can't think straight. I can't look at him ... How could I? I've just seen every part of him naked and let him do things to me, intimate things ... Pleasurable things!*

For the first time in my life they didn't feel wrong, yet I feel the most guilt and shame I've ever felt. It's too much. My head feels like it's going to self-implode, taking my body with it.

The buzzer goes again, only this time longer and repetitive, someone making it clear they have no intention of going away. He thumps the door once more, making me jump, and I hear him storm away, cursing. Whoever is out there is persistent, and he knows they're not going to just leave.

I run to grab a robe, now that I know he's gone. I'm trembling all over and I know it's not just from fear. My body is still reeling from what he did to me; the overwhelming climax that rocked my entire world.

I pull off the remains of my clothes until I'm fully naked and swathe myself in the plush bathrobe, hoping to feel more secure. Hoping to feel a slight releasing of this crazy cold fear.

I hear voices in the room ... I can't make them out, but one is Jake and one sounds like it might be female.

*Who's he talking to?*

My curiosity calms me, suspicion becoming the overriding emotion, pulling me out of my own head. A little green-eyed monster pushing herself out, knowing he's with a woman. At least it means he's leaving me alone, for that I'm grateful, but I need to calm down and pull myself together. I need to get my emotions in check. I've no idea what I'm going to do, I need to think, work out the next course of action, put it all back in the little black box.

I can still hear the voices, they're raised now. I strain to hear, but I'm scared to go too close to the door. I don't know how to navigate this ... I don't know how to fix what I've done.

*What happens now? I don't want to be another one of his play mates, he picks up and drops on a whim ... ... How could that work, when I'm with him all of the time?* I pale at the sudden realization.

He won't want me around anymore, if I'm just another fuck buddy. He never keeps any of them around; he doesn't date anyone beyond a month at most, and never goes back to dating someone he's seen before. Very rarely anyway. It's not his style to back track. We can't work together if this is what we do. Have done. He'll replace me. Fire me.

I'm not sure I want to do that again anyway ... I feel dirty and ashamed for letting this happen. I did what every other female on the planet does. I fell at the feet of Jake Carrero and gave him all of me. I am no better than any other women he has ever had sex with.

*No, in fact I am worse!*

I am a broken, emotionally messed-up woman who turns every little act into a huge brain fuck and over thinks every tiny detail. I am a woman who let herself fall for him, despite knowing what he is.

*Why would he want to deal with all the mess that I am?*

The voices in the room have moved away and I realize they're more muffled than they should be. Whoever is here has been moved to his room, and he's shut the door. I physically slump, he would only take someone whose shared his bed into his room to talk. Someone here in a non-professional manner.

Despite all my inner chaos, this thought causes a sharp pain in my chest. I pull the robe tighter around me and slowly unlock the door, peeking out as I do. I can see his door from here and it's shut, the sitting area is clear. My hands trembling,

I move out slowly, pulling the robe tighter.

I can see the remains of my skirt and panties on the floor nearby and Jake's clothes are still lying in a heap. Whoever came here would have seen them too.

I move out to try and listen. My turmoil held in check for the time being. I want to know who's here and in his room with him. I want to know if it's one of his play mates, even though I don't have the right to care. It's getting to me on extreme levels, jealousy eating away inside. Agonizing.

I get close enough to hear the voices more clearly and freeze as I hear the raised clear voice that's overly familiar to me ... That snarly, whiny, bitch of a voice.

Marissa Hartley!

*Fuck.*

# Chapter 31

I hurriedly pick up the remains of my clothes from the floor and throw them in the bin. I leave his clothes folded on a chair in the room and discard the condom packet in the kitchen waste bin. I don't know why I'm trying to hide this now, she's already seen it, and I'm guessing by the raised voices, she's making it clear.

I feel like a guilty, dirty secret, his mistress and she's the wife. I'm scurrying around trying to erase what I've done, I'm also trying not to listen at the door and my heart is doing some sort of "Cha Cha" as I rush around. I'm completely out of control, all traces of PA Emma banished, my palms are clammy and cold, and I feel physically sick.

I creep back to my room and turn on the shower. I need to clean his smell off me, eradicate the memory of how he felt. I need to wipe away my shame and get back that cool calm PA who would know how to handle this ... That's one of her job skills ... Handling awkward situations.

The water's hot and harsh, but I don't care. I want it to punish me. I want it to scold the crap out of me and take away the lingering feel of his touch, his skin on mine. His kiss, his hands, his smell ... Him inside of me. I can't bear to think about how it felt. Not now. Not ever.

I'm running ... I know I am ... Mentally pulling away at speed and ramming myself back into that tiny box in my head, that safe concealed, controlled box where my life is one long mass of tick boxes and orderly lists. No emotions and no complications. I can handle that life, because I control every part of it, there are no surprises, no unplanned events. No feelings that can rip your soul to shreds. No one to reject you.

Coming to work for Jake had been a mistake. From day one he made me question myself over and over, made me forget and lose my reserve, made me relax too much. He has a way of making me lose sight of who I am and what I am doing. He let that part of me I lock away, slide out, and I hate it; he makes me feel unsteady and vulnerable and I can't do this.

*How can I go back to before? He's unraveled me in so many ways. I'm more broken now than I ever was.*

\* \* \*

When I emerge, I'm wearing my workout clothes, a clear plan in my head and I feel more optimistic. Determined. I'm going to go running, clear my mind and get the hell away from him for a while, until I can reel in my thoughts and feelings. I also need to put a huge sea of space between Marissa and myself, simply because I can't stand her, or the fact she's here with him. I don't know how she fits in, or what she means to him anymore. What I am in this mess. I don't intend to find out. My heart is aching, but my defense system is connecting, and I just need air.

My damp hair is tied up the best it can be, now it's so short, and my sneakers are on my feet. It's quiet. I assume they're still in his room, doing god knows what. I don't even want to think about it.

I open the door, pulling my hooded top on and zipping it over my sports crop top in a distracted movement, but freeze as I see him sitting alone on the couch, facing my door. Pausing mid-movement, and then continuing to haul on my jacket, I try to ignore that he's watching me in an unsettling, silent way. His expression bleak, he's still topless, wearing jeans and bare feet. I gulp.

He looks sexy, ruffled, but totally stressed, his arms are up and resting on top of his head in a pose that just screams "My life is fucking over". I falter, but he says nothing, just sighs; still watching me and I force myself to walk into the room. I look around for his guest and note his door is shut.

"She's in there ... It was Marissa." He says darkly. I say nothing, just chew my lip nervously. My heart's pounding so hard I think I may have a heart attack. I want him to stop staring at me. He's making me even more nervous than I already am, dissolving my resolve.

"Are you done having your after-sex crisis?" his tone droll. I flinch at his words but ignore them.

"I'm going running ... I need some air." I say quietly. Unable to meet his eyes. Focusing on putting my iPod in my holder on my arm, and plugging the headphones in.

"How appropriate, Emma," he sneers at me. I glare at him, but move to the side, to walk around the furniture for the door. He jumps up, leaping easily over the couch and standing face to face with me, blocking my route menacingly. He towers above me, anger on his face.

"I don't think so."

"What? You're going to stop me from leaving?" I reel back in trepidation. A little unsure of him right now.

"If I have to." He looks sardonic.

"You want a cozy chat with me and Marissa, do you?" I can't help with the sarcasm; he's knocked me off balance with his behavior and I'm just reacting.

*Why am I being this way? ... Why is he? What's wrong with us? We should be able to just go back to before.*

He steps back, seemingly stung by what I said and rubs a hand over his face, losing his menacing glare. He scrubs his fingers through his unruly hair, he looks desolate and I feel a twang of guilt and pity, but I steel myself to stay still.

"Things are fucked, Emma ..." His voice wavers, he sounds exhausted.

That's an understatement if I ever heard one, and I'm heartbroken that he's now only realizing this! He lifts his hand, cupping my cheek and runs his thumb across my mouth unexpectedly, causing me to flinch at his touch, at the surprise of such a tender motion. He withdraws as if I've scolded him, puts both hands into his pockets instead. He looks like a child and turns his face away, hunching his shoulders. It makes me ache to reach out for him, but I still my hands by my side. I have more control than this. I need to do this.

"Are you going to fire me?" I ask flatly; I need to know ... I need to prepare myself. Figure out where I go from here.

"Why would you ask me that?" he snaps, his fiery green gaze on me, anger instantly returning.

*Oh ... I don't know maybe because you've another woman sitting, waiting in your bedroom, and coitus is not part of my pre-arranged employment contract.*

"I need to know where I stand." Is all I say, cool and crisp, devoid of my betraying emotions. He snorts as if I've said something outrageous, then mumbles something that sounds like "you and me both". I'm not sure, but I ignore it anyway.

"Why is she here?" I look toward the door behind him and feel that inner twang of pain. Jealousy. He stops for a moment, as if he's trying to find the words, then just says it.

"Marissa's pregnant ... I fucked up."

It's as though he's punched me full force in the stomach, I'm reeling and dying all at the same time ... Unable to really take in his devastated expression fully.

*What the hell?*

I feel the nausea rise quickly and the spin in my head, before I can grasp control. It's as unexpected as the last time I fainted.

"Whoa, Emma." He grabs my arms as I crumble and rights me against him, the familiar feel of his body and heat acting like an anchor for my spiraling mind, stopping me from fully blanking out.

"Sit." He barks, and yanks me down toward the couch beside him, he draws me around, sitting me down quickly. I grasp my face and sink my head between my knees, trying to push the tilting sensation down. Trying to stop the overwhelming urge to be sick.

"That doctor was fucking useless," he hisses.

"I'm fine," I lie. "Stop swearing." I can't lift my head just yet or I may actually die ... I think I'm losing the ability to see. Everything is swimming and heat has washed up from my toes in a sickening wave. My body is tingling and not in a good way.

"You're not fine, Emma ...You're getting seen by someone else."

"Stop it!" I snap and sit up, swaying a little.

"It's dizziness, that's all. I've had a shock okay ... You just told me you're going to be a father, just after we ... For fuck's sake." I snap, and he stops dead; I see him pale visibly, he slumps down and exhales slowly.

"You're not the only one, okay."

*Ironically put.*

"When did she tell you?" I try and sit up, swaying a little, but feeling less likely to keel over. Trying to figure out how long he has been seeing her.

*Did he sleep with me, behind her back?*

"A couple of days ago." He sighs looking down at his lap.

That explains his monumentally shitty mood for the past couple of days, and hints at just how unhappy he is about this.

"What are you going to do? ... Marry her?" my voice falters.

*Why do I sound so childlike? Oh, I don't know, maybe because the thought of Jake marrying her is killing me.*

I'm hushed by the twisted frown he throws at me.

*Okay, maybe we don't live in the nineteenth century anymore, but I'm sure Father Carrero will have something to say about a namesake being born out of wedlock. His father is a traditionalist after all.*

"No, I'm not going to ask her to marry me, because I knocked her up, Emma ... I'm not that stupid." I remember him telling me about his father marrying his mother on a whim and I realize why. Jake has more sense. Thank god.

"What then?"

*Why do I even care? I shouldn't care.*

I've royally fucked over my job, our friendship, and my life. It won't be long before I no longer work for the Carrero empire at all. I shouldn't care about this, I shouldn't be feeling that aching pain in my heart and chest at this fact. I've blurred the lines of how I should feel about him, and I need to bring them back into focus. My head is a complete mess.

"It's complicated." He looks torn. I see that hint of lost little boy and it hurts me. Even after all this, I still care about how he feels. I'm pathetic.

"As complicated as what we just did?" I flush as I realize the voice that said it was mine.

*Mouth, why do you hate me so?*

"Contrary to what your crazy little head tells you, Emma. There was nothing complicated about that," his flat tone and angry expression shut me up.

*What does that even mean? Oh, wait ... It's just sex, Emma ... Right?*

I turn my face away and stare at my hands. Tears burning my throat.

"It was Marissa ..." he says it so quietly that I almost don't hear him.

"What was?" I snap upright, snapped around by his random declaration.

"When I was sixteen ... When you asked me about the girl I loved." He stares at the floor and not at me, his hands flat on the couch. I've nothing to say, no words filter through my brain ... I just gawk at him as he frowns back at me finally. I'm stilled by the shock and heavy thud inside my chest. Nausea swirling back up violently.

*I don't want it to be her, anyone else, just not her. Why did it have to be her? Was that some female intuition all along, inside of me screaming that she's meant more to him?*

"I was with her for a year ... I was mad about her." He sounds like he doesn't believe it himself. A dryness to his tone. I don't want to hear this. I can't bear it.

"What happened?" I croak.

*Mouth? Were you not listening to my brain when it said I don't want to hear?*

He looks uncomfortable and gets up to walk across to the table near my bedroom door. He pushes around some weird modern wooden sculpture there and I can see the tension running through him as he looks for the words. I'm frozen and holding my breath, a sea of emotions aching in my chest.

"She broke my heart, Emma ... She fucked my best friend." He drops the sculpture back in place.

*Oh my god. Why would anyone want to cheat on him? I mean look at him? Why would she want to hurt him?*

I shake my head as if I can't believe it. I don't want her to be the one.

*Is she the reason he's the way he is? Why he keeps women at arm's length, and it's just sex and fun? Did having his first love savagely rip his heart open make him unable to trust women in his life? Keeping them all at a distance, the way I do with everyone else.*

"Why did you start seeing her again?"

*Do I want to hear him tell me how he's never got over her? No, I don't.*

He shrugs and looks at me intensely.

"It's complicated."

*When is it ever not?*

"Stop saying that," I wail. I realize I'm on my feet and I'm angry.

*Why?*

Because he's my Jake. Not hers. I want him to want me, and only me; I know it's never going to be that way and it rages every part of me. Rages and burns that once, long ago she had exactly that and she threw it all away. She was a complete idiot!

"Emma ... What do you want me to say?" he moves at me, and pushes me back to sit down, so he's standing over me.

"You think I planned any of this shit?" he looks broken, eyes damp and face unreadable, yet somehow sad.

"Do you love her?" I ask of him, complete fear gripping me inside.

*Don't cry ... Please don't cry. Not here. Not now. Not in front of Jake.*

A look flashes across his face and I can't read it. I'm scared of his answer, so I cover his mouth. "Don't." I'm shaking my head. "I don't want to know." He grasps my hands and pulls them away.

"Emma, it's not what you think," he pleads, his body trying to cage me in against him.

*No? What do I think? ... What could be worse than this?*

"I can't ... I can't right now ... I just need to go." I push him away, lost in teen Emma mode and rejecting contact, while my heart is crushing in on itself.

"Stay, Emma, please. We need to talk." He's trying to pull my arms to him, but I'm pushing him off. Marissa is right there in the next room, she's pregnant with his baby. She's the first love of his life. She's the reason he avoids relationships. What am I supposed to think? She's the reason I'll never have a chance with him.

"I need air ... space ... Jake ... I need space." I gulp down tears and panic, and finally throw his hands off me. He lets me go and moves back rejected, he's letting me leave, but I don't want to go anymore. I don't know what to do. I hesitate.

He says nothing, just gives me his boyish wary look and deepens his frown. I can't stay here, so I let my body go into automatic pilot. I stalk toward the door, pulling up my hood, and don't look back, knowing that walking out is the only choice I have. I don't look back, even when I hear him say my name.

\* \* \*

I run about three blocks before I stop and let the heart wrenching pain over take me. I cry like I did the night he left me on that boat, and I think I may actually die this time. If my lungs don't self-implode, I think my heart might. The pain is unbearable and raw, and I've never willingly exposed myself to enduring it this way, except that night.

I sit on a bench with my head between my knees and I think I may even throw up; this isn't my life ... My life is calm and easy and straightforward, my job, my apartment, my responsibilities. They all slot into place and I manage them all well. This isn't really happening. I'm in a parallel universe, or I'm dreaming. I'll wake at any minute and this will all have been one long, bad dream. Except I know that it's not. Meeting Jake has slowly changed it all, he is too potent to be around, changing me, changing how I think and live, until I don't feel like I am in control anymore.

*Is this how we got here?*

\* \* \*

I finally start walking back to the hotel, I don't know how long I've been, but I'm calm, and my tears have dried on their own, my face feels tight and swollen, but I don't care anymore. I've been through so many emotions these past weeks, I think I'm slowly losing my mind. I'm definitely losing the grip on my control. I don't even know how to claw it back.

The room is dark and empty, I've been gone for two hours according to the wall clock ticking loudly in the modern suite. There's a light under Jake's bedroom door. It makes me stop. Pain clenching in my chest that he's in there with her.

*Is this how it's always going to be? There's always going to be me, feeling desolate, alone on one side, and Jake on the other side of a bedroom door with another woman?*

Isn't that what this is all really about? Except I know this isn't all on him ... I'm incapable of letting him get close to me, even if he actually wanted to try. I'm afraid of what that means, what that will feel like; too much has happened. Even if he told me he wanted me and only me, then how would that work? I don't see how this could get any better, it's better if we forget it ever happened, it's better if we just act like we did before the kiss in the kitchen and go back to an easier time.

*Can I do that? Can he? Can I bear it?*

I'm going to have to if I want to keep my job, and I do want to keep my job. I love working with him, I love being his right hand, but surely that in itself is half the problem? We crossed the line and now I'll never be able to just be what I was. Because I love Jake.

*Shit. I love him.*

I push the door of my room open and halt suddenly. Jake's laid on my bed, illuminated by the lamp beside him with his laptop on his thighs. He's been waiting on me, his cell tossed carelessly in the center of the bed, beside mine. I guess he tried to call me and found my cell left behind. He flits his gaze from the screen, up to me and closes it silently, without breaking eye contact. He looks every bit like the CEO he was the first time I ever met him. Mature and poised. In control. It makes me ache so badly.

"We need to talk." His voice is steady and deep, hoarse from tiredness. I feel my inner confidence slide silently from deep within and make a quick exit via the door. I swallow and take a deep steadying breath, suddenly coy and afraid.

I'm better than that and move coolly into the room to start removing my hooded top, all control being forced back in place, hiding my inner turmoil, hours of tears giving me some of my facade back. I can do this.

"Can I have a shower first? I'm sweating from my run." That's a lie as I barely ran anywhere, I just don't want to do this. I want him to leave. I need space to function and deal with the unavoidable fact that I'm in love with a guy who can't love me back.

"No ... I've waited long enough." He bristles, and I can feel his eyes on my back. I kick my running shoes off and slide them under the vanity with my toes, smooth fluid movement, giving nothing away about the tension and panic rising in my throat.

*So, this is where Emma has been hiding ... Finally. Great time to make a comeback.*

"Fine, but be brief, I want to go to sleep." The tone is cold. I can't help it, PA Emma is my dominant self, she slides in effortlessly to protect me whenever she feels me falter, and tonight I have fallen so far from my tree. I have fallen in love with Casanova Carrero, and I am drowning.

I can tell by his slow, steady intake of breath his anger is still hanging around between us. He pauses, and I glance in the mirror slightly to see what he's doing, he's looking at his hands, on the bed, and frowning, contemplating his next move and he doesn't look happy. I've rarely seen him lost for words; I feel hopeless watching the anguish rush across his brow, I can tell he's trying to decide what he wants to say next.

"Is this how it will always be, Emma?" he sounds defeated and I cave inside.

*Why can't I just be honest with him for once? Why can't I tell him about the chaos that goes on inside my head? Why can I never just talk to him the way he talks to me? Why can't I tell him that I'm being this way because I love him, and it kills me to know it's unrequited.*

"What do you mean?" I ask steadily and coolly, making slow, deliberate movements to untie my hair, maintaining that outward persona, despite the internal shaking and nausea I feel. I want to wipe this day out and start again, go back to safer ground.

"One step forward, and six steps back," he says quietly and to no one in particular, I hear a tone of deflation in his voice. I can still see him in the corner of the mirror, his body slumped in a non-Carrero way. I can't help but feel a longing for the strong curve of his shoulders to return. He looks so vulnerable suddenly.

"I've called Ryan's, the jet is being prepared to take us back to New York, tonight ... Pack." He slides from the bed, scooping up his laptop and cell and stalks to the door, stopping briefly. He looks at my back; I see him in the mirror and look away. I can see the anger flash across his face. His body locked in a disturbing pose that says he's beyond done with me.

"I used to think all you needed was time ...To learn to trust me, but now I see that talking about this is pointless. You don't need time, Emma ... I was fucking wrong." He storms out, slamming the door and I feel a wave of pain slide over me. I bite my lip to hold the tremble still and push down the threatening tears.

He has no clue how much I trust him, no clue whatsoever. I wouldn't have let him do those things to me otherwise; it's better this way, better that he's pissed. Better that he never knows the truth. We won't talk about what we did, maybe we can start over again tomorrow. We're getting good at sweeping everything under the rug.

*Out of sight, out of mind, right?*

I can at least fool myself into hoping that's how this will be. For now.

# Chapter 32

We get to the airfield in the dark. Marissa is traveling with us, invading my territory and I resent her. She's wearing Jake's sunglasses over her pale face, despite the late hour; I'm guessing she has puffy eyes from crying, and even that tiny little detail causes me so much internal trauma. Those glasses are always meant for me, not her.

She looks effortlessly seductive in a clingy dress, showcasing her curves and long curled hair. She hasn't said one word since the tense meeting in the room as we left and then drove over here.

I avoid looking at her, and him, he's ushering her into the plane like she's some petulant child. His hand occasionally touching her lightly to guide her and burning inside my soul. He's avoided me since he left my room, his manner toward me is cool and distant and I can't stand it.

Maybe it's better like this. There's been icy silence, avoidance of eye contact between any of us and an atmosphere so thick you could slice it with a knife. Marissa is acting like I don't even exist and hasn't once looked my way. Not that I care. That flawless face and pouting mouth only ignite my internal rage and I wonder how she would look with my laptop rammed down her throat.

I sit alone on the left of the aisle and pull out my laptop to give me something to focus on, besides the last few hours. I don't want to open my mind to what I did with him, and I can't bring myself to look at him with her. I don't want to see his blank expression, devoid of any emotion.

They both go to sit over the aisle, facing each other across a small table. I try not to watch as she attempts a reach at his hand. My stomach tightens. He removes it from the table, returning it to his lap coolly and they sit in silence, tension heavy. I want him to move and sit somewhere else, away from her, or across from me instead. He doesn't.

I watch from the corner of my eye, breath held, she's pouting at him, but he ignores her. Shifting in his seat so that he can look out of the window instead, he doesn't seem to have anything to say to either of us. I guess Jake has never had to deal with a messy situation like this before. He never really overlaps women so that any come face to face. And anyone he dates normally knows it's temporary and doesn't make a fuss. This, however, is beyond awkward. Two women who actually love him. Although he only knows about her. I'll never admit it.

* * *

I attempt to work through the flight, I have enough to keep me occupied, to pretend to anyway, and I'm aware of him for the entire journey. His closeness across the aisle, his scent lingering between us. We're not far apart, but it feels like there's a canyon between us. A million miles of vast baron land and he's so un-reachable. I feel like I've lost him.

He's using his laptop, but unlike me he's not as focused

and wired into it the way I'm trying to be, he keeps staring pensively out of the window and fixing a blank gaze at the darkness outside. His mood is preoccupied. I wonder what he's thinking about. It tugs at me. I long to know what's keeping his head busy as he stares silently into nothing.

*Is he thinking about what we did? Or is he thinking about the baby and her? I want to know how you feel, Jake, about all of it.*

I long to be alone with him and have him tell me what's going on in that dark look and still face. I know I never will again, we've reached an impasse. The only way forward doesn't bear thinking about.

I try not to look at Marissa, now sound asleep in her chair, his sunglasses still in place on her overly flawless face. We contrast in so many ways, only our hair color matches. She's small and curvy with deep dark eyes and a sensual mouth, everything about her screams exotic beauty. Her figure curvy, yet not overweight, her breasts larger than average and they look natural. She's a born seductress in every way and I never stood a chance against her.

*How could I ever compare to her?*

I'm small and petite with average curves, average face, average Emma. She's the first girl he ever loved, and now she's carrying his child. She isn't some damaged mess, unable to relax and let Jake in fully, she's not some girl he just screwed out of frustration on the bedroom floor to cure weird tension between us.

That was me!

I look at him longingly, I never stood a chance against him, or with him. How could I? Some worthless little tramp from Chicago with hopes of grandeur, no way of knowing how to deal with the force that is Jake Carrero. I have deluded myself for so long. He's always been out of my league.

# Chapter 33

I finally get home to the apartment in the early hours; Jake had two cars awaiting us at the airfield and I didn't need to share the journey to his apartment first. This was a new move for him, we've always shared cars coming home, so this spoke volumes.

He never looked at me once in our entire trip. At the car, he just guided Marissa into his and left, left me standing in the dark of the airfield with Jefferson. Empty and broken hearted, aching to have him say something, anything to me. I almost burst into tears right then and there.

Sarah's in bed and I know, without checking, that Marcus is here too, I can sense his presence in the house and smell his scent lingering in the air. Cheap cologne and deodorant. The thought makes me feel uptight, but I ignore it and go to bed, taking sleeping pills before I lay down. I'm going to need them; my head is so full to bursting that I know if I even try and extract one tiny piece it will unravel like a chaos of elastic bands. That I'll unravel, and I'm so done with that kind of pain and turmoil.

\* \* \*

I wake to the sounds of Sarah making breakfast, my head feels groggy, but at least I managed to sleep. A dreamless black haze and the usual night tremors waking me early. The after effects of the pills are not great, my mouth is fuzzy, and I feel hungover. I venture through in my robe, seeing her moving from stove to worktop effortlessly. The kitchen has always been her territory and it shows in her graceful, easy movements. She looks different this morning though, tired and uptight.

"Hey," I breathe, she startles at my voice then breaks into a warm smile. I notice the lack lustere in her normally bright eyes and feel the hint of concern unravel inside of me.

"Hey, stranger ... God, I love your hair, when did you do that?" she gushes at me, the tight look dissipating. I automatically reach up and tug on a strand self-consciously, I shrug.

"Felt like a change."

*Has it really been that long since we have been in each other's company?*

"You look so different ... So un-Emma," she giggles and continues to work.

"You hungry?" she goes back to focusing on the batter she's mixed up.

"Not really." I smile tightly. How can I tolerate food while my insides are violently rejecting life? I notice the pile of letters on the surface and rake through, flinching at the ones addressed to Marcus.

"So, were you going to inform me I had a new roommate?" I ask quietly, I see her pause for a second, the whisk stills, then resumes.

"I really didn't think you would care, Emma ... You're

never here ... I get so lonely." Her voice wavers and I'm hit by sudden guilt.

*Lonely? Sarah?*

The bright and sassy soul of the party, surrounded by her chef friends and busywork schedule ... Since when? I look her up and down, my mind racing over recent months, pushing further back ... I guess I have never realized, always focusing on my own turmoil and keeping her at arm's length.

I regret it instantly, as though for the first time, seeing it from a different view point. I've left her alone so many times, assuming she has everything she needs. That she didn't need me. No one else ever did.

"I'm sorry, Sarah," my voice breaks unexpectedly, her head snaps around, looking at me in confusion. I just feel an overwhelming guilt hit me hard in the gut.

"I'm sorry that I've been such a shit friend ... And a worse flatmate." The dam I've been holding back all night bursts, such a small reason to fall apart, yet here it is, that extra nudge of my vulnerable emotional bubble and it pops. Magnificently.

*Truly losing the plot, Emma!*

"Hey ... hey, shhhh." She drops her pan and ladle, rushing to my side and cradling me awkwardly in her arms as the tears start to course down my face.

"Where the hell has this come from, and what have you done with Emma?" she laughs, an anxious edge in her voice, I feel her breath in my hair and it pains me even more, it reminds me of him.

"I'm sorry," I sniff and reel myself back in, embarrassed by my behavior, but in a way relieved. Sarah has never known this side of me, maybe it's time I let her see that I'm not the strong capable shell of a person she has known so long, after all. I am so tired of pretending.

"I'm really sorry, Sarah."

"Emma you're scaring me ... This is so not you ... To be honest, I don't actually know how to react." She looks wary, still holding me awkwardly. We've never hugged before, so this is monumental.

I stand up, pushing the bar stool aside and wrap my arms around her fully, giving her the most Jake-like hug I can muster. I did learn from the best after all. At least he taught me that. This girl has been there in times when I was no one, I've pushed her so far into the background of my life in a bid to forget who I was that I forgot about her, how much she used to mean to me. I've left her floundering in my past and never realized she needed a place in my present. She hugs me back. I feel the hesitation in her fall away and she embraces me with equal vehemence.

When we part, there are tears in her eyes, she looks confused, unsure, but overwhelmed mostly.

"I'm different, Sarah ... things ... Jake ... He's changed everything." I smile through tears, unable to explain. He has no idea what he's done to me, these months, these agonizing few days; he's opened a dam and I can't pull the flood waters back. He's broken me apart and let the parts of me I try to contain leak out everywhere, the cracks growing so wide I can never piece them back together. He's made me feel emotions I have always been so afraid of feeling, or letting other people see. I was selfish. Sarah deserves to see how much I care for her. Always have.

"Emma ... I don't know what he's done or how, but I would really love to give him one huge kiss right now." She grins at me, her eyes full of love and sincerity, but I only crumble. Catching my sob in my throat I begin to pour my soul out through my eyes.

"He's made me fall in love with him ... But he doesn't love me back." I cry at my own admission, broken by it and fall into the arms of my long forgotten best friend. Ready to unload the burden finally.

* * *

Marcus glares at Sarah as he leaves the apartment, his bag over his shoulder as he heads out. She throws him a haughty look and turns her face back to me on the couch, they have been arguing over something pointless, now he is going to work. Apparently, this is normal for them.

We're huddled together under a warm throw, drinking hot chocolate, my emotions calm finally. I haven't been able to tell her everything, there is too much to tell, too much to explain and I am still unable to just open up, even to her.

Baby steps.

She knows the basics of the story, how things built up to the last few days in the hotel room and having sex with Jake; then the appearance of Marissa. The final breaking of my heart.

"What was it like?" she asks, there's nothing in her face, curiosity maybe; trying to understand me, understand what I feel.

"Sex with him, I mean."

"Amazing ... Terrifying ... Heartbreaking." I answer honestly, because that's what having sex with him had been; to fall so deeply under the spell of him, even though I know it will go nowhere. The realization that I can never wipe it away and it will haunt me for an eternity. No one will ever compare, in any way.

"I can't get over the change in you, Ems," Sarah points out in awe, her eyes wide with emotion.

"I feel like I have my old Emma back, but somehow, she's different too. There has never really been this new version of you, despite the heartbreak, you seem somehow, better."

"New version?" I quiz, confused, smiling a little.

"Teenage Emma, only less aggressive." She laughs.

"And yet so much changed ... emotional ... open, and honest ... even warm." She giggles with an apologetic expression.

"You make me sound like I was awful to be friends with." I chide softly, guilt coursing through me again. I lower my lashes, ashamed in a way that I've been this way toward her for so long. So blind to it.

"You have your charms, Ems ... You've no idea the allure you have, even when you're acting the ice maiden." She smiles. "There's always a hint of something more in you ... Like it's just out of reach, I can see why Jake would pursue it ... That elusive prize, always dangling out of reach, that door sitting ajar, waiting to be opened." She grins at me, my face flushing with her version of how she sees me. It's so disconnected with who I am. Who I think I am.

*Is she right? Does Jake see something worth chasing, worth holding on for, and trying to figure out?*

"My messed-up brain." I smile sadly, she smiles back at me gently.

"Have you ever just come out and told him how you feel? He may surprise you." She coaxes, gently placing a hand over mine.

*Why have I never done this? With Sarah I mean, this girly, sharing our problems, being real and letting someone else figure out your heartbreak with you. That shoulder to lean on.*

Because I'm incapable of showing people that I'm capable of being hurt, defensively protecting myself always. Jake has stripped me of my armor, slowly and surely.

"It's too hard." I admit sadly. "I'm scared all the time,

Sarah ... Scared of what he'll say ... Scared of what He's thinking ... feeling ... He's complicated, he sleeps around ... He has women at every city we go to, always at arm's length ... He doesn't do love. I couldn't bear his rejection." The words slice me, I can't think about these women he has sex with, the pain is too acute. She's watching me carefully, sipping her cocoa and thinking.

"You think he wants to be with that girl though; Marissa?"

"I don't know, they have history ... He seemed angry at her, but then he still brought her home with us and left the airport with her." I feel the tears tug at my eyes and push them down. I shift to cross my legs under the throw and cradle my cup closer, in a bid to regain my equilibrium, feeling like the warmth is soothing me somehow. I can't analyze what is there between them, it's too painful.

"How did he take the news about the baby?" she pushes gently, but I just shake my head and shrug, I really am bewildered about all of that, I've barely let my brain process that whole mess.

"He didn't seem happy ... He closed up ... Jake isn't ready for that kind of commitment. He can't even commit to a girl, let alone a baby." I sigh sadly.

*Isn't that where all my self-doubt comes from?*

No ... My self-doubt has always existed, always gnawing at me, reminding me how worthless I am, in the grand scheme of things. Having a father reject you and a mother who eternally put her own needs above you will do that to a person.

I push it down hard, Sarah sighs heavily, mirroring how I feel; there isn't anything much to say on this subject. We've dissected it all endlessly through three cups of cocoa.

Finally, after a brief reflective silence, Sarah cuts in.

"Your mom keeps leaving messages on the answer

machine ... She knows you're never here and I know she has your cell number, so I guess she's not actually trying to contact you directly."

"I spoke to her briefly, she's doing well, her nurse is taking care of her." She smiles at me gently. Sarah text me this all before, and hadn't been surprised at my non-responses to her messages. I remain impassive.

"Did she mention her new beau?" I grit my teeth and slide the mug on the table, full of too many hot drinks, nausea rising. Sarah raises an eyebrow, then lets her comments pass unspoken. I haven't told her about Ray ... About what happened in Chicago. I will, I promise myself to tell Sarah everything, just not right now. This is all new to me, sharing ... talking.

"Are you going to talk to her?" she asks instead, her bright blue eyes focused on my face. I'm avoiding it, looking at my hands in my lap, and I shake my head.

*How can I ever talk to her again? How can I ever go back there?*

Ray ... Sophie ... My past ... Her past. It's one huge ball of string waiting to unravel, and I don't have the energy or the inclination to go there anymore. I have so many emotions about my mother, so much conflict, love and hate. It's not something I can evaluate anytime soon. Especially not with all this new chaos overtaking me.

"What about the little girl?" Sarah asks as though reading my mind. I briefly told her, via text, and the odd call, about Sophie.

"She's doing well ... She's going through the process of being awarded a protection order, so she can stay with her new family without fear of being returned home. Her father will be prosecuted. She's in counseling ..." I smile at Sarah. I have been keeping tabs on Sophie via Leila, Jake's mother and via Sophie herself, in email. Jake told me his brother seems to have taken her under his protective wing, and she seems to trust him.

*Carrero charm.*

"You did for her what someone should have done for you, Ems." Sarah is so direct and spot on that I snap my eyes to her, inhaling lightly. I want to deny it, want to brush it off like old Emma would have, return to cold and controlled, "no one hurts me", but I don't. I bite my lip, pushing away the force of emotion and nod.

"I know." It sounds so sad it hurts me. Sarah's eyes widen, tears filling them, she knows how hard my admission is, how far I must have come to even admit this to her. She has seen the years of denial, bravery and fight in me. She knows me better than anyone in the world ... Well maybe, except for Jake.

"Promise me something." She breathes, a solitary tear rolling down her cheek.

"What?" Right now, I wouldn't deny her anything. I feel responsible for her sadness, and it's aching inside of me.

"You won't go back into hiding ... I want you to talk to a professional ... Take this further, Ems ... Regardless of what happens with Jake." I see the bravery in her eye, she's waiting for my reaction, pushing to see if I really am old Emma after all. This is a request she's made many times over the years. The same request Jake made, which sent me into a rage. I bristle, old Emma habits are hard to kill. I stiffen and feel the defensive response form on my lips but take a steadying breath, exhaling slowly to calm my reaction.

"I'll think about it." It's all I can promise her. I see the elation in the depth of her eyes, the celebratory smile at the realization that something huge has changed within me. I don't think it's something to be all that happy about, but it is what it is.

Jake has ruined all that I was.

\* \* \*

I help Sarah clean the apartment in companionable silence for the rest of the afternoon, we talked ourselves out and I feel there's nothing more to say. I have so much to process.

She keeps catching my eye and shaking her head at me in awe. I don't think she can really accept that this is how I am now, as though she keeps waiting on the old Emma to jump out and throw herself into commandeering, emotionless mode, again. Her attention unnerves me, but I don't want to freeze her back out again, she deserves more. I deserve more.

I keep checking my cell obsessively, but he doesn't call or text; every time I see the blank screen I die a little more inside. I long for one of his song emails, a text, anything! I understand his silence, she'll be with him, he has a lot to think about, talk about; he's mad at me, he's overwhelmed. It doesn't make this any less painful.

I spend an hour going through emails and work files, before throwing it aside listlessly. I'm trying not to focus on him, on her, what we did. It's like trying to turn back the tide in a way, and my head is my own worst enemy. I can't even begin to dwell on what the future holds, my job ... Jake and a baby ... Seeing him again. I feel like I'm in an alternate universe, sitting here in my own apartment, it looks so different to me. The whole atmosphere has shifted since I opened up to Sarah. I feel like I'm home, first time since I moved here, that this apartment feels like a safe haven from the outside world.

I think back to my childhood room in Chicago, I never really felt like it was my home. I never connected with the city, or the people; my own mother ...

Sarah had been a force to be reckoned with, she was shy and small, and looked vulnerable. So, I swooped in to protect her, in a way that I needed someone to protect me. Except, she wasn't really that vulnerable at all. She let me believe it, so that I had a purpose, a focus. That's what I did ... I fixed things, helped others have better lives than me, organized things to make it all so safe and steady and predictable. Much like my mother does for her homeless shelter patrons. I was trying to fool myself, trying to detach myself from my own life.

It's why I excelled at my job, distancing my own needs and emotions and robotically taking control.

*Is that what my mother does? Are we more alike than I care to admit?*

Jake flipped the tables on me, he brought my own life, my own flaws and insecurities into the picture. He didn't want just a brainless PA to do his bidding, he wanted involvement from me. A two-way friendship. To delve into my life and fix things for me, that others failed to do. This insane need in him to pry and figure me out, like a kid with a toy.

He is a child sometimes, hardly surprising that I posed as a challenge and an adventure. I was probably the first young female to grace his presence who didn't want to bed him, who hadn't fallen at his feet drooling. It was probably refreshing to not have a girl swooning and acting demure all the time. I had been real, we bonded as friends and got to know each other. Not posing a threat to one another at all and catching me by surprise.

That's how he got in, by being the one man I have ever met who didn't want anything from me at all. He didn't desire me, he didn't frighten me, his easy, laid back manner, forcing me out of my formal mode. Always pushing the boundaries further into laxness.

I crossed the line, not him, I fell in love with him and in turn I gave him a free rein to chase me as another conquest. He is a hot-blooded male, and that's what he does. I took away the rules to our friendship by kissing him, and opened a can of worms, sending us both spiraling into confusing, blurring the lines of what we are, causing chaos between us, I only have myself to blame.

\* \* \*

Marcus returns mid-afternoon, his short shift for the day over and offers to take us both for a late lunch, which shocks me. The fight between them forgotten and replaced with giggles and hugs.

I still can't warm to him, so decline the offer, feeling Sarah's eyes on me. She's asking me to give him a chance, for her sake. I throw her a look which I hope conveys the message "baby steps", and they finally leave, giving me head space to think. Time to figure out how I'll face Jake at work on Monday.

# Chapter 34

I'm tense as I sit in the office waiting for Jake, he hasn't called or text me all weekend and I've been too afraid to contact him. Apart from after our time on his boat, we've never gone this long with no contact, and it has me feeling overly touchy and emotional. My nerves eating away at me. Already I've snapped at two receptionists when coming through the floor to the office, for the smallest things.

I check my watch repeatedly.

When Rosalie takes up residence in her own area of the office outside of mine I realize it's after nine and Jake still hasn't shown up; he's rarely late. I'm tense and on edge, and I've no idea what we'll even say to each other. All I've thought about all weekend is what we have done. How it felt to have him kiss and touch me that way, what it felt like to let Jake have sex with me, and it brought me to tears over and over.

Despite everything I thought when it first happened, I can't deny that the memory is bittersweet. I felt alive and cherished, sexy and wanton, all in one go, and his touch is the only touch I can ever trust, the only touch I ever want to feel.

Sarah has gotten to me, another long talk, the next

morning, turning my way of thinking. Showing me that I haven't anything to lose, and everything to gain. That my parents have set me up for insecurity and worthlessness in my own mind. Fear of rejection and a warped version of life. She convinced me that it is only in my head that I am not loveable. That only I am convinced I am not worthwhile enough to be loved by Jake.

I've lingered over the memory so many times, I see it every time I close my eyes, remember how he feels, smells, kisses, and I just want him to come in, so we can talk properly. I want to run into his arms and have him take all this pain away. I've already resigned myself to the fact that I finally need to be honest with him, about as much of my past as I can bear. I need to tell him that I'm scared about how I feel about him, and I don't know where it will lead. The chaos which goes on in my head when I seem cold and distant. I need him to truly understand me.

I know one thing for certain after all of this ... I love him hopelessly, and I need to tell him.

Despite how he feels about me, his obsession with casual sex and a stream of women. I need to tell him how I really feel. No matter the outcome. No matter his response. It's expanding inside of me so quickly now that I can identify it; I'll self-implode. Sarah was right about that at least. I need to take a chance and be brave. Give him the opportunity to tell me if there is hope.

\* \* \*

Jake walks in with a man in tow and I feel myself take a sharp breath at his mere appearance, he's in a dark gray shirt, left open at the collar, and dark jacket, dark pants and shades, his face has a little more stubble than normal. He looks perfect in

## Jake & Emma

every way, a seductive cool, confident heart-throb and it makes my heart constrict painfully. His eyes are concealed with Ray Bans as they walk by me in the office.

I long to reach out and touch him as he passes. He keeps his distance, giving me a tight smile, and says nothing; just heads with his male friend to his own office and shuts the door. I feel sick inside. I just want to be alone with him to talk. I just want a chance to explain, apologize, win back my Jake in any small way that I can.

*I want to know what's happening with Marissa. How he feels about it, what the future holds for her, and him.*

I sit at my desk and fidget with everything within reach, but I just don't care. I don't have the strength to be PA Emma anymore. I'm listless, tense, and emotional, and I've fallen to pieces so many times in the past two days that I could cry right here, in front of everyone, and I wouldn't care. I need him.

My hair falls forward into my face so many times I start regretting this hair cut at all.

*Why did I ever change it?*

I smile sadly; my hair is just another sign that I had been letting go. Taking away a piece of the armor, oblivious to the fact at the time. Another small change pushed on me by Jake's looming presence. I tug my fingers from my scalp, I've been tangling them absent-mindedly, and straighten my back.

This is sheer agony, my nerves are all over the place, my mind anywhere but work.

Finally, his visitor leaves, and waves me a passing goodbye and friendly smile. I sit with bated breath, wondering if I should just walk in and try to talk to him. I don't have to ponder over it for long, as my switchboard lights up and he asks me to come into his office.

I hold my breath, my nerves reeling as I get up and slowly make my way in, pushing the heavy door closed behind me once I'm inside. I'm unable to take my eyes off him. He's looking down at his laptop, concentrating, and typing, he's taken off his shades and his jacket, he just looks too good to be real, yet avoiding looking at me.

I ache for him to glance at me and smile in his usual way. Hollywood handsome, but he doesn't. He looks up darkly and indicates I take a seat; all Mr. Business Carrero, devoid of all friendliness, acting ultra-cool toward me.

I can sense the tension already. I do as I'm told, still unable to tear my eyes from him. I can feel my body trembling, waiting for some sign of how this will play out. Something doesn't feel right.

"Emma, this isn't easy for me to say." He looks at me for a long moment, darkness in his eyes, but his face is closed off, giving nothing away. He shifts in his seat so he's sitting taller and closes his laptop slowly, his eyes watching me as intently as I'm watching him. I hold my breath with the nerves he has me feeling.

"We can't work together anymore ... Too much has happened for this to work." He sounds so cold.

I feel myself gasp sharply, as though I've been struck. Shaking my head as I take in what he's just said, I never saw this coming at all. I feel my insides drop.

"What?" I sound dazed, my voice detached from my reeling mind, my body frozen to the spot.

"I've made arrangements for you to go to our headquarters across town, Carrero Tower. To work on my father's floor, Emma ... It's for the best." He looks away and turns his chair to the windows of the office, gazing over New York. His body language completely unreadable, straight and solid and physically dismissing me.

I can't formulate a response at all, I feel like I'm drowning. I can't breathe. I try to speak, but only a sob comes out.

Without any warning I crumble, my face falling forward into my hands and I lose control. I begin crying softly, unable to stop anything anymore, just a shadow of the person I have been playing for so long.

*Jake can't do this to me, to us ... He can't break me this way. Not him ... Not after everything. He's sending me away, and it's ripping me apart inside.*

"Emma, don't, please." His voice waves over me closely, I feel his arms come around me, pulling me from my chair. I can't look up at him. I can only let him pull me around and crush me to his chest, wrapping his arms around me so tightly, I can barely breathe.

"Not now, Emma ... Not like this," he says breathily. I don't understand what he means by that, all I can do is sag against him and let everything flow out of me, all the anguish and heartache and pain of the last few days, basking in the feel of him.

I try and regain control of myself, my sobs finally turning to soft tears as I calm down. Unable to think of any words to fix this. I take deep breaths and try so hard to be calm again.

Finally, I'm stable, still held tightly in his arms, surrounded by strength and his intoxicating smell. Taking solace in the cause of my pain. He feels like a safe haven to me; but how can he be when he's told me I'm to be sent away from here, that I'm done working for him? He's not my haven anymore, he's my destroyer, cause of my desperate pain.

"I'm calm," I finally say, numb and empty. Lifting my hand to wipe my face, my make-up smearing across the back of it, but I don't care. I want him to see how broken I am over this.

I feel the warmth of his breath on top of my scalp, he's been resting his mouth in my hair the whole time, breathing me in as I was breathing him in. Painfully familiar.

## The Carrero Effect ~ The Promotion

"Emma ... This ... Us ... It's toxic ... We just fight and feel angry with each other, all the time." He sounds defeated; my head's screaming at me to tell him, to open up and tell him. That how I've behaved, how I've reacted and held back, is all in the past, that I want him to see the real me. I want him to finally get through my walls, show him the constant inner chaos of my fucked-up mind, but I can't.

Old Emma still has control over my mouth. Old Emma is recoiling in fear of rejection, because he is already hurting me and pushing me away.

He pulls away from me and sits me back down on the chair. I see the look on his face and it stills every word I have brimming in my mind that I want to say. He looks cold, as though he's shut a door and he's trying to gain distance. I know that look. It's my look. Nothing I say will make a difference.

"We don't work anymore." He walks to the windows and stares out, his body tense, he places a palm against the glass and stares outside silently for what seems like an eternity. That perfect body, outlined against the skyline, only serving to torture me.

"We can talk about this, Jake." I finally manage, my voice sounds broken and childlike. I want to get up and walk to him, throw myself back in his arms.

*Tell him, Emma ... Tell him you love him.*

"No ... There's nothing to say." The coldness in his tone kills my voice completely, shutting down the words I long to say.

"It's done, Emma, it's arranged ... Clear out your things today, take the rest of the day off, then report to the HQ offices first thing tomorrow. You'll work for my father from now on." He sounds cruel ... Jake's gone and only the version who left me on the boat remains. I shake my head, feeling a new wave of tears building up inside of me, the panic and hysteria, a chest-crushing pain I've never experienced in my life.

"Jake ..." I can barely talk through the new wave of emotion.

*When will this ever end? It hurts so much.*

I'm like a bottomless sea of tears that I can never empty. I see his shoulders sag and his face moves closer to the window, his breath forming a small steamed area in front of him.

"Don't make this harder on both of us ... Just go," he says it so softly, and so surely, it makes my breath catch in my throat, stilling my tears.

*I really have lost him.*

There's so much I want to say, but I can't. He's closed the door on me. Ironically, after months of me refusing to open mine and his always being wide open, it's now shut in my face and locked tight.

I hold on a moment, in the hope he'll look at me, but he remains where he is. Staring over New York and refusing to move. He wants me to go, it's in every tiny tense cell of his body. I can practically taste it. I feel frozen to the spot, my head reeling and desperate to say so much, but my mouth stays silent. I've lost everything that mattered to me ... I lost Jake. He's all that matters to me.

I stand slowly, self-preservation kicking in, steady myself and turn deliberately. I walk slowly, agonizing each step, praying he stops me; but he doesn't. When I finally open the door, I pause, taking a deep sigh and turn to look at him once more, he hasn't moved. His stiff posture still the same.

"Will I see you again?" I ask softly, my voice full of fear.

"I don't think so, Emma ... What's done is done. It's better this way." His voice is lifeless, empty. It rips the last shred of my heart out and lets it loose on the wind, leaving a hollow space, full of fire and pain. I can't bear to look at his strong tall body, held tautly against the New York skyline anymore; this will be my last memory of him and it's unbearable. I turn and pull the door closed behind me, walk through my own office, shut the door which always stood open. I sit at my desk, concealed from everyone and break down within the circle of my own arms.

* * *

I'm numb when I finally say goodbye to Rosalie. I've packed my personal things and she's having anything else taken to my new office in Carrero Tower later today. HQ across town. No excuse to ever come this way again.

Jake stayed in his office the whole time I packed up, and no matter how many times I stared at that door, willing him to come to me and beg me stay, he did not. My heart's broken into a million pieces, I'm amazed that it hasn't killed me, that is still beats, that I'm still upright. I've nothing left to stay for.

I manage to leave via the stairs. I don't want people to see my scrubbed clean, raw face, and puffy eyes. My hair hides most of it as I walk from the building with my box file, containing everything that is personal to me, everything that connected me to him.

"Miss. Anderson?" I'm startled by Jefferson, Jake's driver.

"Yes?" I ask quietly, I must look nothing like my normal self, but he smiles at me gently and I can see a look of sympathy in his wrinkled gray eyes. He's been there so many times with Jake and I, yet I barely know the man. I've barely acknowledged him. The elderly looking man with a warm face and impeccable manners. This will be the last I will see of him too.

"Mr. Carrero told me I was to wait for you and take you

home, Miss." He leans forward relieving me of my box. I haven't got the energy to argue, so I allow myself to be ushered into the back of the SUV and driven home. Back to Queens, back to the emptiness of my own room and own bed. A Jake-less life.

Sarah isn't home when I open the door to the apartment. I don't even care, I don't want to see anyone. I dump my belongings on the kitchen bunker and set about taking off every piece of PA Emma that is upon me. Hating her, loathing her. An anger building from some deep place that takes over.

I throw my shoes across the floor in rage, I rip off my jacket and skirt, and throw them down the hall dramatically. I strip piece by piece, every clothing item, every jewelry item, stockings and lingerie and stand naked in my own living room, crying my heart out. Wanting to rid myself of every cold, controlled ice maiden piece of me that attributed to losing the only man I have ever wanted. I want to scream and rip my own hair out.

I reach for a throw on the couch and wrap it around me, trying so hard to bring back the memory of being in his embrace. I feel like I'm dying, the pain is so acute, so overwhelming, all I can do is crumple onto the couch and let it over take me.

I'm making up for a lifetime of bottled up tears and emotions, a lifetime of pain and rejection. Heartache. Abuse. Jake cut through all of it and found a beating heart somewhere in the darkest depths of me. He kept trying to bring it to the light and I fought every step of the way.

Look where it got me. Alone and broken and losing the only man I was ever capable of trusting, ever capable of loving. He has a child on the way, maybe he will try again with Marissa now I am no longer a thorn in his side, a constant distraction. He called us toxic ... That hurt to hear. It struck into me like a knife.

I am toxic to him.

*What does that even mean? I slowly poisoned him in some way, until he couldn't bear it anymore?*

I finally drag myself to my bedroom and pull on some pajamas. I haven't worn anything like this in so long, I am amazed I even still own a pair. I climb on the bed, moving the huge bear Jake won for me at a street carnival on one of our trips. It causes a new wave of pain across my chest and I sob into the bears stomach, lying across my bed.

I can't bear this, I should have said something to him, I should have at least tried to tell him how I felt. Maybe if I had, then I wouldn't be here now, crying into a bear's fluffy belly; the only symbol I have of him that I can actually hold this way. I sit up and dry my eyes.

*What would I have said to him?*

*I love you, Jake?*

*What if he doesn't feel the same way? Who am I kidding? He sent me away ... He doesn't feel the same way about me.*

I think back to every time he tried to get me to open up, every kiss, and having sex with me. I let myself wonder if it was all ever about the challenge.

*Had I just been something to conquer?*

No—I don't think I had been. I learned to trust him, saw more than just the Casanova playboy. I had seen the real Jake. The caring, funny, and sometimes vulnerable, Jake. He told me everything about his life. Our bond had been real ... Our friendship. He'd been affectionate and attentive, no one else cared for me and looked after me the way he did. I refuse to believe that none of it was real.

I pick up my iPad and scroll the monumental list of songs we sent one another over the past few months, the jokes, the apologies, the hidden meanings, trying to see the truth behind it all ... I stop on a song, pausing my inner anguish with that of confusion.

*Skylar Grey—"I Know You".*
*I wonder when he sent this?*

It's not one I remember ever being gifted to me, my memory flits back through all our time together and I can't recall him ever sending me this song. Sometimes he just added music to my iPad for me, when we were bored or on a flight. He would sit and leave me songs in humor, or just because.

Because he knew I would listen to them. Was this one of them? I pause and click play on the music file, laying back on my bed to listen to the lyrics.

The haunting melody drifts over me soothingly, but the words strike a pain deep inside me, each word like a message from him, so accurate in every way ... Asking me to let him in, to give him a chance to love me. That he knows I put myself through so much pain, because of my past; begging me to just give him a chance and stop pushing him away. The words make my soul ache and a new flood of tears run silently down my face.

*Why hadn't I listened to this before? Why now, when it's too late? ... What does this mean?*

When the song fades away, and my tears silently subside, I sit up, taking my iPad without hesitation. I scroll iTunes purposefully ... There's a song that I listened to, a dozen times when we were apart, I need to send it to him now. It says more than I ever could. A girl telling a guy that she loves him, despite her walls, she cares. Her memories of him and what he means to her. That she misses him and all his crazy ways. She will do anything to be with him.

Maybe it isn't too late after all, he put that song on there for me to find, maybe he thought I already had and just never told him, ignored it.

*Had that hurt him? Been part of the reason he has withdrawn?*

Finding the one I'm looking for, I forward it to Jake's email before doubt can creep in. Before I can talk myself out of it.

*Avril Lavigne—"Wish You Were Here".*

It says everything I want to say to him.

I sit staring at my mailbox, waiting, watching, praying he opens it and listens to the song. Every lyric equally able to pass a message, as this song just has for me. I pray I'm not too late.

I hear every noise of my room, and the world outside as the minutes drag on endlessly. I feel like I'm holding my breath and even my heart has stopped beating.

I finally get an email notice that Jake Carrero has gifted me a song. Even his name appearing on my screen makes my heart constrict in pain and fear. With shaking hands, I slide my screen cover aside, my heart stills, my breath stops, I open the email, the subject:

*"Always an Avril fan."*

*Jake Carrero has sent you an iTunes gift.*

*"Let Me Go" by Avril Lavigne.*

My world tips into darkness as pain overtakes and I fall onto the bear, crying out in anguish. He doesn't want to know, he's gone and I'm sure I'll die of the pain this time.

# About the Author

L.T. Marshall is a Scottish born and bred romance writer with more than the average person's life experience. She has been a torrent of wild things—including singer in a girl band, animal rights activist and charity owner, worked in radio and offered jobs in TV.

A passionate, restless soul, who has always found peace in writing—the only way to calm that fiery spirit. She uses her wit and dark humor to her advantage in her works and has been an avid reader for most of her life.

Her influences vary, but from early life and a teen stint in journalism, she applies logic to most of her plot lines, is a self-confessed research fiend, and likes a lot of psychology behind her characters actions.

She currently resides in Central Scotland with her two children and fiancé of 13 years, making waves in the book world with her signature "WTF moments" she likes to apply in each story, hints of humor and devastating emotional rollercoaster rides.

## A note from the Author

I hope you enjoyed my book, it would mean a great deal to me if you took the time to leave me a review on Amazon or Goodreads—or even both. My reviews are something I regularly, and actively read, and appreciate you taking the time to leave me one. x

*L.T.Marshall*

## Find the Author online

You can find L.T. Marshall across all social media and she regularly interacts with fans on Facebook.

Website:      ltmarshall.blog
Facebook:   facebook.com/LTMarshallauthor
Twitter:        twitter.com/LMarshallAuthor
Instagram:  instagram.com/l.t.marshall

Printed in Poland
by Amazon Fulfillment
Poland Sp. z o.o., Wrocław